D0119300

05610583 3

"Jagged and quotable ... one can open it on almost any page for pithy, scathing take-downs of life, the universe and everything" *Times Literary Supplement*

"Wildly entertaining ... inspired ... he leaves you inspecting the carnage with a grin on your face" *Spectator*

"Could we have an American Houellebecq? Jarett Kobek might come close, in the fervor of his assault on sacred cows of our own secretly-Victorian era, even if some of his implicit politics may be the exact reverse of the Frenchman's. He's as riotous as Houellebecq, and you don't need a translator, only fireproof gloves for turning the pages" Jonathan Lethem

"[A] thrillingly funny and vicious anatomy of hi-tech culture and the modern world in general ... this book's cleverly casual style, apparently eschewing literary artifice, reminded me [...] of Kurt Vonnegut. But it's the enraged comedy of its cultural diagnosis that really drives the reader onwards. There are so many brilliant one-liner definitions that it's hard not to keep quoting them" *Guardian*

"The Kurt Vonnegut, hell, the Swift and Voltaire of the Twitter age too, why not? He has come up with a satirical novel that, at least while you're immersed in it, makes everyone else's novels look like the blinkered artefacts of the bloated, tech-addled, smilingly exploitative western culture that he so nimbly takes to bits. It's vicious. It's a hoot" *The Times*

"A grainy political and cultural rant, a sustained shriek about power and morality in a new global era. It's a glimpse at a lively mind at full boil ... This book has soul as well as nerve ... My advice? Log off Twitter for a day. Pick this up instead" *The New York Times*

"A brilliant, laugh-out-loud screed against the 'overlapping global evils' that the internet represents, a furious manifesto dressed in the guise of fiction, about a San Francisco artist whose life is upended when a recording surfaces online of her doing the unthinkable. It's an eye-opening look at the world we live in, where our lives revolve around devices made by enslaved children in China, and where the only thing we feel empowered to do about it is complain ... via said devices" *Chicago Review of Books*

THE FUTURE WON'T BE LONG

JARETT KOBEK

First published in Great Britain in 2017 by Serpent's Tail,
an imprint of Profile Books Ltd
3 Holford Yard
Bevin Way
London
WC1X 9HD
www.serpentstail.com

First published in the USA in 2017 by Viking,
an imprint of Penguin Random House

Hand lettering on page 132 by Sarina Rahman

1 3 5 7 9 10 8 6 4 2

Printed and bound in Great Britain by Clays, St Ives plc

A CIP record for this book can
be obtained from the British Library

ISBN 978 1 78125 855 2
eISBN 978 1 78283 359 8

To e.j., wherever she may be on this American continent

SEPTEMBER 1986

Baby's Parents Murder Each Other So Baby Goes to New York

I moved to New York not long after my mother killed my father, or was it my father who murdered my mother? Anyhoo, in a red haze of blood and broken bone, one did in the other. Several weeks were spent filling out paperwork and cleaning up the gore.

After I finished with these burdens, I abandoned my siblings and boarded a Greyhound bus in the parking lot of a corner store on the outskirts of my Podunk little Wisconsin town. Thirty-six hours later, I was in the city.

When I came out of the Port Authority, a building that scared me shitless, I couldn't see the Empire State Building, so I asked a cop how to get to the river. He looked at me and laughed, hard, because of how countrified I was, a real corn poke, and showed me which direction was west.

I walked on 42nd in daylight. No one mugged me. At the end of the street, I made my way across the highway and onto a pier. I looked out at the Hudson River. I looked out at New Jersey. I watched boats on the river. I saw the distant Statue of Liberty and believed in her gaudy symbolism.

People in New York would never understand about my Podunk little Wisconsin town. It was an issue of size. Even in Jerkwater, Ohio, or Backstabbing, Pennsylvania, you still had neighborhoods and streets and thousands of citizens. My Podunk little town was seven hundred people, mostly farmers.

In a place like that, what you do for fun, for amusement, is drive, day in, day out, day in, day out. You cruise the three blocks of Main Street in your car, seeing boys you knew from school, pretending that you want to fuck the girls.

So with the possibility of NYC, I was like, *okay, please.* I am yours. You may conquer me. I submit to your underground system of the soul. Bring me to 241st Street and White Plains Road. Bring me to Coney Island. Bring me to Midtown. Bring me to Morningside Heights. Bring me to Flushing, Gowanus, Wall Street. I am yours. I am yours. Free me from the tyranny of the automobile!

I could walk, at last, I could walk. Back in Wisconsin, you'd drive for three solid hours to buy an album, or a book, or pants, or anything. And that would only bring you to what people back home call a city, a place of maybe ten thousand people.

Oh people, oh the people, oh New York, oh your glorious people. Your Puerto Ricans, your Hebrews, your Muslims, your Chinese, your Eurotrash, that fat little fuck Norman Mailer, your uptown rich socialites, your downtown scum, your Black Americans, your Koreans, your Haitians, your Jamaicans, your Italians, your kitchen Irish, Julian Schnabel, your Far Rockaway and Staten Island white trash. Oh New York, I loved your people. They were all so beautiful! Many of them were hideous, really ugly with terrible teeth, but even the ugly ones were beautiful too! Oh I was in heaven.

And your fags, New York, oh god, your fags. All I hoped was that they would love me.

I was as queer as a wooden nickel, but Wisconsin hadn't offered this yokel much opportunity for erotic love, so what common language could I even speak with the cocksmen and leatherboys?

One day in ninth grade, I made the mistake of blowing my best friend, Abraham. I was afraid to let Abe come in my mouth, so I got him to the edge and made him spasm into his blanket. As punishment, he refused to reciprocate, which was a real downer, but he did give me a handjob, which was okay.

I went home and thought about it. I decided that I'd let my best friend come in my mouth.

The next day, as I received the first blowjob of my life, in walked his mother. She saw everything. Her son, naked, me, naked, my cock in his mouth, my hands on the light down of his stomach. I ran out of their house and drove home. Neither Abe nor his mother ever said a word, but it ruined the friendship and I spent my high school years clutched by fear, worried that I'd need to leave our town in shame.

I never did anything else, not with anyone other than a few girls who were kissed to keep up appearances. Their tongues in my mouth like soft robots, offering abstract interest but no sexual desire, no longing, no need.

And then, New York, there you were, like a homo homecoming queen standing before me, hands on your hips, regarding this shy wallflower.

With your Meatpacking District, your West Village piers and Fire Island. I was yours, crying out, *Oh, take me, take me, take me!*

But before anything could happen, I needed a place to stay.

A guy from my Podunk little town had moved to the city. This guy from my Podunk little town was about three years older than me. I asked the guy's brother for the guy's phone number.

—Watch out, his brother said, we don't talk much with him and I heard he's living in squalor.

Squalor sounded fabulous. I didn't care about the phone bill, so I called New York. His name was David.

A girl answered. I asked for David.

—Okay, dude, she said, hold on.

I waited for about ten minutes. When he came to the phone, he spoke with this high, nasal voice.

—Hey, he whined, is this El Gato?

—It's me, I said, you know me, remember?

But he didn't.

—I'm the one, I said, remember, I'm that guy who set the school record for both the fifty- and hundred-yard dashes in the same day?

—Oh, yeah, he said, you, that guy, why are you calling?

I begged and groveled until he said that if I made it out east, I could stay with him, giving me his address on 12th Street. David explained the crude navigational tools of New York life, telling me to look for the Empire State Building and then head in that direction. Once I was past that giant, north and south could be discerned by looking for the Twin Towers, the relative position of which also indicated east from west. This method was useless for people who went above 30th Street, but come on, David said, who goes above 30th Street? Maybe some assholes for drugs.

I walked from the highway to Times Square. That was some hell of a place. You know all about it. Who doesn't? The sex and sleaze that made its butterfly transformation into a tourist trap, a Walt Disney wonderland. I saw it happen, or, well, I was in the city while it happened, because, really, it was going above 30th Street. Who went to Times Square? Maybe for Club USA. But otherwise?

Moving along Broadway, I took in the stores and buildings. As I was a country bumpkin, I couldn't control my personal space. I stumbled into people with an alarming frequency. Most brushed past without a look back. A few cursed me to the high heavens.

When I got to Union Square, it was a ruin, a park surrounded by hookers and pimps and filled with drug dealers. I didn't know why men kept saying, *Works, works, works, you need some works?*

—Sorry, sir, but I'm not seeking employment.

—What the fuck is wrong with you?

I shut up and walked until I got to 12th Street. Then I headed through the East Village and into Alphabet City. David'd said his place was in an old brownstone between B and C. It took a minute to find because the address wasn't on the building. I knocked and knocked but there was no answer. I tried the door. The knob gave way. I went inside.

The place was burned out and dirty, the color of charred wood, trash everywhere, graffiti on the walls. Exposed wiring, exposed plumbing, exposed insulation. I didn't see anyone.

—Hello, David?

I walked in a little farther and repeated myself. A punk rock-looking guy came out from behind the staircase. Other than album covers and television and pictures in magazines, this was the first time I had ever seen a punk rock-looking guy.

—What do you want? asked the punk rock-looking guy.

—I'm looking for David?

—Who's fucking David?

—David, he's from my hometown. Back in Wisconsin? We talked last week, he gave me this address.

—Try upstairs, said the punk rock-looking guy, but don't steal nothing.

I climbed a flight of stairs to the second floor. Things crunched and broke beneath my feet. I peered inside one of the bedrooms. I couldn't see a thing. I flipped a light switch. There wasn't any power.

—David, David, where are you, David?

Then I heard a weak voice.

—Come here, said the voice from a room across the hall.

I went in.

—David? I asked of the darkness.

—Over here, someone said.

I went toward the voice. A young man lay atop a pile of old rags.

Back home, he'd been beautiful. I remembered his skin with its network of blue arteries. Now, several compacted layers of dirt darkened his acne-strewn flesh, dimming its grim tattoos. Grease matted down his brown hair.

—Who are you? he asked.

—David, it's me, remember? I'm that kid who set the records for the fifty- and hundred-yard dashes?

—Hey, man, you're in New York?

I sat beside David on another pile of dirty clothes. I didn't say much. I hadn't thought this far ahead. Even if he hadn't been living in squalor, what could we talk about? The only thing I knew about David was how hard I'd crushed on him in tenth grade. For two solid weeks, I'd masturbated thinking about his cock in my mouth. It was a cavalcade of semen, real and imagined.

David slumped over, his chin down on his chest. I'd never seen a junky before, so I thought he was tired. Twenty minutes passed. I couldn't take it anymore.

—David, I said, David, wake up.

—Oh man, you're still here? How'd you get here?

—Remember when we talked on the phone?

—No?

—You said I could stay with you.

—I did?

—Yeah.

—Rent's fifty dollars a week.

—Fifty dollars a week?

—City's expensive. Everyone pays. You give it to me, I give it to the boss.

—You didn't mention rent on the phone.

But talking was pointless. He'd fallen back asleep.

I looked for a safe place to put my bag. The room's main features were two separate stacks of old mattresses, around which were scattered several broken tables.

Someone had taped black construction paper over the windows. Dirty garments and plastic food wrappers. I pushed some clothes into the far corner and stashed my bag under the pile. I scattered old cupcake wrappers on top of the clothes.

Back in the hallway, a voice boomed down through the wooden floorboards of the third story. I started toward the first floor but stopped because the shadows moved.

—You do realize that you needn't pay him, don't you? David is as full of it as an overflowing latrine. There is no rent. There is no landlord. This is a squat, darling.

The shadows walked forward. A girl, a year or so older than me, nineteen or twenty, dressed in a checkered gray skirt, wearing ugly yellow sneakers and torn up black tights. Her red hair was crazy, spiky. She'd dyed in a few black streaks.

—No soul in this house of ill repute pays rent, she said. David wants to score. You look like an easy mark.

I blushed. An easy mark?

—My name is Adeline, she said. On occasion, I stay here.

I started telling her my real name, but then I thought, why should anyone know my real name? I moved to New York for the same reasons as anyone else. To escape myself, escape the past, escape all previous knowledge.

—Call me Baby Baby Baby, I said.

—May I call you simply Baby?

I thought for a second.

—Okay, I said, but only as a nickname.

—Baby, then.

Footsteps echoed downstairs, coming toward the front of the building. Two people, a boy and a girl, both very drunk, stumbled through the hallway beneath us. We couldn't see their faces. The boy started shouting:

BROOOOOOOOOOOOOOOOOOOOOOOOOOOOKLLLLLLLLLLYNN NNNNNN. BROOOOOOOOOOOOOOOOOOOOOOOOOOOKLLLL LLLLLYNNNNNNNN. BROOOOOOOOOOOOOOOOOOOOOOOOO OKLLLLLLLLLLYNNNNNNNN. BROOOOOOOOOOOOOOOOOOOOO OOOOOOKLLLLLLLLLLYNNNNNNNN. BROOOOOOOOOOOOOOOO OOOOOOOOOOOKLLLLLLLLLLYNNNNNNNN.

BROOOOOoooOOOOOOOoookklyn.

—I'm going outside, I said to Adeline. I only came into town a few hours ago.

—Walk to Avenue A and then head two blocks south. You simply must see Tompkins Square. It's one of the eight wonders, darling.

—I hope we'll talk later, I said.

—Perhaps we will, said Adeline. You know where I may be found.

Back in Wisconsin, I'd studied maps of Manhattan. I knew if I was over by Avenue C, then the river was the eastern border, making navigation easy. But I panicked and forgot what I'd memorized. With neither the Empire State Building nor the Twin Towers visible, I got lost.

I hadn't paid any attention on the way in, not with my tunnel vision. Moving now in what seemed like all directions, I really saw the area and oh god, this was not the New York of my dreams. David's neighborhood was more like the television news footage of Beirut. About a fourth of the buildings were demolished, empty lots filled with rubble and long grass growing high. Another fourth were abandoned, boarded or bricked up and left to rot. Even the pavement was broken and destroyed, the sidewalks crumbling. Dogshit was everywhere.

One empty lot looked as if its building had exploded, obliterating the walls and ceilings while leaving the interior contents unscathed. Piles of doors and furniture and bathtubs and the scattered plastic of people's lives, trash all mashed together. There was no fence, no barrier between the street and the remains.

My family had been poor, but we were the working poor, people who lived off our land. The citizens of Alphabet City were something below that, living on the streets, in abandoned buildings, in empty lots, in burned-out cars. There was a ghost town quality that would be hard to believe today when every block is crammed with hundreds of people no matter what hour. In those days, the streets were empty. And the few who were there? Well.

I forced my face into a blank, not wanting to betray my shock, letting some of my hair fall down past my forehead. The homeless wouldn't scare me. The punks wouldn't scare me. Neither would the people that my relatives would have called Spanish. Nor the Blacks. I kept my honky blue eyes forward, straight ahead, hoping no one would sniff me out.

After an hour of wandering, I came upon what I assumed was Tompkins Square. Anyway, it was square. What other park could be in the area? I checked the signs and, yeah, it was Tompkins Square. The park was a city of homelessness, a sea of tents and makeshift shelters, with as large a population as my Podunk little town.

People lived up against the fences, sleeping on the benches and its pathetic grass. A large group camped inside a giant concrete structure alongside the 7th Street perimeter. On the side of this structure was a mural of a woman in red surrounded by arcane symbols, but I didn't understand their significance. Months later, someone told me that this rectangle was a band shell. The mural, they said, was called "Billie Holiday and Family Planning."

A teenage girl, kind of heavyset with dirty hair, wearing denim clothes covered in patches, walked over right in front of me. She stopped at a leafless tree, squatted down, and started pissing.

This was no delicate release of urine, not like my own modest streams or the soft tinkling that the patriarchy would imagine for a lady, but rather a deluge, a torrent that dropped from her body like bombs from the bay of a B-29 bomber over a nameless German city.

Gazing into her vacant eyes, with her sodden puddling in my ears, it came to me that, at long last, I had escaped the American Middle West.

I walked back to David's place, my body shaking on wobbling legs, wracked with the dead awful sense of freedom, of absolute and unregulated liberation. Not America's bullshit foundational principles, but a freedom more primal, the freedom to live beyond the margins. A great tug pulling off the scab. The blood flows and reveals daily life as a collection of lies, reveals the bruised, bleeding flesh, the meaningless of human endeavor. You could die, it would be a shame, but your death will not matter. Nothing matters. Nothing ever matters. You cannot achieve a single thing of consequence. No one you know will ever achieve consequence. Your family is as meaningless as empty air. And so are you. That's freedom. That's a teenage girl in rotten denim, squatting beside a tree, making water like a giraffe.

The sun set into blue light. A cold rose up. People were bundled, rushing down the street. *Wimps! Cowards!* I thought. Try wind blowing off Lake Superior on a January morning, an ice chill running through your body at 6 am while you handle the livestock.

Back at David's place, the front door was still unlocked. I went upstairs. The building's power had returned, offering illumination from a few exposed lightbulbs.

David's room looked the same as before, but now I could see the stains. The pile I'd put over my bag had shifted, become formless. The cupcake wrappers were gone. I dug through the clothes, trying not to smell them. My bag was missing. So was David.

I waited.

Every detail of those low hours burned into my brain. People came in and out of the house. Some yelling, some crying, some storming around in rage. One girl wandered through the front door singing. Her slurring words stuck with me, I remember their sound to this day: *Something told me it was over / when I saw you and her talking / something deep down in my soul said cry girl cry / when I saw you and her walking by.*

Laughter, a sick laughter, erupted from upstairs. I thought about seeing who was laughing and why, but I didn't want to miss David. A girl popped her head into the room. —Bobby? she asked before she caught sight of me and turned away.

I have no idea how much time passed before David came back. When he did, his stagger told me everything. I wasn't angry, exactly, because I'd been smart enough to keep my money on my person. But there were some good clothes in that bag. The bag itself was a gift from my mother.

—Where's my bag? I asked.

—Who are you? asked David.

—You know who I am, you rotten thieving son of a bitch, I said. I'm from our Podunk little town. I set our school's records for the fifty- and hundred-yard dashes.

—Right, right, right, he said. You. Yeah, when'd you get in?

—Where's my bag, David?

—What bag? he asked.

David flopped on a pile of mattresses. The springs coiled beneath him, a squeaky sound like mice trapped within a wall.

—I want my bag, I said.

—What bag? he asked.

—You know perfectly well what goddamned bag, I said.

He rolled to his side and rested his head in his hand, his watery eyes shining from the forty-watt bulb.

—Look, man, he said, fuck your bag. If it ain't here, it ain't here. You can't moan about something that's gone. That won't get you anywhere in this life.

I walked to the bed. His pants clung to his legs, loose from sheer wasting skinniness. Tiny scabs dotted the webbed skin between his fingers.

—There were some good clothes in that bag, I said.

—Yeah, he said, well, they're gone. If you need clothes, there's plenty here.

I balled up my fists. I was going to hit him.

A >click< sound. I looked down. David had a little knife, its blade extended. He wanted to menace me, but his motor control was so unsteady that the weapon bobbed up and down like breadcrumbs on water. I could have taken it from him, but why bother?

I went into the hallway and popped my head into the other rooms, look-ing, I guess, for a fight. People sat around, no one saying anything, maybe drinking beer. Laughter came down again from the third floor. Laughter, laughter. Huh huh ha ha ho ho ha ha hee hoo ho ha ha hee hee ho ho ha ha hee hee. That goddamn laughter.

There were about ten steps between the two floors. I got halfway up before Adeline crashed into me. We fell over, but we didn't fall down the stairs.

—Watch out, you oaf, she said.

—Adeline, I said. It's me. Baby.

—Oh, Baby, she said. Baby, I'm leaving. I shan't ever return.

—Who's laughing up on that third floor?

—Never ask about the third floor.

We stood up. She used my arm, revealing the fragility of her body, how light she was, how little weight she had on her frame.

—Are you crying? she asked.

—David sold my things, I said. All I have are the clothes on my back.

—This place hasn't done either of us much good, she said.

She started down the stairs. I watched her, wondering if there was some-thing I should say. I couldn't think of what. *Don't go! Don't leave me! Please! Not among strangers!*

Adeline turned back. I sucked in a breath.

—Where are you from? she asked.

—I'm an old Wisconsin boy, I said, exhaling. Don't hold it against me.

—Wisconsin. Where's your accent, Baby?

—I lost it, I said, to seem more sophisticated.

I'd adopted the dry, flat voice of television, but I never could tell if the ruse was successful. The only evaluative criteria were comments from kids in my high school. But they were hayseeds. You can't trust the opinions of hayseeds.

—You're here all alone? asked Adeline.

—Wisconsin didn't end too well, I said.

She wasn't wearing any shoes or socks. Her bare feet were exposed. I cringed at the thought of her toes curling in the debris.

—What happened to your yellow shoes?

—Forget them, she said. Why don't you come with me?

—Where?

—To my dormitory, she said. I have a single, but there's a spare bed. Come and stay for some little while.

—Okay, I said, but where are your shoes?

Sometimes you can get these intuitions, glimpses of truth that are pure inspiration. I knew that her shoes were on the third floor.

—They're upstairs. I left them with Bobby.

—Who's Bobby? I asked.

—Bobby is, or rather, I thought that he was, my boyfriend. Right now he's upstairs screwing another girl's brains out. He started right in front of me, Baby. Screwing her brains out. I left the shoes.

—Wait here, I said.

I started back up the stairs. Adeline grabbed my arm.

—It's not worth it, she said. He'll murder you.

I made a mocking sound, a cinematic laugh.

—I worked my father's farm, I said. I've seen more death than you can shake a stick at.

—Please, she said. Mommie Dearest is loaded with dough. She's swimming in cash. I can afford more shoes.

I shrugged her off and climbed to the third floor. The layout was identical to the second. The same rooms. The same clutter and decay. I located Bobby by the sounds of him screwing someone's brains out, an irritating high-pitched female whine paired with a substrata of male groaning. I went into the room and flipped on the lights, and there, sure enough, was a girl on top of a guy.

—Are you Bobby?

—What the shit is wrong with you? Get the fuck out of here.

The girl jumped off. She was the same girl who'd stuck her head into David's room. For a moment Bobby lay there, flat on his back, stark naked, his cock still hard and glistening. He was skinny and dirty like David, but old. He must have been thirty. I could see that he was much lower on the social ladder than Adeline.

—I came for Adeline's shoes.

—Are you fucking juiced or something?

I bent over and picked up the shoes. Bobby rose from the bed.

—Don't go near Adeline again, I said.

—Or what? he asked.

—You won't like what happens.

—Let me tell you what's going to happen, man, he said. I'm going to finish fucking this broad and tomorrow I'll find Adeline and fuck her too. And there isn't nothing some dumb fucking good Samaritan faggot from Westchester can do about it.

Another vision. Beneath the dirt and drugs, I saw Bobby as a scrawny boy in tenth grade, wearing a black t-shirt that read SUGARLOAF, praying not to be noticed by the bigger, meaner kids, biding his time until he could drop out of school and get away from his family. God knows, I should have sympathized, I should have been there with him, the queer kid cowering in fear. But I'd set the school records for the fifty- and hundred-yard dashes. I'm a natural athlete. People loved me. I was popular. Bobby'd been in the city for too long, enraptured within his little egalitarian heroin heaven. He couldn't remember high school. He'd forgotten that life has a natural pecking order. No one had ever called me faggot.

The wrinkled lines of his flat face were like a map of my shame. Wisconsin, my family, my father, my mother, my hometown, my high school best friend, his mother, that terrible squat, longing for the boys who didn't know you existed, accidentally hurting the girls who did, David, the loss of my bag, being so lonely, feeling like no one could ever love me.

I hit Bobby until my hands swelled. Then I kicked him.

He rolled on the ground, gurgling in his own blood and spittle. The girl watched. One minute she was giving him the time, the next he was collapsed into his own arrogance.

—Come by tomorrow and look for Adeline, I said. You know what you'll find.

I picked up the yellow shoes again, the fingers of my left hand plunged deep beneath the tongues. Traces of my own blood around the swollen knuckles, where I'd split the skin.

Adeline waited at the bottom of the stairs, standing in this screwball way, left leg twisted around the right, arms coiled in a fold.

—I have your shoes, I said.

She took them from me. Her eyes went wide. She dropped the shoes and put her hands around mine.

—Did Bobby do this to you? she asked.

—I did this to Bobby.

Adeline sat on the bottom step and tied her laces. I thought about how strange it is that shoes exist, that we live in a world with shoes, that their purposes of fashion and protection were so often opposed.

—Follow me, said Adeline.

She rushed to the ground floor. At the front door, I looked back at this piece of hell on planet Earth. I'd wasted a few Wisconsin weeks dreaming that it would be my home.

—Good luck, you morons, I shouted at the empty hallway. Don't forget to send me a postcard, you stupid idiots!

—Baby, said Adeline, you needn't be theatrical.

Back on 12th, the street lights weren't working. With so many empty lots and abandoned buildings, I experienced a new sort of darkness, a city dark. A homeless guy stood near a wire trash can. He was filling it with debris that he'd gathered, shaking garbage out of a bag that he held over the can's open mouth.

—Hey, I said to him, where'd you get that bag?

—Fuck you, he said.

—Can I buy it? I asked.

—Five bucks for you, Dracula.

I turned my back to him and counted out the bills. Adeline had walked on ahead without realizing that I'd stopped. She noticed that I wasn't beside her and came back. She stood a few feet away. I got the five bucks together. I held them out.

—You first, I said. Don't worry, I won't rip you off. I'm an easy mark.

—Take it, he said.

He threw the bag at me and snatched the money.

—Where'd you find this? I asked.

—Trash can on C, he said.

None of my clothes were in the bag, but of course they weren't. Fresh stains decorated both the outside and the interior, complemented by a pervasive scent of urine.

—What the dickens? asked Adeline. Why would you want such a thing?

—My mother gave me this bag, I said. Do you have a washing machine?

—There's a communal one on the fourth floor, she said.

We reversed the path that I'd taken to David's place. At Second Avenue, there was a theater on the corner. Its marquee read: HAVE I GOT A GIRL FOR YOU! THE FRANKENSTEIN MUSICAL.

—Have you seen that play? I asked Adeline.

—Why, she snorted, would I possibly see that? It's vulgar, Baby. But do you know, a friend of a friend lives above the theater. The artist David Wojnarowicz. Are you aware of his work?

—No.

—It's *très* sinister, she said.

We crossed Second Avenue. A surprising amount of women were on the next block, standing alone, wearing garish makeup and scandalous dresses. A few talked with men, creepy older guys with thick eyebrows.

—We've passed through the veil of a prostitution zone, Adeline said. NYU is building a dorm at Third Avenue. The construction has displaced the hookers. They've trickled down, darling.

The prostitutes weren't glamorous and many looked very sad, but this was more like the New York of my dreams. Dirty and seedy but not quite as desperate, as empty, as cruel as Alphabet City. Prostitutes! Whores! I couldn't believe it. The shining sequins on their dresses cheered me up, putting energy back into my walk.

—Is it much farther? I asked.

—Not so very much longer, she said.

—Adeline, I asked, is there any food at your place? Should I buy some before we go in? I'm starving.

—My roommates always keep some scrap of something in the Frigidaire, she said.

We walked into Union Square. I still didn't know its name. We cut through the park, passing beneath an equestrian statue of George Washington. The First President's sword was missing. So was his bridle strap. His curled left hand held nothing. Black spray paint scarred the pedestal, two big bubble letters: SD.

—Can you see that building? asked Adeline. She pointed at the narrowest, tallest building on the park's west side. Green copper ringed its roof. Each storey had three windows facing the park.

—That's my dormitory, said Adeline. Not the whole thing. Parsons only has floors four through eight. I live on the sixth.

When we arrived at the building, I read the words carved along the length of its marble portico. BANK OF THE METROPOLIS. The address was 31 Union Square West, next door to 33, the building where Valerie Solanas fired 32-caliber slugs into Andy Warhol's exploding plastic inevitable torso. But I didn't know anything about Andy. Not then.

Adeline passed through the first door, stopping in the antechamber. Behind a glass window, a tired old man sat at a makeshift desk. He didn't do anything, didn't say anything. Just sighed and buzzed us through the second door, waved at Adeline and returned to his black-and-white television.

The lobby was narrow, with a set of steps at the back. There were two elevators. We rode in the one on the left.

—This is my first time in an elevator, I confessed.

—How do you find it, Baby?

—It's faster on television, I said.

The front door of her suite opened into a big, dusty space that was half living room, half kitchen. The stove was filthy, caked with the debris from years of careless frying and boiling. A small hallway led to the bathroom and two separate rooms. Every wall painted dead white.

Adeline's room was at the front of the hallway. The second bedroom, farther back, was shared by two girls from South Korea, Sun-Yoon and Jae-Hwa. They'd both adopted American names. Jane and Sally, respectively. It fell on Jane to try and keep the suite clean, but some places are too old. Even the carpeting rotted with mold. What could one girl do against decades of urban decay?

—Welcome to 6B, said Adeline.

We went into her tiny room. The floor was bare linoleum. Adeline'd covered her walls with images and photos. Famous people, fashion photographs, cheap reproductions. A poster of Max Ernst's *The Robing of the Bride*. I didn't recognize it. Another announcing performances by Siouxsie and the Banshees at the Hollywood Palladium on June 6 and 7. A full string of Christmas lights stapled around the window, casting a soft glow.

At the room's center stood a ladder that went up a good ten feet before disappearing into a dark oblong space. I climbed up and poked my face through the hole. The ceiling was three feet from the crown of my head. Twin mattress, sans boxspring, on either side, recessed into crude wooden containers.

People lived like this, sleeping three meters off the floor.

—Put down your bag, said Adeline. We'll find you food.

I planted myself on a half-broken couch in the common area, watching her slap lunch meat atop some very dubious bread. I noticed her toenails, their jagged edges and chipped black polish.

Sun-Yoon came out of her room.

—Jane, said Adeline, this is my friend Baby.

—Hi, I said.

Sun-Yoon didn't respond. The mustard bottle made a wet farting noise.

—Baby will be staying with us for some small while, until he gets his act together. He rode in tonight from Wisconsin.

—Hello, said Sun-Yoon. She closed the bathroom door behind her. She turned on the shower.

—Sun-Yoon's food is the one sacred commodity of this suite, said Adeline. She and Sally voice frequent complaints to the head of housing about my scavenging.

Sitting on the pillows in Adeline's room, stuffing myself, it came to me that I hadn't eaten since I'd stepped off the bus. Adeline handed me a cup.

—What's in it? I asked.

—It's liquor, Baby, what else would it be?

I sucked it down like Coca-Cola, burning the back of my throat. Alcohol takes hold fast, but I never know when it's hit. What killed me was the tiny size of her room. There wasn't any shelving for her clothes, so Parsons had provided an upright closet. That, combined with the crummy desk, occupied half the usable space.

The upright closet made me shudder.

We talked, we talked, we talked.

Adeline told me that she was from Pasadena, a city outside of Los Angeles. I asked if her family was in the movie business. She scoffed and said, no, her dad had been a well-regarded dentist and oral surgeon. He'd invested heavily, and wisely, in real estate. He practiced on famous clients. I squealed, asking who he'd worked on, but Adeline couldn't think of anyone other than the time when her dad put a cap on the lower left incisor of two-time Academy Award winner Jason Robards. A few days later her father fell down dead in his office, victim of a burst heart, leaving Adeline alone with her mother.

—A month ago I ran into Mr. Robards, said Adeline. He lives outside of the city, in Connecticut. He hadn't the slightest who I was, but I told him about Daddy. He felt sorry enough that he bought me ice cream at Serendipity. It was so kitsch.

After her husband's death, Adeline's mother sublimated her grief by entering a wild period of excess. I pressed for details, curious about the potential decadences of a middle-aged woman, but Adeline demurred, saying it was old news. Only recently, her mother'd calmed down and settled into a period of comfortable, blurry alcoholism.

—Mother's become a pleasant enough souse, said Adeline, very much like Myrna Loy in *The Thin Man*. But Mother's so much older than Myrna was when Myrna ran with William Powell. It's a bit pathetic.

—Why don't you have a roommate?

—Mother and I conspired, she said. I visited Dr. Jacobs, Mother's analyst. I told Dr. Jacobs that I'd go simply mad if I had to have a roommate.

The good doctor sent along a note saying that I suffer from an unspecified mental condition and must at all costs live alone.

Ashamed that I lacked any good stories of my own, no wild periods of excess, I talked about farming. About the empty lives in the middle of this American continent. Adeline gave me the impression that she'd only ever been in California and New York, leapfrogging her way over the great nothingness of the U.S.A., never confronting the dumb, open faces of this country's people.

Through her window, I caught my first glimpse of New York daybreak, when the sky lightens and strips the earth of its color. Adeline pulled down the cheap plastic shade, plunging us into off-season Christmas illumination.

—Time for bed, she said.

—Adeline, I said, why did you invite me here?

—You're a sailor without any port of call.

—But you aren't expecting anything, are you?

—Expecting?

—You know, I said. Expecting.

She leaned forward. I stiffened, freaked out that I'd made an accidental pass. I didn't want to be kicked out, not now, not after she'd been so nice.

—Baby, she asked, don't you favor men?

My bag was still on the linoleum floor, beside her yellow shoes. A lot of good clothes in that bag.

—Yes, I said.

Which was the first time aloud.

—Then why should I expect anything?

—But how can you tell?

—You put up a decent front, said Adeline, but you won't be able to hide here. This city is queerer than a three dollar bill. Take the spare bed and tomorrow we'll cut that hair and find you some reasonable clothes.

—What's wrong with my hair? I asked, but Adeline climbed the ladder without answering.

OCTOBER 1986

Baby Learns One or Two Things About Life in New York

The next morning, Adeline pulled opened her shade, and I looked out toward Mays and the other stores along the south side of the park. The Zeckendorf Towers were rising.

I did get my hair cut, by the by. Adeline herself wielded the scissors. For years I'd hidden myself beneath a bowl, only another decent lad from the badlands. Adeline chopped away the blond veil, exposing my bone structure and the general shape of my head.

For my clothes, we pilgrimaged around the building, taking alms offered by fashion students. These donations carried me through my first few days, until Monday next when Adeline rushed into the suite carrying several large bags, claiming that she'd gone to the Salvation Army on Fourth Avenue. I picked through the too-clean shirts and pants, noting in silence that someone'd forgotten to take off the price tags from Macy's and Saks.

Six days earlier, I'd been a long-legged hick, a cornpone fresh from the farm. Now I saw myself in the mirror, with new clothes and a juicy haircut. I was dead sexy. And so, so, so clearly gay. I could see it in my lips and my hairline, in the tightness of my facial muscles. God, how did I think I could hide? I was such a homo.

We never spoke of the boy Adeline rescued from a squat in Alphabet City, that child who faded into a *persona non grata*, unmentioned, like a mentally retarded cousin spirited away to a Victorian country asylum.

Weeks rolled by. I wandered New York, its manic energy seeping into my bones. The pavement vibrated, resonating with billions of earlier footsteps, centuries of people making their way, the city alive with the irregular heartbeat of its million cars and trucks, of its screaming pedestrians, its vendors and hustlers. The roar and clamor infected my blood, transforming my walk. Gone was my lumbering gait, now I moved sleek footed and fast as a shadow.

I went anywhere that Adeline asked. I never said no. Art openings, movies, sometimes museums. I remember one film that we saw together, *Peggy Sue Got Married* at the Quad Cinema, a corny fantasy about a woman attending her twenty-fifth high school reunion, directed by Francis Ford Coppola.

As these things are wont to happen, Peggy Sue is crowned queen of the event. She suffers a panic attack at the moment of her coronation, fainting into darkness. When Peggy Sue regains consciousness, she discovers herself transported into her own past, trapped in high school and doomed to re-create the miseries of her youth.

At the film's beginning, Peggy Sue has achieved a belated adulthood and decides to wrest control of her destiny by divorcing her unfaithful husband. By the end credits, she's submitted to the humiliations of her adolescence, the knowingness of a grown woman being no defense against the idiotic mistakes of youth. Peggy Sue reverts to her girlish persona, awakens in the present, and stands by her man. Adeline hated the resolution, calling it antifeminist, but for me, the central premise was the true horror, this idea that the universe could take your life away on a whim, could force you back.

We also caught *The Godfather* at the Film Forum on Watts Street and Sixth Ave., an extended leather fantasy by the same director. The plot is pretty simple. Marlon Brando, the original motorcycle stud, rules over the Corleones, a family of closet cases. All of Marlon's naughty boys are beholden to the eldest, an ultra-butch and hairy James Caan, who ruts around the family estate like a randy bull. Al Pacino gets a hard-on for the lifestyle after a silver daddy police captain teaches him to respect the whip. Al goes wild, dishing out damage on every bitch that he can find. It's much better than *Peggy Sue Got Married*.

Adeline knew everyone, was invited to countless parties. In the East Village, the West Village, Greenwich Village, Alphabet City, SoHo, the Upper East Side, Battery Park, even the outer boroughs. We attended them all.

The only parties I didn't enjoy were those thrown by people from Parsons. Adeline couldn't help herself. Whenever she saw a gay classmate, she'd push us together.

—But Baby, you two have so much in common. Think of the discussions!

Yes, we do, I'd think, but I couldn't, not really, not then. Plus, at a party? Who wants to sleep with someone they met at a party?

That's a pointless question, because Adeline offered its answer. The inevitable narrative justification for our attendance was Adeline's desire for suitable bedmates. In reality, despite her hours of flirting and dancing, she rarely slept with anyone. Which got me thinking about the difference between people's idea of themselves and the way that they truly are, the vast gulf between human aspirations and the hard quirks of personality that nothing can efface.

A lucky few made the cut, earning a chance to initiate themselves in the mysteries of her orifices. Then I'd be out on the couch in the common area.

As a survival strategy, I befriended Sally and Jane. Or tried to, anyway. Jane never warmed up to me, although she appreciated my futile attempts to help her clean the suite. Sally and I got along, despite the language barrier, and she often fed me. Neither complained to the head of housing.

The longest lasting of Adeline's young men claimed to be from Santiago, speaking with a heavy accent, but one time I walked with him across the park, to a deli, looking to buy pop. A Mexican kid worked the cash register. He tried talking to the guy from Santiago. *En Español.* Nothing, not even a response, the guy from Santiago's eyes glazed over, not recognizing the language.

We walked back with Adeline's boy-toy chattering on about American baseball, about the Mets, with whom he'd fallen in love while watching the World Series, about Bill Buckner being a divine gift from Tío Dios. I thought about saying something to Adeline, but why bother? I knew that he'd be gone in a few weeks.

Myself, I was too square, too backwards for rank promiscuity. I assumed it'd come, somehow, probably, but I'd only just admitted aloud my need for other men and their bodies. I envisioned looming decades of erect cocks. My pleasures now were simple. I was Adeline's awkward friend, the quiet type standing beside her as she denounced Jeff Koons to her classmates. It was enough to keep my eyes on the glorious bodies, listening to their banal dialogues, enjoying some kind of wonderful.

I feasted on humanity, on people.

Like that man on the eleventh floor. By that glorious being alone may we describe New York City in the Year of Our Lord, 1986.

How did he appear? Portly, not fat. Tall, graying goatee. Often seen wearing a ridiculous fedora. I espied him on occasion, typically in the elevator, but never attached him with any undue importance. He appeared as only one of many adults wrestling with the unhappy fact that four floors of their apartment building were under occupation by an invading force of drugged and dissolute college students.

And then one day, Adeline pointed at the man from the eleventh floor as he walked out from beneath the portico. She whispered:

—Do you see that fellow? That man's name is Thomas M. Disch. You won't know his work. I gather he's some sort of science fiction writer. Which is a lot of dreadful stuff, don't you think? Robots and spaceships.

Science fiction.

Among his many flaws, my father had spent most of his life as an inveterate aficionado of the genre. Stacks of rotting paperbacks in the barn, yellowing books that he tried to get me to read. I refused. The closest I came was *The Fellowship of the Ring*. Which broke his heart, really, because the old man was a hardliner who believed in a strict division between genres.

One year he left the family behind and drove to MiniCon, a science fiction convention held in Minneapolis. A writer named Spider Robinson was the Guest of Honor. My father loved Robinson's books, all of which I gather take place in a ribald saloon located somewhere in outer space. When the old man came home, he couldn't shut up about the experience. The writers he met, the books they signed, the panels he attended. We got sick of hearing about it. Spider Robinson is a fucking idiotic name.

I started a lonely vigil, keeping an eye out for Thomas M. Disch, imagining that I'd seen his books in my father's collection. But that was wishful thinking, I'm sure, misremembering volumes by Gordon R. Dickson with some hope of a connection to my distant, dead parent.

I saw Thomas M. Disch three or four times, perhaps five. On one occasion, he was in a heated, screaming argument with another man. I'd seen this other man around the building with greater frequency than Thomas M. Disch. From their voices and postures, I understood they were having the complicated kind of fight that my parents took up on blank nights when the television offered nothing and there was no other outlet for their attentions.

A lovers' quarrel. So that was it, then. A queer science fiction writer living at the top of Union Square. A queer science fiction writer with a steady boyfriend. Now I really wanted to talk to Thomas M. Disch, now it went well beyond my father. I wanted to ambush Thomas M. Disch in the elevator and ask *how? how? HOW? HOW?*

How do you live like this, how did you learn this, how did you become a gay man writing about robots? How do you manage your steady beau?

But I was too shy.

I did the next best thing, walking to 12th and Broadway, to the store I'd seen on my first night in the city. Above its plate-glass windows ran flat red rectangular panels with white block letters: STRAND BOOK STORE. EIGHT MILES OF BOOKS. Embedded within the panels were smaller white signs with black lettering: LIBRARIES BOUGHT and OLD RARE NEW.

As I stood across the street, looking at the store, a little man on his dirty bicycle pedaled past, a boombox wedged into his wire handlebar basket. Tinny music rose above the clamor of cars: *Yeah, heard about your Polaroids / that's what I call obscene / tricks with fruit / it's kind of cute / I bet you keep the pussy clean.*

I've originated a baroque theory that the Strand is in some inexplicable way a microcosm mirroring the city's greater social experience. In recent years, they've remodeled the place, made it as clean as an infant's nursery, and opened up the second floor. By contrast, Patti Smith starved there in the '70s.

In '86, it was a studied disaster, fucked up, cluttered and devastated. Entering its single door, there was a bag check at your immediate right, a crap desk surrounded by poorly carved wooden cubbyholes and staffed by the least pleasant person in the building. After passing this modern-day Cerberus, you'd lose yourself on the overstuffed ground floor, wandering beneath green fluorescent lighting, examining books crammed into wooden and gray metal shelves, arranged in arbitrary distinctions that separated 'Fiction' from 'Literature'. The basement was a labyrinth of half-price review hardcovers and all the other weird shit that couldn't fit on the first floor.

A meager science fiction section occupied the far end of the ground floor, between fiction and sociology. Mostly paperback and kept in no sensible order, runoff trash stocked on the off chance some loser might wander in, jonesing for his fix of fruity elves and space opera.

Like me. I was that loser.

Wedged between Mercedes Lackey and Ted Sturgeon, I found an early-'70s reissue of Thomas M. Disch's *Camp Concentration*. Beneath the title and copy advertising THE MOST ACCLAIMED SCIENCE FICTON NOVEL IN YEARS was a painting anchored by the crude torso of a male nude pulled open by its own hands.

The price was penciled inside the front cover. $2. I dodged yuppies hovering around display tables, and took the book to checkout, a long desk that ran parallel with Broadway.

—Next! shouted a ginger-haired girl.

I gave her the book, she looked at it and laughed.

—This looks terrific, she said.

—It's for a friend, I said. I prefer Hemingway.

—Sure you do, she said. It's two dollars and seventeen cents.

NOVEMBER 1986

Adeline Teaches Baby About Marijuana, the Secular Sacrament of California

Everyone in Wisconsin always said they got high, but other than indulgences on overnight trips for track meets, I never saw anyone with weed. I'd been stoned before coming to New York, but I'd never been flat-out baked, never experienced the expansion and contraction of time that encompasses several weeks of smoking pot.

Adeline, on the other hand, was from California. She'd grown up with marijuana as a secular sacrament. In Pasadena, in Los Angeles, in the whole of the Golden State, pot was a kind of social punctuation. Adeline was stoned through the four years of her ridiculous private high school. She hadn't smoked much in college. She said it wasn't a particularly interesting drug, that she preferred hallucinogens and stimulants.

But then, at last, finally, without recourse, at wit's end, Adeline was assigned coursework that she could not complete.

—It's dreadful, Baby. I'm bored. This nonsense is related to French theory.

She wasted a few hours staring into her blank paper, fiddling with sticks of charcoal, but never making a line, not even a smudge. Throwing her hands into the air, she announced her intention. She would get stoned and draw whatever came to her mind. Even if the work produced under the influence was of poor quality, it'd be better than showing up with nothing.

—This woman wouldn't dare fail a completed assignment, Adeline said.

She left the suite and came back twenty minutes later.

—Do you have it? I asked, embarrassed at the excitement in my voice.

—What do you think I've been doing?

—Can I see it?

She laid out two ounces. Skunk weed, but I didn't know it.

—Shall we? she asked.

I nodded my head.

—I bought ZigZag papers at the deli, she said. Isn't it terrible how we regress to childhood at the first sign of trouble?

She coached me as I inhaled, talked me through coughing when the heat hit my lungs, eased me into it. We laughed and rolled around on the dirty carpet. My skin tingled, like there were thousands of metal subcutaneous Q-tips bouncing back and forth against the elasticity of my flesh.

—What about your work?

—Oh that. Ha ha ha ha. Well. Well. Oh, that. Ha ha! I shall draw several portraits of Bela Lugosi.

—Who's Bela Lugosi?

—Why, Baby, he's Dracula! Capes and fangs? 1931? Universal Pictures? Directed by Tod Browning? He doesn't drink wine? In your ignorance, darling, you're nothing but a philistine!

—Is that the assignment?

—Fuck my teacher and fuck her assignment.

Her hand ran across the paper, leaving behind a trail of dark smudges and rough lines.

—There are several bookstores on Hollywood Boulevard which cater to the cineaste. Larry Edmunds, Pickwick, Book City. You can find any number of publications on the cinema. I have quite a library in Pasadena. The Golden Age of film remains in Los Angeles, no matter the grime, if only you know where to look.

I couldn't see any discernible shape in Adeline's drawings, but I found myself peering into and through them, my thoughts going free association.

—Why do you talk like that? I asked.

—Whatever do you mean?

—You speak like someone from the past. But you can't repeat the past.

—Can't repeat the past? Of course you can. Why, Baby, I'm a positive fraud. My accent is as affected as yours. It's sheer insecurity, darling.

Sally came out of her bedroom. We burst into laughter.

—Was he really from Santiago?

—So he said.

—And by their fruits ye shall know them.

—Whatever do you mean? asked Adeline.

—It's just something that someone said once, I said.

Adeline completed ten drawings of Bela Lugosi. I fell asleep, starving, too high to climb down the ladder. In the morning, Adeline was gone, in class. I sat around. My money was disappearing, fast, and soon I'd have to get a job. The thought made me sick.

Around 3 pm, Adeline came into the suite, bursting with success.

—The Belas went over swimmingly, she said. I suspect they'll be my best grade of the semester.

We had two ounces left. You can give it away or you can smoke it. Adeline rolled a joint. I put in my own efforts, but I couldn't achieve the same crisp California finish, my attempts disintegrating halfway through. We got high and wandered the streets, New York looking somehow different. The mundane was not made magical, but subtly altered. Purple clouds floated in the night sky, backlit by inexplicable luminescence.

Then we were just stoned. Adeline may have bought more pot. Which was easy enough, the park was full of dealers. It started snowing. Through the window, I could see every individual flake. I could see past the park, out toward the river, but I couldn't see the river, but I sensed the river, the river lapping against the jagged edges of the city, and beyond the river, Brooklyn, pulsing like a heart, a whole other city that was the same city. A backwater to which we'd only gone twice, on the BMT L all the way to Canarsie. A Polish kid from the design department at Parsons lived there with his family. He'd thrown a few parties. Adeline insisted that we attend. I watched as a blonde illustration student vomited in the front yard, the hacking sound echoing off vinyl siding. I sensed the modest two-storey house, its walls vibrating across the river.

Then we were just stoned. Adeline did schoolwork, turned in projects, read books assigned for courses. She had a copy of George Bataille's *Story of the Eye.* I asked what it was about. She told me. I promptly forgot.

—It should change soon, said Adeline. We're reading the Futurists next.

Then we were just stoned. I watched television with Sally while Jane scoffed. I hadn't watched television since Wisconsin. There was a program called *Alf,* about a furry orange space alien with a huge nose that enjoyed the taste of cats and crashed with a human family. I wondered if Thomas M. Disch watched *Alf.* There was a program called *Golden Girls,* about four nonagenarian female retirees who were crazy horny for all the withered and desiccated flesh of Florida. There was a program called *Starman.* This was my favorite. I have no idea what it was about. Then we were just stoned. I stopped watching television. Adeline read more books.

Our pot ran out. Adeline grew tired of it, I grew tired of it. A week contracted, my brain brittle like a dried-out sponge. We were no longer stoned.

I walked to Rockefeller Center. Workers were in the process of putting up the Christmas tree. It wasn't lit. No one skated on the ice. I thought that the walk would clear my head, cold wind whipping through my absurd clothes and my yellow hair.

I considered taking the subway back downtown, but walked home instead. Broadway between 40th and Union Square is a no man's land, especially at night. I was alone except for the homeless and stray professionals. Closed stores, closed everything.

Back at Union Square, I walked to the south end, checking to see if Adeline's light was on. It was. I didn't want to see her, didn't want to see anyone. I walked down University Place to Washington Square. NYU kids were in the park, along with drug dealers and the tents and punks and junkies. I sat on a bench, remembering this guy named Peter. We'd gone to high school together.

He died in our junior year, victim of an undiagnosed medical condition, born with holes in his underdeveloped lungs. We weren't close but the school was small. Besides, I was an athlete. People always wanted to be my friend. Peter was a guy that I saw, spoke with, waved at. And then he died.

What would life be like if he hadn't? Where would he have ended up? Like his parents, I guessed, the long disappointment after his youth terminated into marriage and kids and a job that he couldn't stand, waking up every morning with a hot spike of acid reflux as he drank his obligatory coffee and then falling asleep with another as he drank cheap whiskey. Peter was a simple guy, an easy case. This was beyond his imagination. All of it. Adeline, Union Square, Washington Square, Alphabet City, Polish kids from Canarsie who attended Parsons, guys who pretended they were from Santiago, illustration students in pink leotards unable to hold their liquor, Peggy Sue's time-traveling panic attack, three solid weeks of smoking pot for no reason beyond general apathy. I'd spent two months in New York convinced of my own righteousness, convinced of the absolute necessity of being here, but what if I was wrong? What if New York was just a different flavor of bullshit?

A homeless couple got into a fight, the woman beating the man, the man crying alcoholic crocodile tears. I thought about walking farther south, maybe all the way to Battery Park, but decided against it, figuring I'd better head back.

At 31 Union Square West, the doorman buzzed me in. His name was Bill. He was about fifty-five years old, maybe a little older. He always wore a baseball cap and a brown leather bomber jacket. Like all the doormen at 31 Union Square West, he was Black. Very few residents of the building, students included, were Black.

One time Adeline and I were stoned, going out to buy junk food. She had her period. Bill stopped us on the way out and asked:—Where you going?

—To the deli, I said.

—What for?

—Candy, said Adeline.

—You don't need to feed that girl candy, said Bill. She's sweet enough.

I opened the door to 6B. Adeline sat at the table, hunched over pieces of paper. She was dressed down. Gray sweatpants, which I'd never seen her wear, and a heavy black wool sweater. She'd brought her turntable into the common area, playing loud enough to shake the whole room: *Let's sway / you could look into my eyes / let's sway under the moonlight / this serious moonlight.*

—Baby!

Adeline turned to the record player and lowered the volume.

—Baby, asked Adeline, wherever have you been?

DECEMBER 1986

Baby Talks to Thomas M. Disch

Presented as the found diary of its protagonist, Thomas M. Disch's *Camp Concentration* moves through the space of about a year. Louis Sacchetti is imprisoned by President Robert McNamara for dissidence during the ongoing Vietnam War. Shortly after the novel opens, Sacchetti is moved to a secret prison by the name of Camp Archimedes, an installation run by scientists in service of the U.S. Army.

Unlike Sacchetti, the other prisoners at Archimedes have been collected for their subnormal intellects. Upon arrival, these unlucky few are dosed with an experimental form of syphilis. In addition to the well-known problematic aspects of contracting the Spanish Pox, this iteration of the disease accelerates its infection time, achieving a near-instant form of its tertiary stage, destroying the normal structures and containments of the human brain.

The end result? Its victims are transformed into the bearers of genius-level IQs. They experience frantic bursts of creative and cerebral spontaneity. Former car thieves and card sharks become great scientists and dramatists. One of them, named Mordecai Washington, develops an ongoing fascination with medieval alchemy.

The book was a long way from Adeline's imagined robots and spaceships, a huge distance from the garbage that my father consumed like daily rations.

When you read a book like *Camp Concentration,* you want to run through the streets, assaulting passersby, grabbing people by their lapels, attempting to shake them from their senescence, spit erupting from your lips, yelling and shouting: *DO YOU KNOW WHAT THOMAS M. DISCH HAS DONE? HE HAS WRITTEN* CAMP CONCENTRATION *AND SOMEHOW ESCAPED BEING PUT IN JAIL! LISTEN TO ME, DO YOU HEAR ME? THOMAS M. DISCH HAS WRITTEN THIS GREAT UNWIELDY THING! THERE ARE OPEN SECRETS IN BOOKS THAT WILL*

CHANGE YOUR ENTIRE WAY OF BEING! HOW CAN LIFE EVER BE
SANE AGAIN?

One morning in early December, when I'd gone out to get Adeline and
myself some coffee, I tried my hardest not to think about Christmas. What
would I do over the holiday? I squeezed my eyes half shut, as if the pressure
would push out the thoughts, and walked past the crumbling, filthy statue
of Lincoln, momentarily distracted, as I always was, by the bizarre sight of
the Great Emancipator wearing a toga.

Nearing the entrance of 31 Union Square West, I watched Thomas M.
Disch go through the first door. I hurried to catch up, coffee sloshing in
each hand. I don't know why, I guess to ride the same elevator. Which I did.
I moved inside and stood beside Thomas M. Disch. I noticed again how
huge the man was, how large in every sense of the word.

He pushed the round button marked 11.

—What floor? he asked me.

—Six, I said.

The elevator began its slow ascent, creaking and wheezing on its way. I
stared at Thomas M. Disch.

—What is it? he asked.

—Sorry, I said. It's just that I loved *Camp Concentration*. I read it a few
weeks ago. I think it's the best book I've ever read.

—Have you read many books? asked Thomas M. Disch.

—No, I admitted.

The elevator reached the sixth floor, going a little high, then readjusting
itself back in line with the exit. The door opened. I hesitated.

—Look, said Thomas M. Disch, you can ride with me up to the eleventh
floor. I'll answer any question you ask, but that's it. You can't come inside
my apartment.

The door closed. We continued our ascent.

—Well? asked Thomas M. Disch. Don't blow it. This is your moment.

I wanted to ask about being gay, ask if his gayness impacted the book,
whether being gay hurt his career as a writer, whether or not he was a writer
because he was gay, whether or not there were a lot of gay writers of science
fiction, about what his life was like, about how he got published, about the
experience of being published, what was it like having an abstracted seg-
ment of his thoughts encapsulated in small bricklike objects floating
around the world in a process that he could not control.

But I couldn't. Heat rose to my cheeks. I felt myself blushing.

—I'm sorry, I said.

—It's okay, he said. It doesn't matter. No one ever asks good questions.

The elevator reached the eleventh floor. When it stopped, Thomas M. Disch pressed the button marked 6. He walked out of the elevator and then turned back and used his foot to stop the door from closing.

—You seem somehow less horrible than other people your age, said Thomas M. Disch, so I'll give you advice that I wish someone had given me when I was young and stupid. Would you be fine with that?

—Yes, I said, please.

He took off his outrageous hat. He looked right through me. Thomas M. Disch stood before me, ruminating, thinking. He coughed a little bit.

And then he said:

—No one is in charge. There is no central authority. There are people who can kill you, people who can put you in prison, people who can ruin you. That's a marked difference from someone who is in charge. It's a wide distance from a person being in control. You have spent your whole life believing in the myth of human competence, of parents, teachers, politicians, accepting the idea that there is a hierarchy of individuals who have worked hard, done the right things, made the proper choices, and been rewarded for such efforts. You think that there is a natural order in which we are each compensated on the basis of our individual merits, that the truly talented and intelligent reside at the top. This is complete fucking horseshit. The people at the top are as moronic, as base and inept as those at the bottom. The ruling class is simply meaner and more ruthless than us troglodytes. If I were you, I'd stop wasting my time with minor novels about experimental syphilis and start paying attention to the way things really work. I'd abandon any hope of a Great White Father who will save you from yourself. I'd stop pretending like your government and your society possess the capacity to handle any of their ongoing existential challenges. They don't. Nobody saves anybody. Everyone flails around. Nothing works. All of life is a horror show. Even the people you love will reveal themselves as little more than bags of shit. The whole world is fucked. You might as well become someone who does the fucking.

Thomas M. Disch pulled his foot away. The elevator door closed. Heat from the coffee burned my hand through the flimsy paper cups.

Twenty-one years later, he shot open his head and blew out his brains. He was still on the eleventh floor. He pulled the trigger on July 4th.

JANUARY 1ST, 1987

Adeline Meets Her New Boyfriend

W e'd just rung in the New Year 1987, an apartment somewheres in the East Village, tinsel and cheers around us. A gauche person actually crooned "Auld Lang Syne." I considered the drug situation, wondering if there wasn't a purse floating about with an '86 vintage of cocaine. Baby spake to me, saying, "Adeline, watch out, that Kurt Vonnegut guy is coming over." I hadn't the slightest, so Baby said, "Come on, you remember, this is the guy who always talks about Kurt Vonnegut." I hadn't the slightest.

"Well, Baby," said I, "this fellow sounds quite the dreadful bore."

We'd struck up a conversation with a girl who'd holidayed in Florida with her family and returned on a commuter flight. "The Sunshine State," she said, "is fucking white trash, but the weather is way better."

"East Coast people don't know anything about the cold," said Baby. "Go out to the Midwest. Lake Superior will freeze off your nipples."

"I shouldn't much like that," I said.

This apartment somewheres in the East Village was as dark as unlit thickets, as boggy as Grimpen Mire. Pitch radiant, people dancing and talking, black light and disco ball and very primitive laser. One of those awful, terrible parties where the insuppressible stench of alcohol seeps from everyone's pores. Strong enough that the odor was noticeable even to myself, and darlings, I was three-and-a-quarter sheets to the wind.

"Did you go home for Christmas?" the girl asked.

"We stayed in the city," I said. "I couldn't begin to imagine a return to Californy. I've only just started to understand New York. Everyone in California is dead. D-E-A-D. As a doornail. Deader than dead. Ne plus ultra dead."

"So it goes," said a voice behind us, with a baritone so deep that it shook my bones. Baby made a face. "So it goes," said the voice again. A young man of about the same years as myself. One couldn't imagine that deep of a voice from such a youthful body.

His fashion was neo-retro, Edwardian frock coat meets the pastel colorations of the 1980s. A New Romantic in the wrong year and the wrong country. His travesty hair was mouse brown and limpid. I shouldn't have been surprised to learn that his mother doubled as his barber.

"I beg your pardon, but that's some rum talk," I said. "Whatever is your name?"

"We met last month," he said. "You're Adeline. I remember you. Why don't you remember me?"

"Adeline's memory is the worst," said Baby, rather unhelpfully.

"Pay no regard to this disagreeable young homosexual," I said. "And speak your name."

He mouthed the word, but a scream from the far side of the room engulfed his sound. Music ended, gasps and silence. I pushed my way through vile bodies towards the commotion.

There, beneath purple light, two wretched boys did battle. Professional pugilists these fellas were not. Arms, legs, headlocks, kicks, punches, all awkward. One bled from his forehead.

"Ain't it an appalling spectacle?" I asked Baby, but Baby wasn't beside me.

"Busy, busy, busy," said the unknown boy with mousy brown hair.

Both contestants were ejected with force. I watched from the window to see if they'd continue their battle in the street, but on the pavement they embraced, perhaps crying about the awful pain of existence, and walked arm in arm towards Greenwich Village, singing an off-key and wobbling rendition of Queen's "We Will Rock You."

Human variety, said I to my own self, will never cease to amaze you.

The boy with limpid hair went by the name of Kevin. We talked no small amount, regrettably much of it about the Kurt Vonnegut novels *Player Piano* and *Jailbird*, neither of which had I read. I informed Kevin that I'd breezed through *Breakfast of Champions,* which was a dirty lie, and Kevin sneered, "Oh, everyone's read *Breakfast of Champions.* To really understand Vonnegut, you gotta read his others!" I rolled my eyes, perhaps not visibly, at the suggestion.

I invited Kevin back to our suite. On 9th Street, Baby pulled me to one side and whispered, "Adeline, not him!" but I psshed and tssshed and sssshed. For his part, Kevin did not regard the mild controversy, being rather enraptured with the manner in which his shoes struck the cement.

When we returned to 31 Union Square West, our old Bank of the

Metropolis, poor Baby suffered yet another exile on the couch. Kevin climbed up the ladder, crawled into my bed, removed his clothes, removed my clothes, and proceeded to screw out my brains.

Now, reader, had this been an ordinary night in the adventures of your narratress, our Vonnegut-inspired friend would have departed in the light of sober morning and not made his reappearance. Yet it was New Year's Day. Holiday spirit overtook me.

Kevin exuded a certain appealing quality. Sleeping buck naked except for a graying tube sock on his left foot, the rise and fall of his bare chest with its scraggle of hair, a clicking sound emerging from his throat each time that he exhaled.

One sees in this boy one's own age, immature, poorly dressed, terrible haircut, offering little in the way of conversation. Somehow, something about this acnefied picture makes a convincing argument. One ends up smitten.

And if that ain't sympathy for the awkwardness of being male, what is?

This, you see, is how I ended up with my second college boyfriend.

FEBRUARY 1987

Suzanne Comes to Visit

Ringing phone at 7 am on a Friday morning in February, climbing down the ladder in a half-conscious fury, answering to the shrill voice of my inebriated mother.

"Adeliiiiiiine," said Mother. "You'll never guess where I am!"

"Where?" I asked, weary.

"The International Terminal at JFK! I took the red-eye!"

"Uhm, why are you, like, there?" I asked.

"Adeliiiiiiiiine," said Mother. "I'm in New York for the week! I couldn't let you miss Christmas and not get any presents! I've even brought your gifts from Dahlia and Charles!"

"You're here?" I asked. "In New York?"

"Yes, dear," said Mother. "And for the whole visit, I'll speak entirely in a Noo Yawk accent! Fuggedaboutit! What street do youse live on? Tirty tee and uh tird!"

"Have you been drinking?" I asked.

"Only uh few highbawls on da foist-class aeroplane," she said.

"Mom," I said. "Please stop. I can't take it."

"Adeliiiiiiine," said Mother. "I'm waiting for my baggage and then I'll get a car into the city! I'm staying at the Plaza! I know you'll come to lunch, won't you!"

"Whatever," I said. "What time?"

"Nooooon, Adeliiiiiiiine," said Mother. "I'll be waiting in the lobbbbby!"

"See you then," I said and hung up.

Enrolling at the Parsons School for Design was clearly an attempt to escape Mother, to escape Dahlia and Dahlia's awful husband, Charles, to escape greater Los Angeles, to escape the Crossroads School for the Arts and Sciences and the genius vision of its founder, Paul Cummins. I'm quite certain that somewhere in the primordial stew of my ridiculous brain, as I considered my acceptance letters to various educational institutions, a voice had spake, saying, "Adeline, darling, consider matters. Two thousand four hundred thirty-nine and seven-tenths of a mile is a looooooooong way from home."

Yet this voice had not contended with the dread reality of Mother.

Despite her many depravities, the woman rose each morning and willed away the ritualized hangovers. Smearing a thick patina of lipstick and rouge across her face, she soldiered into her office and managed the daylights out of her business affairs.

We'd only grown richer since Daddy's death. Money, that great barrier to so many dreams, proved no impediment. Mother could visit whenever the fancy took her. My one surprise was that she'd waited this long.

I imagined scenarios by which to dissuade her from future holidays, considered a perilous visit with the hopheads and roughs down by Ray's and the Pyramid, then, with more deliberation, abandoned it. Mother would find the lower orders so charming, so quaint, adore their patched denim and their disease-encrusted syringes. She'd coo over the bold graphic type of the *Newsday* slogan on Ray's awning: TRUTH, JUSTICE AND THE COMICS.

The night prior, I'd finished reading an uncorrected proof of Bret Easton Ellis's new novel, *The Rules of Attraction*. I'd uncovered the proof in the Strand, deep in a pile of nonsense and novels.

It often seems that when one reads a book, the events of one's life take on a distinct resemblance to the fictional narrative.

The Rules of Attraction played through my mind like the blurry hurdy-gurdy filmstrip of a Kinetoscope. A scene in which Paul Denton is called to New York by his mother, who is taking her own jaundiced bite from the Big Apple.

I climbed up the ladder. Baby in the spare bed, his slumber undisturbed by the ringing. What a blessing is ignorance, thought I to myself. What an absolute delight.

Perhaps he should accompany me to the Plaza. But Mother would love Baby. It was impossible to miss. What if Baby anchored her? What if she came back for him?

White paint of the ceiling. Engines moving around the park, the horns of traffic, the rising voices of pedestrians. Thousand thread-count against my legs and arms. Morning breath in my mouth, dry cotton tongue. Noxious fumes, diesel, gasoline, uncollected garbage. Another scent as well.

Kevin.

*

"Why," asked Kevin, "do I have to meet her?"

"You'll simply adore her," I said. "She possesses every favorable quality you can imaginate."

In the backseat of a cab motoring towards the Plaza. People could make cruel comments about Kevin, and God knows that Baby surely did, but, if nothing else, the boy offered reliability.

"How were you occupying yourself? What else could possibly be filling your time?" I asked.

"Studying," he said. "I have an exam on Monday."

Kevin attended New York University, pursuing his undergraduate degree. I simply cannot remember what it was that he studied. Literature, perhaps, or some other putrid nonsense.

I put my hand on the back of his head. I'd grown fond of his haircut. "What's all this, then," I asked in an atrocious cockney accent. "When 'ave you attended class, guvnor?"

"My grades are a lot better than you'd think," he said.

We disembarked by the drab equestrian statue of William Tecumseh Sherman and Wingéd Nike. We ran across the street during a lull in traffic.

Mother was nowhere within the lobby's confines. After some exploration, we uncovered her in the Oak Room, where she'd pickled herself in some very choice brine.

My sudden appearance elicited a screeching sound that one associates with oversized birds of prey: "Adeliiiiiiiiiiiiiiiiiiiiiiiiiiiiiiiiiiiiiine!" She grasped me in her claws, swallowing her daughter into a sloshed hug.

Mother pulled away and spoke to Kevin. New work had been done on her face. Perhaps an eye lift? Her bronzed flesh too taut, too outré, too close to the same inhuman visage shared by all Angelino women of a certain age and social standing. I longed for the original true face of my mother, the smile destroyed by a decade of surgery.

She made an effort at afternoon tea, but I insisted that we find a place more authentically Noo Yawk. A tiny pizza parlor off Fifth Avenue, the tomato sauce of our slices matching Mother's garish red power suit.

"Adeliiiiiine," said she, stuffing her face, "New York has the best pizza in the world!"

"It sure does, Mom," I said.

"Keviiiiiin," said Mother. "How do you know my Adeliiiiiine!"

"We, like, met at a party," I said.

"On New Year's Eve," said Kevin.

"Don't you dare provide details," I whispered.

He ignored this demand, talking about the party, about what we had done, about how long we had been dating and many other inessentialities. The timbre and bass of his voice vibrated me to the absolute verge.

"Have you read much Vonnegut?" he asked Mother.

"No," she said. "But Adeliiiiine's father was friends with the producer of the film adaptation of *Slaughterhouse-Five*! You remember Jennings Lang, don't you, Adeliiiiine!"

"Uhm," I said. "No?"

"He died last year!" said Mother.

"Okay," I said.

"I envy you," said Kevin to Mother. "Adeline and I only get these books in a single dose, when Vonnegut's career is in its final stages. But you're old enough to've seen them come out one by one, and experience the dialogue between author and audience."

He may as well have painted a crucifix on his back, bathed in the blood of lambs and thrown himself down amongst the lions. Mother stiffened, her smile evaporated. She stopped speaking in exclamation points. To talk about her age! A perfect faux pas.

Having proved the weight of his salt, Kevin tagged along for all subsequent encounters. Our questionable troika visited the Met, FAO Schwarz, the Museum of Natural History, uptown, downtown. Once, while Kevin contained his self within a public restroom, Mother inquired as to why he was such an indelible presence and I responded, as sweet and sickly as I could muster, "But Mom, I'm, like, in love!"

FEBRUARY 1987

Suzanne Goes Home

On the day that Mother left, Baby and I sat in the common area, he at the table, myself on the couch. "Are you glad she's gone?" he asked.

"It isn't that I don't miss her," I said. "But she's simply exhausting. All that theatrical training. Daddy discovered her waiting tables at a two-bit coffee shop on Wilshire Boulevard. Her tips paid for acting classes. She's been schooled by the very best in the fine art of sucking up the atmosphere in any room."

"Why did you let Kevin meet her? Why not me?" he asked.

Speak of exhausting. How often Baby had asked and how often I had told him that it was not a matter of preference but a choice of expediency. I considered my fifteenth version of the same response when my thoughts were scattered by the buzz of the intercom.

"Yes?" I asked, holding down the microphone button.

"Your moms is here," said the doorman.

"Adeliiiiiiiiiiiiiiiiiiiine, it's meeeeee!" cried my mother, faint and distant.

"Send her up," I said into the intercom. "Now, young man," I said to Baby, "you'll discover what happens when a wish comes true."

There is always a looooooooong period between the interaction over the intercom and the moment when a guest arrives in the flesh. This is an empty space, a meaningless moment that exists outside the realm of conventional time. It is impossible to fill, and any individual who acts with nonchalance upon their guest's arrival is, at best, a damnable liar. No one is calm nor collected within that liminal zone. Everyone always waits, rife with anxiety.

Mother. Knocking.

"Adeliiiiiiiiiiiiiiine!"

I imagined her on the other side, staring into the blue door, looking at the gray carpets, at the awkward angles of the hallway, weighted in thought, discovering where her money went.

"Hi, Mom," I said, weakly smiling.

"Adeliiiiiiiiiiiiiine!" she said, pushing in, hugging me. "I couldn't leave without seeing where you live! Kevin isn't here, is he!"

"No," I said. "He's not."

"Oh good!" she said. "We need some girl time!"

"Mom," I said. "I'm, like, not alone. You should meet Baby."

The world ended.

Baby squirmed in discomfort, aware of the pause, the shaking, the silence. I worried that he would find her faintly ridiculous, with her drumskin face and her pillbox hat. Of course he didn't. One thing that I adored about Baby. He was never cruel.

"Hello?" he asked Mother.

"And who are you?" she whispered.

"Mom," I said, "this is Baby. He's a stray. I took him in. He, like, lives here."

"I'm sure that he does," she said. "I need to sit."

She put herself on the couch.

"Baby," she said. "Where did you come from?"

Baby went on and on and on and on about Wisconsin and whatever dreadful little hamlet he's from, soliloquizing about the Rust Belt or the Dust Belt or the Must Belt and cheese and farming and dairy and the difference between raising chickens and tending cattle and how no one in Wisconsin will call a drinking fountain a drinking fountain, how instead Wisconsites will call a drinking fountain a bubbler.

My eyes floated, my focus of vision drifting throughout the room, avoiding Mother's too-tight face as it twitched with suppressed emotion.

She stood and said, "Adeliiiiiiiine, Baby is going to wait here while you show me your roooooooooom."

Mother looked at the ladder, at the twin lofted beds, at the desk, at the closet, at the throw pillows, at the cheap decorations, at the artwork, at the Christmas lighting, at a rain lamp that I'd acquired a few weeks earlier. It was turned on, illuminated, beads of oil dripping down around a reasonable copy of Athena Parthenos.

"It's so charming, Adeliiiiine!" she said. "But this friend, this Baby, where did he come from?"

"In a squat down in the East Village."

"Just like a movie!" she said. "And he's alone in this world!"

"He doesn't talk much about the past," I said.

"It's a good thing, angel!" she said. "Hold on to him! But Adeliiiiine!"

"Yes?" I asked.

"I know you hate taking my advice! Please just listen! One or two gay friends are fine, all women do it, but don't make it a habit! No one likes a fag hag!"

Baby and I escorted her out, riding down in the elevator, passing beneath the portico. She'd kept a Town Car waiting, idling in front, a black Lincoln with a Middle Eastern driver.

She hugged me goodbye, threw her arms around Baby, saying, "I'm so glad to have met you! I'm sooooo glad Adeliiiiine found you!"

Mother crawled into the backseat, lowered her window, waved at us, shrieked out her pterodactyl goodbye. The car took off, heading south on Union Square West before dissolving into nothingness. I started to cry.

I couldn't believe it, couldn't believe that Baby was bearing witness. He put his arms around me, pulled me into a tight embrace, and then, God help him, Baby started crying too.

"Why are you crying?" I asked.

"I don't know," he said.

A few people looked at us, and I wondered if it wasn't because of my own outlandish outfit and tears and Baby's farmfed looks. A swish middle-aged man, clad in sable from head to toe, sauntered over and said, "Don't worry, we're all dealing with it. Everything will be all right, you two. These things happen. Don't take it so hard."

"Dealing with what, exactly?" I asked.

"Why are you crying?" he asked.

"We haven't the slightest," I said. "Some maudlin reason that involves my mother."

"Oh," he said.

"Why," asked Baby. "What's happened?"

"You haven't heard?"

"No," said Baby.

"He's dead," said the swish man. "He's really dead."

"Who's dead?" I asked.

"Andy Warhol," said the man. "Andy's really dead. He died this morning in a hospital."

MARCH 1987

Adeline and Baby See *Nightmare on Elm Street 3: Dream Warriors*

B aby," I was saying, "haven't you ever noticed that Mormons have trouble closing their mouths? It's because their ridiculous teeth are too big for their thin lips."

"I've never met a Mormon," said Baby.

"Oh Baby," I said, "you must come out West. We're lousy with Mormons."

We were walking back to Union Square after attending a screening at the Gramercy Theatre.

We'd considered *Wild Strawberries* on a double bill with *Autumn Sonata* at the Thalia SoHo, and *Angel Heart* was playing at Movieland on 8th, but I'd seen the latter on a date with Kevin. After some argument, it fell to either *Evil Dead 2: Dead by Dawn* at the RKO Art Greenwich or *A Nightmare on Elm Street 3: Dream Warriors* at the Gramercy.

Baby argued for *Wild Strawberries,* saying, "Everything we see is so lowbrow. Can't we watch an actual art film for once?" I convinced him otherwise, saying, "Horror films are the art films of the '80s. The whole world is deluged with blood. The only valid films are about men who replace their hands with chainsaws or bladed claw gloves. *Wild Strawberries* is so tired, so passé, so borrrring. It's the portrait of an old man dying."

I suspect that Baby disliked *Dream Warriors*, but he didn't say. Myself, I found its denouement very powerful. Coming after two films in which Freddy Krueger has wreaked misery upon the dreams of countless teenagers, *Dream Warriors* suggests an internal escape from the series' central idea. A group of suicidal kids discover that they too can shape their nighttime reveries, if only they give over to the concept of lucid dreaming. They experience differing degrees of success, but the underlying glue of their sleepy efforts is a transformation of their inadequate selves into hyperevolved adolescent fantasies.

Which is how it would be, don't you think, if teenagers had to fight a monster from their dreams? They'd never imagine practical solutions, but rather construct youthful responses best suited to the challenges of high school. In *Dream Warriors,* the group Poindexter actually rises from his semi-crippled state and starts shouting, "I AM THE WIZARD MASTER!" whilst green bolts of lightning fly from his hands.

"We've got to find something else," said Baby, after the film, passing the outskirts of Gramercy Park. "We need new hobbies."

"Shall we increase our attendance at parties?" I asked.

"I'm tired of seeing the same forty people," said Baby. "I need something new."

"What you need," I said, "is a righteously good shagging. It ain't English for a boy of your age to be without the taste of flesh. You could always engage with the mysterious world of human sexuality."

Through the locked gates, I stole a glimpse of the statue at the park's center. Edwin Booth. I hadn't yet made ingress, the park being private and requiring a key, so at that very moment I hadn't the slightest of whom the statue offered a likeness. But imagine, darlings. Your brother shoots America's favorite President at point-blank range and your eventual fate, through the tumults of society and fame, is perpetual memorialization within Manhattan's most exclusive green space. Welcome to New York.

"I've told you a thousand times," said Baby. "I'm not like you. I can't hop into bed with anyone who asks."

"Baby," I said, "you are dangerously close to calling me a slut."

MARCH 1987

84 Second Avenue

I woke in the morn and washed away the night's grime. My first class was one that I'd come to dread, an utter absurdity titled "History of Art: World Perspectives."

What proved the real drag was not the professor but my fellow students and their questions and earnest strivings. Being a freshwoman, I was trapped in the amber of Parsons's storied Foundational year, imprisoned alongside the hoi polloi as they inebriated themselves with newly discovered freedoms and excesses.

Darlings, you'll believe me when I say that in such a heady environment, your Adeline heard some very dubious questions being asked whilst even more dubious theories were floated. My fellow students sent me. They really sent me.

But self, said I, you must be patient with these people and their striving. You are different than they. You have had advantages unknown to the plebs. You are an alumna of the Crossroads School for the Arts and Sciences.

Crossroads had originated as an outlandish educational experiment of the 1970s. Reeking of incense, peppermints, and a whole helluvalotta hashish, a group of educators and likeminded parents banded together in the shadow of the Vietnam War, seeking methods of instruction which would not grease the gears of the military–industrial complex with their children's blood. The goal being development of the individual as an individual.

By the time of wee Adeline's arrival, the doped ambitions of the hippie era had given way to an increasing '80s institutionalization. Culture clash as waves of cocaine, celebrity, and money washed over the student body. The liberal vision grew fainter, harder to explicate in the era of Unca Ronnie Reagan.

Yet it remained a good school, saving me from parochial Pasadena oubliettes. The faculty avoided the pantomimes of Johnny Law, treating us like adults and encouraging our independent study. We were allowed to go idiotically idiosyncratic, running up and down the Alley, wild at heart. On

Monday you'd smoke unnamable drugs, on Tuesday you'd read *Dubliners*, on Wednesday you'd play hooky, on Thursday you'd bake oatmeal cookies, on Friday you'd lie on a carpet beside Jim Hosney, listening to *The Kinks Are the Village Green Preservation Society.*

The experience bestowed upon your humble narratress both the ill luck and good fortune of having passed through her late adolescent personality transformations loooooooong before receiving her high school diploma. A tough road to haul as she sat in classes beside newly-out dykes discovering the world's injustice and grotesque boys who spent most of their lives drawing and redrawing and redrawing and redrawing and redrawing images of Batman being punched by Superman.

At lunchtime, I called Kevin from a payphone on the third floor, asking if he wouldn't like to meet. The lad said it sounded divine and suggested I come to his place after classes.

He'd given me keys to his apartment at Second and 10th, diagonally across from the old church. I walked up the two flights of dirty stairs, fixated, as ever, by the dusty broken mosaic tiling.

"Kevin?" I called out, stepping across his threshold. "Art thou home, sirrah?"

The man wasn't around to receive visitors, likely having jaunted downstairs to purchase his daily ration of cigarettes or some other inessentiality. I sat on the futon in what I suppose constituted his living room.

He didn't own a television, which was delightful as I can't stand the dreadful stuff, and his walls were sparsely decorated with a few posters, the most prominent being a blood-red threesheet for *Jules et Jim.* There were books, the endless books and records that poured out of the bedroom, splashing up against the walls of the living room and its attached kitchen.

When Kevin returned, he carried a brown paper bag, wherein he'd stashed a six pack. "I didn't think you'd be here so soon," he said. "Don't you get out at seven?"

"An off day, dear boy," I said.

"Want some Schlitz?" he asked. "It made Milwaukee famous."

We spent the next hour on his futon, each consuming three cans of the tasteless rot. I couldn't begin to tell what was said, either by he or I, but I do recall thinking about how strange life could be, about how one could end up in a crumby apartment with one's boyfriend, a silly little fellow whom one hardly knew and how life expected one to pretend as if this was not the strangest of all possible worlds, as if one's actions were perfectly normal.

After some small while, my head was buzzing like the busiest bumble-bee in Boston. Kevin climbed atop of me, tongue jutting into my mouth, his soft, unlabored hand on my stomach.

"I'd love it, darling, but I simply can't. It's the New Moon."

"So what?" he asked, sighing with impatience, flopping beside me. "Who cares about astrology?"

"The womb cares. It's that time of the month, old sport," I said. "It's like the Red Sea down there. I'm bleeding like a dinosaur."

"I'm not afraid of blood," he said.

"Honey," I said, "no one asked you to play Moses."

We went for a mosey. New York was still new enough that I could ambulate around the tiny blocks of the East Village, day in, day out, and never experience boredumb. The Schlitz had me blotto enough that as we passed the St. Mark's Bar with its unflattering mural of the Rolling Stones, I sang out lyrics from a shitty radio song, doing my very finest male baritone: "'Cuz I know what it meaaaaans, to walk along the lonely street of dreaaaaaams, here I go again on my owwwwwwnnnn . . .'"

Kevin was mortified. I'd embarrassed him before the souses and dope pushers. He ushered us up 5th Street, turning left on Second Avenue, navigating around the piles of dogshit.

"Do you see this?" he asked, pointing to a curtainless window on the second floor of an unremarkable building.

A tuxedo jacket hung on a tailor's dummy, beneath a drape of rotting plastic. The jacket's style was ooollllllllld like shag carpeting, like it'd been sewn concurrent with the Nixon Administration. Beside the jacket, at the center of the window, hung an extinguished neon sign: DRESS SUITS FOR HIRE, the ITS broken and dangling at an extreme angle.

"This is legend," said Kevin. "No one's really sure what happened. Something terrible. But it's been like this for years. Someone told me that the woman who ran the tuxedo rental shop got raped and killed. You see all that dirt on the window? That's dust from the police investigation, when they were looking for prints."

The ground floor was more empty glass, two doors on either side. Beside the right door, numbered #84, there was a sign, black glass with red lettering: MEN'S ENTRANCE DRESS SUITS TO HIRE.

"I guess her family owns the building," said Kevin. "They've left it like this. Some people say it's haunted. Have you ever met Brown Tony? He said he saw a ghost up there."

That night, back at 31 Union Square West, our old Bank of the Metropolis, I was trying to fall asleep and listening to Baby's breath. The only things in my head were the tuxedo and the neon sign.

I bunked class and went to the library on 42nd Street. I hadn't the slightest about research, so I asked a librarian for any instruction that she might offer. She suggested cross referencing the address in their card catalogue index of the *Times*. Which I did, darlings, but found absolutely nothing. I inquired again for more help. The librarian asked for the address and went away and returned and went away and returned. She handed me a piece of paper with the words NEW YORK TIMES written on it, and a date scribbled beneath the paper's name. January 14th, 1974.

The librarian sent me to the microfilm rooms. Another librarian, much ruder than the first, retrieved the appropriate microfilm and gave me a brief refresher on how to use the ridiculous machine.

I scrolled through page after page, occasionally transfixed not by the articles but by period advertisements, until, by luck, I chanced upon the very brief article I sought. Page 37.

METROPOLITAN BRIEFS

From the Police Blotter:

The nude body of a 40-year-old woman proprietor of a tailor shop that rents tuxedos on the Lower East Side was found bludgeoned to death. The victim was Helen Sopolsky of 84 Second Avenue, near Fifth Street, whose shop is one flight up from that address. The motive of the attack was not determined immediately . . .

I returned to the first librarian.
"Is this it, have you any more?" asked I.
"That's all I got," she said. "You could check the other papers."

APRIL 1987

Adeline Discovers Baby's Employment Status

I never inquired as to the activities in which Baby partook whilst I was out being a student of paramount performance, but your Girl Friday uncovered very definitive evidence that her best pal wasn't, shall we say, having much of an active social life. Little things, like returning from school in the evening hours and finding Baby's shoes unmoved from the previous night. A general wasted look of lethargy across his face.

Not long after the 84 Second Ave Incident, matters shifted. I noticed telltale signs and signifiers of Baby experiencing life beyond our little hothouse.

Many nights, Baby would be missing. Out in the world! When he did come home, long past midnight, he evaded questions about where he'd been, merely chanting, "Wandering. Hither and yon, yon and hither."

The abstract subterfuge worked me into a tizzy, desperately curious about Baby's adventures in the Big Shitty.

I resolved on a course of action. I decided that I'd wait for my next off-day, Thursday, when I typically left the suite at 1 pm, and hide across the street.

When the day came round, I left late, making a ridiculous excuse about being simply unable to find work that I needed for class. Once I was outside, I sat in the park, obscuring myself behind the Temperance fountain. An hour ticked away. Wherever was that boy?

As I slowly surrendered to despair, Baby emerged from beneath the portico.

I followed him across 14th Street, moving past the Palladium. What a gentle soul was Baby, unable to imagine himself victim of plotting and machinations, ambling along through the city, clueless, the same familiar gait as ever.

He turned onto Third Avenue, past Disco Donuts, and then, to my everlasting astonishment, Baby walked beneath the marquee reading

VARIETY PHOTOPLAYS, stopped at the ticket booth, and spoke with the person behind the glass.

We'd passed the Variety a thousand times. I admired the soft pink and teal of its ancient neon marquee, and remained amused by the girlie posters that hung above the entrance and rested on its freestanding easels, but I could not imagine patronizing such an establishment. Yet there was Baby, nonchalant as a nun in November, strolling inside!

I regained my composure. At the ticket booth, I spake with an evil-eyed fellow behind the glass. "One, please," said I.

"You sure you got the right place?" he asked.

"Absolutely, old sport," I said. "I've never been more certain."

"You don't look much like the girls who come here," he said.

"That's entirely all right," I said. "I don't expect I think much like them either."

I passed two dollars under the glass. He slid a ticket in my direction. Another man stood, smoking his stupid cigarette, by the open-framed doorway.

"What's on the bill?" I asked this second man, forcing myself not to stare at the unsanctified shape of his ears.

"Girl, who knows?" he asked. "I don't have a fucking clue."

Staircases on both walls of the lobby led to a balcony that ran atop the double theater doors. Considering the melancholic blue paint of the walls, I presumed that Baby would stick with the ground floor.

Beyond the double doors, I entered an antechamber filled with ancient vending machines. I pushed through another doorway into a surprisingly well-lit theater. There weren't many seats, perhaps 150 divided into three sections. The same blue paint.

I darted into an aisle seat in the back row.

The movie was pornographic. One white woman bent over, taken from behind by a white man, her face rhythmically pressed into another white woman's mons pubis. As the film was from the late 1960s, its image contained quite a bit of sociological content. Archaeological evidence of lost hairstyles, makeup, and body types. Scratches distorted the quality of projection, as if the print had rotated without end from the day of its release.

When my eyes adjusted, oh reader, I could see the other patrons, and it became clear that the Variety was a suck and fuck theatre, the likes of which I'd only heard about in fond whispers of New York in its halcyon time before AIDS. Many men masturbated in their seats, a soft sound like a thousand ceiling fans. Groans rained from the balcony.

There were two doors at the bottom of the theatre, on either side of the screen. Men moved in and out, often in pairs, often alone. I decided that it must be the bathrooms.

But where was Baby?

Mid-scene, the film changed. Gone was the pornography, up was a delightful black-and-white Western from the 1950s, starring Gregory Peck as a character named Jimmy Ringo. This film started on its third reel, somewhere in the middle. The audience, transfixed in various states of pleasure, paid no notice. The ceiling fans spun on.

A would-be rube gunslinger attempted to start a gunfight with Jimmy Ringo, asking him to a settle an argument. "Why should I?" replied Gregory Peck. "I say Mac waters his whiskey," said the rube. "Then you're kinda dumb to be drinking here, aintcha?" said Gregory Peck. "Well, you ain't very sociable, are ya?" asked the rube. Down at the far left, one man was bent over a row of seats, another man behind him grunting with every thrust, the front of his legs slapping against the first man's buttocks.

I'd grown so accustomed to the rivers of flesh flowing through the aisles that I didn't hardly notice when an old man, perhaps sixty or seventy years of age, moved beside me. Only the sound of his unzipping pants roused me from the cinematic experience.

Don't you know that his penis was out?

"Hello," he said.

"Put that dreadful thing away," I said. "You're embarrassing yourself."

"You look so pretty, here," he said, "in the glow of the movie house."

"Sir," I yelled at top volume. "Remove yourself! Gather up your decency and march to the bathrooms where I am certain that you will find any number of degenerates looking to service you in the manner you see fit!"

God help the sorry sot but he listened, and as he fumbled with his fly, the man was blindsided by a blond freight train. Baby Baby Baby. A full fury of fists. The pathetic old gent down amongst the semen and soda stains.

"Baby! Stop! Enough!"

Baby beating the man, the house lights coming up, a whole menagerie of old men peeking their heads up from the rows and running out of the bathrooms, another man pulling Baby away from my assailant, Baby being told that he was fired and needn't return, Baby and I walking home, Baby not speaking to me whilst I offered profuse apologies, Baby refusing to parley for several days, refusing to sleep in the bed beside mine.

Yet as the Ancient Greeks understood in the days of their hotstepping hoodoo, silence as a long-term habit never wins many acolytes.

We reemerged, gradually, into true dialogue, though at first I didn't dare stray towards the topic of Variety Photoplays. When Baby laughed and I laughed with him, I inquired plainly as to what the hell he'd been doing at that dreadful cinema.

"I needed money," he said. "So I went looking for jobs."

"At a suck fuck movie palace?"

"That was the appealing part," said Baby. "The open fucking, Adeline, it's so foreign, but there's actually something really beautiful about two men coming together for anonymous sex."

"Baby, tell me, please," I said, "that you did not have sexual intercourse with those men."

As soon as the words leapt from my tongue, I regretted it.

"And if I did?" he asked.

"I'd burn with worry," I said. "Hedonism of that kind died out with disco."

"Don't worry. I've spent my whole life being told that having sex is death. I've learned the lesson."

Baby engaging in sex with a fellow patron of the Variety was as likely as Mother wrestling the sun down from the high heavens.

I took no pleasure in his abstinence, a sadder outcome than if he'd received blowjobs in the bathroom. Imagine our Baby, randy as a dunghill rooster, hiding in the dark corners of Variety Photoplays, too afraid, too shy, too bashful, too interested in, I suppose, monogamy. Too ashamed to be blown by an old closet case from the Lower East Side.

I let the topic die, resolving to take control of Baby's quixotic sexual misadventures. I remembered the purple blossoms on Baby's swollen hands after the night that we became first acquainted.

APRIL 1987

Adeline Convinces Baby and Kevin to Have Sex

One night I was at Kevin's apartment, discoursing with that feller about no matter in particular, meaning, obviously, the long borrrrrring drag of literature. Kevin conversed as best he could, on a human level, by talking my ear off about the books he loved, ones that I would never read.

"It's really kinky," said Kevin. "Tom Ripley's got a love affair with this much younger boy, Frank. At one point, Ripley dresses in drag and visits a gay bar."

"Who in all of creation is Tom Ripley?" I asked.

"Adeliiiiiiiine," said Kevin, sounding disturbingly close to Mother. "You know exactly who Tom Ripley is, remember?"

He went on and on and on and on about Tom Ripley this and Tom Ripley that and Tom Ripley there, reciting some rotting nonsense about someone named Dickie Greenleaf. I paced about his apartment, pretending to listen, examining piles of books pushed up against the baseboards, stacked atop every available surface.

I came across *Queer* by William S. Burroughs.

"Whatever is this?" I asked, holding it up for Kevin.

"Oh, he only got that published a year or two ago."

"Darling, why are you reading this?"

"I don't like Burroughs," said Kevin, "but no one can shut up about him. So I read a few of his books. *Junky* is okay. *Queer*'s the one I like most."

"Yet you aren't much more than a pussy hound," I said. "Why should you care about queers?"

"That's an offensive thought," said Kevin. "Aren't we all a little bisexual?"

"Don't count me amongst those ranks," said I.

"I'm sure you've been attracted to women," said Kevin. "Most girls have a secret desire for other girls. Everyone is attracted to everyone. I've been attracted to men."

"Have you?" I asked.

"Sure," he said. "Who hasn't?"

In that instant, I birthed my wicked plan, knowing that it could be achieved, long suspecting that Baby's hostility toward Kevin was rooted in more than a simple clash of personalities. The only questions were those hallowed rules of good journalism: who, what, where, when, how, and why?

And then word circulated about school that a delightful girl named Luanna Potrero was hosting a party the next weekend, a themed monstrosity. The Dress Like You Go to a Normal College party. I informed both Kevin and Baby, saying that I burned to attend, like I'd caught a terribly painful dose of the clap, and mentioning that I had no desire to bring their counterpart, but what could be done, the news had leaked, and now it was a destiny shared amongst us three.

Themed parties are terrible bores. I refuse to participate in their ridiculous narrative justifications. For Luanna's party, I wore my own clothing, an outrageous pink vinyl dress I'd picked up, and teased out my hair, yellow and blue shadow above my eyes, ultra-thick mascara. I looked amaaaaaazing.

Baby treated the party with utter gravity, electing to play the square. He donned the same drab clothing he'd worn when first we met, almost a year earlier, the white letters of his ugly red sweater reading INDIANA.

"Why didn't you incinerate those rags?" I asked.

"I'm sentimental," said Baby.

Kevin met us outside of our old Bank of the Metropolis. He too had entered into the spirit of the occasion, dressing supremely preppy. "My brother goes to Yale," he said. "This is pretty close to what he wears every day."

Luanna Potrero's apartment wasn't far from our abode, being a one-bedroom at 9th off University Place. Outside the redbrick building, I espied a gaggle of gals from Parsons. We joined them in the elevator, riding up, up, up in strained silence.

On the fifth floor, inside the party. A nightmare New York television view of America. All the country's grotesque fashions and meaningless cultural artifacts caricatured by a group of big-city art students.

Kevin ventured into the bathroom, where Luanna'd packed ice and beer into her bathtub. He played healing Jesus and fished out bottles. I guzzled mine like an Arab at an oasis.

The party's subtext highlighted our presumed superiority to Americans beyond the boundaries of Manhattan. It was literally ironic as the cruel streak meant to distinguish us from the herd only demonstrated our un-breakable bonds with the triumphant beast.

I was sure that out in them contiguous forty-eight, a goon was throwing a Dress Like You're in New York Party, and a blonde from Cheese Country had opted to go highwire and doll herself up, and the costume she'd devised was identical to what I was wearing.

Luanna shimmied and twisted on the makeshift dance floor, and I envied her, wondering how she could be so unselfconscious. The song was about a year old, "Kiss" by Prince, detailing how Prince did not want a girl with any specific human qualities beyond the ability to suck on his face.

Myself, I weren't much for dancing. When Luanna broke from her undulations, I engaged her in a conversation.

"Beer is fine for the proles, darling," I said, "but where do you keep the hard stuff?"

"What, you mean like cocaine?" she asked.

"Not quite yet," I said. "Where is your liquor, have you any tequila?"

"I've got some José Cuervo hidden in my bedroom, like under my bed," she said. "But don't drink it all, I want some later."

There I was, down on my knees, hands under Luanna's bed. A scene beyond imagination when I boarded the plane at LAX.

I filled Kevin and Baby with shots, attempting to bring them to that holy place of tequila enlightenment where buffoons are damnably drunk and superbly sober, where the drinker becomes, momentarily, an incarnation of Cary Grant. I wanted those lads stinko.

I kept the bottle in a Donna Karan bag that I'd bought months earlier, giving the boys each one shot every thirty minutes. Soon they were mad for life, deranged with liquor. Baby started dancing, and do you know, even in his perilous state, the boy had rhythm. Kevin, poisoned by the dreaded blue agave, pushed me into a dark corner and groped like a sophomore at a drive-in.

When they tottered on the verge of uselessness, I rounded them up, saying good-bye to Luanna Potrero, and pushing my menfolk out the door. Baby sang a deliriously off-key rendition of Cyndi Lauper's "Time After Time."

The elevator door opened. We stumbled into the street.

"I'm going home," said Kevin. "I'm too fucked up. I can't deal with Union Square."

"Young man," said I, "you are coming with us. I will brook no dissent!"

Back in our suite at 31 Union Square West, our old Bank of the Metropolis, Baby sat at the table, Kevin and I on the couch. Baby and Kevin talked about, of all possible things, basketball. I stopped listening to their nonsense, which I gather was about the Bulls and the Knicks, and tried to discern a way by which their bonhomie might be manipulated, but I couldn't see the angle. I decided on a simpler technique.

"Baby," I said, "don't stay up on account of us. Kevin isn't staying over, so you might as well go to bed. I'll come in soon enough."

Baby walked towards the bathroom, forgetting to shut the door. We heard the soft sound of his splashing urine. He said goodnight and went into our bedroom.

"I wasn't going to say anything while he was around," said Kevin, head lolling on the back of the couch. "Why did you make me come here if you aren't letting me stay?"

"Don't trip yourself up on a pretext, old sport," I said.

I told him the plan.

I argued against his protestations, suggesting that he was a prude and calling him bourgeois in his morals, saying that he was nothing like his great literary heroes, asking him if he thought that he could understand literature if he wouldn't act like a person made of literature. Still he objected. I posed the question: "Don't you care at all?"

"How can you even ask?"

"If you care, you'll do it," I said.

"But how?" he asked.

"I suggest that you get up, open that door, climb that ladder, and crawl into bed with him. Once there, I imagine you'll figure out the rest. The basic principles are the same. Go and give him the time. You're horny, aren't you, so why not?"

"Won't you be jealous?" asked Kevin.

"I haven't the slightest what you mean," I said. We went back and forth. "Either you do it or you can leave. Soon he'll pass out. Your window for homoerotic pleasure is fast closing."

"Fine," said Kevin, getting up.

For the first time, I suffered exile on the couch.

I woke with Baby standing over me, grim, his face looking down from the most awful perspective, giving him a droopy double chin. Reader, your friend Adeline doesn't very much care to see anyone from that view, let alone a person upon whom she's foisted a great deal of liquor and the offices of her boyfriend.

"How ever long have you been there?" I asked.

"About ten minutes."

"Please, in the future," I said, "let's try and avoid being creepy."

I sat up, gradually, my body aching. Which was rather unusual as I'd been a nun the night before, barely touched a drip of that rotten demon alcohol. Perhaps it was a psychic, telepathic, emotional resonance off of Baby. Or perhaps it was exhaustion from shepherding an idea to fruition. Or perhaps the simple discomfort from sleeping on the futon.

"So?" I asked Baby.

"So," he said.

"Kevin?" I asked.

"Gone," said Baby. "Before I woke up."

"Did the boy speak no words? Or leave a note of good-bye?"

"He snuck out," said Baby, "with the first light of day."

"Busy, busy, busy," I said. "How was it?"

"Personal," said Baby. "I don't think I can talk about it."

"It's your funeral," I said, going to the bathroom. Then I scoured the kitchen, seeing if my South Korean roommates had any coffee, which they had, a glass jar of Folgers Instant. I brought the kettle to a boil and poured two cups over the grainy powder. I intended one for Baby, but he'd fallen asleep on the couch.

Halfway through the second cup, I noticed that my keys were on the table, offering a somewhat reduced appearance. I examined the ring. Two keys lighter. Kevin's, removed. I assumed by him.

I'm not of a morbid mind. I avoid reading symbolism into daily life, but the subtext seemed indisputable. I telephoned Kevin. There wasn't any answer on his end of the line.

That evening, when I assumed that he wouldn't be keeping social appointments, I made my way to his apartment. I buzzed his apartment. No answer. I buzzed again. No answer. I buzzed a third time, looooooooooooooooooooong. No answer.

My fingers mashed against the buzzer for every apartment but Kevin's. A crackling voice across the speaker. I responded with a blurry nonword, a rough imitation of English. The door unlocked.

I climbed the stairs to Kevin's floor, and stood beside his door, knocking and knocking and knocking and knocking.

"Kevin," I said. "Answer this door at once! No man may hide forever!"

There was no answer. I felt the great fool, like a 1950s hysteric who's just discovered that the boy next door has knocked her up.

I chalked Kevin's behavior up to the mysteries of human experience. I was new with knowledge. The orchestration of sexual liaisons between one's boyfriend and other men was not, perhaps, a step conducive towards building a stable relationship. What did I care, really? The city was awash with boys, and my bestest had eaten from the tree of knowledge.

Back at home, Baby continued his refusal of any discussion. I poked at him with my finger, pushing into his ribs, giggling madly, until he said, "Fine, fine, I'll tell you something, but only one thing, okay?"

"Pray continue, dear boy," I said.

"What really surprised me," said Baby, "was how warm it was. It burned in my hand."

I let out a shriek, appalled and amused. "Oh my God!" I said. "Baby, you send me, you really send me! You finally did it!"

MAY 1987

Adeline and Baby Move to East 7th Street

Life continued apace, as it does, as it will, as it must. The very merry month of May arrived, with warmer days and looser clothes. My final projects came due, all focused on the 84 Second Avenue Incident. The imagined crime scene, the moment of absolute loneliness, of being helpless and not having a single person to stick up for you, of dying raped in New York in the annus horribilis of 1974, of Helen Sopolsky appearing but once in the *Times*, of her family leaving the storefront untouched, a memorial hovering over the East Village, rebuking the indifferent city, rebuking a place that let its women die miserable deaths, rebuking the great urban organism that allowed the killer to go free, case unsolved, never apprehended, a tableau openly mocking the idea of justice. I earned straight As.

Having opted not to take summer courses, I received word from the bureaucrats that I must evacuate the dormitory at the end of the spring semester. Poor Baby! He'd only just settled into gainful employment at an actual, respectable cinema in the West 20s, and now, as it does, as it will, as it must, life crept upon him, demanding that he abandon his home.

I had no intention of leaving the city and suggested that we venture into the world and acquire an East Village apartment.

"Adeline," he said, "I won't have much money to pay rent."

"Cease your prattling about lucre," I said. "You'll pay what you can and Mother will cover the rest."

Typical of all endeavors in real estate, our timing was poor. Gone were the days of 2,500 square feet for $300 a month. Not that money itself was any object, but I rather enjoyed being cutthroat with the gruesome landlords of NYC.

Baby had no stomach for haggling, so I removed him from the matter, searching for apartments in the *Village Voice* classifieds until I uncovered a large space on 7th between Second and Cooper Square, diagonally across the street from McSorley's. A two-bedroom third-floor walkup. The landlord, a Neapolitan named Stefano, informed me that the apartment was rent stabilized, but I hadn't the slightest what that meant. $700 a month. There was no buzzer for the apartment, so guests would have to scream our names from the street.

It was time to bid adieu to 31 Union Square West, to Sun-Yoon and Jae-Hwa, to the students that we'd encountered in the elevators, to the tenants who hated us merely for breathing, to our view of Union Square and the slow construction of the Zeckendorf Towers, to our old Bank of the Metropolis.

School rules required a check-out with the RA, but I was raised in opulence and privilege and believed myself exempt. Sally and Jane could take care of such matters. I wanted to leave as soon as possible, well before the other students, desperate to avoid witnessing the humiliations of all those would-be artists packing stereos into their father's station wagons.

"I'm going to miss it," said Baby.

The new apartment was ridiculously decrepit, with an old pull-the-chain toilet stuck inside a closet and our bathtub located in the kitchen. I thought it was chaaarming, a very nice welcome to living away from any protective power. No parents, no dormitory, no rules, no nothing. Tell me, reader, what coarse beast wants their first apartment to have class?

With Baby toiling away at the cinema, I drifted like a dandelion, crazy as a daisy, sally in the alley. Don't you know that I invented a new role for myself? I spent the summer as the best little homemaker in all the East Village.

I found our beds, our couch, our lamps, our posters, our art. I even found us a cat, a twenty-seven-pound Maine Coon that I renamed Captain Jenks of the Horse Marine.

On St. Mark's, I bought a copy of *Liege & Lief,* a terribly folky album with the most remarkable gatefold sleeve depicting different instances of the English ritual calendar year. An image of the Burry Man sent me to absolute distraction.

Friends dropped by, girls and boys from school. We imbibed, mostly alcohol, some marijuana. Baby even made acquaintances at his job, one or two of whom weren't horrendous. They'd pop in and the boys would talk, at nauseating length, about Leonard Cohen and Trotsky.

Basically, it was home.

JUNE 1987

Spider-Man Gets Married

A friend from Parsons, Jeremy Winterbloss, paid us a visit. A rare occasion, as he was very busy with his internship at Marvel Comics.

"Tomorrow will be nuts," he said. "I have to go to Shea Stadium."

"Whatever for?"

"They're marrying Spider-Man before the game. Stan Lee is officiating. All of us interns have to make sure the costumed characters don't die from heat exposure. I'm the Incredible Hulk's handler."

It was all part of a publicity stunt in which Spider-Man married his longtime girlfriend, a buxom redhead named Mary Jane Watson who was given to saying things like, "Face it, Tiger, you just hit the jackpot!" and "Eat your heart out, Gwendolyn! This time little Mary Jane's in the spotlight!"

The marriage occurred in *Amazing Spider-Man Annual #21* and in the newspaper strip. Somehow this had been tied into a baseball game. Don't ask me, darlings. I've read Guy Debord and I still don't understand late-period capitalism.

"One good thing, though," said Jeremy, "is that they're having Spider-Man's reception at Tunnel. Have you gone?"

"I've yet to attend," said I.

"Why don't you come?"

Jeremy opened his canvas messenger bag and removed a thick piece of pink paper. An invitation to the reception, with this awful little drawing of Spider-Man in a top hat, right hand swinging on his webbing, left hand clutching Mary Jane around her waist. The important words: "This invitation admits two guests."

"I stole a few from work," said Jeremy. "Tom DeFalco'll never notice the difference. You should come and watch Captain America eat a piece of wedding cake."

Baby and I selected clothes. Fashionable but not so bizarre that we'd stand out amongst individuals whose livelihood involved drawing Spider-Man punching Doctor Octopus.

When the jolly clock jolly well struck ten, we hailed a cab, disembarking at 27th and Twelfth. I shoved our way through the drooling masses who stood behind the velvet rope.

Baby worried that the hired thugs might shake us down for IDs, us being underage, but I laughed at my ingénue and said, "Honestly, Baby, you've got four corners and four equal sides! We're special guests at this hellhole. They wouldn't dare."

The bouncer didn't throw us a passing glance.

The owners had taken an old industrial train tunnel that ran through a warehouse and transformed it into a barebones dance floor, girders and beams exposed. The long passage ran the length of a city block. You could go to its end, put your fingers through a metal gate, and see tracks disappearing into darkness. Catwalks up above, and rooms running off the main drag, each with its own specific design. The bathrooms, such as they were, were crude unisex stalls, unglamorous shelters containing the great human tide in all of its indecorous horror, some things coming out of bodies and other things going in.

"Adeline," whispered Baby. "What is this place?"

The invitation specified that Spider-Man's wedding reception would take place in Tunnel Basement, the exclusive club-within-a-club. We found the entrance and again showed our invitation.

We were down beneath the Earth in a dark pit with a pathetic stage fronted by a minuscule dance floor, pressed against the filthiest couches that a human mind could conceptulate. Neither hide nor hair of Jeremy Winterbloss.

The strangest thing, reader? The superheroes dancing, surrounded by a crowd of unfortunate men and even more unfortunate women. If one wants to imagine the appearance of an afterlife in which the wicked are punished, one would do well to picture the Incredible Hulk boogie shuffling at Tunnel.

"What we need is strongest alcohol," I said. Baby wandered off, leaving your old friend Adeline in a solitary stare, gandering with Clara Bow eyes at the dance floor, yet again reconsidering her choices in life.

After Kevin's disappearance, I'd experienced dwindling interest in parties, in dance clubs, in the endless monotony of music and the movement of the human form. I had the growing sensation that this part of my life was approaching an inglorious end. Spider-Man began his electric slide.

A creeeeeepy middle-aged man struck up a conversation, telling me that he was an inker for Marvel. "What in the name of the Holy Trinity and the Prophet Mohammed," I asked, "is an inker?" He droned on and on and on and on, saying something about the artwork of a man named Herb Trimpe.

On the other side of the room, Baby talked with what I assumed was another of Marvel's creations come to life. When I drew upon them, I saw my mistake.

He was in deep conversation with a very swish young man who sported a Technicolor dreamcoat.

"Oh, I just love comic books," said the young man. "I loooove fantasy and sci-fi and all of that! Have you ever seen the old soap opera *Dark Shadows*?"

"I'm glad you came over," said Baby to me. "Meet Michael. He's a party promoter."

"How are you, gorgeous?" asked Michael. "I looove your little dress!"

Reader, take note of this unfortunate and disagreeable boy. His name was Michael Alig. By the end of this book, he and a friend will bash in the head of a drug dealer named Angel, pour Drano in the mouth of the dying man, leave the corpse to rot in the bathtub for over a week, chop up the body, put its remains in a box, and throw it into the Hudson River.

AUGUST 1987

Adeline Runs into Kevin at the Kiev

There I was, dour as a penniless Irishman on St. Paddy's, walking out of the Kiev, a Polish restaurant at the corner of 7th and Second Avenue, where I'd eaten a heapload of pierogies in the back room, trying and failing to read *The Slaves of New York*.

My concentration was bustville because a geriatric woman wouldn't stop yelling at the waitress, and the waitress, being a coooooooooold Ukrainian babushka, was hollering right back. I finished eating and paid my bill at the register.

I walked outside and directly into Kevin.

Every dramatic moment of my life seems to coincide with menstrual cramping. How does one describe waves of something within twisting into knots, trying to push its way out? I'd suffered it earlier that day, but it'd been slightly tempered by the distraction of my swollen breasts. The pain was why I'd gone for Kiev comfort.

The adrenaline rush of seeing Kevin brought on the full cramps, splitting me with the weight and the pressure.

"Darling," I said, struggling not to grimace. "Funny seeing you here on, back on Second Avenue."

"I thought you'd be in California," he said.

"California is such a bore," I said. "Besides, I couldn't leave Baby."

Don't you know that Kevin turned red?

"We have an apartment," I said. "By McSorley's."

"That place is all right," he said. "I've been a few times."

"Do you really want to talk about McSorley's?" I asked.

"What else would we talk about?"

If you can believe it, there was a tight feeling in my chest, dissimilar from the pressure within my womb, like my body informing me that it had missed Kevin, that I'd sold him short, that I'd suppressed emotion.

"I have questions about your disappearing act."

"What's left to talk about?" he asked.

"You never got in touch," I said. "I worried."

"There wasn't anything to say."

Running my hands through that terrible hair, the way he slung his legs over mine when we slept, the freckled skin on his knuckles.

"Do you want to go somewhere?" I asked. "And talk, I mean."

"I've made that mistake once," he said. "I won't make it twice."

"What mistake?"

"I don't think you ever even considered me," said Kevin. "You never knew me. You never wanted to know me. I was like a character in the television show of your mind. You're a bad person, and worse than that, you're a lousy lay."

"We can talk it through," I said.

"You can't repeat the past," said Kevin.

"What do you mean you can't repeat the past?" I asked. "Of course you can."

FEBRUARY 1988

Baby and Adeline Go to Pasadena

I learned a lot from Hollywood, but nothing so much as the need to see matters through. Consider, for instance, getting fucked in the ass. At first it's a deeply uncomfortable sensation, plunging into pain, but with a little hard work, you discover a world of pleasure, demanding *more, more, MORE!* It was Jaime who schooled me in that erotic art, screwing my brains out, and the streets of Hollywood were a blueprint, a machine designed to manufacture Jaime's life.

Our woeful autumn of 1987 was dominated by Adeline suffering from a nervous breakdown, giving over to her basest impulses and paranoia. I came home every night and found her chain-smoking clove cigarettes, surrounded by strands of hair that she'd pulled from her head.

Her fixation on 84 Second Avenue had blossomed into true madness. She'd discovered that, in the late 1800s, the building served as a boarding-house for homeless women. The Unfortunates. Adeline saw real significance in this connection, as if a malign force permeated the centuries, as if the property itself wreaked havoc on women.

The body of her research and knowledge went into a self-published zine, a Xeroxed work on which she labored with real obsession. For weeks, she sat arranging and rearranging artwork, fretting over it like a jigsaw puzzle, hoping to find the exact configuration by which she could unlock the mystery and free herself from its influence.

The title of this publication?

DRESS SUITS ON FIRE.

And of her conversation? The circuitry of her dialogue, the recurrent themes, the nonsense, the imagined persecution? Don't even start me talking or I'll tell everything I know.

When Christmas rolled around, I argued for time off. I suggested going to Los Angeles, to inexplicable Pasadena. Adeline demurred until I asked her to do it for me, saying that it was me, not her, who needed a jaunt to the

West Coast. That it was me, not her, who couldn't brave winter in NYC. *Why don't we stay with your mother?*

It meant quitting my job, but I'd find another. The city's managerial class loved a honky who submitted to menial labor. That was the terrible fact of life: my white ass would always be hired ahead of Black kids and Nuyoricans.

On February 1st, we boarded an airplane at Kennedy and zoomed across America, the Captain tucked beneath my seat, his feline brain zonked out on a fifth of a Valium. I ate the other four fifths, the drug lulling me into a fitful, unsatisfying sleep.

I woke thirty thousand feet above the Earth's surface, peering through the window at the thick carpet of clouds, beneath which lay the flat expanse of the American heartland. I had no idea of our location but was dead certain that we were passing over my old home.

We disembarked. Adeline's mother was waiting, her black Mercedes convertible parked at the terminal curbside.

—Adeline, she cried. Adeline, over here.

She needn't have said a word. Her outfit was its own clarion call. Helen Keller couldn't have overlooked that insane blue hat and its orange flowers.

—Baby! cried Adeline's mother, throwing her arms around me.

The hug lasted an uncomfortable length. I let it linger as long as she liked.

—Oh my God, isn't that a darling cat?

My mushy brain couldn't comprehend Los Angeles. Billboards, ten-lane freeways, tunnels, endless cars, hours of asphalt, general stink of the air, thick gray smog destroying visibility, anemic palm trees hovering above the road. It went on forever, rolling before me like piss-poor video art. Adeline's mother zoomed in and out of traffic, honking her horn, mumbling in exasperation at her fellow drivers.

—I'm so happy you guys are home. Baby, call me by my name, Suzanne. Will you do that for me?

—Sure, I said.

—Tell me everything about New York, said Suzanne. Tell me about school, about all the boys you've met, about your apartment, about the things you've seen. Don't skimp on any details!

—I don't really know what you, like, want from me, said Adeline. But I guess I can, like, tell you about school or something. It sucks. And uh the city? It sucks too. And uh boys? They suck the worst.

I giggled in the backseat, amused whenever Adeline lost her accent.

—You can sulk however you want, said Suzanne, I'll talk to Baby. So Baby, how do you like New York?

—It's the greatest place on earth.

—Pasadena won't offer much competition, said Suzanne. Maybe you'll find something or someone out here that you'll like just as much.

Their house sat on a side street off South Orange Grove Boulevard. A high wall of vegetation rendered the building invisible from the street. While the telltale landscaping of the other homes was ostentatious, the buildings themselves were, essentially, normal. The kinds of houses found anywhere in America, in any city or town with a decent neighborhood.

Adeline's house was the outlier, a gray nouveau-riche monstrosity, a sprawling rectangle with random peaks and haphazard Italianate windows. Back in the American Middle West, you encountered houses like Suzanne's only when you made the mistake of reading Booth Tarkington. There sure wasn't anything like it in New York.

Our first concern was establishing the Captain. Suzanne, or someone working for her, had purchased a litter box and food. We opened the Captain's carrying case. The great giant lumbered out, sniffing at the air. I picked him up, getting a face full of paws, and showed him that we'd put the litter in a pantry, and that his food was in the kitchen. He looked bored and ran off.

—We had a dog, said Suzanne. His name was Brownie, a German Shepherd mix. Don't you remember how much you loved Brownie, Adeline? You used to call him No-no. I'm too busy, really, to have another pet. It wouldn't be fair.

My room on the second floor, two doors from Adeline's, exuded a creepy antiseptic aura, the wood too polished and perfectly dusted, the bedding folded too crisp, too perfect. I tried out my mattress, a soft contrast with 31 Union Square West and East 7th Street, wanting to rest, but I couldn't sleep within the total silence of Pasadena.

Each room of the ground floor opened into at least two others. I followed echoes of the human voice until I discovered Adeline and Suzanne sitting by a fire in the living room, surrounded by sofas.

—We were catching up! said Suzanne. But I have an appointment on the other side of town. You know how terrible traffic can be. There's food in the fridge.

She grabbed my shoulder, nails digging in. Her footfalls went up the stairs.

There were bookcases but not many books. Mostly ceramic sculpture, plants, and records. So many records. One shelf hosted a cluster of family portraits. Photographs always bore me, and I don't like thinking about family, but I'd never encountered a likeness of Adeline's father, so I examined the collection.

And then I fucking saw it.

—Adeline, I shouted. What the fuck is this?

She walked over, almost catatonic, looking at what I held in my hands, a silver-framed portrait of Adeline, Suzanne, a man that I took for Adeline's father, Adeline's sister, Dahlia, and an unknown blond youth. The photographed Adeline was, at most, ten years old.

What unmanned me, driving cold shiver splinters up my spine, is that, accounting for changes in fashion, the blond youth could've passed as my twin.

—What does it look like? she asked. It's a family portrait.

—But who the fuck, I asked, is this guy?

—That's Emil, she said. My brother.

—You don't have a brother.

—I did.

A miserable story poured out. Emil, her brother, born queer, born theatrical, with a penchant for old movies and vaudeville, out of place in 1970s Los Angeles, haunting the Silent Movie Theater. There was a minor scandal. Emil picked up and arrested while soliciting male tricks on Selma Avenue, rousted in a routine bust. His name ended up in the *Pasadena Star-News,* beneath the reproduction of his mug shot, a photograph in which, for whatever reason, Emil wore a white tuxedo. Wracked with shame, tormented with guilt, naked, exposed, he threw himself to his death, leaping off the Colorado Street Bridge down into the Arroyo Seco.

—So what else could I do, asked Adeline, when I saw you standing there, looking like a lamb about to be eaten by wolves?

FEBRUARY 1988

Suzanne Changes Baby's Life

Suzanne sat at the kitchen table. Adeline was somewhere on the property. The kitchen was cavernous, a gigantic island stationed in its middle, cookware hanging from the ceiling.

—Baby! cried Suzanne. Just the person I wanted to see!

— I'm so tired, I said.

—Jetlag, said Suzanne. You'll get over it. Everyone always does. Do you want any breakfast? We've got cereal or I could make you some eggs.

—Cereal, I guess.

She put the bowl in front of me. Heaps of shredded wheat floated in staid milk, a change from the sugar and chocolate abominations of my childhood. Suzanne sat beside me, staring, making me self-conscious, as if I was about to put too much into my mouth, as if milk would drip off my chin.

—Baby, she said, do you ever think about college?

I dropped my spoon into the milk.

Did I ever think about college? Did I ever think about college?

Living with Adeline was like sitting sidelined at the big game, watching the team rush toward victory. While she grew into an adult, an intellectual, someone with a future, I cobbled together the autodidact's consolation prize, an education patched together from Eurotrash art films, hand-me-downs, and science fiction paperbacks.

—Did you know that Adeline's father attended NYU for his DDS?

—Adeline's excellent at keeping secrets, I said.

—We've been great friends to the university. Have you taken the SAT?

—We didn't take the SAT, we took the ACT.

—But you took an admissions test?

—Yes, I said.

—And did well?

—Yes, I said.

—And your grades in high school?

—I did very well, I said.

This was true, but who knew if my academic prowess was won through my own merits? Being an athlete lent itself to favorable interpretation of assignments and class participation. The faster that I ran, the higher my grades. I pulled in an A average.

—I called NYU this morning, said Suzanne. You're well past deadline, but I asked if there wasn't a way to bend the rules, considering how promising of a student you are, and bearing in mind the amount of money that this family has donated. They're faxing an application to my office. You'll need your high school transcript and two letters of recommendation. Adeline's father was good friends with one of the trustees, so he'll write you one, and you'll have to ask an old teacher for the second, and then we'll see about getting you accepted.

—Can you do that? I asked.

—Do what? she asked.

—Ignore deadlines?

—The only reason to be rich, said Suzanne, is to avoid the little details that ruin most people's lives. Otherwise, what's the point of having money?

MARCH 1988

Stacie

One night, I lay in bed, atop my blankets, finishing *Là-Bas,* a novel by the French decadent Joris-Karl Huysmans, whom I'd discovered through a passing reference in H. P. Lovecraft's "The Hound." Before leaving New York, I'd checked a few bookstores to see if they carried any Huysmans.

One surly clerk at the Strand remembered that Dover Books published several editions of Huysmans. I walked down to 180 Varick Street, to the Dover Bookstore, and there, sure enough, on the ninth floor among the gray metal racks, were limitless copies of *À rebours* and *Là-Bas.*

The latter recounts the story of a nineteenth-century Parisian aesthete. Ennui forces him toward a scholarly investigation of the Middle Ages, focused primarily on the personage of Gilles de Rais, an anointed nobleman and compatriot of Jeanne d'Arc, a man who helped chase the English out of France. With the war finished, Gilles's bloodlust did not subside, driving him into a phase of outrageous debauchery. Alchemy, unspeakable sexual rites, demonology. All culminating in the murder of hundreds of children, their bones thrown into his moat. Huysmans's protagonist follows his subject over the edge, immersing himself in a world of contemporary French Satanism, culminating in sexual encounters at a Black Mass beneath the shadow of Notre-Dame.

A high squealing laughter sprung from Adeline's room. I followed the sound. A blonde girl and Adeline sat on the floor, like teenyboppers from television, giggling and laughing and gossiping. The Captain supine in the blonde's lap, furry stomach turned upward.

—Do you remember Rebecca, the fat one from seventh grade? She, like, lost all the weight. She's like a model now. I heard she's dating Rob Lowe.

—Darling, someone's always dating Rob Lowe. It's a universal constant.

I coughed and pushed myself into the room.

—Stacie, said Adeline, this is Baby.

—Baby? asked Stacie. What kind of name is Baby?

It's shocking the shit you stumble upon while living in another person's house. Suzanne had saved every photograph, every crummy Polaroid, every coffee-ringed snapshot, every pictorial memento. This mania went beyond albums and framing. Stray images were scattered through the house.

—It's his name, said Adeline. What kind of name is Stacie?

—I can defend myself, I said.

—It's not you I'm concerned about, said Adeline. It's her. What if you, like, beat her?

—Why would he beat me? asked Stacie.

The most interesting photographs were of Adeline's time in high school. Pictures of a sophomore, a junior, a senior, dressed as late-late-late punk verging into protogoth. All black clothes, black boots, black lipstick, black eyeliner, black mascara, dyed black hair in strange croppings, sticking up and out at random, no rhyme or reason.

Some of these photos were taken at Crossroads, or as I liked to call it, Misfit High, surrounded by a motley crew of freaks.

After we got to Pasadena, I'd asked Adeline why we hadn't whittled away time with her fellow mutants. They were all gone, she said. Everyone was at college. Or dead.

Stacie was something else, a friend whom Adeline'd known since junior high. Before it all, before the death of her father, before the black makeup.

A very special kind of California girl. Too perfect and too sharp, as if she spent hours each morning in the bathroom, standing before her mirror like a minor Fascist bureaucrat, removing every trace of any possible flaw. Her face was almost unnatural, as if she weren't real, as if she were a hologram projected from a higher dimension into our familiar three.

—Baby's got a mean streak a mile wide and twenty fathoms deep, said Adeline. You wouldn't know it looking at him.

After beating a retiree at Variety Photoplays, I resolved myself against violence, a vow kept for nine months until I pounded the sense out of this asshole from Staten Island who told Adeline that he could smell her pussy.

Being quick to anger was so goddamned embarrassing, as it revealed my belief that the best solution to every problem was to find the biggest person in the room and hit him until he cried.

—What do you guys, like, want to do tonight? asked Stacie. Should we, like, go dancing or something?

—Yes! I shouted.

—Where should we go?

—What about Marilyn's? asked Adeline.

—Marilyn's is, like, so passé. We're adults now. That's kid's stuff.

—I haven't been in years.

—It's all ages. Do you know what that, like, means?

—Let's do it, said Adeline. We won't even drive. We can walk.

—We're too old for Marilyn's, said Stacie. You can't repeat the past.

—Can't repeat the past? asked Adeline. Of course you can.

I changed my clothes while Adeline and Stacie smoked pot. The sickly scent wafted into my room. I rushed back to Adeline's boudoir.

—Adeline! What if your mom smells it?

Adeline made a disapproving click with her tongue.

—Is the big bad pot monster scary wary for Baby waby? she asked. Are you going to cry?

She was right. Why would Suzanne care? Suzanne didn't care about anything. She'd probably danced naked on Malibu beaches while the radios of cherry station wagons blasted out "Mockingbird," toking dope and getting her brains screwed out by surfers. Deep down, I wasn't much more than a cotton-pickin' chicken picker, shucking corn and squeezing teats. I'd never be sophisticated. I'd never keep up. I took a few hits off the joint, letting it seep straight into my brain chemistry.

The first fifteen minutes of our walk were through an upper-class heaven, lush greenery and beautiful homes. At what seemed like a random intersection, Adeline pivoted.

—Where are you going? asked Stacie.

—You know, said Adeline.

—Oh, said Stacie.

We followed Adeline down a long street, stopping before a modest two-story dwelling. The lights were on. The living room was visible. Two children played inside, chasing each other back and forth.

—Why are we here? I asked.

—I grew up here, said Adeline. Mother bought her present home roughly four years ago. Daddy would never have tolerated such a vulgar place.

—It's not so bad, said Stacie.

—It's vulgar, said Adeline.

We retraced our footsteps, heading back to the intersection and entering a business district. The streets grew wider, the traffic became heavier, the trees sparser, the buildings uglier.

To look at Stacie, to hear her speak, I wouldn't've imagined that a thought could enter her head unless it was blown into her skull with a gun. But here she was, crossing Colorado Boulevard, beneath a cement bell tower, telling us that she'd decided to major in Classics with a focus on the Ancient Greeks.

—Why Classics? I asked.

—It's, you know, like, I thought I like wanted to do foreign policy but at USC, we've got to, like, take prerequisite courses, you know? So one of them is on the history of philosophy and so, okay, we were, like, reading a lot of Plato, you know, and then we like got to the *Symposium*. And it was, like, the funniest and most interesting thing I'd ever read, you know? So I read more and more about the Greeks, like, as much as I could.

—What of the Romans? asked Adeline.

—The Romans not so much, said Stacie. I don't really, like, like them.

A purple awning hung over the entrance, bearing white script lettering: MARILYN'S BACK STREET. The entrance was in the rear of a strip mall. We walked around the block, going through a parking lot full of teenagers. They squealed and chuckled. Different than New York teenagers, the ones who menaced with nothing more than a stare. These kids were easy. Soft faces, soft bodies, soft eyes. I could've stolen their lunch money.

The club was dark, its décor time-warping to the late 1970s. Packed, crammed, jammed, wedged, lodged, stuffed, chock-a-block with every adolescent in a twenty-mile radius. I could smell the hormonal insecurity. I could hear pimples popping.

After Spider-Man's wedding reception, I'd returned to Tunnel. Three times. Without Adeline. Michael Alig threw parties in the basement. The best were Larry Tee's Celebrity Club. I dug the vibe, part circus, part freak show. I wouldn't have admitted it, but as much as I liked Michael's scene, I preferred the regular Tunnel. The basement was performance art. Upstairs it was pure dance. I could lose my mind with the physicality, with the sound of the beat.

Adeline moved over to a wall, staring at the dance floor, glaring at these poor kids, most of whom were about six years her junior. She lit a clove cigarette.

—Why did we come here? she asked.

—You insisted! said Stacie.

The DJ put on "Faith" by George Michael.

—I love this song, I yelled. Come on, let's dance!

Adeline wouldn't. Stacie would. There we were, a pair of twenty-year-olds shaking ourselves silly among an awkward throng of high schoolers. Nothing in the club ever means anything, but here in Marilyn's Back Street there was an especial lack of consequence, because there was no chance of seeing these people again. And if we did, what did it matter? They were dickheads from high school! In Pasadena! I danced harder, faster, thrilled by the anonymity.

A song came on, one that I'd heard before, "No New Tale to Tell" by Love and Rockets, with some very sexy lyrics: *You cannot go against nature / because when you do / go against nature / it's part of nature too.* The flute solo. The kids waved their arms and jumped like epileptics. So did I. So did Stacie.

I yelled at Stacie: —I'm exhausted!

—Me too!

Soaking wet with sweat, clothes sticking to my skin. Stacie grabbed my hand, pulling me off the dance floor. We couldn't find Adeline. We went into the parking lot. Adeline was leaning against a gray El Camino, smoking.

—Why are you, like, out here? asked Stacie.

—I couldn't, like, take it, she said. So I've been talking with the kids.

—What did the kids say? I asked.

—Absolutely nothing, said Adeline. The kids never say anything. They never have.

We walked home.

—You know, said Stacie, that song's right, you know. There really is no new tale to tell. Like, I was talking about earlier, you know, like the *Symposium*? It's, like, a big gay orgy, where all these Athenian intellectuals hang around getting drunk with Socrates, talking about the different meanings of love, and of course it's, like, some of them are very carnal, and then some of them are, like, ethereal, and then at the end, this beautiful youth of Athens, Alcibiades, storms into the party, and he's, like, upset, because he can't, like, figure out how to fuck Socrates. So his definition is, like, the opposite of a definition, it's just, like, a list of all the things Socrates says he knows about love, but how he won't ever, like, actually, you know, do anything about it. Like, he won't fuck Alcibiades.

—Hooray, said Adeline.

She walked upstairs and went to bed.

—The last few months were pretty rough, I said.

—Adeline's always like this, said Stacie. She's a depressive.

I brought Stacie into the kitchen and made us ham and cheddar sandwiches. We sat beneath the dim track lighting, stools pulled up to the island, talking about this and that, that and this. The Captain strolled in, giving us a sideways glance before he visited the pantry. I heard him digging in his litter box.

—What about the *Symposium,* I asked, made you want to major in Classics?

—It's Socrates' definition of love, you know, like, Platonic love? If you read it closely, what he's really saying, you know, is that love is, like, just friendship and the way that friendship, like, nurtures a love of the good. And, like, I loved that, you know? Like, I liked the thought that there was a culture somewhere that valued friendship. That there was a book which told you that you could have friends.

MARCH 1988

Baby Dreams

With the first few dreams, I thought that I was talking to my mirror image. As the nights went on, it became clear that my dreams were of Emil, as if his ghost haunted me through sleep. One dream kept reoccurring. Emil in the living room, on a couch, watching television. I came in from behind, drawn by the noise of the idiot box.

Emil turned.

—It's you, he said.

—It's me, I said.

—Or is that me?

—Or are you me?

I sat next to Emil. We watched television together. Emil explained that the program was about Hell and Heaven, and had been filmed on location.

—Everyone's very interested in the afterlife these days, he said, so it's a brilliant idea to make a documentary.

—Yes, I said.

—Do you want to see where I am? They filmed outside my apartment.

—I don't believe in Heaven.

—Who said I was in Heaven?

—I don't believe in Hell, either.

—What if Hell believes in you?

I'd jolt awake, sweating. It happened every night.

APRIL 1988

Baby, Adeline, and Stacie Go to Scream

Stacie called, suggesting that we go to Scream, a club located in Los Angeles proper. I demanded that Adeline say yes. We'd been in Pasadena for nearly two months and I still hadn't seen Hollywood. Not even the sign!

—You won't like it, said Adeline. Hollywood's even more of a sewer than New York. It's east of Eden and west of garbage town.

—I want to see the Walk of Fame, I said.

—Jesus, she said. You've got to be kidding.

—Adeline! I want to see La La Land!

Stacie came over. We got stoned. They decided that I should drive us into the city, despite my license being, at best, only semi-valid. Adeline wanted to take the 134 to the 2, but Stacie insisted that I drive on the 110, a terrifying road with little lanes and everyone speeding about forty miles an hour too fast. The darkness of the new moon didn't help, and I almost crashed three or four times. Zipping around curves, moving through dark tunnels.

And then, after the final bend, there it was.

Rising cluster of anemic skyscrapers and endless expanse of built-out humanity. I'd seen New York, I'd lived in New York, I'd loved New York. Nothing looks as good as the Manhattan skyline. Nothing impresses like New York.

But Los Angeles! Those lights!

—Fuck, said Adeline, my heavy flow is supposed to be tomorrow, but it's coming on strong.

—Did you bring extra? asked Stacie.

We took the Wilshire exit, passing through a straight shot of emptiness, nothing but office buildings, strip malls, and homeless people. Stacie told me to find somewhere to park.

—Where's the Hollywood sign? I asked, as we walked.

—Calm down, said Adeline. We'll see it when we're, like, done with the club. These things've been there for, like, decades. They aren't going anywhere.

We parked and walked toward the club, joining a crowd that thickened with each step, an ant trail ending at an enormous cement building, a slab monolith festooned with Art Deco angel statues holding swords and torches in their folded hands. The entrance was an intricate metal gate rising about two stories, topped with a superbly ornate clock. Words carved into the building, running above the metal: ALL THINGS WHATSOEVER YE WOULD THAT MEN SHOULD DO TO YOU, DO YE EVEN SO TO THEM.

—And by their fruits ye shall know them.

We passed through the metal entrance, moving into a beautiful lobby with a grand carpeted staircase at the back of the room. Two wings ran off either side, pounding music coming from each. People all over the stairs, standing around, talking, smoking, drinking. Rock'n'rollers, mods, rockabilly, death rockers, punks, goths, freaks, weirdos, losers.

—I'll find you guys later, I said.

A rhythmic looping sound, like waves crashing, the earth itself quaking. I followed it into the dark room. A ghoulish malnourished guy with giant ears was at the microphone, playing a guitar and singing, a cute girl on the keyboards, and two other men, bass and drums. The voice coming from the lunatic was deep, grating, irritating.

Hard to see what the hell was happening. People doing an awkward dance to the drone. Some people can dance to anything. The song ended. People cheered.

—Wedding song! Wedding song!

—The wedding song? asked the vocalist, speaking with an accent.

—Yes! shouted a guy from the audience.

—The wedding song.

—What's the wedding song? asked the bassist, also in an accent.

—The generic wedding song. Just any wedding song will do. White wedding, perhaps? Would anyone care for that? Rock and roll.

—Rock and roll wedding, said the bassist.

—Okay, uh, this is uh, said the vocalist.

—Can I have some more bass in my monitor? Please?

—This is our theme tune.

Slow gloomy guitar. Drums wild. Bass. Keyboard hard to hear. More and more people dancing. This sexy guy next to me, dusky, tight white shirt, ripped-up old jeans, longish hair, wool knitted hat on his head. He moved with ease, in his own world. And I flashed on him, quick. Us naked, us fucking, my cock in his hands, his cock in my mouth, both of us coming every which way, the tips of our cocks pressed together, sweat rolling down his chest into my mouth, grunting.

—Okay, uh, said the vocalist, this is "Marry Me." The wedding song. As it, as it, the generic wedding song. By properly request.

Faster than the last. The sexy guy danced, doing this thing with his arms that should have looked idiotic. But he waved with grace. Perfect.

—"Some Velvet Morning," said the vocalist.

I moved close. The sexy guy didn't see me, still dancing, faster during the verses. Slow during the chorus: *Learn from us, very much, look at us, but do not touch, Phaedra is my name.*

The song ended. I took my chance.

—What's this band called? I asked.

—These Immortal Souls, he said. That guy used to be in The Birthday Party.

—The Birthday Party? I asked, but another song started and he started dancing.

A natural drift, the crowd pushing us apart. I wandered back into the lobby. Even more people on the steps, ashing their cigarettes into the rug, grinding their heels against the fabric. A goth couple on the bottom steps, making out, wet tongues visible in open mouths, her sucking on his, his licking hers. I watched, rushed with embarrassment, and went in the other direction toward a different kind of music, entering another dark room.

Projections on the walls. Violence, malice, hatred, death. All very cartoony, detached from the actuality of suffering. So many skulls. The DJ was spinning "Just Like Heaven" and the crowd sang along, a great writhing mass. What the hell, why not? I danced into them, sticking out eleven more songs, none that I recognized, one of which had a mad man for a vocalist. *How about a nice cold hug before mommy comes home?*

I broke from dancing and went to a corner. Hoping to catch my breath. Adeline, standing alone, smoking a clove cigarette.

—Baby, said Adeline.

—I'm exhausted, I said. Where's Stacie?

—Out on the dance floor.

—What about you?

—O, Baby, she said in the old voice, you'd as soon catch me jumping over the moon with a pack of cats in tow than you would find me dancing to Bauhaus. Not amongst this ragtag pack of hooligans.

—I need to use the bathroom, I said. Should we leave soon?

—Whatever, she said. It doesn't matter.

Back in the lobby, looking for the bathroom, the goth couple still at it. I stopped again, similar to Variety Photoplays, abstractly fascinated. Human sexuality could manifest so publicly. I couldn't imagine.

A hand touched my back. I turned, expecting one of the girls, but finding that sexy guy. He looked even better in the light.

—Hey, he said, you fucking split. We were still talking.

—Sorry, I said.

—Why'd you do that?

—I'm not sure, I said.

He smiled at me, big teeth, parted lips.

—My name's Jaime.

The DJ played "Ballroom Blitz" and the lights came on, revealing the filth accumulated through the night, the debris of deranged rockin' rollers loitering in a Jazz Age ballroom. Stacie didn't want to sleep, and I'd promised Jaime a ride, and I hadn't seen Hollywood. Arguing, drunken, babbling stoned nonsense.

I agreed to drive to Santa Monica, to the beach. We took the 10 the whole way, the freeway empty of traffic. I pushed 100 miles an hour, crazy from Jaime's scent filling the car, too insane to care about the police or my fucked-up license or my fucked-up brain.

—Do you know this song? asked Jaime, singing the lyrics, rich, clear, beautiful voiced: *I would go out tonight, but I haven't got a stitch to wear.*

No one answered. Jaime didn't notice.

—So, like, said Stacie, the theory of forms is this idea that, like, in the, you know, higher realms, there's this place called the plane of forms, and, like, everything we see in our mortal world are lesser copies of the idealized forms of things that are, like, on the plane of forms. So if you see, like, a table, it's, like, you know, a lesser version of the form of the table, which, like, explains why some tables are really nice and others are so shitty. Because some tables are, like, better copies of the form of the table. So that means, I think, that somewhere there's a Baby or a Jaime or a Stacie, a more perfect version of ourselves that are just there, like, in the world of forms.

So you are just a terrible copy, like a counterfeit Gucci bag, of your higher, most perfect self.

Adeline navigated us toward a small park alongside the beach. Jaime ran ahead, running in the sand, taking off his shirt. Too dark to see his body, but I could feel it, pulsing, sending out radio signals to the antenna of my cock.

—Do you think he's gay? I asked Adeline.

—A little bird once told me that everyone's bisexual. There's but one way to find out.

Jaime in the water, pants rolled up, shirtless. The shadow of the pier behind him. I kicked off my shoes and rolled up my own cuffs, the waves lapping against my ankles.

—It's the first time, I said, that I've touched the Pacific Ocean.

—My family took us here all the time, he said. Me and my sister loved that Ferris wheel. I haven't been here in, like, five years.

What did it matter? What the fuck did anything matter? All of us would die. There'd be no trace of me or Jaime or Adeline or Stacie or anyone we'd known, we'd be nothing but food for worms, piles of ashes. The human race would be gone, lost to the universe, the planet too. What would my shame mean then? What was the point of not doing what you wanted while you wanted?

—Can you see me? I asked.

—Not that good, said Jaime.

—It's getting lighter, I said. The sun is rising.

I walked closer to him, trying not to shiver.

—What about now? Am I any clearer?

—A little, he said.

—And now?

—Yeah, he said.

I reached out, my rough palm on his cheek, my heavy fingers going below his chin, pulling his head toward mine, leaning into his mouth, our tongues against each other, soft parade of lemon of sapphire of stars of flesh of lust of sweat of honey of some velvet mornings. My hands on his body, his quivering skin, running up and down.

—Do you want to come home with me? I asked, after we pulled apart.

—Where's home?

—Pasadena, I said.

He nodded. I nodded.

Stacie was on the hood, half asleep. Adeline was leaning against the trunk, smoking clove cigarettes, looking into the buildings on the other side of the street.

—It's like watching ten televisions at the same time, she said. Really bad television. People are so boring.

—Let's go, I said.

—Don't you still want to see Hollywood? she asked. The sign is waiting for you.

—No, I said.

I recognized the way back, getting us from the 10 to the 110, which exploded into Pasadena, only needing directions to Adeline's house. Pulling into the driveway, the world pink with the risen sun. Suzanne wasn't home.

—You, like, live here? asked Jaime.

—For the time being, said Adeline.

Stacie crashed out on a couch. Jaime and I walked up to my room.

APRIL 1988

Suzanne Demonstrates the Pitfalls of Alcoholism

Adeline's spring clean was as inevitable as a funeral. Down came the framed photo of Groucho Marx, down came the poster of Marlene Dietrich in *Blonde Venus,* down went all the books from their shelves. A mini-history of Hollywood boxed up and hidden away.

—I'm tired of it is all, Adeline said. Childish things.

—But there must be something you want to keep? I asked.

—A few books, maybe, but I don't know, why bother? What's the point of any of it?

—Tell me one thing, I said. What's your favorite book?

She sat on the floor, back against her bed, and opened one of the boxes. Here we may consider the circular reality of the bibliophile, because as she dug through her books, I caught sight of a volume that, years later, I would purchase. *Masters of Menace,* a joint biography of Peter Lorre and Sydney Greenstreet. I still own it. I've yet to read it.

Adeline pulled out a garish, oversized paperback. Its purple cover comprised of crudely cut black-and-white publicity stills. In green letters read its title: *Classics of the Horror Film.* Authored by William K. Everson.

—This one, said Adeline. It meant a lot.

—Can I read it?

—I guess, she said. Do whatever you want. It's all trash anyway.

In truth, I had no interest. I'd always found Adeline's interest in the horror film to be the least interesting aspect of her personality. But the time would come when the enormity of what she was doing would overwhelm her, when she'd be struck with an insatiable nostalgia for her old possessions.

I brought the book into my room, thinking about Jaime, wondering if I should call him. We hadn't seen each other in a few days. All my thoughts were of him, of the sweet way that he smiled, of his mewling as he slept, of his unnatural calm.

No one answered. I still didn't know where he lived. Somewhere in Hollywood. I guessed that he lived alone. Or maybe had his own phone line.

Smelling him in my bedclothes, I considered beating off, but the night was early. I preferred coming right before sleep, after the buildup of daily hormones. The force of orgasm that much more powerful.

I read *Classics of the Horror Film*. The early chapters were the best, about silent films and the '30s. Lugosi in *White Zombie,* Boris Karloff in *Frankenstein,* and oh so many photographs of Tod Browning's 1932 masterpiece, *Freaks.*

The latter film serves as a vehicle for the prolonged display of actual, identifiable human deformities. Siamese twins, the human torso, midgets. Three deeply distressing pinhead girls, sufferers of microcephaly with tiny little bodies and elongated skulls, hair shaved except for knots at the top of their heads, inversions of a monk's tonsure.

The rest of the book was a bummer. The Hayes Code had destroyed the horror film. I was looking through the last few pages, reading about *The Exorcist,* when I heard the front door open.

CRASH!

Running to the hallway, I bumped into Adeline.

—Was it another earthquake? I asked.

A blood cry from downstairs.

—ADDDDDDDDDDDDELLLINNNNNNNNEEEEEEEEEEEEEEEEEE
EEE! ADDELIIIIINNNNNEEEEEEEEEEEEEEEEEEEEEEEEEEEEEEEE
EEEEEEEEEE!

—Oh no, said Adeline.

Suzanne was sprawled on the floor, a black party dress hiked up around her waist, one pump on, one pump off. She'd broken a heel. A man in his early 50s stood over her, penny loafers, blue jeans, black sports jacket. His shirt was open at the top, bony breastbone visible, sun damage and freckles.

His teeth, every last one, were perfect. They blazed white.

—Your mom had a little too much to drink, he said.

—Obviously, said Adeline.

—I'm going to help her upstairs, said the man.

—No, said Adeline. You're not.

—Adeliiiine, groaned Suzanne. Adeliiiine.

My parents had problems, but neither were this pathetic, this drunk.

—Time for you to leave, said Adeline. We'll help my mother.

—Adeliiiine, noooo.

—It doesn't quite sound as if the lady'd like for me to leave.

—What's your name? asked Adeline.

—Call me Stu, he said. I'm a friend. I'll help her upstairs.

—I'm not moving, said Adeline. You aren't going upstairs.

Stu bent over and tried to lift Suzanne, whispering into her ear, but his efforts came to nothing. He'd pick her up, she'd slip back down, like he'd tried to grasp water with his bare hands.

—You'd better leave, said Adeline.

—I'm not going anywhere.

—Baby, she said.

The toxic reek of alcohol drifted from Suzanne, wafted off Stu. I didn't know Suzanne's age. I guessed maybe fifty. I hoped I wasn't like this when I was fifty.

—You have to go, I said to Stu.

—Who the fuck are you? he asked.

—I'm the guy who'll make you leave.

—Sure you will, sweetheart, he said. Won't you worry about breaking a nail?

It was interesting. I didn't feel the same instant anger that had fueled previous encounters, but a tormented person can manufacture rage with the reliability of an industrial product. All you need do is tap those deep reservoirs of misery and memory. Think about your past and something'll raise your ire. You find your hands clenched into fists, grabbing a middle-aged man named Stu, bashing Stu's head into a wall, lifting Stu by his age-inappropriate pants and throwing him face-first into the front yard.

—I'm not doing anything else to Stu, I said. I could kick him a few times, but why bother?

—Much as I'd like it, said Adeline, I'm not sure he's worth it.

I hefted Suzanne over my shoulder and put her on a couch. I worried that she might choke on her own vomit. Adeline assured me that Suzanne was a weathered veteran of this particular war, too much of a soldier to die in her sleep.

Unconvinced, I lingered. Adeline went upstairs. Suzanne was awake, her watery eyes unable to focus.

—Hi, she said.

—Hi, I said.

—I drank too much bourbon, she said.

—Looks like it.

—I think I'll sleep now, she said.

—Okay, I said.

—Goodnight, Emil, she said.

—Goodnight, I said.

I found Adeline on the floor of her room, listening to a record that I didn't recognize. To see her mother like that. To see Adeline, see her see Suzanne.

—I don't want to be like her, she said.

—You aren't, I said.

I lay next to her, the carpet bristling against my flesh, my arms around her. We didn't say anything. I hugged Adeline until she fell asleep, her face against my chest. The record started skipping. I turned off the player and put a blanket over Adeline.

Jaime didn't answer. Where could he be? I didn't own him. Or want to own him. But I wanted him with me, right there, right in that moment. Would have given anything to hear him talk about the stupid things that he liked. About skateboarding or Dungeons & Dragons or beer or anything.

I beat off.

MAY 1988

Baby Gets into NYU

Then there was the time when I got into NYU.

MAY 1988

Adeline Makes a Decision

I was downstairs, watching a VHS recording of *The Wonder Years*, a television show about a junior high student in 1968. The idea is that this kid, named Kevin, narrates from an indeterminate point in the future, presumably 1988. The whole thing is an excuse for Baby Boomers to remind everyone yet again about the irrefutable Monumentalness of the 1960s.

This particular episode hung on Kevin's love interest, an eleven-year-old girl named Winnie Cooper who wears fishnet tights and go-go boots, and her older brother, Brian, an incredibly sexy nineteen-year-old. He's presented as an archetypical all-American midcentury rebel, but anyone with even a rudimentary knowledge of queers would spot Brian as an ace player for our team. Kevin has an adolescent hard-on for Brian, describing him as "sweaty, greasy, working with his hands . . . Whatta guy!"

Brian goes to fight in Vietnam. And like anyone who ships out to Vietnam in film or on television, Brian returns in a body bag. Kevin finds Winnie hiding in the woods. She's staring into the abyss of existential meaninglessness. Kevin takes advantage of her sorrow and confusion. Kevin scores a kiss. End of episode.

Click. Clack. Rising over the television show. Click. Clack. Click. Clack. Click. Clack. Click. Clack. The credits rolled. I paused the VCR. I went upstairs. Click. Clack. From Adeline's room. Her door half-shut. Click. Clack. I pushed it open, a little, and peeked inside.

She sat on her bed in a lotus position, legs folded, left hand pointing downward. Click. Clack. Her right hand held a child's toy. Two plastic balls equidistantly suspended from a string, with a handle in the middle. Click. Clack. Through vertical motion, the balls crashed into each other on a horizontal plane. These collisions sent them in the direction opposite their previous vertical movement, where they'd crash into each other again on another parallel horizontal plane, repeating the process. Click. Clack.

Adeline's eyes were closed. She never lost control of the balls. Click. Clack. They went up, they collided. Click. They went down, they collided. Clack. Like a train over tracks.

I watched another episode of *The Wonder Years*. Click. Clack. Winnie Cooper's family buried her brother. Click. Kevin attended the wake. Clack. The last time that he saw Winnie Cooper was when they kissed in the woods. Click. His future self reflects that his adolescence is ruled by the strongest forces of human existence, Eros and Thanos, love and death. Clack.

I fell asleep. I don't know for how long.

Adeline pushed me with her feet. The television was off. *The Wonder Years* was over.

—Baby, she whispered. Baby, wake up.

—What is it? I asked.

—I'm done being miserable, she said. I'm done being neurotic. I'm done with a life of unending strife. I'm going back to New York.

—When? I asked.

—As soon as I can, she said.

—What about me? I asked.

—Stay if you want, she said.

—But why? I asked.

—You know why, she said.

—Yes, I said. I do.

Suzanne didn't come home until 10 pm. They fought. Adeline packed.

I sat up, reading, thinking about Jaime. I called him, told him the situation, asked him what I should do. I wanted Jaime to scream, to holler, to demand that I stay in California, to stay with him, to never leave.

—Your choice, he said. I'll miss you if you go.

—But you think I should? I asked.

—Your choice.

We got off the phone. A soft knock at my door.

—Come in, I said.

Suzanne. It was the only time she'd been inside my room.

—She hates me, said Suzanne.

—No one hates you, I said.

—She does, said Suzanne.

I wondered what it was like having this for your mother, someone who would conspire with her daughter's best friend. I smelled the booze.

—Where did I go wrong? asked Suzanne.

—Parenting is hard, I said. You're much better than mine ever were.

JULY 1988

Baby Meets Jaime's Friends

As Adeline was in New York, Suzanne rarely appeared. Without the narrative justification of family, the house became an expansive storage space for her earthly possessions. We only saw each other on the occasions when she needed a change of clothes. She'd give me money for expenses.

My real human contact was with the maids. They arrived every few days, these two lovely women, Maria and Rosalita. They barely spoke English. I hardly spoke Spanish. When they realized that I wasn't part of Adeline's family, they started laughing at me, a gentle laughter like running water. They made strange food, and shoved plates at me, saying, "Eat! Eat!" I'd creak out a *gracias*.

Jaime slept over about five nights a week. I'd pick him up in Hollywood and drive him to Pasadena. We never went anywhere, never saw anyone. He'd sit around Suzanne's house, telling me stories about his childhood, about going to Venice Beach, about seeing Guns N' Roses play a frat party at UCLA before they got famous, about how he didn't really like that Sunset Strip bullshit.

Then we'd fuck. We fucked in every room. We fucked in rooms that I didn't know existed. We probably created these rooms, demanding that they burst into existence as venues for our lust. Old, unused bedrooms cluttered with junk. In the kitchen. In the living room. In the den. In the backyard. In the front yard.

He wouldn't talk about his family, only saying that they lived near Pasadena, somewhere in Highland Park, a place name that I recognized from driving on the 110.

This went on for months.

One night, after we'd fucked, our arms wrapped around each other, I asked why he hadn't introduced me to his friends. Or shown me his apartment.

—You, like, wouldn't fucking like it, dude, he said. It's not your scene or something.

How the hell did Jaime know my scene? We argued. I wouldn't let him get away. Wearily, exhausted, he sighed and said I could come to his apartment. I could meet his friends. I asked when. He said tomorrow.

—You mean it? I asked. Really?

—Sure, he said.

I pulled him back. His flesh against mine, not even sex, just that moment of electricity, of one body against the other. We rolled and tumbled for hours.

Around noon, I drove him to Hollywood and Vermont. He told me to return, later, in a few hours, at six o'clock. He gave me his address.

—One thing, he said. You've got to, like, realize we can't like be physical, okay? Not around my friends.

—Oh, I said.

—You have to say yes, okay? he asked. They don't, like, know. I haven't told them. I wanna. I really, like, fucking want to tell them.

—Okay, I said.

I drove through the streets on instinct. Los Angeles is as easy to navigate as New York, both cities being enormous grids. I went up on Sunset past the Marlboro Man and parked at Tower Records. Running along the building's sides were large reproductions of album covers. The only one that I recognized was Michael Jackson's *Bad*.

Tower was a junk shop that sold one kind of junk. Popular music at the exact transitional moment when compact discs began replacing the vinyl record. The CDs came in long cardboard boxes, the discs and their plastic clamshell cases occupying about one third of the length of the boxes. Two boxes could be placed side by side, forming the same shape as one vinyl LP, allowing record stores to avoid the cost of new shelving.

Inside that garish yellow and red building, it was clear which side had won. CDs were on almost every rack. Tower was terraforming.

A pair of girls stood by the doorway, talking loud, both wearing extremely vivid makeup, their hair teased out to unfathomable lengths, media stereotypes that I couldn't believe existed beyond television.

—I heard, like, this is where, like, he used to work, said one girl.

—Really?

—Yeah, like, when they were totally broke. Like, he used to like sleep underneath the steps because he, like, didn't have an apartment.

The albums in Tower seemed so grotesque. Late-adolescent, final-period rock 'n' roll. Bravado about sex and women.

Giving up, I walked on Sunset, landing at Duke's, a coffee shop, sitting for an uncomfortably long time, eating and drinking while I lingered over the *LA Weekly*. I read the listings for live music, enthralled and appalled by the sheer scope of human ambition, at the thousands of bands performing that week. Would any gain recognition? Were any good? Was it the folly of youth, the folly of America, the folly of an impossible dream? Looking at the names all up against one another, I got a flash that these bands were comprised of the underclasses, of people without Adeline's opportunities. People scraping by on marginal talent, hoping the spark might light a fire, hoping to transcend into our social betters. Why did people try? Why do people do anything?

Two hours later, my waiter banged fresh silverware on the table. It wasn't long until 6. I left a tip and went to my car.

I stopped at a gas station on LaBrea and asked for directions. The attendant told me what to look for and where to go, finishing every sentence with the words *hee haw!*

—Wilton? That's way up past the freeway off Hollywood, *hee haw!*

—Thank you, I said.

—You take care, *hee haw!*

Jaime lived off Franklin Avenue. Other houses on the block were in good condition, but his property displayed the scars of a rental. Chipped paint, broken driveway, crabgrass. Years of neglect and abuse by an absentee landlord.

I rang the doorbell. A girl answered.

—Hi, I said. Is Jaime home?

—Yeah, she said. He's home.

She stopped, saying nothing. She wasn't even looking at me, but past me, focused on something over my shoulder. I smiled. She didn't smile back.

—Can I come in?

—Come in? she asked.

—Yeah, I said. Come inside and see Jaime.

—Oh, she said, sure, come in.

She melted away. I stepped into the sitting room of a California

Craftsman. Trash littered throughout. Old vinyl couches that someone'd stabbed, slits running down their back cushions, stuffing pushing out. Broken children's toys. A long crack along the length of one wall.

I stood there like a grinning idiot.

—Where's Jaime's room? I asked.

—Oh, his room.

—Yeah, I said. His room. Jaime's room?

—Jaime's room's off the kitchen.

What's the German word for the moment when you discover your lover in his bedroom, shirtless, holding a crummy acoustic guitar, surrounded by two men roughly your age, also shirtless? What's the German word for that?

—Hi, I said.

—Oh dude, said Jaime. You made it. Awesome.

—Yeah, I said.

—Baby, he said, this is Tommy and that's Raoul.

Tommy and Raoul were a specific kind of Hollywood, very polished and very dirty, as if they'd spent some great portion of their lives refining their appearances only to then roll in the dust.

—Hey, man, said Raoul.

—Hi, dude, said Tommy.

Jaime's room was spartan. A crummy desk and a Murphy bed, pulled down from the wall, Jaime sitting on its edge. Tommy and Raoul on metal folding chairs. Garbage on the floor, debris, old candy wrappers, and empty soda cans. Jaime's unwashed laundry was on his desk.

—What's happening? I asked. Should I take off my shirt too?

They all laughed, with their big moon eyes. Not at the joke.

—What? I asked.

—It's nothing, man, said Jaime. Don't worry.

—Something's up, I said.

They laughed again. That old anger, the rage, boiling up.

—We flipped, is all, said Jaime. No big deal.

—Flipped?

—Acid, dude, he said. You know, flipped acid?

The conversation ended with Jaime's fingers placing two tabs of sacramental blotter on my tongue. The acid was called Magic Mountain. Jaime showed me the sheet, stamped with a repeating pattern of a mountain, a radiant Eye of Providence superimposed over its peak. The paper tasted like chemicals.

—We flipped about thirty minutes ago, said Raoul.

There was a period of terrible anxiety, waiting for the outcome. I'd inflicted this thing on myself. The next few hours were unavoidable. Imprisoned by the drug.

Another taste in my mouth, disgusting dryness. Rotmouth. A trickle of cool sweat leaked from my left armpit.

—I'm going to look at your backyard, I said.

Too many trees. A lemon tree at the back struck me as someone's prize. I have no idea why. The lemons vibrated. I couldn't look at the leaves, not without trails coming off them, their shapes warping. There wasn't any grass on the ground. Patterns in the dirt, mounds and valleys and footprints. Something was definitely going on upstairs.

—Hey, said Jaime. How are you feeling?

—Jesus! I yelled.

—Calm down, dude, he said. It's all okay.

—When did you get there? I asked. I didn't hear you.

—I've been here for a few minutes, watching you.

—How are you feeling?

—It's really starting, he said. I've done it a thousand times. It's always different and always the same.

Raoul played a song on Jaime's guitar, voice drifting through the open window: *It was Staggerlee and Billy / Two men who gambled late / Staggerlee swore he threw seven / Billy swore that he threw eight / Staggerlee said Billy / Oh please don't take my life / I've got three hungry children / and a very sickly wife.*

On the last word, my head spun. Raoul's voice dragged out, slow like molasses, thick like syrup. Wiiiiiiiiiiiiiiiiiiiiiiiiiiiiiiiiiiiiiiiiiiiiiiiiiiiiiiiiiiiiiiii iiiife. I wasn't in the backyard, I was inside Jaime's room.

—Why's it happening so quick?

Staggerlee he went down to the devil / and he leaned up on his shelf / he said come out here Mr. Devil / I'm gonna rule hell by myself / well the devil called his demons around him / Lord, let's climb this wall / He said here's a bad man, Staggerlee / and he's going to kill us all.

Orange light filled the room, licked with invisible flame. My jaw ached, I couldn't stop clenching, biting from the back of my mouth.

—Jaime, why's everything on fire?

—What? he asked.

He was on fire. His face demonic.

—Dude, he said, you don't look so good. We'll go for a walk and get you some air.

Me and him, side by side, stumbling along Hollywood Boulevard. I saw the street signs, anyway, and walking was good because walking prevented me from focusing, walking wouldn't let me fixate. My brain broken, made stupid. I wanted to express my thoughts, but nothing came out, not the right way. I wanted to tell Jaime what I saw.

—Dude, he said, you've got to stop.

—Stop?

—Dude, he said, you keep saying *hee haw! Hee haw!* It's freaking me out.

—*Hee haw*?

—Yeah, he said. *Hee haw.* You keep saying *hee haw.*

—Am I laughing or am I crying?

Standing on a bridge over the freeway, looking down at the traffic. I could read the drivers' minds. The woman driving the red car was cheating on her husband. The truck driver was a murderer. The taxicab drove itself, lacking any guiding presence, no person behind the wheel. I heard their thoughts. *What's for dinner? I wonder if he still loves me. Will I get that promotion? How will I afford the mortgage? I'll have to kill the bitch.* Dark night, the car headlights flashing green and amber.

—Come on, said Jaime.

People on the street. I don't know them. Who was I? Did they fear me as much as I feared them? Someone walked by, leashed to a two-headed dog.

Jaime talked, but the words came out silent, dialogue balloons from comic books, air writing in luminescent lettering, falling apart before I could read. Down into a thick alphabet soup on the sidewalk. Dissolving.

—Are you listening?

—What?

—I was dude I was saying that I can dude I can see the, you know, the wires behind the world. I can see who's pulling the strings. It's not God. There is no God. God is the wires. We are the wires. So are we God?

Every new block was a descent, misery on all sides, tunnel vision, loss of ego, loss of self, until we reached the next street sign. The world rang back with clarity, with totality, sounds of bells. BRONSON, GOWER, EL CENTRO, VISTA DEL MAR, ARGYLE.

Stars on the sidewalk, names I couldn't read. I stopped, scrambling the letters into place.

—What does it say? I asked Jaime. Does it say Stagger Lee?

—No, he said. It says Tod Browning.

—Tod Browning? I'm standing on Tod Browning?

VINE.

—I'm at Hollywood and Vine! I'm at Hollywood and Vine! I'm at Hollywood and Vine! THERE WERE A LOT OF GOOD CLOTHES IN THAT BAG.

The buildings sang songs. The lampposts too. I could see down the Boulevard, fire at its farthest end, past the castle, past the mystical palm trees. I could see through a building, to the other side. I read a name. ANGELYNE. Image of woman, huge-breasted, blonde, red lips, futuristic sunglasses. Her mouth opened, the building speaking through Angelyne, her bosom jiggling, four words. What Time Is Love?

The city burning, I smelled the city burning. Jaime took my hand and pulled me toward the flames. I screamed, in a fit. In the fire, I could see it, I could see Frankenstein's monster stomping Hollywood, lightning shooting from bolts in his neck, buildings crushed. I could, I could, I could. I looked at the people around me, to see if they could see it, but I couldn't see Jaime anymore, the only people that I saw were the pinheads from *Freaks*. I'd wanted to see famous people in Hollywood, but mercy god please not like this. The little girl pinheads dancing in their pink floral dresses, their black open broken mouths highlighting rotten yellow teeth, waving at me and calling out my name, but they weren't saying my name, they were shouting out, *HEE HAW HEE HAW HEE HAW HEE HAW HEE HAW HEE HAW HEE HAW HEE HAW HEE HAW HEE HAW.*

Crashed into blackness beneath a jet coal statue. My eyes wouldn't focus but I read the words. ERECTED IN THE MEMORY OF RUDOLPH VALENTINO 1895–1926.

—Where are we? I asked Jaime.

—You were, like, freaking out, he said. So I brought you here. No one's ever in this park at night.

—What time is it? I asked.

—Almost dawn, dude. You can see the sun rising.

—The sky's the wrong color. Everything is the wrong color. Why are my pants wet?

—You pissed yourself.

—What happened to my shoes?

We walked toward his house. The fluidity of thought returning while the physical sensations of the drug lessened. Trails, color and visual distortions. But now it was almost pleasant, I controlled the drug. Rather than the drug controlling me.

—Can I come inside? I asked at Wilton and Hollywood.

—That's not a great idea, he said.

—Why? I asked.

—You can't handle your shit, he said.

—Oh, I said.

—Sorry, it's just how it is.

AUGUST 1988

Baby Calls Adeline

I called Adeline.
　　—I'm coming back, I said.
　　—I'm waiting, she said.

AUGUST 1988

Adeline Receives an Unwelcome Tutorial
on the Nature of the Police State

Unbeknownst to me, Baby'd gone and matriculated his silly self to New York University. He emerged from the West Coast in late August, plunging into freshman life. Orientation, course registration, purchase of textbooks. I inquired as to how he could possibly afford such an education.

Baby explained that he'd been classified as a financial independent. His grades in high school were exceptional, his income pitiful. NYU had bestowed a merit scholarship upon him.

"A gol' darned free ride," he said.

"Good for you," I said. "Never pay for nothing."

Having dawdled with Jaime and bandied about with childish notions of love's sweet blossoms, Baby's return occurred a bit too late.

A fortnight earlier and he would have been on scene, thick in the mud, for the moment when the world changed, when the city metamorphosed itself with a sacrifice of blood, becoming a dark Satanic mill in service of real estate developers.

Fourteen days earlier and he would have been home for the riot at Tompkins Square.

The Lower East Side, its traditional boundaries including the East Village, spent most of the '70s and early '80s as a plague pit soaked with spittle and jism, a grotesquerie of drugged-out decadence. Heroin reigned, the substance of choice.

By the mid-80s, the crown was in dispute, with crack staging an insurgency. Crime and personal safety became grave issues.

Compounding matters, the blocks themselves were shifting. It began with the East Village art explosion, sending out a beacon to the first wave of gentrifiers. Truth be told, these people who were akin to yours truly.

Ecstatic epigones and daffy dilettantes. Yet most of that first cohort cultivated a healthy respect for the dirt in which they rocked and rolled.

They came because the neighborhood was filthy, because it was interesting. They did not seek to shift its balance, even if that's exactly what they did.

The first wave always brings a second. Trouble erupted in '86. On the corner of 9th and B, an ancient building suffered conversion into luxury condos. The Christodora House.

Other East Village buildings had fallen to the same ugly fate, but for one of those unknown intangibilities, the previous renovations had flown well under the radar.

Christodora. Offering a different kind of luxury to a different kind of person at a downtown price, and being on the corner of Tompkins Square, sounded the initial cannon shot of a loooooooooong war.

The park's unofficial residents passed the livelong day by pissing, shitting, fucking, fighting, drinking, shooting up, smoking crystallized cocaine, burning trash, dying. All in the daily sight of Christodora residents, in the front yard of these bleeding-edge units *du jour*.

The propertied classes are born to complaint. They simply live to make their displeasure known. I know my own, darlings.

City officials felt the Great White Pressure. A decision was made. For the first time in living memory, there would be a park curfew. The city landed on 1 am.

At 9 pm on August 6th, 1988, a police brigade assembled around the park's perimeter. Horses, infantrymen, light artillery, helicopters. This gradual amassing of the troops constituted fair warning. The implicit message being that if one were foolish enough to wander within the perimeter after the curfew, then one would receive no quarter. The police were offering the beating of a lifetime.

1 am came and went. The people did not leave Tompkins Square. They rallied against the police.

What followed was a scene that evoked all the delicacy and tactful refinement that we've come to associate with urban police work.

Cops wild, instigating and provoking the melee, spilling into the streets around the park, coming up 7th, chasing people through St. Mark's, pushing outwards along Avenue A. Beating civilians, kicking the phlegm out of photographers for the *Times*, clubbing reporters from the *Daily News*.

That very night, unawares, your humble narratress attempted to ignore the stifling heat, pacing her fingers through a battered copy of *Blood and Guts in High School* by Kathy Acker. It proved an impossible re-read with the cacophony of helicopters and sirens.

I gave up, headed downstairs, and stepped into 7th Street. People ran past my door towards Cooper Square. A young woman was smeared in her own dark-clotted claret. I asked a man what was happening.

"The cops is killing us down in Tompkins Park!"

An inner voice spoke, Self, you're curiouser than a cat at Christmas. Self, it said, you must surely journey down to the place of pain.

I needed to see, but I shouldn't much like it if the cops were killing me down in Tompkins Square. I changed into a neutral outfit. Dressed down, conservative, a power jacket and well-cut slacks, bestowing the appearance of a person with means. Beneath the jacket, I donned a moth-eaten t-shirt that I'd purchased from an LA death rock band called The Castration Squad.

A steady stream of people pushed up 7th, their faces and heads split open, sweat diluting the blood, clothes torn. At First Avenue, I couldn't get any closer. Mounted cops on horseback blocked further access.

Over to 6th and down towards A, right into the action, at the very intersection where the tidal wave of punks, skinheads, freaks, and homeless crashed up against the police line. People shouting at the cops, hollering, screaming. Coagulate gore in the streets. Whistles being blown, horses galloping. Helicopters overhead, motorblades kicking up dust storms, spotlights illuminating the Avenue. Chants. Men on the rooftops, throwing M-80s. Bottles, cans. Violence from above. I moved off to the side, watching the NYPD discipline and punish a great swath of unarmed individuals. Four cops smashed a slight woman against the Con Edison substation, kicking her, bashing her face into the brick. Other cops stood guard, preventing rescue. A Catholic priest attempted mediation, demonstrating the direct relationship between organized religion and the state. "Come now," he said in this lilting Irish brogue, "but ye'll be knowing in your heart, won't ye, that violence t'isn't our way now?" A man knocked off his bicycle, beaten with batons. The gash in his forehead, bits of bone.

Disoriented by the blood and the exploding firecrackers, I turned and bumped into the chest of a lone police officer. He was my age, perhaps a year or two older.

Truncheon out, blue shirt, yellow badge, riot helmet. His eyes ran over my body. *So this,* I thought, *is death.* I supplicated myself with a tepid come-hither glance, hoping that he'd rather fuck a comely young woman than destroy her beauty. He lowered the baton and ran off in another direction.

The cops couldn't get past 6th Street. Neither could the citizenry. Heads were cracked for hours but the line held.

At sunrise, the police received orders to abandon the park, returning it to the very people they'd evacuated.

Think of it, reader, won't you?

In that month of August, in that year of 1988, the New York Police Department, the great dreaded NYPD, couldn't manage the elementary task of rousting hobos and hoodlums. They couldn't wrest control of a ten-acre park. A massively superior force retreated from the unarmed resistance of society's lowest.

Think you now of thirteen years later and mark the passage of time. Mohamed Atta and his unpleasant pals crashing aeroplanes in the World Trade Centre. Cops on every corner, a complete shutdown of the city. Effortlessly. Without resistance or complaint.

The change started at Tompkins Square. That was the moment.

The bloodied masses retook the park. A blackguard contingent stormed the Christodora, trashing its lobby, pulling out its plants, breaking the glass of its front door. All the while screaming, "Die, yuppie scum, die!"

I walked home, dazed, clothes stained with other people's blood.

AUGUST 1988

Adeline Meets Daniel Rakowitz

S hortly following this unwelcome tutorial on the nature of state power, I made the acquaintance of a homeless pot dealer named Daniel Rakowitz, encountering him at a Justice Rally in the park.

By the end of 1989, dear reader, Rakowitz will have murdered Monika Beerle, his Swiss roommate, who was a dancer at Billy's Topless. He'll have dismembered her body, boiled the skin off her bones, hidden her skull in a locker at the Port Authority, and made a stew of her flesh which he will feed to the homeless contingent in Tompkins Square.

The way some people live.

OCTOBER 1988

Минерва

I undertook a healthy interest in an odd character at Parsons, a young woman in the Fine Arts department named Минерва. Her reputation around school was that of a dyed-in-the-wool anarchist.

Through her first two years of higher education, Минерва produced explicitly figurative work, owing a massive debt to Francis Bacon and demonstrating a distinct Neo-Expressionist influence.

Returning from the '88 summer break, she'd entered the realm of didacticism, stripping away pictorial elements and focusing on the presentation of messages rendered in simulated type.

A great number of art students travel down this ghastly road, but Минерва's work exuded a special quality. Most of the kiddies in their third year will attempt clever aphorisms. LET'S ALL PRETEND WE'RE WORKING CLASS. WHEN THE BOMBS DROP, NO ONE WILL REMEMBER WHO YOU FUCKED. THE ONLY GAY THING AROUND HERE IS THE DANCING.

Минерва's canvases were stark gesso white, with meticulously rendered statements in black boldface serif. The language was graphic, employing a stilted English. My favorite was a three-by-four-foot canvas that read: SHIT IN YOUR OWN COCKS, BASTARDS! Another favorite: PUSSY POWER FOR PUTRID PRINCESS!

I watched as the latter canvas emerged into being, slow parthenogenesis over a four-hour studio session. A miniature blonde Soviet in her filthy denim jacket and ripped-up leather pants, painting crude obscenities. Oh, darlings, Минерва was divine.

Whilst she packed up her materials, I asked if she'd like to go somewhere.

"Fucking shit," she said. "What you think? My life so empty there is nothing I must do?"

"Darling," I said, "I imagined it might be fun to get a drink."

"Alcohol, hm?" she asked. "Fucking why not, bright girl? Let us drink until our thighs sweat with human toil."

We landed at the Continental Divide, on Third Avenue, a restaurant-slash-bar recently redecorated in a style best described as Dinosaur Chic. Ten-foot-high murals depicting scenes out of *One Million Years B.C.* sans Raquel Welch and her cohort. Shrieking pterodactyls that could only remind yours truly of Mother, tyrannosaurus rex rampages, moronic little dioramas inside cubby holes. Above the bar, a shelf hosted children's toys. Godzilla, Dino from *The Flintstones*, a brontosaurus.

"Do you like Parsons?" I asked. "How's the new work being received?"

"Fuck faculty in bloodied assholes," said Минерва. "Terrible shits who understand nothing. Those who cannot. Fuck them. But I am pissing so much money on degree. And I love New York City, even if is much better ten years ago."

"Everyone in New York complains about how the city was better ten years ago," I said. "Or some indeterminate period before their own arrival, whichever comes first. But it's never better, not really. It's always the same."

At that very moment, darlings, this terrible fellow walked into the bar. I'd had a fling with him about two years earlier. Back then, when he was begging yours truly to dole out handjobs as if his name were George Whitney, this fellow had dressed beaucoup très preppie, but now he'd grown out his hair and was wearing a Megadeth t-shirt. Megadeth!

"Sweet thing, would you mind terribly if we left?" I asked Минерва. "Someone who I used to watch neigh and whinny whilst in the throes of orgasm has just darkened the establishment. My apartment's only a block over."

"Sure thing," she said.

Walking across St. Mark's, Минерва pointed to a huge mural painted on the north side's tallest building. "You see this?" she asked. With a pure black background, a neon blue cartoon outline of a young man's head, cigarette dangling from his outrageous oversized lips, his hair done in white paint. A blue patch covering the right eye. Painted across the bottom, in loose red script, was the word GRINGO.

"I've considered this icon before," I said.

"Is from film called *Gringo*," she said. "Is title credit, done cheap. Local asshole play character of Gringo, local junky scum. Maybe you see on his skateboard? My friend give blowjob. Starfucker. No thanks. Fuck him. Only mural matters. Looks over us, at gateway of Village, watches our existence. Unchallengeable eye. You read *Great Gatsby* in high school?"

We'd been assigned the book back at Crossroads, but I'd caught the film adaptation on television and faked mightily off my knowledge of Robert Redford's lackluster performance.

"But of course, old sport," I said.

"Myself," said Минерва, "I believe Gringo is Cyclops of Doctor T. J. Eckleburg in vale of ash. Gringo sees all. Gringo knows all. When Gringo go, so go East Village. Game is up when there is no more Gringo. Doctor T. J. Eckleburg is only good thing in bullshit capitalist fantasy. Is Judeo-Christian god? Or emptiness on which proletariat worker projects meaning?"

Baby wasn't home, it being the time of day when he was either in class or working at the Theatre 80 St. Mark's.

"Roommate?" asked Минерва.

"He isn't present."

"Is student?" she asked.

"At NYU," I said.

"Fucking NYU," said Минерва. "I tell stories about NYU. Real prick institution."

I offered Минерва some food, but she declined.

"New York ten years ago is real place," she said. "All since is monkeys who fling shit. You and I are nothing."

FEBRUARY 1989

Baby Invites Adeline to Bret Easton Ellis's Apartment

Our holiday break did not include a sojourn to California. Mother telephoned on several occasions, but she hadn't much to say, still smarting with the unspoken and implicit implications of my abscondence.

Baby was clubbing rather heavily and regaling me with tales of Mykul Tronn, Magenta, Brandywine, Oliver Twisted, and the other baroque drag queens and club kids that he'd met in the sweat-stinking bomb shelters and filth pits around the city.

"Bully for you," I said. "Have a grand old time. My only request is that you refrain from bringing riff-raff into our apartment."

I'd fallen upon the simple conclusion that Adeline and nightclubs were like the repelling ends of two magnets. The ridiculous jangling limbs, the open mouths and grinning faces, the repulsive joy of people who were oh, sooooooooo happy! to be there, in that moment, shaking and grinding. Some things in this world were not intended for yours truly.

So it was with no small amount of surprise on that February night when I answered our Mickey Mouse telephone at 1:47 am and heard Baby on the other end, demanding that I meet him at an apartment belonging to some fool whom he'd met at Palladium.

"Baby," I said. "Surely you can't expect me to trot out at this time of night? It's freezing!"

"Listen to me, very carefully," said he. If wires could transmit odor, it was a certain bet that I'd be flooded with his boozy breath. "I'm only a few blocks away. You do not want to miss this. I promise."

"I'd rather not," I said. "I'm reading. Plus, you know. Club people."

"Adeline," said Baby. "When do I ever ask you to do anything? When do we ever do anything together anymore?"

A voice shrieked behind him. The shattering of glass. The cheers of a small crowd.

"Do you have Queen Rex with you?" I asked.

"No," said Baby. "I wouldn't call if she were here."

"Okey-dokey," I sighed. "What's the address?"

"114 East 13th, between Third and Fourth."

"What's the apartment?"

"2D," he said. "There's a doorman. He'll let you up."

"A doorman? Jesus Christ, Baby. What sort of animal are you associating with?"

"Come here," he said. "You will not regret it."

"I very much doubt that," I said.

I fortified my nerves with two swigs from a bottle of ultra-cheap tequila. I hadn't wanted to consume that rotten stuff, but a gut-level sixth sense informed me that survival would require stiff intoxication.

The tequila was an artifact of Jeremy Winterbloss's last visit. He'd made his appearance on the pretext of lending me certain comic books, but the true purpose of this visit was for Jeremy to grow drunk and complain about his love life. "Girls around school don't seem interested," he said. "Or maybe I'm not interested in them."

"What sort of woman are you seeking?" I asked.

"I have no idea," he said. "Someone who seems like they have a clue what they're doing with their life?"

He presented me with two trade paperbacks. *Watchmen* by Alan Moore and Dave Gibbons. *The Dark Knight Returns* by Frank Miller. Both published by DC Comics.

"Aren't you a Marvel man?" I asked. Jeremy'd transitioned from his internship into a part-time job working for Larry Hama, the writer on *G.I. Joe.*

"I guess," he said. "But Marvel can't do something like *Watchmen.* Our corporate culture doesn't reward excellence. Other than Larry, the only good writer we've got is this woman named Ann Nocenti, who's doing *Daredevil.* And most of the office hates her work."

"Because she's a woman?" I asked.

"Because she's interesting," he said.

Walking up Third Avenue, my stomach burned with the old tequila churn. I examined a construction site. A new NYU dormitory. Those were the days when NYU was always erecting a new dormitory on Third Avenue.

I'd asked Baby how he felt having matriculated into an organization with the stated goal of our neighborhood's complete transformation. "To be honest," he said, "I haven't thought much about it."

In the lobby of 114 East 13th Street, I informed the doorman that I was ascending to apartment 2D. He was one of these self-important little men who cannot help but invest their jobs with an undue amount of gravity, the kind of person who acts as if they themselves own the establishment. He wouldn't let me up. He insisted that we buzz the apartment.

A drunkard answered, slurring out the words, sure, go ahead, send her right up.

I waited for the elevator, standing by a redbrick wall. On the other side of some glass doors at the lobby's rear, there was a well-kept garden. A private garden in the East Village. How quaint. How absolutely divine.

The apartment door was ajar. Human clamor drifted out with the smoke of cigarettes. I didn't bother knocking, sweeping in from the tiny hallway, moving past the makeshift home office.

It was a one-room studio, bordering on loft. Sparsely decorated, prewar high ceilings. Walls painted white. Very little furniture, the bare minimum. A desk with an electric Olivetti typewriter. A futon bed up against the wall.

Three drag queens were in the throes of acrobatic entertainment. A jumble of colored tights, feather boas, and makeup so outrageous that even yours truly wouldn't dare the attempt. Two on the floor, on their hands and knees, with the third standing on their backs, one foot on each queen. The top mama warbled out a song by Dean Martin, about a marshmallow world in the winter. "The world is your snowball, see how it grows!"

A loose circle of seven people surrounded this human pyramid, everyone holding cigarettes or a drink. Baby and his friends stood out, younger than the rest, fresh faced and stupid. Baby was wearing a pair of unfortunate lamé pants and a shining gold shirt, and his friends were done up in green-and-purple polka-dotted spandex cutoffs that emphasized their white tube socks and black hi-top sneakers.

"Adeline!" Baby cried out.

We hugged. His bloodshot eyes confirmed my suspicion that he was halfway between the sun and the moon.

"I see the a-a-a-ac-crobatics have st-st-st-started," I said. "Is this why you dr-dr-dr-dragged me here in the middle of the n-n-n-night?"

"Can you stop doing that?" asked Baby. "It's really annoying."

"S-s-s-s-sorry," I said.

"Anyhoo," he said. "You've got to meet the host. He was just here, talking to his girlfriend. The actress, Jayne Dennis?"

"No idea," I said.

"She's on *Days of Our Lives*," said Baby. "Oh, there he is!"

A decently sized young man emerged from the bathroom, his suit sleeves stopping well before his wrists. A few buttons of his shirt were undone, exposing his undershirt. There was a wet spot on his stomach. He wasn't wearing any shoes or socks.

"Come on," said Baby, pulling me across the apartment.

We came to a halt before the man, who stared at us, confused, unfocused. He'd been partying all night. Perhaps several nights. Perhaps with no sleep. Perhaps he never slept. Perhaps he didn't know that sleep was possible.

"Meet my friend Adeline," Baby said to the man. "She's from Los Angeles, too."

"Hey," said the man. I'd been mistaken, confused by the suit. This was no man. He was a boy, about our age, plus two or three years. A boy like all the boys in my life, like all the little kiddies.

"Adeline," said Baby, "this is Bret."

"What school did you attend?" I asked, knowing my own kind, a fellow traveler in the privileged halls of private education.

"Buckley," said Bret.

"You appear somehow familiar," said I to him. "Were you acquainted with George Whitney?"

"I'm friends with his older brother, Timothy. Did you go to Buckley?"

"No," I sniffed. "I went to Crossroads."

Nothing evoked my interior snob like someone who'd paid for a traditional education, throwbacks to the days of company men, to doctoral candidates in engineering at Caltech and Stanford, men who would graduate and build missiles for Lockheed.

"What are you doing?" hissed Baby.

"Baby," I said. "How many of these dreadful boys do you imagine that I've met in my short lifetime? Timothy Whitney! I used to give handjobs to his kid brother!"

One of Baby's friends positioned himself atop the kitchen counter. Someone had turned on the enormous stereo, which blasted out "Only in My Dreams" by Debbie Gibson. Baby's friend danced, avoiding any semblance of the beat, performing a drunken facsimile of the cha-cha with occasional Rockette kicks.

Baby pulled me into a far corner, by the bed.

"You don't understand," said Baby. "That's not just anyone, Adeline. That's Bret Easton Ellis."

"What?" I asked.

"That's why I invited you."

"What?" I asked again.

"Look!" said Baby, indicating the zigzag bookshelves on the wall over the bed, wherein rested multiple copies of editions authored by Bret Easton Ellis. Foreign language translations. *Menos que cero. Moins que zero.*

"He's so young."

"Don't worry," said Baby. "He's too drunk, I think, to have noticed. I've been keeping pace and I'm well past the point of being affected by social slights. Just talk to him again."

"I'll wait until the proper moment transpires," I said.

Such transpiration did not occur for some time. Mine eyes played witness to human bodies stampeding through the motions of fun.

Great amounts of insipid conversation, far too many Billboard Hot 200 songs, and an awful lot of that terrible drunken party laughter which always forces one to consider what's wrong with oneself and then forces one to wonder what's wrong with everyone else.

About two thirds of the assembled congregation lacked any sense of Bret Easton Ellis as an author. He was simply the man who owned the apartment. The other third could not cease from peppering him with inanities. "Did you really go to Bennington?" "Is it exciting to be a writer?" "What's Robert Downey Jr. really like?" "Where do you get your ideas?"

They'd ask these questions as they drank his alcohol and then, before he could offer a reply, shouted out follow-up statements. "My father went to Bennington!" "I've always wanted to write!" "I heard he's an asshole!" "I've got so many ideas but I just don't know what to do with them! Can I tell you a few?"

Here he was, our famous author, surrounded by the hottest accoutrements of the American 1980s. A downtown apartment, an enormously powerful stereo, an immaculate kitchen with stainless steel refrigerator, the obligatory Olivetti typewriter, a *Les Mis* poster, bookshelves stuffed with his own work, a suit cut so right that it was wrong.

For the life of yours truly, I could not see why the man had bothered. Suffocation by plastic wasn't any better than shitting one's self with the DTs and crying out to the great gods of dope for mercy hot shot of heroin. He seemed so very lonely.

The young author stepped out onto his balcony. I darted around a drag queen falling asleep on her feet and followed him outside.

"Would you spare one of those?" I asked.

"Why not?" said Bret Easton Ellis.

"I don't want to bore you," I said, returning his lighter. "But je t'aime *The Rules of Attraction*. It's a to-die-for fave."

"So you're the one," said Bret Easton Ellis. "Did you know that Tom Cruise lives in this building?"

"And?" I asked.

"Don't you think it's interesting that Tom Cruise lives in this building?"

"Not particularly," I said. "No."

Every apartment on the east side of his building had its own balcony, but none were close to the size of Bret Easton Ellis's veranda.

"One night," said Bret Easton Ellis, "I watched two gangs fighting down on the street. One gang had chains. The other gang had a guy with a car. The guy with the car kept trying to run over the guys with chains. It was kind of fabulous. Have you ever eaten at Cave Canem?"

"No," I said.

"It's across the street from the Lismar Lounge. It used to be a famous bathhouse, the Club Baths. They had parrots and palm trees inside. The city closed it down, you know, because of AIDS. My friend Hayne Suthon bought the building and opened a restaurant. She kept the décor but cleaned out the cum. Now they serve authentic Roman dishes, circa 79 AD. It's very yuppie."

"I know Cave Canem. They're simply not my sort."

"I attended the opening," said Bret Easton Ellis. "Did you really like *Rules*? The *Voice Literary Supplement* gave it a horrible review."

"It's excellent," I said. "Though it demonstrates the same characteristic weakness of *Less Than Zero*."

"And what's that?" asked Bret Easton Ellis.

"You exhibit an undeniable strain of American squeamishness," I said. "You believe in the venality and shame of sexuality and drug use, as if the clockwork of our blue planet stopped and started on what people under the age of twenty-five shoved into the various holes of their bodies. But brother, that's okey-dokey, the world requires its prudes."

"One of those queens has some cocaine," said Bret Easton Ellis. "You could go into the bathroom and shove some sparkling white lines of co-caine into the holes of your body."

"Why not," I said.

MARCH 1989

A Radical Shindig at the Anarchist Switchboard

I bleached out my hair and dyed it pink, courtesy of Tish and Snooky, then had it snipped snipped snipped into a Marilyn Monroe by Mark the Barber over at Open til Midnight. Later that very same evening, Минерва rushed into our apartment.

"Big change," said she.

"George Herbert Walker Bush is our President. One must adjust to the new era," I said, looking at myself in the mirror. "Like all things, this too shall fade."

She planted herself on my bed, talking as I dressed.

"Interesting thing about New York, bright girl," she said. "I think Americans are not knowing how much Uncle Sam exports hatred to rest of world. Soviets hate Blacks because Hollywood hates Blacks. Ronald Reagan loved putting Negroes in cages. When I come to New York, I see race is myth. темнокожий are no different. Some terrible, of course, but when is teenaged male not terrible? When was last time great hymn and high Hosannas written to virtue of horny seventeen-year-old? And in person, I see many are quite attractive."

"I thought you were a lesbian," I said.

"Passing phase," said Минерва. "No more nights at Cubbyhole. Enough kitty cat for one lifetime."

"Are you looking for a boyfriend?" I asked.

"Eh," said Минерва. "Maybe boyfriend is looking for me."

I donned a black dress with matching jacket and gloves. I wrapped a tiger-print shawl around my neck. I tied old chains to my wrists like bracelets. Just above my right breast, I attached belt buckles like a soldier's medals.

"This is more than enough," I said, regarding myself in the mirror, worried as ever that I'd added poundage in the posterior. "Let us journey out into the evening."

*

Revolution was in the air, pollen clouds shaken loose by the riot's whirlwind. Минерва, sensing my interest, suggested that I accompany her to a radical shindig at the Anarchist Switchboard.

On our way, my dear Stalinist pal inquired about Kommie Kalifornia, asking if it were better than New York. "The weather is primo," I said. "But LA is real dullsville."

"What of San Francisco?" she asked.

"I've only been thrice, in high school. The people appeared a bit confused."

"Fucking hellfire," she said. "I am looking for graduate studies. Otherwise visa trouble."

The Anarchist Switchboard wasn't much more than an uncomfortable room painted stark bleeding red in a dingy little basement on 9th Street. Bare light bulbs offered illumination. People sat on broken couches and metal chairs.

Some were flat-out radical intellectuals, their lives consumed by multiple re-readings of Bakunin. Others were bearded weirdos, leftovers from the radical '60s. A handful were obvious addicts, nodding off into psychoactive oblivion. The rest were kids dressed in the media-manufactured uniform of The Punk. They sent me. They really sent me.

We occupied two open cushions on a couch, the broken springs jabbing into my meat. Sitting beside yours truly was an older woman, a bottle of schnapps emerged from her coat pocket.

"Bad time keeping," Минерва said, looking at her Swatch watch. "Fucking anarchists."

An older man in a Yankees baseball cap started the meeting. We were there, he said, to consider whether or not the indictments of a few police officers made a lick of difference. "Show trials!" said the old woman, schnapps blooming as she opened her mouth. "Enough talk! I want to know what we're going to do!"

"At least someone's being prosecuted, right?"

Hisses and boos.

The Yankees aficionado mentioned that the city was making cash offers to victims of the Riot, all below $15,000. "It's an insult!" shouted the woman.

She was not alone. People blurted out whatever ideas traipsed through their silly little heads.

Behind us, a young man spoke with a noticeable accent. New Jersey. Not particularly thick, but surely noticeable.

"The problem as I see it," he said, "is that we've been living on borrowed time. There was a collective delusion fueling the Lower East Side, that we could exist here with impunity, that we were free to run wild and that our way of life was sustainable into perpetuity. We were mistaken. You can't break the rules and get away with it forever. They're going to steal it from us, slowly, over time. If you think it'll end here, you're wrong. It won't be finished until every poor person is driven out of the city, until they transform all of Manhattan into something that we can't recognize. We're doomed. Sitting around talking revolution in an East Village basement is as good as twiddling our thumbs. The reason why the poor always get shafted is because we're victims of human nature. We'd much rather squabble amongst ourselves than go the distance with the rich. The only reason the rich are the rich, as far as I can tell, is that they lack the social mechanisms of restraint. They do what they want. They tell poor people to jump and poor people ask, 'How high?' One thing I like about this neighborhood is that we've transcended restraint. We need to harness that energy and transform it into distinct political action."

"Fucking Jon de Lee," whispered Минерва. "Of Inverted Bloody Crosses."

"Do you know him?" I whispered back.

"I fucking do," she said.

"Would you be good enough to introduce us?"

The speeches petered out. Constant recycling of anger. Минерва and I ascended to 9th Street, in the freezing late-March weather, and there I was, talking with Jon de Lee, him looking at me, and I thought, oh great God be damned, what a God damned attractive ruffian. I asked if he had a girlfriend and he laughed. I asked him what was funny and he said, I'm in a band. I'm an anarchist. Anarchist band members don't have girlfriends. They don't believe in relationships. I said that sounded like masculine bullshit. He asked what I was doing tomorrow.

And that is how I ended up with my third and final college boyfriend.

MARCH 1989

Adeline Goes on Three Dates

Sitting in a booth at the Jones Diner with Jon de Lee. Watching as he ate a $1.50 cheeseburger deluxe. My fingers picking, gingerly, at his soggy French fries.

The single previous time that I'd dared cross the establishment's threshold was on the evening that Jean-Michel Basquiat died, five days following the bloody brouhaha at Tompkins Square. Word of the artist's passing spread via telephone, particularly amongst the more motivated students at Parsons. Someone mentioned that our hometown hero had overdosed in his loft on Great Jones Street.

A handful of us drifted to his building. The corpse was long gone, putrefying somewhere in a morgue, undergoing a coroner's autopsy. There wasn't anything to see but a handful of crack addicts. As we stood in the street, one daft soul couldn't cease her prattling about how this old rock star, Bucky Wunderlick, had lived on the block waaaaaaay back in Ye Olde 1960s.

"Bucky's stuff is really a wonder. Even now," she said. "Have you heard the Mountain Tapes? People think he's crazy because he converted to Islam for a while and made annoying albums like *Abu Dharr's Tears*, but that was only a phase. The most recent aren't as preachy. The last one's kind of weird. Bucky seems like he's gotten super upset about NASA."

Then another of our holy fools suggested eating at the Jones Diner. So that's what Parsons' Finest did on the night that old Jean-Michel gave up his ghost. We stuffed our faces with the most grotesque food you can imaginate, only a couple of hundred feet from where they'd wheeled out the body.

Do you wonder, reader, why had Jon de Lee escorted me into the diner's confines? The answer is very simple. We were on our third date. The diner was his idea of fine food.

"So you're rich, right?" he asked.

"The family has money," I said.

"And Mommy gives you the cash?"

"You might say that."

"For what, college and your clothes and food?" he asked.

"You might say that."

"So really," he said. "You're another gentrifier who believes for no apparent reason that the East Village is a place she can make her own."

"What a charming line of inquiry," I said. "Darling, a man who's adopted the name Jon de Lee shouldn't criticize the pretensions of others. It ain't as if you were born within the ringing peals of the Most Holy Redeemer. Red Bank is a long way from the Lower East Side."

"I was born working class," he said. "It makes sense that I would gravitate to another working-class neighborhood. I know these people. I don't see them as local color."

Our first date, if it may be so called, had occurred on a Tuesday night when Jon de Lee invited me to witness the hallowed event of his band playing the Pyramid Club.

The Inverted Bloody Crosses shared the bill with Collapsed, Bold, and Nausea. I hadn't the slightest. I somehow convinced Baby to come along. "You're a groupie now?" he asked.

The Inverted Bloody Crosses sounded horrible but were the proper sort of awful, constructing signs and signifiers of post-riot LES discontent. Pronouncements, *sans musique*, about the cops, about the rich, about wars against the working poor. All delivered by Jon de Lee. Vocalist and lead guitarist. In the short moments between his prolonged bouts of ranting, the band cranked out dense eruptions of noise. Jon later explained that the Crosses were thrashcore, elaborating on the various punk subgenres and their distinguishing features. I tuned him out, bless his pretty little head.

"So what," said Baby, "you're going to fuck this guy because you saw his band?"

"Cease your judgments," said I. "Only the good Lord Jesus Christo knows what shenanigans you've experienced at the Pyramid."

"Adeline," said Baby. "You can't repeat the past."

"Can't repeat the past?" I asked. "Of course you can."

When the music finished, Baby begged off. I protested, but when I took in the scene on Avenue A, I was happy for my roommate's evanescence. It was pathetic, and I was a contributor, one of several slags crowding the bands, desperate to chat up musicians. *But these are punk people!* I thought. *Punk people should be above mere cock-rock bullshit.*

"The cheeseburgers here are the best in the city," said Jon de Lee. "Greasy and good and cheap."

"I suppose," I said. I did admire the diner's interior. The walls and the vinyl were abortion-clinic green, one long room contained within brick, a counter with stools up against it and five booths. Through our half-circle window, the emptiness of Great Jones and Lafayette, perfect view of a parking lot.

When Jon de Lee floated the idea of a second rendezvous, I refused to attend another live event, insisting rather that we do something, together, alone, as two acolytes sharing a moment in time. The concept perplexed him: "Isn't the date a bourgeois fallacy designed to reinforce the myth of natural marriage?"

"It could be," I said. "But we're going all the same."

He invited me on a constitutional around the city. So we perambulated, talking. He pontificated his usual bullshit, obviously, more rants about war against the poor, about police power, about the unrighteous applications of the state. But he talked, too, about his family and his early life.

His name wasn't Jon de Lee. An adopted *nom de guerre*. He'd been born Jonah Lieber, a Jewish boy out in Monmouth County. "My parents," he said, "divorced before I was born. Growing up, it was me, my mom, and my sister. My brother didn't live with us. My father was gone but sent child support. Then there was school, which went fine until junior high and my bar mitzvah, when I started noticing a difference between me and the other kids. They were too Jersey, I guess. Or I wasn't Jersey enough. I never gave two fucks about their gold chain bullshit. I dropped out and came to New York. I've been on the Lower East Side ever since."

"You're well spoken," said I. "For a dropout."

"Why should an intellectual be academy educated? America has a long tradition of self-made men," he said.

"You don't believe in America," I said. "You're an anarchist."

"A foolish consistency is the hobgoblin of little minds. I believe in the dream of America."

"What's a hobgoblin?" I asked.

"Like Puck, you know, in *A Midsummer Night's Dream*."

"Never seen it," I lied. "Or read it."

"It's all right," said Jon de Lee. "I prefer *The Tempest*. We have a song about Caliban called 'Dildo Lies Bleeding.' Caliban washes up on the East River and becomes a heroin addict in Alphabet City. I got the idea after reading Hart Crane's *The Bridge*. There's a section about Edgar Allan Poe on the subway, and I thought, that's so true. Because Edgar Allan Poe did look like a waxy-faced subway pervert."

We landed at Wall Street. "In all my days living in New York City," I said, "I've never been to Wall Street."

"There's nothing interesting down here," he said. "Just assholes on portable phones."

A statue of George Washington stood before Federal Hall. Our nation's Founding Father on a pedestal, the likeness a little too dandified. Smears of dried blood ringed the pedestal. The rotting corpses of small animals littered the pavement.

"In all of tarnation," I said. "What are these things?"

"Haven't you seen this before?" asked Jon de Lee. "There's a cult out in Flatbush. They think the founding fathers are voodoo loas. Or something like that. It's never been clear. Now that you know about it, you're going to see this shit constantly."

I agreed to a third date but insisted that Jon feed me. Thus the Jones Diner. Thus the drastic sight of Jon de Lee sucking down a cheeseburger deluxe.

"So why the fuck are you in college?" he asked, pounding on the flat end of a ketchup bottle.

"It's simply what's done," I said, playing my role to the hilt. "People of my social status are destined for college."

"But you're an artist?" he asked.

"Something like that," I said.

"Aren't you going to eat?"

"I ate your fries," I said. "That's enough for me."

"I hope you aren't suffering from anorexia nervosa," he said. "There are people in this neighborhood who actually can't afford food, who don't have the luxury of starving themselves."

"Oh, Jon," I said, "can't we just let them eat cake?"

When he finished his meal, we walked east. I showed him 84 Second Avenue. I informed him about the existence of *Dress Suits on Fire*. He knew the story. "Her family still lives here," he said. "I've talked to one, her sister,

I think. It's tough, you don't want to ask too much. I know someone who saw a ghost up there."

"Brown Tony?" I asked.

"No," he said. "It was Spacer."

Around then I decided that I'd take him into the boudoir, but his status as an anarchist played on my worries. I didn't feel any particular investment in monogamy, but I had pride.

"So your ethos, darling, your creed of a propertyless utopia, prevents you from commitment?"

I asked before the wrought-iron gates of the Marble Hill Cemetery. A gaggle of the homeless had taken shelter among the dim remains of the dead. They incinerated wood in barrels. A few tents erected, no doubt filled with needles and glass pipes.

"I didn't say that."

"You did indeed," I said. "On the first night we met."

"I talk a lot of shit," he said.

MARCH 1989

Adeline and Jon Have Sex

When one suffers a long and protracted illness, it's possible to lose all memory of good health.

Like myself. I am a prime example. I hadn't the slightest of how sick I'd become, not until I took the cure.

Consider the many instances of my short life involving intercourse with doltish young men, idiot boys and their scrawny bodies. Sex without any erotic charge, akin to favors offered to a friend.

Reader, mistake me not. Your old pal Adeline was not one of these hopeless young nymphets doomed to fornicate like a bunny rabbit with pleasure always just beyond her reach. There were moments of enjoyment, instances of genuine good. Fumbling fingers and tortured tongues. Nervous orgasms. It happened. This I shan't deny.

Sex with boys was disconnected from possibility. A kind of friendly masturbation, a semi-mutual achieving of physical release.

Memories of these previous encounters became distant, remote, erased once I got down to brass tacks with Jon de Lee.

With Jon it was communication, a dialogue between two bodies, electric impulses transmitted over wires of flesh and bone. Words one cannot speak, words that can only be heard. Skin that became skin that became skin anew.

We made love and we had sex and we had sex and we made love. But reader, again, I implore. Mistake me not. I am not your Pollyanna, I am not your sweet princess. We fucked, we fucked, we fucked, we fucked, we fucked, we fucked. We fucked in the effluvia of our bodies, we fucked in the scent of it, in the sheer stench of it, in the garden of our human flowering. Stained sheets, stained clothes, stained souls, stained towels. Fucked until my pussy ran dry and was rubbed raw, fucked until the Captain yowled outside my door, his gray paws smacking against the wood, fucked until Jon's daily erections withered into nothingness, unable to support a third or fourth condom, fucked until the arrival of my period, pausing only until the heavy flow ceased, then fucking as Jon's penis turned cartoon red with my discharge, fucked until celestial bodies rotated on their axes and reversed course in the Heavens, until the bed broke, until the building itself became hypercharged by orgones. Our fucking was a pulsing wave, a holy burst of scared geometry, a congress of wonder.

Between sessions, Jon would proffer half-baked Marxist analysis, saying, "What I admire about you women, and where I've got a powerful sympathy for your kind, is in the amount of effort you put into sex."

"Whatever do you mean, old sport?" asked I.

"Take yesterday, after I couldn't deal with the condom, and you used your hand and your mouth. I couldn't help it, but I felt like a factory boss and like you were the worker, and I kept you from the means of production, because there was no fruits you could reap from your labor."

"It's not a job," I said.

"Was it a gift?" he asked.

"I've had gift sex," I sighed. "That was nothing like gift sex. You're too much of a dude, dude. You'll never understand."

Bret Easton Ellis telephoned while we fucked, leaving a message on our slightly dysfunctional answering machine. "Adeline," said the machine. "It's Bret Easton Ellis. Sorry to call on such short notice, but I've got a thing uptown. Jayne can't go. I was wondering, would you come with me? There'll be free drinks, of course. Jay McInerney'll be there and he's an absolute fiend for frozen watermelon. Call back if you get this before seven. Thanks. It's Bret Easton Ellis."

I was in love. I'd even used the word, said it to Jon de Lee and heard him say it back. And love conquers all. Or saves the day. Or conquers all. Or saves the day. I didn't return Bret Easton Ellis's phone call. A shame, but I couldn't leave Jon. Not with work to be done.

I imagined Bret Easton Ellis worrying about his social function, the enfant terrible in his social milieu, telephoning a young woman who lay beside a punk rocker from Jersey, a man who resided between C and D in an illegal apartment, who existed beyond the confines of the cash economy.

Both men were on the same island, separated by nine tenths of a mile. For practical purposes, they may as well have been on different planets.

APRIL 1989

Minerva ♥ Jeremy

Jeremy telephoned one afternoon, inquiring if I was free. He wanted to pop over for a visit. I said that I'd be delighted. I rang Минерва. I suggested that she drop by.

When he entered our domicile, Jeremy handed me a small pamphlet. *The Hepcats Jive Talk Dictionary*, priced 25¢, published in 1945. On the cover, a woman and her fella are dancing an anemic jitterbug, her skirt swirling waaaaaaaaay up past the knee, revealing an ultrascandalous bit of slip.

"Why, whatever is this?" I asked.

"I bought it at a comic convention on Long Island," he said. "Turns out that a fifth of the definitions are slurs for Black folks. And that, Adeline, is some shit I've been hearing my whole life. That's one set of terminologies for which I don't need a dictionary. I thought you might like it."

"Are you implying that I have a need for racial invective?" I asked. "What shall I do with your hepcats and their jive dictionary? Stage a Klan rally?"

"I'm implying that you enjoy awkward vocabulary," he said.

Минерва shouted my name from the street, her thick accent bounding off the buildings of East 7th Street. I walked downstairs, opened our front door, and let her in.

I made her introduction to Jeremy. The silence was absolute, like sudden and mysterious teleportation into the total vacuum of space.

"Jeremy works at Marvel Comics," I offered.

"Marvel?" asked Минерва. "How is Red Ghost? Still he has his apes?"

"How do you know about the Red Ghost?" asked Jeremy Winterbloss.

Sometimes it's that easy.

They departed, together, concocting plans for the next day.

Reader, allow me to remove any hint of foreshadowing. Of the many comings and goings within this book, be assured that Jeremy Winterbloss and Минерва comprise the one pairing who will not suffer any undue tribulation. They will remain connected until their bodies crumble into dust.

MAY 1989

Adeline Gets Sick

The night after his spring semester ended, Baby returned from an orgy of unrighteous clubbing, shivering and covered with dank sweat. I demanded to know what drug had induced such a nightmarish state, but he assured me of his sobriety.

This wasn't drugs, it was physical illness. *Obviously,* said I to myself, *he'll catch death in the clubs, rubbing up against all those people. It's like an incubator for germination.* But consider, darlings, that your world-weary pal Adeline was oblivious enough that she did not think of AIDS. She imagined a pedestrian illness, like virulent influenza.

Baby burned with fiery fever. Then came the congestion, the running snot and thick phlegm. He lost his voice.

I assumed the role of Florence Nightingale, nursing him, wiping down the molten forehead with ice-cold rags. Never once did I believe myself vulnerable to his disease. I considered my physicality impenetrable, a sentinel incapable of being laid low by Apollo's arrows. This was, by the by, the absolute heights of delusion.

His body healed itself on the tenth night, something of a spontaneous miracle, as his summer courses began the very next morning.

The next day, while he attended classes, I manifested all of his symptoms. Simultaneously. Lost voice, copious production of phlegm, fever deliriums.

Patient Zero was too busy with his book learning to offer much nursing, so he telephoned Jon and said, "Jon, if you love your lady, you'd better come over to our swinging pad."

One of the Lower East Side's premier thrashcore vocalists, in whom I'd invested my affections and affectations, sat at my bedside for many long days, suffering my every outrageous complaint.

Alas, none of his tender ministrations helped, no matter the attempt. On my seventh day, he said, "You won't find someone who hates the medical establishment more than me, but you've got to go to a doctor."

"I don't know how," I said. "I've never made a doctor's appointment."

"Should I call your mother and ask about your insurance?"

"No, not Mother!" I said. "Just find a doctor, please."

He scheduled an appointment. He slept beside me throughout the fever-soaked night.

The doctor was a woman in her earlier fifties, dyed auburn hair hanging flat on the sides of her head. She inquired how long I'd been sick, to which I offered a truthful answer.

"What is it with you people?" she asked. "Do you need to lose an arm before you get help?"

She prescribed a weeklong course of antibiotics. Jon helped with the pharmacy.

"Don't you have somewhere to be?" I asked.

"I'm pretty fucking sure this is where I should be," he said.

By their sixth day, the antibiotics cleared my infection. On the seventh, I hoped to rest like the Good Lord Almighty, but this proved impossible.

An itching in my vagina prevented peace. Urination became an episodic visit to pain. On the eighth, the discharge started. What pleasure it is to have corporeal form!

We hadn't fucked since I'd taken sick, entering into our third week of enforced abstinence. Jon was like a starving animal hungry for raw meat, pressing for it, voicing inchoate complaints about losing the summer.

I was too ashamed to explain why we simply couldn't. What do you offer to the man that you love? "Sorry, sonny Jim, but at this very moment my vagina is expelling chunks of clotted cream. This state of affairs probably renders the area rather inhospitable for your own genitalia!"

I called Минерва and asked if she wouldn't accompany me to the doctor. "Trouble?" she asked. "Yeast infection? Is nothing. Doctor will fix." But would she come with me? "Okay, Joe, why not? I experience American medical practice. Plus is good excuse. Winterbloss wants see *Batman* movie."

The very same doctor came into the examination room. I worried that she lacked recollection of yours truly, so I spake, "Doctor, I hope you'll note that I scheduled my appointment very promptly!"

"What's the problem?" asked the doctor.

"Her pussy is yeasting," said Минерва.

"It's true," I said. "My cup runneth over."

"Young lady," said the doctor. "It's my firm belief that women generally know more about what's going on with their bodies than anyone else. If you say it's a yeast infection, I believe that it's a yeast infection. I could do the swab and slides and prepare a culture, but I have a feeling that it'll only confirm what you're telling me. Let me ask you, do you want to go through the process, or do you just want a cure?"

"The cure, please," I said. "I won't stand for another minute of this terrible itching."

She prescribed the weeklong application of a topical solution. Under no circumstances should I attempt intercourse.

"Doctor," I asked, "what do I tell my boyfriend?"

"Tell him the truth," she said.

I was sure Jon'd seen more infections than I could imagine, his natural scene involving junkies and crackheads, two groups not renowned for robust health.

Yet I'd begun thinking of myself as an island of sanity in the madness of his life. I'm not a blushing robin, I'm not afraid of the horrible things that my body can produce, but in the end, one simply need face reality. Body-positive feminism fails at the yeast infection.

I dissembled, I dissimulated, I performed an outrageous amount of oral sex. By the end of the week, all evidence of infection disappeared. Terrified that those unfortunate white stains would return to my underwear, I kept Jon leashed for another seven days.

AUGUST 1989

Daniel Rakowitz

On August 19th, at 6:30 pm, in Gramercy Park, a subsurface Con-Edison steam pipe went kablooey. An eighteen-storey geyser, steam and mud thrown high above the city, windows blown out, cars destroyed, the park splattered with filth. Edwin Booth covered with Manhattan's subterranean muck.

If I'd ventured out of doors, ambulated up to Cooper Square and looked north, I would've seen a steam cloud rise above the city like an ill-tempered djinn menacing Baghdad. Yet it was an awful drizzling New York night, the air thick as molasses. I refused to leave our apartment.

At roughly the same moment, Daniel Rakowitz was brutally murdering the Swiss dancer Monika Beerle in a dilapidated building on the corner of C and Ninth.

One version of the story says that Beerle, who may or may not have had drug problems, invited Rakowitz to live with her. Another version says that it was Rakowitz's apartment, that he invited Beerle to live with him, that she paid the back rent and assumed control of the lease. Either way, following a short period of cohabitation, Beerle wanted Rakowitz gone, splitsville daddy-o, like oooout of her life.

Who can blame her? Rakowitz must have been hell. The man spent most of his days in the environs of Tompkins Square, arguing for the legalization of marijuana, growing ever more unhinged, telling people that he was the Risen New Lord, a living god whose followers would triumph over America.

The storefront at 335 East 9th Street housed the Temple of the True Inner Light. Anyone could attend Sunday service and be given a free dose of DPT, or dipropyltryptamine, a legal hallucinogenic. The sole requirement for receiving this head-chugging charity was that its recipient must consent to suffer a lecture about the true nature of Christ, some silly nonsense about God's incarnation within lysergic acid.

There is a story that Rakowitz visited the temple. When he ambled through its garish front, did he admire its tripped-out yellow and red primary colors? Did he stop to look at the plywood covering its display window? And if so, did he take note of the vast mandala painted thereupon? Did he read the words beneath? "The Psychedelic is The Creator." When he opened the door, did he notice the magic mushroom painted above the address? And did those feet in ancient times walk upon Manna-hatta's daughters' green?

Rakowitz ranted at the tiny cluster of true believers. Antichrist, dead animals, 696, fascist uprisings, the exact location of the soul within the human spleen.

The monologue grew dark enough that the adherents brought him outside and checked his bag for weapons. What did they find? His pet rooster, named Rooster, and a German-language copy of *Mein Kampf.*

So again remember Beerle, spending fourteen days in a cramped two-bedroom apartment alongside this creature. She did the sensible thing, informing Daniel that he must leave, as her sister was soon to visit from Switzerland.

Rakowitz, high on marijuana and tripping on LSD, punched Beerle in the throat. This may or may not have killed her. If it did not, he strangled her with a cord. He dragged her body into the bathroom, abusing it with a knife.

For about a week, the bathtub held some portion of Beerle's body.

There occurs an influx of people, their number unknown. Some witness Monika's head on the kitchen stove, where Rakowitz is boiling the meat off her skull. Sylvia or Shawn, the previous roommates? Perhaps Crazy Dave, the building superintendent? Others?

One rumor has it that Rakowitz cooked and ate a portion of Beerle's brain. Another story was that he boiled her flesh into a soup and then served it to the park's homeless population.

Perhaps this begs the question of why would anyone accept soup from a lunatic like Rakowitz. It turns out that for all his flaws, he believed in charity. He had a history of cooking large dinners for the encampments.

The unused portions of Beerle's flesh are flushed down the toilet, her offal joining with sewer waste. Within a week of the murder, stories begin circulating through the neighborhood.

Jon always had a common touch. Rumors gravitated to him. We were in Le Snakepit, across from the park. I bought a gaudy pentagram belt. As we left the establishment, a dirty junky teen, ripped denim and sweat stains, stumbled from Tompkins and called Jon's name. We waited as this boy crossed the street. He talked with Jon, ignoring me.

"Did you hear that shit, man," he croaked, "that shit with fucking Daniel, man?"

"Yeah," said Jon de Lee. "I heard."

"Wait," I said. "Daniel who?"

"Daniel with the fucking chicken," said the junky. "He was in the park earlier today, talking all kinds of bullshit about being a fucking god. Someone says, 'Does God have the right to take a life?' and he goes, 'Of course. I have made that decision.'"

"Daniel's a fucking freak of nature," said Jon de Lee. "But I don't believe he did it."

"You heard about the soup, right, man?"

"Yeah," said Jon. "Everyone's heard about the soup."

"I haven't heard about the soup," I said.

"Never mind about the soup," said Jon.

"Did you know her?" asked the kid.

"I saw her around," said Jon.

When the junky stumbled away, I pressed Jon, he demurred, I pressed harder. He told me the story, what the neighborhood knew, what the neighborhood didn't, who'd seen what, who'd eaten what. I couldn't believe it.

"The rooster guy? Really?" I asked.

"Yeah," said Jon.

"What about the girl?" I asked.

"Her name was Monika," he said.

"Why hasn't anyone called the cops?"

"Don't be so fucking middle class," he snapped. "The pigs are kicking the shit out of us every goddamned day. Who trusts the cops? What neighborhood are you living in?"

With the riot well in the past, and the media's attention drawn elsewhere, the city had escalated its campaign against the neighborhood.

There began almost weekly raids on the homeless of Tompkins Square, their settlement now called Tent City. A routine took hold. The police rushed in, destroyed the shelters, arrested a few protesters, and made a retreat. The homeless came back and rebuilt anew. See ya next time, officer.

The squatters fared no better. One grew accustomed to massive police presences attempting to evict residents who were occupying derelict structures.

These collectives fortified their buildings against state intrusion, leading to scenes of open warfare. Siege engines versus punk rockers with bottles and firecrackers. The cops almost always won. Hundreds of people lost their homes.

"We're living here because we want freedom from the police state," said Jon. "We're at war with organized government. We can't run to the police. If the stories are true, then the neighborhood will take care of it. In the neighborhood's way."

"What does that mean?" I asked.

"What do you think it means?"

I wandered for the next several days, seeking any hint of the murder, about Daniel Rakowitz, about Monika Beerle. I overheard people discussing, openly, details of the killing.

"He cut her head right off, he's got the head on a stove! Crazy Dave saw it."

Supposedly, before Rakowitz committed the act, he stood in the park telling people that he would kill Beerle. The day that he did the deed, he came back and discussed his crime. When he split her body apart, he told people. Everyone knew what happened. An entire neighborhood shrugged its collective shoulders. The same old story. Another dead woman on the Lower East Side. More dress suits to hire.

I made Jon take me by Rakowitz's building. I wanted to see it, I said, for reasons of morbid curiosity, a sick desire to inure myself. "Jon," I whined, "I want to be exposed to the true brutality of capitaliiiiiism."

Someone had vandalized the door:

> 700 CLUB E. 9th St.
> Home of "THE FINE YOUNG CANNIBALS"
> She drove me crazy
> so I KILLED HER!

"This can't last," said Jon. "Something is going to break."

He couldn't have known that what would break was the patience of yours truly. After we said goodbye, I went home and called the 9th Precinct. I explained, calmly, rationally, that a murder had occurred at 700

East 9th Street. I gave them the name of the victim and the name of the murderer. I described Daniel Rakowitz. I asked what would happen.

"I can't say, lady," said the man on the phone. "We'll take it under consideration."

He hung up.

I'd watched cops from the very same precinct savagely attack and bludgeon the citizenry, but I truly believed that with a murder they might make some effort.

Days ticked by. Nothing changed. Rumors swirled. Was it possible, really, to trust anyone? The people didn't care. The cops didn't care. Who cared about Monika Beerle?

Later, it emerged that others had tried convincing the police, but the authorities knew Rakowitz, considered him a local harmless nut and did not find the rumors credible. Or maybe they saw Beerle as nothing special, one more dead stripper in a neighborhood full of corpses. Who could keep track? There was even a rumor that Rakowitz had worked as a police informant.

Stories like the death of Beerle lose their horror, become amusing, slide into the background tapestry of the neighborhood. Become another craaaazy thing that happened in this craaaaaaazy place.

Classes started. I hardly cared. Weeks passed.

One day, I encountered Rakowitz, walking towards me, coming up St. Mark's. He wore his denim jacket and jeans.

An acid reflux strike from my stomach up my throat. I jumped out into the street, almost being run over by a Coca-Cola truck. From the safety of the other side, I watched him walk past, oblivious to the world.

Then, like that, in an instant, weeks into September, the police picked him up, and asked if he'd killed Beerle. He admitted that he had. They asked where the remains were. Rakowitz brought them to the Port Authority, where he opened a locker. Inside the locker was an army duffel bag. Inside the duffel bag was a plastic bucket. Inside the bucket was Beerle's skull, her bones, and a whole lot of cat litter.

Jon came over, telling me the news. I lay across my bed, reading a copy of *People* magazine that someone'd left at Parsons. Don't ask why I'd brought it home. I haven't the slightest.

"I thought you'd be happy," he said.

"She's still dead," I said. "It's one of those things."

Baby was in the kitchen. He'd been the one who heard Jon shouting in the street, and the one who'd gone downstairs.

"Listen," said Jon. "Do you want to see it?"

"See what?" I asked.

"The apartment," he said.

I shouldn't have, but I did. I said yes. We walked the few blocks, through the park and the latest iteration of Tent City. It seemed fuller than ever. No one cared that Monika Beerle was dead. No one cared that Daniel Rakowitz was insane. It was around then that the sensation rushed up at me, emerging from the concrete of New York. At last I understood that life was not a game which one could win if it was played with enough skill.

The graffiti remained on the building's front door. I was too disturbed to wonder why the door wasn't locked. We climbed several flights of stairs and came to the apartment. Someone had written on Rakowitz's door: IS IT SOUP YET? And WELCOME TO CHARLIE GEIN'S SPAUN RANCH EAST. Flowers hung, crisscrossed with police tape.

"People have been coming in and out of here all day," said Jon. "We just have to slide under the tape."

A month later, the *Village Voice* ran a six-page article about the crime. Called "Blood Simple," it was written by Max Cantor, the actor who played Bobby in the film *Dirty Dancing*.

The meat of the text came from interviews with Sylvia and Shawn, confirming the worst rumors. They weren't living in the apartment, but Sylvia did see Beerle's head on the stove. She had refused to turn in Rakowitz. That's friendship.

"Jon," I said. "I can't. I thought I could but I can't."

"Wait here," he said. "I'll check it out."

He opened the door and disappeared inside. For the briefest of moments I saw the interior. Another tiny East Village apartment.

1988, 1989, 1990

Some Things That Happened to Baby
During His Nervous Breakdown,
Presented in a Random Order

Then there was the time when Baby went to an after-hours party at Cave Canem. He'd come back from California with indisputable evidence that he was terrible at being gay, that his social skills needed work. It was a moment, he resolved, to be with other men, to learn how to be around those who were openly celebratory of their faggitude. Men who weren't afraid of their desires, who didn't hide their selves away.

As was his wont, Baby solved this problem in the craziest possible way.

He called Michael Alig.

Cave Canem was on First Avenue near the corner of 2nd Street, next door to the Ortiz Funeral Home. Around 4:30 am, Baby followed a trickle of humanity inside, going to the basement level, where a dance floor sat beside a four-foot-deep pool of water. Baby wondered if the exposed ersatz columns were Doric, Ionic, or Corinthian.

The DJ played an old song. For the first time in Baby's life, he listened to the verses: *Some boys take a beautiful girl / and hide her away from the rest of the world / I want to be the one to walk in the sun.*

Willfully misinterpreting the lyrics, Baby imagined the vocalist to be in possession of a superhuman ability that allowed her to walk on the sun's molten nuclear surface.

—Baaaaaabyyyy, cried Michael Alig. What do you have on? You don't look very fabulous!

Alig was wearing a bikini mail-ordered from 1965. His face was painted with bright yellow makeup.

—I don't feel very fabulous, said Baby. California broke my heart.

—Jesus Christ, said Michael Alig. You're such a drag! Did you come here just to be depressed? I thought girls wanted to have fun!

He gave Baby a pill.

—Here, take this, he said. It's pink, it's fabulous!

—What is it? asked Baby.

—Who cares? It's mother's little helper!

Baby swallowed the pill, chalky like uncoated aspirin, sticking in his throat on its way toward his stomach.

—I see some people who really matter, said Michael Alig. People who aren't glum glusses! I'll check in with you after the drug takes effect, Baby girl, and we'll see if you aren't a little less sour.

People filtered in, the music played louder. Baby stood by the railings. A girl came over, smiling and saying hello. He couldn't remember if he knew her. He looked at her for a moment too long.

—Have we met? he asked.

—We haven't talked, she said, but I'm in your philosophy class.

—Oh, said Baby. Yes. Yes, you sit in front. I always sit in back.

—Why are you here? she asked. Don't you have school in a few hours?

—Don't you?

—Sure, she said. But I'm a bad student. I'm destined to fail.

Her name was Regina. In the clubs, she preferred Queen Rex, a nom de guerre bestowed upon her by Michael Alig. She told Baby about Cave Canem, the name of which was Latin for "Beware of the Dog." A decade earlier, the building was a famous gay bathhouse, its interior done up like a tropical paradise. City officials shut it down during the dark days when they believed that AIDS was a transmittable cancer. The new owner, Hayne Suthon, from New Orleans, had convinced her family to buy the building. The premise being that stewardship of a restaurant would curb Suthon's wild nature and transform her into an upstanding citizen. Such dreams were short lived. Hayne filled the pool with water and let Michael Alig promote parties.

—How do you know Michael? asked Queen Rex.

—We met a while back, said Baby.

—Why haven't I seen you around?

—I've been out of town. How do you know Michael?

—I'm one of his club kids, said Queen Rex.

—What the hell is a club kid? asked Baby.

—Didn't you see the story in *New York*? Michael made the cover. We're all his puppets. Where've you been?

—Los Angeles, said Baby.

—Gag, gag, and triple gag, said Queen Rex.

Queen Rex convinced Baby that they should dance. During the second song, an uptempo track about sex, the drugs took hold. People never looked so beautiful. Music never sounded as good. The bathhouse walls radiated remarkable light.

More people filtered in, a different crowd. Outrageous people who kept shouting out Michael! Michael! Michael! Through the waving limbs of the dance floor, Baby saw these people surround Alig, as if he were Christ and they his disciples. *He really must be famous now,* Baby thought. *Why the hell did he return my call?*

Queen Rex hugged Baby. Baby hugged back, a clean hug, an easy clean hug.

The music and the lights and the Roman walls came together in an overwhelming burst. Baby felt happy that he'd come to Cave Cavem, that Michael Alig invited him. Very happy indeed to meet Queen Rex. Or Regina. Whichever. Would he call her Regina at school? He supposed that he would.

People stripped off their clothes and jumped into the pool. Ghost images trailed before Baby. He knew it was the drug, but he also imagined that it was a psychic resonance of the bathhouse days, that these people splashing against each other, screaming, with dirty water the only barrier between their embraces, all of this worked as an erotic sorcery summoning up the ghost of Old New York, of the days when men fucked freely without fear, of a time when his sexuality wasn't being equated with death.

—Why, he asked Queen Rex, are they doing this?

—People need to do something, said Queen Rex.

—But aren't they worried? he asked. Aren't they worried about AIDS?

—No one has sex anymore, said Queen Rex. Sex is so passé. It's everything but. I'm going in the pool. Are you coming in?

—Maybe in a minute, said Baby.

Queen Rex stripped out of her odd leather costume. She jumped into the water. Her hands ran over a man's body. A couple grinded against each other. Baby stood three feet away, brain spurting neurons, intoxicated by his lack of concern. *The '80s are the decade of fear,* he thought. *But the '80s are almost over. Is this what the '90s are going to be like? Drugged-out people almost fucking in dirty swimming pools?*

—Baby! shouted a voice beside him.

Michael Alig. The bikini top off, hair and skin soaking. Makeup smeared down his face.

—Baby, said Michael Alig, what kind of bitch comes to a person's pool party and then refuses to get wet?

—I'm a rabid dog, said Baby. I'm afraid of water. I'm that kind of bitch. *Cave canem.*

—That's so hilarious, said Michael Alig, because I'm famously rabid and I'm not afraid of anything.

Michael Alig tackled Baby. As they plunged into the lukewarm liquid, Baby wanted to be angry, attempted to will himself toward rage, but it was like a wall in his brain blocked the chemical receptors responsible for negative emotions. He wasn't angry. He was happy, happy at being touched and happy with the liquid, happy that his clothes were soaking wet, happy that Michael Alig was trying to push his head under water, happy that people were cheering and touching him.

—Who am I? he yelled above the splashing water.

—You're Baby Baby Baby, someone said. You're a rabid dog. Now bark like one!

And Baby barked, grabbing the body of a sweet man beside him, this slick-skinned, waterlogged Adonis of the Lower East Side. They kissed and Baby's head exploded with waves of pleasure coming off the tongue, his body attuned to nothing but this moment, like his erection was the only constant in an ever-changing universe, a holy erection akin to those housed by the pantaloons of Walt Whitman in the month of March in the year 1855, like Baby'd journeyed to the fifth dimension and looked down at time, like his atomic particulars were not newly configured but had always been from the Big Bang at the beginning, pressed against this man, in this pool, in this city, with beautiful humanity around him, listening to this terrible song that was the best song ever recorded, *don't stand in the corner waiting for the chance, make your own music, start your own dance,* that was the only song ever recorded.

—Oh please, whispered Baby into the wet mouth of this Greek divinity, never let it stop. Never ever let it stop.

Then there was the time when Michael Alig and Michael Musto, the gossip columnist for the *Village Voice,* attended the 1988 *Dark Shadows* Festival at the Vista International Hotel, beneath the Twin Towers of the World Trade Center.

When the dust settled, Michael Alig phoned Baby, furious with Musto, who'd scored full green room access and left Alig among the common attendees, the actual scum. Most of who were incredibly ugly and disgusting.

Fat old hairy men and women who hadn't considered personal style in decades.

—And if you can believe it, said Alig, Musto wormed his way to Jonathan Frid! They had themselves a nice fucking little lunch!

—Who's Jonathan Frid? asked Baby.

—What are we even talking about? Don't you know anything? He's the actor that played Barnabas Collins!

Weeks earlier, Michael Musto had visited Tunnel, going around asking club kids questions about the history of Western Civilization. Who was Homer? Who is Richard Nixon? Who was Nietzsche? Who wrote *War and Peace*? Who's the Vice President? Most people couldn't answer. This didn't surprise Baby. He'd spent enough time around Alig's misfits to realize that their candles did not burn with the brightest flames.

With Michael Alig watching, Musto asked Baby about Baudelaire. Baby spoke about the French poet at some length, faking off the jacket copy he'd read on a translation of *Les Fleurs du Mal*.

—You know, said Baby, Baudelaire's fine and everything, but honestly? I prefer Rimbaud.

Baby hunted down the next installment of the *Voice,* desperate to read Musto's column, which appeared under the title of "La Dolce Musto." The writer dedicated two inches to his impromptu pop quizzes, critiquing the Downtown resurgence, suggesting that it was staged by New York's lesser minds. There was no mention of Baby's discourse on French symbolism.

Michael Alig read the same column and telephoned, shrieking into Baby's ear —Do you see? Do you see what he's like? He's the stingiest AIDS case in all of New York!

The point of clubbing, or, rather, one of its points, was to be noticed by Michael Musto, to be registered by the living barometer of city life. Musto aped the vamping style of classic columnists like Hedda Hopper but subverted the genre through an intense queerification, giving as much focus to the denizens of the demimonde as he did to genuine celebrities. Queens like Lady Bunny and LaHoma van Zandt received treatment equal to that of Marlon Brando and Madonna.

Musto had taken note of Alig on several occasions, the latter's name appearing alongside Burt Reynolds and Jack Nicholson. In print, who could say which person was more important? Everyone was bolded. Everyone mattered.

—Who's Barnabas Collins? asked Baby.

—He's only the fucking vampire! shouted Michael Alig. He's the whole fucking point of the fucking show! No one's watching *Dark Shadows* in 1988 for fucking Quentin Collins, are they? Why don't you ever listen?

Whenever he talked with Michael Alig, Baby focused not on the words being said but on their hidden meanings. Baby parsed every vocal inflection, every shift of mood, aching and hungry to solve the great mystery. *Why is Michael paying attention to me? I'm a nobody. The whole city lies at his feet.*

Then there was the time when Alig revealed that he'd grown up in Indiana, in South Bend. That city was significantly larger than Baby's Podunk little town, but the two bore more resemblance to one another than either did to New York. Both men were products of that great nothingness known as the American Middle West.

Michael Alig escaped the gravitational pull of South Bend by enrolling in the architecture program at Fordham University. He dropped out soon into his first semester, entranced by the lure of club culture, picking up work as a busboy at Danceteria. The rest was history.

—Okay, said Baby. He's the vampire.

Alig hung up, still fuming.

The next Tuesday, Baby picked up the newest *Voice*. Michael Musto dedicated half of his column to the *Dark Shadows* Festival. He wrote about intimate chats with the stars. Of lunch with Jonathan Frid, there was no mention.

Musto wrote not a word about Michael Alig. Baby imagined his friend poring over the column, burning with outrage, looking for a soul upon whom to vent his spleen.

I hope it isn't me, thought Baby. I hope he calls Magenta.

Then there was the time when Queen Rex and Baby took a cab to the Chelsea Hotel, with the intent of visiting a queen named Christina.

—Do you actually know Christina? asked Queen Rex.

—I went to her birthday party at Tunnel, said Baby.

—She's crazy, said Queen Rex. But strangely sweet. I like her. Don't mention the birthday party.

Queen Rex buzzed their way into the Chelsea. Baby kept up with her stride, denying himself the opportunity to examine the artwork that covered every inch of the lobby's walls. Queen Rex talked to the desk clerk sitting behind a glass enclosure.

—We're here to see Christina, she said. Room 323.

—Sure, said the clerk. Just take the elevator.

Queen Rex knocked on Christina's door. Baby wondered why he'd asked to come to the Hotel Chelsea at 11:57 pm on a Wednesday. They had class in the morning.

Regina never cared about class, which was a great mystery, considering her precarious relationship with the university.

In the beginning, Regina had come on aristocratic, treating NYU like an institution unworthy of her serious consideration, as if school were just another experience into which she'd stumbled, like she was an upper-class twit from F. Scott Fitzgerald's wretched early work. This illusion was maintained for some while, delicately balanced within the rooms of Baby's memory palace until it toppled beneath the accumulation of too many stray facts and inconsistencies.

For instance: Regina said that she lived uptown. Everyone assumed this meant the Upper West Side, but once she let slip that she lived in Washington Heights. For instance: the New York accent breaking through her controlled voice, on occasion axing youse a question. For instance: she talked about her high school in a manner that made it sound like an expensive private school, but Baby read a *New York Times* article describing Midwood as one of the city's elite public schools. For instance: her clothes were always two seasons old, a style which everyone believed intentional until Brandywine remarked that she'd never seen Regina in anything new.

Baby axed Regina to tell him the truth. She admitted that she was paying for NYU through a mixture of student loans and wages earned waitressing at Primola. Baby couldn't understand. *I'm the one who's been given everything,* thought Baby, *so why's she throwing it all away?*

From behind the door, a muffled voice:

—O, yes.

Locks twisted and unlatched. The door opened, revealing Christina, long blonde wig, tight blue minidress, torn stockings. Mere description of her attire conveys no sense of the main event, of Christina's ravaged body. Her bloated face buried beneath an excess of lipstick and mascara, her huge gut straining at the fabric, the too-visible hint of testicles, her broken teeth, her watery yellow eyes that barely opened.

—O, O, O, Regina, is that you?

—Hi, Christina, said Queen Rex. I wanted you to meet my friend, Baby.

—O, O, isn't he delightful? Isn't he something that you could just eat, really?

Christina's accent was an affectation, the world's least convincing German accent, the voice long and drawn out in an ultra-masculine bass. Baby'd met a lot of queens, their voices ranging the entire spectrum, but never one who sounded anything like Christina.

—Isn't Christina's apartment beautiful? asked Queen Rex.

Baby could think of many words for the clutter and debris that filled the one-room suite. He would not have chosen beautiful.

—Yes, said Baby, it's lovely.

—O, O, O, did I tell you about the woman who lives above me? She is an electronic insect, really, you know, is a creature from another world. O, O. Do you want something to drink, Baby? I mean, really?

Christina hobbled to the kitchen, limping on her left leg, carrying a black cane.

—O, O, Baby, said Christina. Come here and get your alcohol.

She handed him a dirty mug bearing the word OPIUM in gilded letters. Queen Rex stood next to an electronic keyboard synthesizer, looking at paintings hung on the walls.

—You've got to see these, said Queen Rex. They're all so wonderful. Did you do all of these yourself, Christina?

—I mean, really, Regina, someone has to do them, don't they?

The signifier of the mug helped Baby conclude that Christina was a queen with a heroin problem. The slurred speech, the non sequiturs, the jaundiced eyes, the disregard for physical appearance, the algebra of need.

Her paintings were executed with skill, demonstrating an ease of line that one would not expect from a drug addict faking a broad Teutonic accent on the third floor of the Chelsea Hotel. Each image featured an idealized depiction of the artist. In one, Christina looked like an ingénue of the 1950s, clad in a long black dress. In another, she'd rendered a simple line drawing of herself reclining on the sidewalk outside of the Chelsea Hotel.

Her best canvas re-created the label of Beefeater gin. Instead of the Yeoman Warder, Christina had drawn herself in full fantastic drag before the Tower of London. Baby'd seen this one before, hanging on a wall in the basement of Tunnel. At her birthday party.

—This is wonderful, said Baby. I love the wit.

—O, O, O, O. Is my favorite gin, really. O, O. Have you been to London? It's full of wretched people, you know, and the world would be a better place if the Nazis bombed them into nothing.

Christina's television, in the middle of the room, was turned on its side. The black-and-white image ran against the vertical orientation. No sound emerged from its speaker, but the image played on, blue gray and snowy, set to Channel 13, showing images of the Brooklyn Bridge.

—O, O, O, isn't the television hilarious? Is actually, well, I'll explain it to you soon. Is actually about the way in which we are all disgraced, and the bridge is pointing to the left now, you know, really.

Baby moved a few fashion magazines off a metal chair and sat down. Long ago, he'd mastered the art of wielding his drink like a shield. With careful observation of a dialogue's participants, and with maintenance of proper beverage placement at key moments, he could spend an entire evening without saying a thing.

Baby inspected a milk-white vinyl record hanging on the wall. NICO. BEHIND THE IRON CURTAIN. Christina had drawn herself on its label.

—The same effect as so many other airliner, you know. Speak of the film, put it in your left ear, just left the other one hang there, with Walkman you can watch film birthday well, you really won't eat any more response to the, you know, the occasional woman who go 'How you get that kid to get that off his head because he can't hear any of these really important instructions?' You know, instructions that she's obviously memorized. And the woman comes up to you and goes like, 'O, you must take those off during takeover.' And you go, 'O, I didn't know that. Excuse me.' That's sort of, it really is the next worst thing that can happen to you. O, Dutch is a method of transmission for a film for people who read in triangular pyramids, which doesn't happen to be on right now.

After Christina explained her idea about blowing up New York with the help of her former landlord, Queen Rex suggested that she and Baby would depart. Christina walked them to the elevator, pressing the call button.

—O, this is the elevator that Sid Vicious died in. No, no, his ghost would always come up in this elevator. And that's the only room I've ever seen Sid Vicious in, is within that elevator. He used to come in and attack me sexually and suck on my nipples. And he still did. He's not in that elevator, I mean, after all, he made so much money off his money. I mean a lot of people make money off of film. I mean, after all, I'm dead. O, O, O, did I tell you about the time when I saw Andy Warhol's ghost?

Outside on 23rd Street, Baby thought of seven different questions about Christina, but before he could speak, Regina threw her arms around him, hugging him.

—Baby, she said, can I stay with you tonight?

—I'm not sure about Adeline, said Baby.

—What if I'm quiet? asked Regina. What if I'm as silent as a mouse?

—I don't know, said Baby.

—It'll help me, said Regina. Because I can wake up and we can go over to school tomorrow. Otherwise I've got to take the train all the way up and then back down.

At 7th Street, the apartment lights were out. Adeline'd expressed her extreme displeasure about Baby bringing home club people in general, and Regina in particular.

—Can't you keep these creatures within their natural habitats? she'd asked. Why must you allow your scum entrée to our humble abode?

Regina and Baby snuck into the dark. Adeline's door was shut. Baby led Regina into his room. They slept, his arms draped over Regina.

Then there was the time when Baby met Loretta Hogg, a receptionist named Dean who became reasonably popular with people in the know. Among the many shticks of clubland, Loretta Hogg distinguished herself by going out every night wearing a fake pig nose. The effect, taken in concert with her long stringy hair, left Baby greatly disturbed.

There was the time, at Red Zone, when Loretta Hogg sat on a table all night with an apple in her mouth.

Then there was the time when Baby ate MDMA at The World, a club on East 2nd Street near Avenue C. The drug hit strong, sending unusual waves from his brain, different from the normal vibe. No sensations of delight in the people around him. Instead a deep fear, high anxiety. He remembered reading that the original definition of panic was the sensation of being lost in a dark woods, a terror brought on by the Great God Pan. Pan-ic.

Pushing outside, he bumped into the doorman, a friend of Michael Alig's named James St. James.

—Watch it, honey!

Several blocks away, far from the club, Baby continued to hear the echo of the dance floor. Synthesizers, pounding beats. Hi-hats and handclaps. Haunted by house music.

Over to Broadway and up to West 4th Street. Baby walked to Washington Square Park, sitting on a park bench near the red monolith of NYU's Bobst Library, the building reminding him of his own relationship with the university. A warm reassurance of belonging, strong enough to bring Baby into contemplation.

Los Angeles. Jaime, yes, but something else, too, some unknown occurrence within the missing hours of his acid trip. An unknown amount of his life lost, gone, disappeared. Who knows what he'd done? Costing him the boy that he loved. His broken heart. Did something else break, too? Some part of his psyche fracturing during ego death.

The park grounds were dirty with litter and filled with an assortment of the homeless and criminals. People tried selling Baby drugs. Smoke, smoke, smoke. He ignored them, moving toward the white marble arch. He'd never before noticed that its statues offered two separate depictions of George Washington. Blood was smeared beneath both, chicken bones scattered.

Baby rounded to the arch's west side, where he discovered a door cracked open, light coming from within. There was no reason for indecision. He went inside.

Industrial illumination cast shadows across the interior brick walls. A spiral staircase at the other side of the chamber. Baby climbed up, body attuned to the mortar and masonry, the bricks breathing with him. Up and up and up.

He came to the attic. Cluttered with junk. Too dark to discern. Baby continued ascending until he came to the trap door above him. He pushed through and emerged on top of the arch, looking south toward the giant aberrations of the World Trade Center.

North, up the infinity of Fifth Avenue, buildings dissolving into a vanishing point. From the ground, tricks of perspective prevented the pedestrian from comprehending the arch's true height. Baby experienced the real thing through atmosphere, seven stories up, the winds whipping around his ears.

He sat, back against the marble, eyes closed. Sequences of lights played in the darkness, his body shivering with the stone. If he tried hard enough, patterns emerged in the lights, shapes, almost celestial bodies. Earlier that day, he'd read a poem by Robert Lowell. "Skunk Hour."

The narrator drives up the central hill of town, sneaking up on lovers in cars. His mind isn't right. Radios play the song "Careless Love." *I hear my ill-spirit sob in each blood cell, as if my hand were at its throat.* Then, as

Baby's professor pointed out, the poem quotes Milton: *I myself am Hell.* Nobody's here. Love o love, o careless love.

Baby looked over the side, peering down. The lamps flickered as if illuminated by gas. There were thousands of spirits, shimmering figures, wandering through the park. *What are they?* Baby wondered. *Are they ghosts? Is Emil among them?*

Moving with care down the spiral staircase. Still too high to go home, to deal with Adeline. At the bottom, walking outside. The park returned to normal. The dull light of electric lamps. No shimmering ghosts, only the debris of humanity. The starving, the drug dealers.

He sang a song by Patti Smith. "Pissing in a River." Baby couldn't remember the lyrics. Words came out strange, improvised, wrong and broken: *My vowels sound heavy, bleating your foul. What door will I hand you? Honey I can't say. What more can I say to you, to make you stay?*

James St. James hadn't left the door. Baby knew him, slightly, introduced by Michael Alig, who'd said that James was the old guard, positively one of those tired nasty mid-'80s Celebutantes. Desperate for relevance, and proving that an old dog can learn a new trick, Jimmy had transitioned into being a club kid. Michael Alig assured Baby that no one minded, not really, if James was so old.

—Honey, you ran out on me! said James to Baby. Where've you been?

—Washington Square, said Baby.

—There's nothing there but disgusting tramps! You missed Brooke Shields. I escorted her, personally, to the VIP speakeasy! And do you know what she did? She asked for my address! She wants to send me a gift! Can you believe how fabulous she is?

Inside, Queen Rex stood beside a disco ball and a peacock-shaped pane of glass.

—Where have you been?

—Out, said Baby. I couldn't take it.

A middle-aged man with a video camera approached. He kissed Queen Rex's cheek, calling out, Regina! Regina! Regina!

—Baby, do you know Nelson?

—I've seen you around, said Baby.

—Baby, this is Nelson Sullivan. Nelson is a friend of Christina.

—Oh, said Nelson, I love Christina.

—Nelson's a club kid!

—I'm more like a club parent, said Nelson. Well, bye-bye, I'm going upstairs.

Almost 4 am. Queen Rex grabbed the arm of a queen named LaHoma van Zandt, a skinny-bodied blonde. She was beautiful. Baby stared at her, wondering if she were really this beautiful or if the drug was altering reality. The most beautiful queen. LaHoma van Zandt. Baby hung on her words, each spoken in a syrupy Southern accent.

—Let's go to Robots, said LaHoma. It's less than a block away!

Other people were dragged along, including Nelson Sullivan and James St. James. Everyone except for Nelson was drunk or high. Screaming in the streets. LaHoma wearing her tiny yellow dress, hopping up and down on wooden heels.

—It's so amazing! she shouted. It's so funny!

Save the Robots was situated in a storefront on Avenue B. LaHoma knocked on the gray door. The Judas window slid open. LaHoma pushed her face up to the opening. The doorman let everyone in, despite his reservations about Nelson Sullivan's camera.

—Do you record everything? asked Baby.

—Day and night, said Nelson. There's just so many gorgeous people here in Downtown and I'd hate to miss a single one.

Thursday when Baby went out with Regina. Friday now. Thankfully no class in the morning. Sleep the whole afternoon.

Baby ended up downstairs, looking at exposed piping and the empty dance floor, which was covered in sand. Still early. People would be arriving until 8 am. Emptiness of the basement, the emptiness of an occupied storefront, giving drug clarity into the nature of the 1980s. A difference from the era of true disco and Studio 54, when proprietors would transform their spaces into works of wonder. Then the idea had been to pull people from their minds, transport them to other worlds.

Save the Robots, The World, Tunnel, Mars, Red Zone, Limelight. Consciously designed to keep the remnants and echoes of their earlier occupants. An old warehouse. A train tunnel. Part of the appeal, to know that the dance space existed only because capitalism had failed. New culture sprouting up like weeds feeding on the old corpse.

Then there was the time when Michael Alig threw a party at McDonald's in Times Square. Actually, the invite was for the Burger King across the street, but the management had refused to host the illustrious event. Michael Alig improvised, giving a thousand dollars to the people at McDonald's and making a few unlucky messengers stand outside Burger King to direct human traffic to the new location.

Baby convinced Adeline to come along, overriding almost all of her objections by pointing out that this party, for once, wasn't happening in a club.

—I don't even think there'll be music, said Baby. McDonald's sure won't pump it through their speakers.

—Zowie! Swellegant! said Adeline. You melt me, Jackson.

Adeline's friend Jeremy Winterbloss had given her a copy of a 1940s slang dictionary entitled *The Hepcats Jive Talk Dictionary*. Adeline had digested its contents, tormenting Baby for two weeks with its lingo.

—I have no idea what that means. Are you coming or not?

—Don't summon your hexes from Texas, Baby. Of course I'm going.

—Everything's copacetic?

—Lamp into my spotters, she said. Ultra copacetic. Everything's grand.

Baby and Adeline dressed. Baby didn't understand why Adeline bothered getting done up. She had a boyfriend. She hated club people. Who was left to impress?

They smoked pot and took a cab to 46th and Broadway. When they arrived at Burger King, a crowd of obvious club people were walking across the street. Baby and Adeline followed, assuming that these people were in the know.

In coming years, the club scene would be a mortar of high fashion, the pestle of money crushing every possible problem of accoutrement. Watching the crowd drift across Times Square, Baby couldn't help but notice the threadbare state of everyone's outfits. They were like Halloween costumes. Fright wigs and goofy makeup. Everything looked so cheap.

The ground floor of McDonald's was tiny, with only a counter and queue for food. The upstairs dining room area was accessible via a staircase to the immediate right. Baby knew that he'd arrived at Michael Alig's party when he saw the bouncer and velvet rope blocking off access to the stairs. Baby couldn't imagine the indignity of being bounced from McDonald's.

—If this guy doesn't let us in, said a voice in the crowd, I'm going to bend him over and fist him. On second thought, now that I've got a better look at him, I might fist him even if he does.

No one was denied entry. They were the right kind of freaks. Baby held

Adeline's hand, pulling her upstairs, making sure that she didn't get lost in the crush.

Baby spotted James St. James, Michael Musto wearing a cow-print fur jacket, Nelson Sullivan with his camera, Michael Alig with his face painted with blue and red dots, Michael Alig's boyfriend DJ Keoki wearing an ugly silver jacket and a risible hat embossed with silver letters that read KEOKI, Julie Jewels of *Project X* magazine, Christopher Robin, Olympia done up like Marie Antoinette, and a whole host of other people whose names Baby did and did not remember.

—This rockpile sends me, said Adeline. Gun all the able grables and creampuffs. There must be three hundred indexes! B.T.O.

Regina wasn't there. Family obligation. She'd called complaining. Baby didn't mind. It allowed him to include Adeline.

They approached James St. James.

—Hi, honey!

—Jimmy, this is my roommate, Adeline.

—Well, isn't she just fabulous?

—This cat's a real snow from Fresno, said Adeline. Ask the cake eater if he's a boiled owl and if he is, can he mash?

—What? asked James St. James.

—Don't even, said Baby. It's too complicated. But Jimmy, are you holding?

They ended up with two tablets of Ecstasy. Baby ate one. Adeline ate the other. Baby momentarily questioned the wisdom of taking drugs in a badly lit McDonald's on Times Square. On the other hand, the pot was wearing off.

Michael Alig came up the stairs, carrying boxes of food. Everyone screamed. Michael! Michael! Michael! Michael! He stood on a booth table and threw food at the crowd, like the Anti-Christ distributing loaves of poisoned bread. People climbed over each other, fighting, desperate to get their hands on cheeseburgers and Big Macs and French fries.

So lovely, really, so nice to be with these people. All of them knew Baby. Some better than others, but he knew them and they knew him. Something wonderful about that, about being recognized and accepted, about being part of the thing. Adeline was smiling, laughing, touching him. Baby thought, *Oh, wow, it's her first time doing MDMA.* Had things changed so much? Why was there a drug that he'd done before Adeline?

—Why, Baby, said Adeline, I do believe that I'm understanding the appeal of these vile people. They're all so charming, in their grotesque little carnival way.

Michael Alig and his club kids had gone through a phase where they ran around town with whistles hanging from their necks, blowing them throughout the clubs. Baby caught the tail end of this period and was glad for its demise. The sound drove him crazy. But here the whistles were again, blasting away inside McDonald's.

Right before the food fight, Baby and Adeline started a conversation with Kenny Kenny and Armand. Kenny Kenny had served as the doorman at every club in town. Her head was completely shaved other than a red topknot kept under a silver hat. Looking at the knot, Baby shuddered, thinking of the pinhead girls from Tod Browning's film *Freaks*.

Adeline talked at Kenny Kenny and Armand for several minutes, the four of them sitting together in a booth. Baby couldn't keep track of it. Across the restaurant, they were singing "Happy Birthday." Whose birthday was it? Armand said something to Adeline about Louise Brooks. Baby interrupted them, as gently as he could, trying to steer the conversation toward something interesting. As he spoke, he found himself even more boring than Adeline, watching himself from the outside, watching him bore his audience, wishing that he could stop it but being unable.

—All right, okay, you've got to understand, said Baby, that Thomas M. Disch . . .

—Not him! said Adeline. I haven't thought of that dreadful man and his dreadful books since our old Bank of the Metropolis!

—Anyhoo, said Baby, Thomas M. Disch is one of the finest writers who emerged from the Science Fiction New Wave. Probably his best book is *The Genocides,* which is about an alien invasion of Earth by these giant trees that colonize every square inch of the planet. Most humans have died, and the ones that haven't are being hunted by these flesh-incinerating machines. Anyhoo, the novel follows the last group of survivors, this creepy community of Bible thumpers with a freakish patriarch who is either Noah or Lot, you pick, and the whole thing is very Biblical in this queered way. Most of the action takes place underground, when the people escape the machines by running into a cave and becoming, basically, worms that live inside the plants' root network. Oh yeah, I forgot, the plants are kind of edible.

—How does it end? asked Armand.

Armand's face. Baby couldn't stop. He had to answer.

—Badly. Everyone dies. The plants are the food for a race of beings who never appear in the book. They used Earth for their farmland.

—Honey, said Armand, that's about the most boring thing I've ever heard.

—Why would you even bother? asked Kenny Kenny. I mean, books? Who reads? Who cares? We're at a party and you're talking about books?

Adeline stood up, letting them out of the booth. Michael Alig was behind them, watching, his furrowed brow bending the painted dots.

—I overheard your charming little story, said Michael Alig. It reminded me of *Dark Shadows*. Have I ever told you about the Leviathan?

FOOD FIGHT. A melee erupted, fried food tossed in every direction. Adeline threw a Big Mac across the room, hitting the right side of a queen's face. The queen spun around to see the origins of this missile, but as she attempted to trace the trajectory, another hamburger hit her in the nose. French fries fell like arrows at Agincourt.

Everyone had to leave, under threat of the cops being called. Michael Alig yelled that they couldn't call the cops, not really, they had a business arrangement. But everyone was gay, in drag, high. No one wanted to deal with cops.

Then there was the time when Baby started noticing how many bald women hung around the clubs. *Why are they all shaving their heads?*

Then there was the time when Michael Alig explained how to rule the world.

—Don't be such a bitch, he said. Shut up and fucking listen! Think of Andy Warhol. What did Andy do when they wouldn't let him inside? He said, Who cares? Then he looked at what he had around him, which wasn't anything other than a bunch of fucking faggots, queens, and speed freaks, and Andy said, these fucked-up faggots are the center of the world. This is where it's happening. There's nothing out there in the real America, where people work for a living, and live in suburbs, and make straight babies and own stupid ugly disgusting cars. The center of the world is here, on 47th Street, in this filthy fucking building filled with these filthy fucking people! It's the rest of the world that's outside. And Andy was right. No one has to spend their whole life as a fucking victim! Anyone can change the world. You just decide that you're what's hot, you're the new fabulous thing, and then tell other people. And keep fucking telling them! They'll laugh at first, because stupid ugly people always laugh at everything, but if you repeat it enough, sooner or later they're going to come around and they won't be laughing. Because if there's anything that's true, it's that no one wants to be left out of the party. They'll ask for invitations. They'll want drugs. They'll want to fuck beautiful young boys. And you'll be the one with the invitations, you'll be the one with the drugs, and it'll be your boyfriend they're trying to slip the tongue. You'll have all the power. You say yes or no. You decide who makes it and who's as nasty as old dog food. That's how you take over the fucking world! It's the simplest fucking thing. America is the original nightclub. All it takes is time and patience and a good doorman.

Then there was the time when Adeline graduated from Parsons, earning her Bachelor of Fine Arts. Baby asked if she planned on inviting Suzanne.

—Mother doesn't belong here, said Adeline.

—She pays for everything, said Baby. I can't think of anything lonelier than not being invited to your daughter's graduation.

—Why must you always take her side? asked Adeline.

—I lived with her for the better part of a year, said Baby.

Don't speak to me of Mother.

When the day did roll around, Adeline didn't attend the commencement ceremony. She wanted to mark the occasion in her own fashion, deciding that simply the very best way to celebrate would be to eat MDMA and watch a movie. For this outing, she brought along her querulous Russian friend, Minerva. And Baby.

The latter noted, silently, disgruntled, that Adeline's disapproval of his friends did not extend to those times when she desired intoxicants. At such moments, the dreadful club folk were pure swellegance.

Baby scored four tablets of MDMA, giving one each to Adeline and Minerva, eating two himself. Of late, he'd upped his dosage. The cause of increase was this one time when he drank some Ecstasy Punch at Limelight. Party promoters employed this noxious brew as a marketing device, crushing a huge number of tablets into a watery fruit-flavored drink. Distributed for free. Baby ended up with an overload, bringing him to an enlightened understanding regarding the psychic parsimony of eating only one pill. MDMA was not LSD. He need not fear it.

Despite her lack of familiarity with the television program on which the film was based, Adeline decided they should see *Tales from the Darkside: The Movie*. She'd read that it starred Debbie Harry, lead singer of the defunct band Blondie. This casting was recommendation enough.

The film was playing at the Loews 34th Street Showcase. A relatively recent addition to the city, the theater was a squat building with three screens. During Baby's first few months in New York, he and Adeline had attended a screening at the Showcase of *Star Trek IV: The Voyage Home*, projected in glorious 70mm. Baby now had no memory of that film beyond the aging faces of its protagonists and a dim recollection of humpback whales traveling through outer space.

Playing one of the basement theaters, *Tales from the Darkside: The Movie* was unusually bad, even by the dubious standards of the horror genre. A portmanteau film, its scant framing story begins with Debbie Harry living the façade of a normal suburban wife. It is revealed that beneath the veneer, Harry is a witch with an eight-year-old boy caged in her kitchen. She plans to host a dinner, going through the trappings of food preparation, with the child intended as the main course.

She gives the boy a book entitled *Tales from the Darkside*. Surprised by his disinterest in the tome, she informs the boy that the book was a favorite from her own childhood. Crazed with the desperation of the damned, the child suggests that he read Debbie Harry stories from within the book. She readily assents. Baby couldn't imagine why she would. The book is hers, she's been reading it for decades. Why would any of the stories be interesting? Even worse, the child can barely speak. There is no appeal in his elocution.

Each of the three tales dissolves into its own short narrative film. The first is about a mummy brought to life by career opportunists. The second is about a hitman hired to kill a cat. The third is about a man who witnesses a gargoyle committing murder and then strikes a deal with the creature to avoid his own death.

The drug disrupted Baby's ability to follow the narratives in any linear sense. Flashes of images came at random, disjointed. The mummy's head cut off and burnt in a fire. The smile of the gargoyle. An old man's face covered in blood. An interracial marriage. Zombies.

A twist of the old man's lip, beneath the stage blood, reminded Baby of the time when he'd met Quentin Crisp at Tunnel. Crisp'd written a book called *The Naked Civil Servant,* a memoir of his life as a flame queen in London around the time of World War II. Through the machinations of fate, he'd ended up as the club scene's elder statesman.

Baby and Crisp spoke for the better part of an hour.

—Do you know, you charming boy, said Crisp, that in the days of Studio 54, the great-grandson of Abraham Lincoln would come up on the train from Virginia to partake in the sheer excess? It's absolutely true. I've had it from multiple sources. His name was Robert Todd Lincoln Beckwith, but they called him Bud. Bud! Bud Lincoln! Isn't it charming? He was a terrible old man with a degenerative disease of the muscles that left him quite incapable of walking. He would be wheeled in by some lovely young stud, and then he'd spend the night talking with Liz Taylor and Mick Jagger. They were fascinated. Wouldn't you be? When the time came to return to his hotel, he'd pick up a coterie of lovely young things. Boys, girls, transvestites, queer, straight. Those distinctions didn't matter in the slightest to the progeny of Honest Abe. Bud brought them back to his hotel and made them fuck each other silly. He'd only watch, as by this time the poor thing's flower could no longer bloom. People've told me the most outrageous stories about his face, about the drooping geriatric visage that leered and drooled while the nubile bodies cavorted and capered in the arms of Aphrodite. The tired old thing died several years back. It goes to show, doesn't it, my little one? Even in the best families.

The film ended. The trio stumbled outside. Minerva, who did not like Baby, pushed off, leaving the roommates with many daylight hours. Adeline was at a complete loss, the MDMA reducing her to a half giggle, enchanted by the empty lot across the street.

—Did you like the movie? asked Baby.

—Oh Baby, said Adeline, I'll assume it's your state of mind that's made you ask such a dreadful question. I thought we had a pact. No obvious questions after a film!

—Let's go to Grant's Tomb, said Baby.

—Shall we? Where is it?

—Way uptown, said Baby. We'll have to go to Penn Station and take the IRT local.

They rode the 1 up to 125th Street, getting off at the elevated station. As they walked down the long stairwell, Baby experienced dislocation, unable to find the right direction. Drug absurdity. The green trees of Riverside

Park were visible, but it took some moments before his brain could issue the cognitive instructions. Adeline was of no help, humming to herself, head tilted upward toward the rusting metal.

—Oh, wow, she said. It's so beautiful. It's man-made, but what if it's always been here? What if it's ancient?

Baby took her hand.

Like every other open space in the city, Riverside Park was a cluster of homelessness and drug addiction. Some on the nod, others doing the telltale shuffle, one step forward, two steps back.

The dome of Grant's Tomb burst through a canopy of trees. Baby and Adeline passed over crumbling granite embedded with the shattered remains of crack vials and broken bottles. Two large eagle statues stood guard on either side of the entrance, their beaks demolished.

Admission was free. There wasn't much inside other than a rotunda from which visitors could look down at the sarcophagi of Grant and his wife. A handful of people were visiting, quiet tourists, shell-shocked look in their eyes. They'd come to visit the moldering bones of an American President, the country's finest nineteenth-century general, and found themselves walking through a park strewn with graffiti and human shit.

Adeline peered from the gallery at the red porphyry of the sarcophagi, polished, reflecting dull light.

—Dude, she said, this is, like, the craziest thing, but I can't read the names. I can only see my own face.

Ulysses S. Grant, who was incapable of imagining the debasement of his Commander-in-Chief's great-grandson, an aged man visiting New York to abuse himself among the nubile cocaine-fueled bodies of the twentieth century. We of New York are like space whales of pleasure and debauchery, the cocks and cunts and powders and liquids of unknown vistas. Ulysses S. Grant, eighteenth President of these States United, there is no way that you could imagine to what uses Bud Lincoln would put his famous name. You cannot conceive of Bud Lincoln's fleshly needs, of Bud Lincoln's disco nights.

—Here we are, Adeline said, and I haven't the slightest about Grant.

—He was a terrible drunk, said Baby. Why not buy a book from the gift shop?

—There's a gift shop? she asked.

—That rack by the front door, said Baby.

No books were offered for sale. Adeline purchased several packets of reproduction Confederate currency. A dollar per cluster of counterfeit cash.

They left the mausoleum, heading north through the park. Adeline opened a package of her faux money, pawing through the bills.

She handed Baby a hundred-dollar note. His eyes saw the bill in negative, its form without context. A series of engraved lines. Baby couldn't recognize the patterns of the intended images.

—What is it? he asked.

—Pure Southern charm, she said. They put slaves on their currency. It's three down-home nigras hoein' cotton.

—Why isn't Jon here? asked Baby.

—Ask the man yourself, said Adeline. I'm sure he'll offer you an answer that simply fascinates.

She wandered ahead. How many years since California? Two? When had Baby last been in anything like nature? The bluest sky. The whitest clouds. Grant's Tomb. Grant, the Great Drunk, the failed President. Grant, who understood human weakness and indulgence and intoxicants. Could it be that he would, in the end, evidence some sympathy for Bud Lincoln? Was it any surprise that his tomb should attract lotus eaters? His body called them, a magnet for the broken and the mad. The secular patron saint of addiction. The secular god of drugs.

Waves off the building, the dome attuned to the upper stratosphere, shooting energy signals into the outer reaches of space. Hyperkinetic emergences of Ulysses S. Grant and his beloved wife, Julia, the bones of their corpses arranged to amplify transmission of messages to the whales. Visit us, conquer us, enslave us. Take this vile world away. No man or woman is fit. Spare us the knowledge of our own evil. We surrender, we surrender. We are Bobby E. Lee. We surrender.

—Baby! Come over here at once!

Adeline stood across the road by a tiny white urn on a pedestal.

—Read the inscription, she said.

ERECTED TO THE MEMORY
OF AN AMIABLE CHILD
ST. CLAIRE POLLOCK
DIED 15 JULY 1797
IN THE FIFTH YEAR OF HIS AGE

*

Then there was the time when Christina had her birthday party in the basement at Tunnel. Michael Alig called Baby with an invitation.

—But why would I go? asked Baby. I don't even know Christina!

—Oh, please, said Michael Alig. Who cares? No one can ever know anyone else.

The scant number of attendees convinced Baby that he'd been wrangled in the hopes of filling out the crowd. The Tunnel basement hadn't changed. It wasn't much more than dirty tables and ugly furniture in a space unfit for human habitation.

Christina, wearing a red dress and stockings, sat under a spotlight. A painting behind her read BEEFEATER. Baby got roaring drunk in the taxi up to 27th Street, sucking down four short dogs in the backseat. As far as he could tell, Christina had agreed to give a performance, singing some songs, and for whatever reason, once the event began, had expressed her total disinterest in doing anything other than sitting and sulking. Nelson Sullivan floated around her, his camera alternating between Christina and the audience.

People demanded that Christina sing "Jumpin' Jack Flash." A queen named Hapi Phace was on the microphone, performing a sloppy comedy routine with another queen named Taboo. A birthday cake was brought out. It read: HAPPY BIRTHDAY CHRISTIAN.

An unknown queen whom Baby didn't recognize took the microphone. Black leather jacket over black dress, black sunglasses, hair dyed cut and shaved post-punk. She claimed that each of Christina's ass cheeks were tattooed with an M, and that when Christina bent over, her ass spelled MOM. Christina asked the queen how much she wanted to be the next Madonna. Throwing the microphone to the floor, the queen said: —Girl, it's not that I want to be the next Madonna. I simply am.

More screams for "Jumpin' Jack Flash." Lady Bunny on the microphone, asking for the song. Christina would not move.

Baby looked away. When he looked back, Christina had a hammer. Then Keoki took the hammer away. Then Christina asked for the hammer back. The unknown queen brought it over. Everyone started singing happy birthday, while a handful of people yelled at Christina to eat the cake.

The unknown queen picked up the cake, strutting before Christina. She pushed the cake into Christina's face. Frosting mashed into her wig, Christina had the hammer, but she wasn't swinging. Sulking, sitting, the cake dripping off her face. Hammer in her hand. Nelson Sullivan videotaping.

—How do you like the party? asked Michael Alig. Isn't it just great? Such drama!

—I'm not cut out for this, said Baby.

—Everyone's only having fun! Don't be such a nervous Nellie!

Then there was the time when Michael Alig introduced Baby to his mother, whose European accent made her sound like Christina.

—Baby, she said, everyone is someone's baby! Even you, Baby! Michael is my Baby!

This introduction occurred on the dance floor at Mars. Michael Alig's mother had flown in from Indiana.

—Baby, she asked, do you have any nose candy for Mama?

Then there was the time when Baby and Queen Rex went to a porn shoot in a warehouse near the corner of Ninth Avenue and Little West 12th Street, very close to Nelson Sullivan's house.

The interior of the warehouse was in a converted meat processing plant. The pornography was specialty. All bondage, all domination. No sex.

A red-headed woman, track marks visible. An overweight man disrobing her. One of the production assistants whispered to Baby and Regina that this was the thirteenth installment in a series entitled *Hammer of the Witches,* after the *Malleus Maleficarum,* a witch-hunter's manual published in 1486. The authors, Heinrich Kramer and Jacob Sprenger, describe the utility of employing certain tortures and techniques in determining a suspect's familiarity with the dark arts. The producers of *Hammer of the Witches* had modified these methods to less lethal extremes, subjecting their female stars to adapted versions of the same historical indignities.

Beneath the aging effects of narcotics abuse, the red-headed woman looked about the same age as Adeline. Every four years the city cycled in a new crop of would-be film directors, would-be writers, would-be artists, would-be models, would-be actresses. Baby'd been in New York long enough that he'd begun encountering a second generation of aspirants. There was never any shortage of human flesh, never any shortage of young women and men degrading themselves in the name of commerce or art, never any shortage of dissolution and drug addiction, never any shortage of idiocy or naiveté, never any shortage of raw material for the great grinding gristmill.

The overweight man applied a modified version of the thumbscrew, then attempted to measure the woman's buoyancy by dunking her in a tank of water. After several more of these endurance tests, the shoot ended with the determination that the woman was indeed a witch. The production assistant told Baby that they'd burn the actress in post.

In the street, outside, Queen Rex and Baby smoked KOOL cigarettes.

—It's been ages, cried Baby, since I've had sex! Absolute ages! I'm an attractive, swish young man who haunts clubs full of drunkards and dope fiends! Why am I not having more sex?

—Welcome to the new normal, said Queen Rex.

—I am absolutely going to get fucked tonight, he said. I don't care how or where! Let's go to a club and find some stupid beautiful boy! Or else I'm going to burst!

—We'll go to Palladium. There's always some young thing waiting to make a mistake.

Walking along 14th Street, Baby looked up toward 31 Union Square West and wished, in a way that he could not articulate, a deep wordless wish down in the dank of his bowels, that he could move back into the building.

There wasn't a line at Palladium. Baby didn't recognize anyone. The club was so passé, but that was its charm. All the outward trappings without any inherent pressures. Regina suggested that they skip the club and go upstairs to Julian's Billiards. Baby said okay. Regina said that she was only kidding.

Regina went to get drinks, leaving Baby against a wall. He thought about sex. He thought about fucking. He thought about screwing out someone's brains. He thought about someone screwing out his brains. He wanted to give someone the time.

Two kids came up to him.

—Don't you know Michael Alig? asked the one wearing a frilly white lace shirt, his bleached blond hair hanging from a red plastic bowler.

—Michael who? asked Baby.

—Obviously he knows Michael, said the other. He's Baby Baby Baby! He's an authentic club kid!

—How fabulous, said the first. My name's Polly.

—And I'm Esther. How are you, Baby?

—Uh, said Baby, I'm waiting for someone.

—Honey, are you waiting for Michael? Is Michael here?

—No, said Baby. I'm waiting for Queen Rex.

—Oh my God, Queen Rex? How fabulous! I can't wait to meet her.

Club life. The world's most self-obsessed people playing out their existences as if on an infinite stage, with every moment a performance. These people were delusional enough to believe that they had a secret audience, that they were always watched.

In New York City, in the so-called Downtown Scene, everything was fabulous. Everything was always fabulous.

Regina came back, visibly disgusted by Polly and Esther, examining the black letters on their identical white backpacks: ALCOHOL KILLS and STOP CORRUPTION.

—Who are these people? she asked Baby.

—I'm not sure, said Baby. They recognized me. They want to know if Michael's here.

—They recognized you? Why would anyone recognize you?

—The article in *Project X*, I guess, said Baby.

—They did an article about you in *Project X*?

—Jesus, Regina, I wrote the article, said Baby. It was my first publication! Everyone's read it. Even Adeline. Why haven't you?

—School, said Regina.

—These little boys don't have a clue about your identity, said Baby. You're a complete mystery.

—Something needs to be mysterious in this shithole, said Regina.

Polly and Esther talked Baby onto the dance floor. He resisted, not wanting to be seen, but then decided, who cares? It's Palladium. No one will know. He tried to follow the groove, but Polly and Esther stuck close and wouldn't stop their terrible dance. Without grace, limbs wild, ignoring the song, inappropriate voguing, outrageousness being the full and only point.

Baby shrugged off and went to find Regina. She sat at a table, drinking a Cape Cod. Polly and Esther came from the dance floor. Regina exhaled pure indignation, stood and left.

Baby took stock. They weren't cute but they weren't hideous. He asked where they lived. They had an apartment on 11th Street. He said, let's go. They said, okay. They said, do you think you could call Michael? Baby said, well, maybe, but let's go to your place, you've got a phone, right?

Inside the apartment, Baby told Polly and Esther to remove their clothes. They obeyed without haste. This is what it must be like to be Michael. To say jump and watch people leap.

—Are we doing this in your bed? asked Baby.

—We can do it here, on the floor, said Polly.

—Wherever you like, said Esther.

—Who needs a bed? asked Baby. Do you have any nose candy for Mama?

Polly and Esther kneeled, their mouths on Baby's penis. Then Esther's mouth was on Baby's testicles. Then Esther's mouth was on Baby's penis. Then Polly's mouth was on Esther's testicles. Then Baby's mouth was on Polly's penis. Then Baby pushed Esther onto all fours. Then Polly retrieved KY Jelly from the bathroom medicine cabinet. Then Baby covered his penis in KY Jelly. Then Baby's penis pressed against Esther's anus. Then Baby's penis was inside Esther's rectum. Then Baby told Polly to put his mouth on Esther's penis. Then Baby told Polly to get behind Esther. Then Polly put KY Jelly on his penis. Then Polly's penis was against Esther's anus. Then Polly's penis was in Esther's rectum. Then Baby's penis was in Esther's mouth. Then Baby bent Polly over. Then Baby's penis was against Polly's anus. Then Baby's penis was inside Polly's rectum. Then Esther's mouth was on Polly's penis. Then Polly shouted out. Then Esther moaned. Then Baby's hand was on Esther's penis. Then Baby's penis was in Esther's rectum. Then Polly's tongue was on Baby's anus. Then Polly's tongue was in Baby's rectum. Then Baby groaned. Then Baby thought of James Boswell, of the man's hidden journals detailing endless encounters with prostitutes in public places, of Boswell's need to ejaculate after watching a public hanging. *Not even the finest English writer of the 1700s knew such decadence as this*, thought Baby. *The twentieth century has democratized lust.* Then Baby's penis evacuated semen into Esther's rectum. Then Baby told Polly and Esther to put their penises in each other's mouths. Then Polly's penis evacuated semen into Esther's mouth. Then Esther's penis evacuated semen into Polly's mouth. Then Esther spit Polly's semen onto Polly's stomach. Then Esther sucked Polly's semen back into his mouth.

Baby lay on the dirty wooden floor. *I hope I don't catch AIDS.*

Esther rolled over, penis dripping seminal fluid down his inner thigh.

—Are you going to call Michael? asked Esther.

—No, said Baby. Absolutely not. Not now. Not ever. Not for you.

Then there was the time when Christina overdosed at the Chelsea Hotel. A rumor went around that she'd called Nelson Sullivan and asked him to film her death. Nelson refused. Five days later, the stench of her rotting corpse forced management to break down her door. The human form in such a state of advanced decomposition that identification required dental records.

Another story went around, about a performance that occurred not that long before the overdose. Christina was on stage at the Pyramid, her top off, singing "I'll Keep It with Mine," a song written by Bob Dylan and recorded by Nico. *I can't help it if you might think if I am odd / If I say I'm not loving you for what you are / But for what you're not.*

An audience member didn't appreciate her rendition. He booed, he heckled.

Christina picked up the microphone stand and threw it at his face. People said that she'd taken out one of his eyes. Baby could not believe it. Too outlandish. Many people said that she'd been brought up on attempted murder charges.

She overdosed in June. Everyone said that Nelson Sullivan was broken up. Baby never had a chance to ask him about Christina. On July 4th, Sullivan died of a heart attack. He was forty-one years old.

Then there was the time when Limelight hired Michael Alig to put on a Wednesday night party called Disco 2000. How things change! Baby remembered this one time when Michael Alig was banned from Limelight for owing someone $700.

The owner of Limelight was Peter Gatien, a middle-aged Canadian who wore a patch over his left eye. He'd owned a string of successful clubs in other cities before buying a deconsecrated Gothic Revival church at Sixth Avenue and 20th Street. Gatien's previous clubs all had been named Limelight. The church took the same name. Opening in 1983, it limped through a few mediocre years before collapsing into the utterly passé.

Gatien turned to Michael Alig. Go ahead, he said, you're one of the young things making the most noise. Take the dead night of Wednesday. I'll bankroll you.

—I finally have what I've always wanted! said Michael Alig. All of my dreams are coming true!

Michael Alig disappeared, entering into furious preparations for his premiere in late August. Rumors swirled. Something about costumes, the club as carnival, like Larry Tee's Celebrity Club but on a whole new scale. Putting away of childish things. This would be different. This would be formalized. The real deal.

On opening night, Baby received a telephone call, making sure that he'd go.

—I wouldn't miss it, Michael, said Baby. Regina's going, too. Everyone's going.

—Even that bitch Musto said he's coming, said Michael Alig. I hope he doesn't spoil everything!

—It'll be fine, said Baby. Trust me.

—Oh, said Michael Alig, what do you know? Why should I trust you? You're nobody!

Baby called Queen Rex. Her mother answered. Baby hadn't met Regina's mother, but they'd spoken countless times.

—¿Aló?

—Hola, said Baby. ¿Regina es allí?

—¿Quién es?

—Es Bebé.

—Baby, said Regina's mother, laughing. Baby! Baby!

Children screamed behind her.

—Baby, Regina no es home. Regina es . . . es . . . at . . . at . . . disco!

—Gracias, Mami, he said, hanging up.

Baby ate two tablets of MDMA. He went into his closet and gathered every belt that he owned. He asked Adeline if he could borrow all of her belts.

—Why ever do you want them?

—I'm going to make a costume, said Baby. For the first night of Disco 2000.

—Are you high? she asked.

—Yes, said Baby.

—On MDMA?

—Yes, said Baby.

—I wish you could stand on the rock where Moses stood and take a look at yourself. Something has gone very wrong. You aren't the young man that I remember.

—Times change, he said. You can't repeat the past.

—What do you mean you can't repeat the past? asked Adeline. Of course you can.

Baby put on a base layer of black clothing and tied the belts over his arms, legs, and torso. In the mirror, the effect worked better than he'd imagined. He looked like a Rainbow Mummy.

—I hope this isn't too Leigh Bowery, he said to himself.

Baby took a taxi up to 20th Street. Kenny Kenny was at the door. Baby skipped the line. Limelight was made anew. Michael Alig had rented live monkeys, which were scattered around the lobby, shitting and screaming in cages. James St. James had been given a cage of his own, wearing stage makeup and a sign over his head: WARNING: DO NOT FEED THE DRUG CHILD. He cried out for a bump! Just a bump! Any bump!

And then there were the costumed characters. Clara the Carefree Chicken, an oversized yellow avian with a predilection for off-beat dancing, pushing people around in stolen shopping carts, groping their genitals. Hans Ulrich, the leather dog. I. C. the Bear. Handmade signs announced these creatures' names.

—Baby! I love your costume!

—Regina! Darling!

They hugged.

—Isn't it wonderful? she asked.

—I'm really really really high right now, said Baby. Is it as amazing as it seems?

—What did you take? she asked.

—Ecstasy, what else?

—A girl over there has Special K. I haven't done it, have you? It's all the rage. All the kids say it's divine. Should I get us some?

—You go enjoy, said Baby. I don't like mixing pharmaceuticals. I should find Michael.

—He's upstairs, said Queen Rex.

Baby made his way across the club. Michael must be pleased with the turnout. Baby darted around a pack of six or seven kids. One grabbed him by the arm.

—Baby! said a female voice.

He looked at the woman. She was petite, wearing a long silver wig, big ugly black boots, thick black belt, and a camo bikini. He sighed, not wanting to deal with another groupie.

Having written several articles for *Project X*, Baby was experiencing increased visibility. He hated it. Honey, said James St. James, that's the terrible price of fame! Baby didn't want fame. He just liked writing.

—Helllllooo, he said.

—Baby, it is me, said the girl.

—Who's me? he asked.

—Me, Baby. Jae-Hwa, Sally.

Baby scrunched up his face. Beneath the makeup, beneath the wig, beneath the bikini, beneath the silver. He saw her. It'd been almost four years, the spring of 1987. Then she'd dressed sub-preppy, with no style. A lot of khaki slacks and pink sweaters and self-cut hair.

—Sally! What are you doing here? asked Baby.

—I am a real club kid now, she said. Ecstasy is in my blood. Do not call me Sally anymore. Call me Sigh.

—Sigh? asked Baby.

—It is my new American name, she said. I have been reading your articles.

Baby asked Sigh if she'd graduated. She hadn't, she wouldn't ever graduate. She'd been thrown out of Parsons in her junior year. She'd struck up an interest in clubbing and stayed out every night, partying through the semester without producing any work.

A portfolio review was scheduled in the final week of classes. Overcome with despair, Sigh roamed the Parsons building on Fifth Avenue, stumbling across a stack of paintings in the basement. She stole the artwork and presented it at her review. The scheme would have worked, she said, except that one of the faculty members happened to be the person from whom she'd stolen the work. Those are my paintings, he said.

—Yet my father is rich, she said, so I continue to party!

They danced together, for a while. Drugs making the music much better. As always.

He said goodbye to Sigh, knowing that they'd run into each other again. She glowed with it, with the intangible aura of someone hooked on club life. The aura of an indigo child. Certain people were made for nightclubbing. But Sally! Who knew? He couldn't wait to tell Adeline.

Other people recognized him, stopped him, talked with him. Air kisses and hugs and declarations of how fabulous they found his belts.

In the Chapel, beneath stained-glass windows, Michael Alig held court, surrounded by Michael Musto, LaHoma, Peter Gatien, and a bunch of kids that Baby didn't recognize. Gatien turned toward Baby, unnerving void of black eye patch.

—The attendance isn't really what I wanted, said Michael Alig, but it's close. We'll get there. This is my moment, Peter. I'm sure of it. This is the big one. No one can ever take this away! Not even you!

Then there was the time when Baby went by himself to Red Zone. It was Saturday night and Baby ate two tablets of MDMA before taking a cab to West 54th Street.

Getting out of the car, he spun on the pavement and bumped into this gorgeous guy. The guy smiled at Baby. Baby smiled back. They talked. The guy's name was Erik. Baby told Erik about listening to an LP of the Shangri-Las' *Greatest Hits*, a record that he'd bought for $2 at the Salvation Army. *Oh God,* thought Baby, *why the fuck can't I just fucking shut the fuck up?*

—There are the obvious songs, said Baby, like, uh, 'Remember' and 'Leader of the Pack,' but the one that I love the most is 'Past, Present and Future.' It's not even really a song, it's more like a long monologue addressed to an unknown boy that goes through the three stages of the title's temporality. But where she kills you, where she gets you so hard, is when she tells the boy, twice, 'That will never happen again.' It's the finality of it. It's the doom of relationships. It's the human fucking condition. It's so awful. It's such a sad thing thinking of those girls.

Erik reached out and touched the side of Baby's face, fingers running along the line of jaw, thumb on cheekbone.

—I'll be your girl if you say it's a gift, said Erik.

And it was here that Baby, which is to say me, myself, it was here, after many moons, that I found my path back to personhood.

JANUARY 1991

Adeline Comes Back from a Trip with Jon

Jon dropped me off outside of my 7th Street quarters. We exchanged pleasantries. Jon drove off to New Jersey. I unlocked the front door. Down the block, a drunken lout was vomiting his lungs into the gutter. New York City. Home.

Climbing the stairs, I imagined Baby and Erik losing all sense of self, delirious with delight at having the space to their selves and indulging in a reckless carnival of homo acrobatics. My one hope was that they'd emerged from their lust and cleaned up the semen and lubricants.

The apartment was untouched, spotless. Imaginate my surprise. The Captain rubbing his winsome against my legs. Louder purrs I have not heard. I dumped my bags on the kitchen floor and stooped low to pet his head, happy for the consistency.

"Baby?" I called out. "Baby? Are you home?"

My bed displayed no evidence of anyone screwing out anyone else's brains. I lay down. The Captain climbed beside me, his left paw and head on my stomach.

It couldn't have been more than ten minutes of peace. The front door opened. I remembered my bags, and was about to warn Baby not to stumble over them, when there came the most wretched crunching sound of my adult life: "Adeliiiiiiiiiiiiiiiiiiiiiiiiiiiiiiiiiiiiiiiiiiiine! Adeliiiiiiiiiiiiiiiiiiiiiiiiiii iiiiiiiiiiiiine!"

Sensation in the lower stomach, clenching with nervous energy, the shock of it. I wanted to hide, but where? I swallowed and trudged into the kitchen.

There she stood. Crazy as a daisy. Sally in the alley. Mother. Baby was beside her, keys in hand, shit-eating mouth.

"Mother," I said. "Why ever are you here?"

"Adeliiiiiiiiiiiiiiiine," said she, her appalling new haircut making her face too round, "I hadn't heard from you in so long! So I came out here! Baby was nice enough to let me in! I'm so happy to see you!"

She threw her claws around my back. Too shocked, too appalled to say anything. Too stunned to push her off.

"I don't expect much from her," said I to Baby. "From you I expect decorum. I expect some modicum of loyalty."

"Adeliiiiiiiiiiiiiiine," said Mother. "Don't blame Baby! I ambushed him in the street! What could he do!"

"I can contemplate several things," I said. "I can think of several things indeed."

"Adeliiiiiiiiiiiiiiine," said Mother. "Something's different about your voice!"

"Where are you holed up?" I asked. "The Plaza?"

"Of course, Adeliiiiiiiiine!"

"I've only now returned home from a long trip," I said. "I'll meet you tomorrow at 4 pm in the lobby. Don't be late. I won't mount an expedition to find you in the bar."

"But Adeliiiiiiiiiiiiiiiiiine," said Mother, "I thought we could get dinner!"

"We can't," I said. "You must leave. Tomorrow. 4 pm. The Plaza lobby."

She departed. Not without passive aggressive protest, insisting that Baby walk her to the street. He obliged. I pressed up against the kitchen counter. Footsteps announced his return.

"How was Graceland?" he asked, smiling.

"Tacky," I said. "Why the fuck did you let Mother inside our apartment?"

"She literally jumped me on the street," he said. "No one's more shocked than I am. I didn't have any time to think. You know how she can be."

Back in my bedroom, lying on my bed. I'd returned from the South with no small amount of placidity, the last five hours of driving filled with resolve earned through new experience, exhausted by travel, as if I'd sweated out all mental poisons. As blank as unused paper.

That was gone, ruined, stolen by Mother, a malign spirit summoned from the past, ink staining the paper. I'd journeyed two thousand miles, changed my way of thinking.

Yet one can never change because there is always another desperate to recall one's old self. Too much change, too much transition into a new person, and this other will lose sense of their own identity. One becomes their unit of measurement.

I excavated Fairport Convention's *Liege & Lief*. I lowered the stylus upon the second cut. "Reynardine." Ethereal sound coming off sparse guitar, spectral voice of Sandy Denny moving through protoplasmic transmission. I'd listened countless times and couldn't begin to speculate as to the song's meaning. I hadn't the slightest. I fell asleep reading *The Hearing Trumpet* by Leonora Carrington.

Dumb luck is a skill one can cultivate like any other. In the sad days before Jeremy Winterbloss and Минерва packed up and moved out to Northern California, I'd been wandering along Fifth Avenue, my brain addlepated with misty thoughts of Blackberry Lane. A voice cried out my name. It was Luanna Potrero.

We exchanged pleasantries. Her graduation occurred the year before my own, and she'd fallen into print illustration, doing spot work for magazines in Midtown. I inquired as to the pay rates. She said they were fantastic.

"I can get you work," she said. "I've got more offers than I know what to do with."

I hugged her, sinking my fingers into the excess of her flesh, and thanked her kindly. I said I'd think about it, which was only dissimulation and pretext.

That very night, reader, I gave her a ring-a-ding-ding and informed Luanna that I wasn't the kind of girl who'd pry the equine mouth and count teeth.

Perhaps you wonder why. Ain't ol' Adeline fixed for life?

Consider the long haul after graduation, strung out with anxiety. I could Nostradamus the future. I'd graduated with a degree in Fine Arts, and my family was lousy with beaucoup bucks.

These twin maladies typically produce one of several unfortunate *dénouements*. A terrible marriage. Substance addiction. Country home in New Canaan. A Francesca Woodman suicide.

So I said yes, of course, obviously, Adeline will raise high the banner of the righteous. She'll do the work.

Luanna had a studio in the West 20s, from which she and a rotating band of illustrators pounded out material at a healthy gallop. There was no house style.

My linework soon appeared on the newsstands.

She had arranged everything, talking with editors, doling out pieces, taking her cut off the top. Our arrangement was flexible. If I wished to disappear for a week and become a Californy transplant gone to seed down in Dixieland, I needn't do much but call my friend and let her know.

The money was good enough that I was able to sever most ties with

Mother and her deep reservoirs of filthy lucre. This isn't to say that your faithful friend wasn't still eating a certain amount of the family's pie.

A year before his death, Daddy had gone and visited his trusts and estates lawyer, and established a certain payout for both Dahlia and myself. Barring incompetence on the part of the trust's administrators, we'd both pull in some cash for the rest of our lives.

But it wasn't Mother's money. That was the key. Great God All Mighty, I was free at last.

Which was, of course, the reason for her impromptu visit. Mother was rather shaken when she realized that without the IV drip of her liquid assets, I wasn't very much beholden.

Thus the ambush, darlings.

The next day I took a cab to Central Park. The driver let me out by the statue of William Tecumseh Sherman. When last I'd looked upon the general's likeness, it was a dull rotted color. Now it blazed with a bright gold leaf that defied the winter late afternoon. I couldn't fathom why the authorities of Central Park had transformed Sherman and Wingèd Victory into disco icons.

My period was upon me. The stress of Mother had thrust me into my heavy flow. The morning was spent plagued by cramps, shitting out my guts.

The woman was not in the Plaza lobby. Despite my vow, I went on an expedition and found her imbibing in the Oak Room.

"Adeliiiiiiiiiiine," she said. "Have a drink with your mother."

"How many have you consumed?" I asked.

"Only three so far," she said.

"Bloody hell," I said. "Why not."

I ordered a vodka tonic. I suppose there was symmetry in it. How insane Mother was! She believed in the appropriateness of our setting, in the righteousness of stewing herself in the Oak Room beside her deeply estranged daughter.

"Did I ever tell you about the first time that we stayed in the Plaza? I think it must have been in 1970," said Mother. "Your father and I flew out to New York. I didn't know anything about the city, but your father insisted on the Plaza! He said only the best for his girl! Your father had some business with the university. Don't ask me what! After he was done with that, we went to Madison Square Garden and we saw Blind Faith. You remember Blind Faith, don't you, Adeliiiiiiiine? It used to be your favorite album when you were an infant. You made us plaaaay it and plaaaaaay it. You'd cry so much if we turned it off!"

We need not be friends but we also needn't be enemies. Blame the alcohol.

"Adeliiiiiiiiine," she said. "Why can't I meet Jon!"

One could always trust Mother to chase away your weakness.

"You're on very shaky ground simply meeting me, Mother," I said.

"But Adeliiiiiiiiiine," she said. "You know I love to take an interest! Baby says he's a nice young man! Much better than that nasty Kevin!"

"Whenever did you find the time to talk with Baby about Jon?" I asked.

"It's a very long walk up those stairs," she said. "And I'd had a few drinks, which made it even longer!"

"Mother," I said. "You mustn't ever come back. You know that, don't you? Cease thinking of us even as anything like acquaintances. Our time together is over."

"Adeliiiiiiiiiine!" she said. "You don't mean that!"

"You've pressing things to which you must attend. You live in Los Angeles. I'm in New York. That's enough distance. Waste your affections on Dahlia. She'll always be there."

"But Dahlia's so boriiiiiiing!" said Mother. I walked away. She ordered two Greyhounds, reminding the bartender to salt the rims.

I instituted a hard rule about the answering machine. We had the thing for a reason, I told Baby, so we'd be damn sure to use it. Every call must be screened. People could announce their selves through the speaker. If they were not Mother or some other malefactor, then we would answer. Otherwise, we'd let the horrible woman ramble.

Weekly dispatches from Los Angeles were invariably delivered at times when Mother was too tight to comprehend the difference in time zones. She developed a great range, finding new excuses to call. Each message existed in a vacuum isolated from all previous efforts.

"Who knows," said Baby. "Maybe she doesn't remember."

In the fine art of giving offense, the woman was a dynamo savant. Her first message expressed interest in my love life. The next was about her confusion as to the mail that arrived in my name, offering financial advice about credit card applications. In another, she spoke about encountering one of my old high school friends at a soirée. They'd asked after me. She wasn't sure how to respond. Could I return her call and provide instruction as to making these encounters less awkward? She'd appreciate it.

The worst, reader, was when she'd convinced herself that I'd flown back to Los Angeles with the sole intent of vandalizing her home.

"Adeliiiiiiiiiiine," she intoned, "I don't know why you want to torment your poor mother like this, but that's fine, if you want to be like that, then you can be like that. But I will not have you coming into our home and throwing things around. Don't think that you can go around destroying other people's property! It's not riiiiiiight, Adeliiiiiine! This is very childish!"

APRIL 1991

David Wojnarowicz

Darlings, don't believe for the smallest little minute that Adeline doesn't know how booooring you consider politics.

I'm right with you, old sport, my eyes running white in the sockets whenever some dreary creature starts on and on and on and on about the winner of an election, or the horrors of Congress, or the latest cruelty wreaked upon some poor unfortunate by the municipal government. I ain't no nattering nabob of negativity. I couldn't give two hoots of a hangman's holler. Tiny miseries are the glue of other people's existence, the sticky stuff adhering together the dull papers of their lives. But not mine.

So you'll simply indulge, trusting in me, won't you, as I relate a bit of the ol' ultraviolent American history? This is the good stuff, the politics that matter.

I'm speaking of the three or four years in which the East Village played host to one of the major combatants in what were once called the Culture Wars. The unhappy late period of David Wojnarowicz.

Say what you might about the man, and many have remarked upon his occasional forays into cruelty, but Wojnarowicz woke up one morning and found himself embroiled in a kind of Jahannam that I would not wish upon my worst enemy. What made him remarkable, and what warmed me to him, was the grace that he displayed after being thrust into the inferno.

It starts, I suppose, with the death of Wojnarowicz's lover, Peter Hujar. Another East Village artist struck down by AIDS. In those days, simply everyone who was anyone died of the disease, and America, being America, politicized the illness with its finest traditions of hypocrisy and bigotry.

A subspecies of the human primate believed that the virus was sent from the high heavens, YHWH's direct retribution against the sodomizing sybarites in the New Gomorrahs of these States United. Why not?

The disease's victims offered easy targets for scoring cheap political points. The poor, the queer, and the drug addicted. Those with an excess of melanin.

As best as I can tell, Wojnarowicz's great anger over Hujar's death, over the death of so many that he knew and loved, reached a crescendo when the artist received his own diagnosis. His own death sentence.

He'd always been angry. Now he was furious. His work moved into the realm of the survivor who knew that he himself could not survive.

A bit later, Wojnarowicz contributed the catalogue essay to an exhibition at Artists Space in Tribeca. A ferocious piece attacking a variety of anti-homo political figures. His targets, blessedly, have passed out of cultural memory into the Gray Havens. They are dead old white men. I shall not name them.

This particular show, titled *Witnesses: Against Our Vanishing*, had received funding from the National Endowment for the Arts. When the head of the organization read Wojnarowicz's essay, he withdrew the money.

Instant furor. Instant controversy. Instant scandal. Mr. Wojnarowicz thrust into the public spotlight. He had not anticipated it, nor was it desired. Yet there he was. The man at the center, the queer cause of all that bother.

Following some outcry, the NEA caved, reversing its decision and restoring funding on the condition that its money not pay for the catalogue. Other sources of filthy lucre were found. The show went forward.

Wojnarowicz became a figure of national import, his name appearing in every major newspaper and countless smaller ones, his essay spotlighted on national television. It was a time when reactionary forces hunted scapegoats. There he was. Big, gay, T-cell count in the toilet. Positively, absolutely, willfully offensive.

An organization named the American Family Association, headed by the Reverend Donald Wildmon, discovered that the NEA was funding a show of Wojnarowicz's in Normal, Illinois: *Tongues of Flame*.

The decision to have the show was made well in advance of the controversy at Artists Space. The money was out the door. There was no going back.

The show's catalogue made its way into Wildmon's grubby hands.

In response, he authored his own pamphlet entitled "Your Tax Dollars Helped Pay for These 'Works of Art.'" Within this well-reasoned publication, Wildmon included slight details from Wojnarowicz's work, cherry-picked to highlight any intimation of homosexuality or drug use.

Thousands of these pamphlets were mailed to every member of Congress and media outlets.

Instant furor. Instant controversy. Instant scandal. Wojnarowicz grew more famous, the subject of further news reporting.

Remember, too, reader, that we speak of one of the East Village's own. For all of its virtues, the transgressive art scene was not a breeding ground for individuals with great social facility. No one ever accused Nick Zedd of oozing politesse and great linguistic facility.

Wojnarowicz was different.

So when confronted by this very unusual situation, he did the least expected thing. He sued Wildmon and the American Family Association. Even more unexpectedly, he won his case, blocking publication of the pamphlet. Though he earned only $1 in damages, the victory stood.

His fame grew. More news coverage. Constant media. Here, too, he shone. Wojnarowicz could articulate himself without giving ground, could speak of his work in such a way as to get across the sense that he'd done nothing wrong, that his artistic endeavors were legitimate pursuits.

All the while, the man was dying. His only recourse was to swallow AZT pills and hope that the treatment would not be worse than the disease. His body rebelling, he was out in the media, fighting the good fight that a thousand others should have fought before him.

I'd read articles in the *Times,* in the *Village Voice,* in the trades, in magazines, watched PBS, listened to NPR. I kept myself aware of the man, had thought of reaching out. He was only six blocks away. Yet I was intimidated. By his articulation, by his disease, by the situation. I've no small opinion of my own self, but what could Adeline say to Wojnarowicz?

An old friend from Parsons, a Turkish blackguard named Nayip Otağalu, had years earlier developed a friendship with the artist. Of its nature, I cannot speak. Nayip conveyed one or two things about Wojnarowicz, details both gossipy and humanizing, before the Turk disappeared after our sophomore year, never reemerging from the wilds of summer break. Presumably stuck forever in Gaziantep.

Jon knew Wojnarowicz, but theirs was no friendship. Sometime in the early '80s, they'd gotten into a fistfight outside of the Pyramid Club. Jon's band of the moment, Ligature Lycanthropee, was on the same lineup as 3 Teens Kill 4, Wojnarowciz's avant-experimental group. There was an argument about allocated stage time. From the way Jon spoke of the incident, I received the unmistakable impression that the fisticuffs had not ended in his favor.

Being old hands of the East Village, they had many friends in common. Word drifted in through Jon about the artist's condition, about the ups and downs of his health.

Wojnarowicz was getting sicker. People wondered how much longer he would live. Feeling the limits of time, I inquired if Jon couldn't perhaps arrange a meeting.

The shrill sound of our telephone.

I'd been reading a crumbling mass-market edition of *Ride the Pink Horse* by Dorothy B. Hughes. One of Baby's many books. Despite my aversion to the mystery genre and its hardboiled offspring, I found the title wonderfully suggestive.

More important, I owed *Playboy* a cartoon of George Bush driving a Jeep Cherokee through an urban ghetto. I was desperate in my procrastination, so there I was, darlings, reading about Sailor in Santa Fe at the time of fiesta, of burning Zozobra.

I stood and gazed deep into the answering machine. The Mickey Mouse phone depicted the character as he existed in the black-and-white cartoons of his origin. Pie-cut eyes and two-button shorts.

The machine picked up. Jon. "Adeline, are you there?"

"Dear boy, here I am," said I, lifting the receiver from the Mouse's clutches. "Where are you?"

"Never mind," he said. "Do you want to meet Wojnarowicz?"

Funny hearing the name pronounced aloud, radically different than how it read in my mind.

"Indubitably," said I.

"Don't say I never did nothing for you," said Jon. "You can meet him tonight at 7 pm. He lives above the theater at 12th and Second."

"I'm aware of his location," I said. "Thankee kindly."

Anxiety and wonderment. I had nothing to say. Would I simply sit and stare, hoping that the artist would perform like an animal desperate for a handful of peanuts? Worse yet, what to wear?

When the hour came, I'd passed through several sets of clothing before choosing a modest black ensemble. Of late, all of my outfits were modest black ensembles. I'd gone conservative, retiring the hair dye and ripped stockings. No longer did I dress like a psychedelic kaleidoscope. I could pass as a legal assistant, running from deposition to deposition, plagued by romantic anxieties that brimmed over whenever the senior partner failed to telephone after our latest indiscretion.

I walked up Second Avenue. I looked at Kevin's building, attempting to peer with X-ray vision through the brick and mortar. Could he possibly have kept the same place? Did the collected works of Kilgore Trout remain his fixed point of reference?

It was only several weeks earlier that they'd reopened the Second Avenue Theater as a movie house. I somehow had convinced Baby and Erik to attend a screening of *Scenes from a Mall* in the main auditorium, a turn-of-the-century Yiddish theater with an unspeakably beautiful ceiling. I retained no memory of the film other than its action taking place in the monolithic Beverly Center, a mall in Los Angeles that looked as if it'd been designed by Albert Speer, and in the parking lot of which I'd once given George Whitney a handjob.

The marquee read: DEFENDING YOUR LIFE, FANTASIA, SUPERSTAR: THE LIFE AND TIMES OF ANDY WARHOL, MR & MRS BRIDGE, MR JOHNSON, THE BRITISH ANIMATION FESTIVAL.

At the entrance to the apartments, a bespectacled older gentleman with brown hair stood before the door. I thought nothing of him until I examined the buzzers, attempting to figure out which button to press.

"Are you Adeline?" he asked.

"I am," I said.

"I'm sorry you had to come over like this," he said, "but David's too sick to see you. He's really sorry but he just can't do it."

"I understand completely," I said. "Tell him that I said hello. Tell him that he's in my very deepest."

"I will," said the man. He let himself into the building. I stood, waiting, thinking that perhaps he'd come back down and inform me that it'd all been a gaudy prank, a test to see if I were worthy. *Your patience,* he might say, *is indeed a virtue.*

Five minutes expired. It was just about the worst feeling that I've ever had. The finality of it, I suppose, the sense that I would never be asked back. I hate being excluded.

I did what I've always done when there ain't no place in this world for me anymore. I went to the movies. *Superstar: The Life and Times of Andy Warhol.*

Très cliché seeing a flicker about one New York artist after being rejected by another, but the other films were so dreadful. Even *Fantasia*. Nouveau riche Walt Disney meets Stravinsky. Bleeghh.

I watched the full hour and a half of Warhol, a collection of talking heads and contemporary footage, adding up to a beaucoup banal portrait of the man and his coterie of speed-freak drag queens.

I didn't learn a single thing, but the shots of his digs invariably included imagery of 31 Union Square West, which jumpstarted a round of contemplation about our old Bank of the Metropolis, and the day that Warhol had died, standing outside in the street, crying about Mother. All of those people congregating outside of a building that the man hadn't used for years. Human variety, says I to myself, will never cease to amaze you.

I walked back down Second Avenue, passing the Kiev, and then passing 6th Street. I couldn't stomach going home and telling Baby my sorry tale, nor could I possibly telephone Jon and inform him that his efforts were for naught. That I'd been robbed by a disease.

Don't you know that it was sheer selfishness? If I felt like this for no reason other than being told no, then what was life like for Wojnarowicz? He was thirty-three years old and every day inched him closer to the coffin.

Who knew how many were like him? Thousands? Millions? Tens of thousands withering across the five boroughs, driven insane by poison disguised as medicine consumed from a fear of doing nothing. We hid the sick in hospital beds, in sequestered apartments, in houses, in the poorest neighborhoods. I wanted to build a fire on the roof of every building where a hapless soul was consumed by the disease. The city would light up, ablaze, the funeral pyre of a culture.

All those sad people. I imagine that most are dead now.

I landed across the street from 84 Second Avenue. DRESS SUITS TO HIRE. Helen Sopolsky.

The humiliation of the human experience, of being trapped within a body. There was no good way to die. That filthy mannequin with its rotting tuxedo, the fashion getting more baroque with every year. The real artists of New York were not Warhol nor Wojnarowicz, but the unknown relatives of Helen Sopolsky.

I always imaginated that I would be one of the lucky few who received spiritual visitation from the building, one of the people who saw a ghost darting back and forth behind the mannequin. It didn't happen. It still hasn't.

JUNE 1991

Stacie Visits New York

S tacie had telephoned the morning after cessation of U.S. hostilities in the Persian Gulf. Operation Desert Storm was over.

Led by President George Herbert Walker Bush, this military escapade was directed against the Iraqi dictator, Saddam Hussein, who'd invaded the Arabian country of Kuwait.

Yours truly was one of the very first Americans to hear about Hussein's invasion. I'd been up all night, working on a problematic illustration, with the television droning a rerun of Quincy Jones hosting *Saturday Night Live* when the screen went solid blue, reading only the words SPECIAL NEWS BULLETIN.

Coming in the middle of a comedy program known for its satire of contemporary affairs, I assumed that I was watching a very poor gag, but soon realized that this was legitimate product. No images, only the lone voice of whoever was hanging around the studio at 12:45 am, announcing the Iraqi invasion of Kuwait.

Stacie said that she had an empty month at the beginning of the summer and inquired whether she might not stay with us for a week. I said, why, yes, honey child, you may.

Televisions and radios and newspapers crowed about American military superiority, but it hadn't been a Good War where all the citizens buckled down under the weight of collective sacrifice. It wasn't even a Vietnam, with the American poor and dispossessed mangled by freedom fighters. The war was a video game in real time on a global scale, in which we unleashed billions of dollars of weaponry on a bunch of ill-educated Arabs.

These battles were massively unpopular around our neighborhood. Gutter punks and hippies ran in the streets, arms interlocked, shouting, "No blood for oil!" Other protests occurred, simultaneously, spontaneously. In New York, in the Bay Area, in cities across the country.

Each eruption demonstrated the hopeless delusions of the American political left.

In general, The Power Mongers paid zero mind to the shrill ululations of San Francisco faggots on the topics about which, it may be assumed, the San Francisco faggots possessed some degree of expertise. Like a decade of dead gay men. Why then would our Dark Masters suddenly muster two fucks of a feather regarding a subject about which, it may be assumed, the San Francisco faggots knew nothing?

Outside of America's liberal hotbeds, the country was transfixed by a creeping jingoism. The great unwashed masses proudly wore t-shirts that read DESERT STORM and BONK BONKS SADDAM HUSSEIN and IT'S NOT OVER TILL STORMING NORMAN SCHWARZKOPF SAYS IT'S OVER! and BE A PATRIOT, SUPPORT YOUR SCUDBUSTERS!

The bloody affair lasted four months before the military ran out of Arabs to turn into charred meat. By Stacie's arrival, the Gulf War was as faint as memories of last Sunday's dinner. The sole visible remnants were the tattered remnants of yellow ribbons, syphilitic chancres that had erupted when the fever ran its hottest, symbols of support for the troops that now frayed under the effects of weather and air pollution.

Stacie had never been to New York, a happenstance that she neglected to mention before her flight. Had I known, I would have met the lass at her terminal gate. As it was, I simply gave her directions regarding the subway, telling her which trains to take and to where.

The girl managed, arriving on 7th Street with jumbo-size luggage in tow, hollering my name from the pavement. I thrust my head out of our window.

"I'll be right down," I said.

"Hurry!" she cried. "I've got to pee!"

Some brute had left an empty cardboard box on the second flight of stairs. I tripped over it, but caught my balance before I brained myself against the wall. I threw open the front door. Stacie and I hugged.

"The toilet is the far closet," I said. "You have to wash your hands in the kitchen sink."

"Ew," she said.

She asked if she might lie down. I stationed her in my boudoir. She promptly fell asleep.

I'd put Baby on notice that his presence was expected, demanding that he come home as soon as possible. I had no idea what to do with this creature who'd washed ashore. The reappearance of another old face from the Californy past was the absolute least of my desires.

I sat at our kitchen table, cobbling together work. The locks turned.

"Where's Stacie?" Baby asked.

"Sleeping," I said. "How's life?"

"Classes, boyfriend, films, literature, writing. The five pillars."

"As salaam alaikum." I asked, "What do we do with her?"

"I have no idea. I'm practically a hermit. Ask what she wants when she wakes up."

"Oh, Baby," I said. "You're no help at all."

Not long after he closed his bedroom door, the melodic pounding of Baby's typewriter filled the apartment. When first we met, Baby typed with two fingers, but over the years he'd developed fluidity on the keys. The sound was like horses running across sand, like an earthquake, like waves crashing, like a visitation of Neptune.

Stacie emerged, bleary eyed, yawning. "What's that noise?"

"Baby," I said.

"He's home?"

"Through there," I said, nodding at his door.

"Baby!" she cried, rushing into his room. Their shadows, on the wall, merged into an exaggerated hug. I wondered if Baby was happy to see Stacie, or if it were pantomime. That boy never could say no.

I reclaimed my bedroom and managed about twenty minutes of work before Baby and Stacie interrupted me.

"Change your clothes," said Stacie. "We're going out!"

"What's wrong with what I'm wearing?" I asked.

"We're going to Limelight," said Baby.

"Must we?"

"Baby says it's, like, the best," said Stacie.

If there was any obvious reason to applaud the influence of Erik, Baby's new beau, it was how quickly he'd diminished Baby's interest in Michael Alig. It'd been over eight months since the last foray into clubland.

Baby donned an uncouth approximation of what he thought the kids might be wearing, squeezing into a pair of silver pants and a shimmering shirt made from bargain-basement sequins.

I refused to change. My options were looking like a legal assistant or looking like a legal assistant desperate to assimilate within club culture.

We walked. I told Stacie about Jon. Baby told her about Erik. We asked Stacie if she had anyone in her life. "There was this one guy, but you know, he turned out to be a fucking jerk," she said. Following the inevitable breakup, she'd applied to graduate school and entered the philosophy PhD program at UC Irvine. She'd spent the last two years reading.

The doorman at Limelight recognized Baby but turned up his nose at mi amigo's reappearance. Baby's outfit was hopelessly out of date, having left the fast lane. All the bright young ones now wore outfits of significant complexity and expense. Baby looked as relevant as a middle-aged man in a leisure suit.

Stacie had no problem. No capitalist ever turns down a half-naked woman. Only age devalues the currency of human flesh.

"Now I could let you in," said the doorman to Baby, "on the basis of who you were. But the question is, who are you now? The distance between here and there can be very small or it can be the longest trip of your life. How should I know? And anyway, you're shedding sequins."

"My God," I said, growing sick of the argument. "Let him in. You will in the end. What's the point of this? Open the goddamned door."

"Okay," said the doorman. "He can go in, but you can't. Not dressed like that."

"Why the hell can't she?" asked Baby.

"She looks like a cop," said the doorman.

Baby turned to me. His eyes scanned over my outfit, focusing on the hem of my skirt.

"You two go," I said. "I must work."

"But I came here to see you," said Stacie.

"We'll reminisce on the morrow," I said. "Baby is a much better choice for nightlife. I'm simply boring after dark."

One hopes that others will protest when one asks to be left behind. Yet it was but a single strophe and antistrophe before Baby and Stacie disappeared within the church walls.

The doorman said, "You're really very pretty, you know, but you've got to do something about those clothes. You look like you're from Staten Island."

"Dear boy, what a coincidence," I said. "I am from Staten Island."

"Too bad," he said. "The worst scumbags come from Staten Island."

"You know what they say, don't you?"

"No," said the doorman.

"And you never will," I said, twisting on my heels and sauntering off into the night.

I hailed a cab. The driver was Armenian. It was like being back in Los Angeles.

In the humble experience of yours truly, cabdrivers the world over make a habit of flirting with the hapless young women who pour themselves into taxis. I was waiting for it.

Yet Papik Topalian expressed no interest. I gave him my address. We traveled in silence, catching a Zen moment of Manhattan traffic, one of the beautiful bursts that occur only under the cloud of darkness, when the streets are empty of cars and a vehicle can pass through multiple intersections with nary a hesitation. The green lights are like beacons that call one forward. Faster! Faster!

New York appears its best when one is in transit. Leaving the city, entering it, or simply riding within its confines. These are its best moments.

Our apartment came as purest relief. What had happened over these years? Why was I dressing like a legal assistant? Why was I so pleased to avoid a party?

Perhaps, said I to meself, you should cultivate stupidity as your new hobby. Perhaps you should become one of those horrible people trapped in perpetual adolescence, delighted to bounce up and down in dingy spaces, clapping your hands, listening to atrocious music and smiling like an infant feasting on applesauce. Wouldn't that be the bee's knees? Wouldn't that be divine?

I checked Baby's room to see if he had any cannabis. He hadn't. How boring he'd become! Almost as bad as yours truly. Perhaps the common denominator was being in a relationship.

I collapsed into my bed. The Captain sat on my chest, purring with the full force of his oversized body. I fixated upon the ceiling, stared beyond it, thinking about Stacie. Her urchin face ripped me right back to Los Angeles. Of all my friends from home, only she had met Emil. I couldn't think of a single soul besides Stacie and blood relations who could testify that my brother too lived. I imagined his life if he hadn't destroyed himself by leaping into the Arroyo Seco. He could have been happy, I was sure, if only he'd let himself. It wasn't that my own life was a crucible of joy. The only important thing I'd learned from New York City was to shape one's perceptions of life's inevitable cruelty. People with blazing disabilities lived reasonably pleasant lives. Cripples who loved every day of their existence. Why not me? Why not Emil?

Stacie roused me from sleep at 5 am, crawling into my bed. She stank of bitter stale sweat and cigarettes and alcohol. A human perfume permeating every square inch of Limelight. The scent of depravity. "Ugh," I moaned, "comport yourself with some decency."

"Push over," she said, shoving me.

"Where's Baby?" I asked.

"Passed out in, like, his room, I guess," said Stacie. "He did a lot of drugs. Me too."

"No after-hours party?"

"Too tired," she said. "So much jetlag. So much cocaine. Have you ever done Special K?"

"No," I said.

"We did it tonight," she said.

"How was it?" I asked.

"Interesting," she said. "God, you know, we don't have anything, like, you know, Disco 2000 or Limelight in California. I thought we were sophisticated because we grew up on the streets of Hollywood, but shit, we aren't, like, anything, you know? Nothing we have back home is like Disco 2000. You know they have a human freak show at the end of the night, where people get naked for fifty dollars and then this one dude pisses into a bottle and drinks his own pee? And there's this amputee woman who takes off her leg and starts dancing around with it? I was like, 'Baby, how is this fun?' and he was like, 'Stacie, just do another bump and you'll figure it out,' and you know, he was right. It got really fun."

"May we sleep?" I asked. "I'm exhausted."

"Sure," she said. "I hope so, anyway. I might be too high to sleep."

Her tossing kept me awake, long sun-kissed legs kicking against me as she sighed, exasperated, pulling my bedclothes. She ran to the bathroom every forty minutes, her body frantic to flush out unholy toxins.

We didn't sleep until about 8 am. Sheer ruination. I was up by noon.

When the evening hours rolled around, we sat in Baby's bedroom, talking about *Pump Up the Volume,* a movie that, incredibly, all five of us had seen.

Meself, Baby, Erik, Stacie, and Jon. The quintet was thus.

The unusual factor was Jon. He never saw films, especially those made in Hollywood. Especially those starring actors like Christian Slater.

Pump Up the Volume offers the story of an Arizona high school student. Under the *nom de guerre* of Happy Harry Hard-On, he operates his own pirate radio station. He broadcasts tepid social subversion to his classmates. These children of suburbia are bored with their lives, bored with school, bored with America, bored with each other, bored with life. They take to this anonymous unknown broadcaster and his message. Society comes down hard. Teachers, principals, cops, the FCC. Tears and lamentations.

"It's such bullshit," said Jon, sucking down a shot of tequila. "Another bourgeoisie vision of rebellion and youth gone wild."

"Be that as it may," I said, "I liked it."

"You like everything," said Baby.

"She always has," said Stacie.

"Even if one strips away all the terrific clichés and demands of the three-act screenplay, there is something enormously appealing about Christian Slater establishing that radio station in his parents' basement. One doesn't often see that in film, one doesn't often see private worlds, disconnected realities built by outsiders through force of will, constructed with taste and abstention."

"I enjoyed it," said Erik, long brown hair running along his shoulders.

"He also likes everything," said Baby.

"Why'd you like it?" asked Stacie.

Erik was one of those mad people who are fully functional. They maintain jobs and operate in the wider world without difficulty, but their inner lives are overrun with divergent thinking. These people take their sweet time before revealing the full scale of their lunacy, by which point one is sucked into their sphere of influence.

"It's all just Christian allegory, isn't it?" asked Erik. "It's the Crucifixion without the Resurrection. Or maybe it's about Jesus after his return, when he rises from death and is so different. Maybe Happy Harry Hard-On is the resurrected Christ of the 1990s."

"What the hell are you talking about?" asked Baby.

"Think about it," said Erik. "He preaches a message that outrages the power structure. He slums about with the lowest and the worst of society. He performs miracles, heals the suburban soul. His demise is a ritualized slaughter. No one ever listens to me, but it's true, Happy Harry Hard-On is the new Jesus."

"Oh, Erik," I said.

We'd run out of tequila. I ventured into the kitchen, hoping to discover more. Baby followed. I rummaged through our cupboards, looking for remnants of previous debauches.

"We're out," he said. "Drier than a dry county."

"I'll purchase more."

"Wait for me," he said. "I'll go with you."

We left behind Erik and Stacie and Jon.

"What a crew," I said to Baby on the stairs. "What a bunch of misfits."

In the deli, we debated different brands of tequila and vodka before settling on a bottle of each. We went as cheap as possible. The bill came to about $20.

I said good-bye to the man behind the register. I wasn't sure if he'd grown fond of us, but at the very least he must appreciate our faces. He saw us almost every day.

"What in the world do you think Erik was saying? Nuevo Cristo?" I asked.

"I've learned to not anticipate what comes out of Erik's mouth," said Baby. "Should I worry about this Christian Slater thing? What if it's an early warning sign of Evangelicalism?"

Erik was in the kitchen, reading a paperback of *The Yellow Wallpaper*. I worried that he might unfold the story's secret meaning. Another Christian allegory, with Gilman's protagonist as the repressed female psychotic Christ of the nineteenth century.

"Hello," he said.

"Where are Stacie and Jon?" I asked.

"They're still in Baby's room," he said, shrugging towards the open door.

I removed the bottle of tequila. At Baby's door, I heard Stacie talking, saying, "It's, like, okay, what you're talking about, with your music, right, like how it can't fulfill you anymore and how you're wondering, like, if something hasn't changed, like, if you're all fucked in the head because you don't think hardcore can work in the '90s, like, the thrill is gone, right? What you're describing, really, is an experience that Kierkegaard would call the transition from the aesthetic to the ethical, which is, like, this moment when one is forced to choose between good and evil, not in, like, an absolute sense, but is forced to, like, understand that there is a choice and that choice must be made. The aesthetic personality is, like, a passive participant, while the ethical person is an individual who is actively reclaiming their actual, innate sense. Achieving the ethical isn't really about choosing good over evil, but rather like hardening yourself toward the necessity of that choice, okay? And it isn't that the ethical means you can no longer be aesthetic, it just means you're, like, moving up to the next level of experience."

Baby came over and stood behind me.

"God in Heaven," I whispered. "It's like tenth grade all over again. It's like Jon is Ian fucking Covington. Absolute déjà vu."

"You could be right," said Jon. "That's great insight. You seem very wise."

"Who is Ian fucking Covington?" Baby asked.

"He was my boyfriend," I said. "Stacie screwed his brains out."

"I totally understand what's going on," said Stacie. "I've been told I'm very perceptive, especially by, like, really sensitive people. And I can tell you're really really sensitive. You're, like, an artist. I admire artists."

"This isn't the past," said Baby. "You can't repeat the past."

"What do you mean you can't repeat the past?" I asked. "Of course you can."

"It's hard being creative," said Jon.

"Why don't you go in there and say something?" asked Baby.

"I should," I said. "Really, I should. Yet it's a funny old thing, Pooh Bear. I'm not jealous. I've never been jealous about anyone but you."

"And by their fruits ye shall know them," said Baby.

JANUARY 1992

Baby Beats Jon in the Street

Jon screwed out Stacie's brains, really giving her the time, but for many months this tryst was an unrevealed secret that haunted us like Communism or the plot device of a minor Gothic novel.

Their frenzied coupling occurred on the last day of Stacie's visit, a few hours before she hailed a cab and disappeared from our lives.

That very afternoon, I'd arrived home, dropping off books between class and work, and found the dynamic duo. They were, supposedly, waiting for Adeline. They said hello, smiling, innocent, angelic. Flushed faces. The rife humidity of sex hung over the apartment. But what could I say? I hadn't one inch of proof. I couldn't go and smell the sheets, could I?

Months later, on a January night, the universe revealed its fractal nature, sucking me into a fourth-dimensional quantum entanglement with this illicit rendezvous.

I'd come home with the hope of getting some writing done. Unlocking the front door and going inside, I saw Jon's dirty denim jacket over a kitchen chair. Adeline's door was closed. I assumed they were in her bed, busy with their drab vanilla flavor of hetero love.

I started typing, writing, pounding the keys, entrancing myself with the thin wild mercury machine music of my fingers. The story was titled "As Sure as Eggs Is Eggs." It's about an alternate reality, the historical departure point being the British defeat of the colonial rebels during the American War of Rebellion.

No United States, no Constitution, no Bill of Rights. The Louisiana Purchase still happens, but the land transfer occurs as part of the Treaty of Amiens. There is no War of 1812. William Wilberforce and Thomas Clarkson end slavery throughout the Empire, its final abolition occurring in 1833, thereby averting the American Civil War, saving the lives of 600,000 potential soldiers. The brute force of this extra-human capacity mixes with British ingenuity, causing a volatile reaction that sparks a massive scientific and technological revolution. Every major advance of our twentieth century occurs before the death of Queen Victoria.

Which all sounds great, I admit, but there are downsides, too. The English caste system solidifies in the Americas, taking on new and disquieting forms.

By unconscious social agreement, all colonials carry upon their person the freshly laid egg of a chicken. Social distinctions are judged upon the thickness of shell, the quality of color, size, and visual heft.

The shelled accoutrement is a fact of modern life. As part of Her Majesty's social welfare programs, every individual on the dole is issued a bargain-basement chicken, dooming the poor to a lifetime of undersized, yolkless eggs. The upper middle classes are trapped within a cycle of perpetually purchasing new hens, desperate for the latest innovation. New breeds emerge with daily frequency. A secondary market of accessories serves individuals who desire not only luxury but personalization. One key accessory is the mandatory opaque white cube carrying case with self-generated spotlight illumination, highlighting the smoothness of the egg's curve and accentuating speckles.

The North American continent is absolutely lousy with egg knowledge. The Western British Empire is crazy with poultry experts.

I hadn't gotten any further than establishing setting when Adeline's voice shattered the thunder of my typewriter. She sounded positively apoplectic, shouting: —Just get the fuck out! Just get the fuck out! Just get the fuck out! Just get the fuck out! Just get the fuck out!

The front door slammed.

I peeked my head into the kitchen. Adeline stood by the bathtub, face as red as her hair.

—What the hell happened? I asked.

—Oh, not much, she said. Jon merely fucked my childhood best friend.

—What.

—Stacie, she said. He fucked Stacie. When she was visiting.

—What.

—Do you need the photo developed and framed? asked Adeline. Jon screwed out Stacie's brains.

I floated above my physical self, my spirit tethered by an invisible umbilical cord, a silvery ectoplasmic tendril. I watched myself throw open the front door. I watched myself barrel down the stairs.

Jon was walking toward Second Avenue, contemplating his transgressions, only halfway down the block. A book in his right hand, jacket thrown over his left shoulder. He heard my footfall, turned back, saw me and started running. Adeline came outside, shouting, but I was too crazy to understand her words.

He rounded the corner, past the Kiev. I gave chase, bursting through the locked hands of a love-struck couple, shoving the man up against the restaurant.

—You had better run, I shouted. I'm going to hold you down and paint you green.

Jon leapt into Second Ave. I barreled after him, not giving a damn about oncoming traffic. My rage could bend steel, would crumple hoods.

—Leave me alone! he shouted.

—You can't outrun me! You fucking asshole! I set the school records for the fifty- and hundred-yard dashes!

He turned down 6th Street, gaining a frantic burst of speed as he ran past the Indian restaurants, ignoring the Bangladeshi barkers who invited him inside with offers of free wine.

Jon dropped his book and his jacket, hoping to lighten his load, but the jacket tangled in his legs. He crashed against the crumbling pavement, right before the entrance to Shah Bag. He lay dazed, bleeding from a gash across his forehead.

The Christmas lights of Shah Bag lit his body. As part of their business model, all the 6th Street Indian establishments kept these lights hanging year-round. I stood above Jon, thinking that it was interesting how he'd managed to fall into the Xmas penumbra during the only time of year when the illumination was seasonally appropriate.

I picked up the book. A hardcover entitled *Defiant Pose*, authored by Stewart Home.

Jon lifted himself on the flats of his hands, crawling like an infant.

Using *Defiant Pose* as a makeshift weapon, I hit his head with as much strength as I could muster. The book was light, only 167 pages, but the lead vocalist of The Inverted Bloody Crosses had been weakened by his tumble, and was leveled by a modest hardcover debut.

He collapsed into the sidewalk.

A waiter came out of Shah Bag. I'd eaten there several times. The waiter looked at Jon, looked at me, and spat on the ground.

Then there was the time when I beat the living shit out of Jon.

Also, I kept his book.

FEBRUARY 1992

Baby Gets a Letter from Parker Brickley

There was Erik, there was NYU, there was Adeline, and there was my burgeoning career as a writer of science fiction, a literary subgenre that in those days still held some water.

During sophomore year, I'd taken a survey course in La Belle Époque with a professor named Jindrich Zezula. In the last week of the semester, I'd sat down at my typewriter with every intention of finishing my final paper on Émile Zola.

Four hours later, when I stood up, I'd written the first half of an exceptionally dubious short story. Two thousand words of unrefined excrement inflicted upon the English language. I destroyed the evidence.

Others followed. I couldn't stop. Ideas poured out of my head, but writing did not come naturally. Writing was work, writing required an apprenticeship. I spent a year doing little but fucking Erik and shitting out terrible short stories.

After committing twenty-seven of these crimes against humanity, there was a new coherence, an awareness of construction and flow. The language no longer impeded the intent. In my arrogance, I began mailing out manuscripts.

My first sale was to Gardner Dozois at *Isaac Asimov's Science Fiction Magazine*. Entitled "Heroin of the Masses," it was a shamefaced conceptual theft of *The Rise and Fall of Ziggy Stardust and the Spiders from Mars* by David Bowie. By the time that it appeared in print, I couldn't even read it, unwilling to relive its youthful naiveté.

But that's life. Sometimes your parents die in outrageous circumstances that force you to leave town. Sometimes your brother throws himself off the Colorado Bridge in Pasadena, California. And sometimes you make your literary debut with the questionable pop eschatology of an alien singing lead vocals in a post-post-post-post-post-post-post-post-post-post-post-post-post-post-post-post-post-post-post-post-post-post-post glam band, on stage at the Pyramid Club, a book of prophecy in his right hand and a dirty syringe hanging from his cephalic vein.

*

Then there was the time when I was browsing books at the Strand and came across a biography of Johnny Appleseed, a pioneer who seeded apple trees across the American Middle West. In addition to his agricultural efforts, Appleseed was an adherent of Emanuel Swedenborg, a radical free-love mystic who'd ascended to heaven in the eighteenth century and came back to Earth full of saintly knowledge.

I grew up hearing myths about the man who planted trees, but what if all along he'd been sowing a different crop in warmer soils? What if his true purpose was spreading doctrines about the transcendent union with Christ through sexual abandon?

I wrote a story called "The Sun That Sleeps Too Long." It was about a twenty-fourth-century analogue for Swedenborg, a character whom I didn't bother giving a new name. I called him Swedenborg 2.

Like his namesake, Swedenborg 2 ascends to heaven, but the mechanism of his journey is alien abduction. The extraterrestrials probe him. They dissect him. They subject him to stress tests. They torture him. When the aliens exhaust their bevy of abuses, their advanced technology allows them to reconstruct Swedenborg 2's body.

In the process of reconstruction, they implant Swedenborg 2's brain with nano-tech that will allow the aliens to track him through the galaxy. Unfortunately for everyone involved, the implantation is scheduled on the first anniversary of $\Omega\Omega\Omega\Omega\Omega$'s death.

$\Omega\Omega\Omega\Omega\Omega$ was the mate of $\Phi\Phi\Phi\Phi\Phi$. $\Phi\Phi\Phi\Phi\Phi$ is the technician tasked with implanting nanotech in Swedenborg 2's brain. In the hours before the operation, $\Phi\Phi\Phi\Phi\Phi$ gets rip-roaringly drunk. $\Phi\Phi\Phi\Phi\Phi$ botches the job.

Swedenborg 2 returns to earth. He discovers himself capable of performing miracles. He heals the sick. He raises the dead. He turns water into wine. He performs exorcisms on swineyards.

He also can't stop talking. He babbles constantly about the alien abduction, which he has mistaken for Heaven, and establishes a new gospel based on infinite and endless sex. This holy horny glossolalia is another side effect of the implant, crammed into Swedenborg 2's left anterior cingulate cortex, leaving the new messiah in a state of perpetual arousal. His dick becomes a dowsing rod, a holy celestial wand.

He attracts a great number of followers.

At the dawn of the twenty-fifth century, Darius 2C Danko, a Nuevo

Swedenborgian, wanders the galaxy in a clunky spaceship. His mission? To plant space apples and spread the gospel of polymorphous perversity. The narrative follows his peregrinations, working a somewhat heavy-handed allegory about American political figures. I also threw in a nonsense mystical overlay, drawing a parallel between Appleseed and the Greek god Bacchus, finding resonance in the spread of vegetation and wild love.

I submitted the story to *The Magazine of Fantasy and Science Fiction*. The editor, Edward L. Ferman, sent a letter of acceptance, informing me that my work would appear in the July 1991 edition. Months later, I received a package containing a check and my contributor's copies.

As far as these things go, the cover illustration was not a disaster. A half-translucent panther's head hovered over a mountain landscape. I opened to the table of contents. There I was, between "Autumn Mist" by Nancy Springer and "The Pan Man" by Elizabeth Engstrom.

They'd changed my title.

I was the proud author of "Johnny Cyberseed."

Regardless of this abuse, people loved the story. The magazine forwarded complimentary letters, kind words from the readers. Their cloying language made me decide that most of my correspondents were very lonely. Nice, but lonely.

In February, a note came from Parker Brickley. A literary agent working at William Morris, he'd been trying to find my phone number. But that was impossible. I was invisible East Village scum living under one pseudonym and writing under another.

Brickley's office was uptown. I called him. He invited me to lunch.

That simple, that easy. All you need do was write. Even if the editors changed your titles. Even if the world believed you responsible for "Johnny Cyberseed."

Life was going well. Too well. I'd forgotten that human existence is a waveform moving up and down through time and space, and that fortune's wheel never stops turning. Good or ill, there's always change coming.

MARCH 1992

Patrick Geoffrois

Baby, said Adeline, don't you know that I bumped into Jon on First Avenue? The mere sight of his face drove me to infuriation, so I gathered some of my menstrual blood and threw it at him.

—You threw your period at your ex-boyfriend? I asked.

—Yes, she said. But I simply fell short, my volley landing at his feet. Jon stood there, not comprehending what I'd done. I told him exactly what had happened. I told him that I had aimed for his stupid face.

—How is that even possible? I thought you used organic cloth.

—Darling, don't you know that I switched to the Keeper months ago? I bought mine at Magickal Childe.

—I had no idea.

—It's much more efficient. I've been using my blood to feed the plants.

Following the dissolution of her affair with Jon de Lee, Adeline had taken up new hobbies. She'd reverted out of her schoolmarm outfits and become, as best I could tell, a regressed punk. She dyed her hair purple, shaved the sides of her head, and was now wearing unfortunate amounts of denim. There was a lot of talk about anarchism as a viable political philosophy. She hid away her Steeleye Span records and the *You Made Me Realize* EP, and took up early punk like *(I'm) Stranded* by The Saints and the X-Ray Spex's *Germfree Adolescents*.

The album that she played most was *Legacy of Brutality* by The Misfits. I'd been with her when she purchased it. Had I known what it meant, I could have stopped her.

But I didn't know that I was about to live through months of brutish New Jersey ambition, courtesy of Glenn Danzig né Azalone. I can't estimate how many needles Adeline destroyed listening to that record, but I know exactly how much of my patience she ruined. All of it.

In terms of her social life, she fell in with a fucked-up Frenchman named Patrick Geoffrois, a street hustler who kept a table outside of

Twardoski Travel on St. Mark's. He'd been a fixture for years, telling people's fortunes, reading palms and spreading the Thoth tarot.

Geoffrois was one of those street characters who cannot be ignored, a gaunt ghoul with piercing blue eyes, no teeth, slicked-back blond hair hanging to his shoulders, black clothes accessorized with hokey jewelry like pentagrams and, irony of ironies, inverted crosses.

Adeline made his acquaintance in the same way that she made all of her bad decisions, via a fixation that was part intellectual, part emotional, entirely crazy.

In February, the man's face had appeared on the cover of *Newsday,* a cheesy picture in which he held a sword's pommel over his left eye. Beneath this grim visage was the headline: CULT PROBE WIDENS.

It went back to Daniel Rakowitz. Although two years had passed, the Manhattan District Attorney's office and the NYPD's Occult Crimes Unit had concluded that Rakowitz murdered Monika Beerle on the order of Geoffrois, as a ritualistic human sacrifice to Choronzon or Duke Focalor. Satanic panic done New York style, with leaks to the press and grandstanding detectives discoursing on demonism in Far Rockaway accents.

No one disputed that Geoffrois was an occultist. But there's occultism and there's occultism.

Anyone who'd been on the Lower East Side for more than two weeks knew Geoffrois for what he was. A huckster, a conman, another pathetic street performer trying to earn his bread. If he controlled a coven, and if he could routinely summon supernatural forces, why would he waste years freezing and begging on St. Mark's?

When Adeline saw the cover of *Newsday,* she walked a block over and encountered the Frenchman at his folding table, sitting where he always sat, doing as he'd always done. She never detailed the exact nature of their first conversation.

I'll hazard a guess.

A recovering junky magician speaking in his slightly accented English about whatever hocus pocus floated in the deep recesses of his brain, dismissing Rakowitz as a hanger-on. Adeline going on about Dress Suits to Hire and the violence inherent in the urban experience, attempting to delve into New York's random cruelty and murder, asking the self-styled black magician for help discerning the hidden meanings of coincidence.

Adeline started visiting Geoffrois's apartment on 11th Street, where he lived with his wife and her young daughter. My roommate returned from these salons with a head full of bizarre ideas about the universe's mystical undercurrents. She began reading books by Aleister Crowley. *Diary of a Drug Fiend. Magick in Theory and Practice.*

Out of morbid curiosity, I opened her copy of *The Book of the Law*. It heralded the Dawn of a New Aeon through Egyptian sex Magick.

Remembering Geoffrois's entrée into tabloid media, I noted one section in which Crowley suggests that Human Sacrifice is a Necessary Act for the Achievement of One's own Will. It was that kind of book, one in which words underwent an enforced capitalization. There was no will in Crowley. There was only Will. He was that kind of Writer.

If Adeline's interest appears silly, what else could she do? Throw herself into a series of punishing one-night stands? Win back her cheating boyfriend?

MARCH 1992

Baby and Erik See *Kiss Me Deadly*

Theatre 80 was showing *Kiss Me Deadly*, a 1955 film directed by Robert Aldrich. I invited Adeline and Erik. He accepted. She declined.

—Why, Baby, she said, don't you think that I've seen it a million times? It's the very best film about Los Angeles! Keep an eye out for the heavy. His name was Albert Dekker. He's one of those très tragique Hollywood stories of a motion picture star dying in distressed circumstances. I won't tell you how it happened until you see the film, otherwise you'll spend the whole time thinking about his death, leaving you simply unable to concentrate. And don't you know that it's the best American film of the 1950s? I'd feel oh so terrible if I removed you from the narrative.

Adapted from an execrable novel by Mickey Spillane, *Kiss Me Deadly* stars Ralph Meeker as Mike Hammer. The film opens with Meeker in his car, nearly running over a deranged female hitchhiker. She's young, naked, and D-list beautiful. A convoluted plot spills out, oozing with the grimy trappings of the noir.

The real thrust is in the presentation of character, focusing on the twin protagonists of Mike Hammer and the city of Los Angeles. Hammer comes off as the world's most amoral creep, the noir antihero taken to its termination point. A scuzzball private detective who uses his secretary, with whom he has sexual relations, as bait for wayward husbands in divorce cases.

Los Angeles is Hammer's mirror. Every dusty nook and cranny is explored, every boardinghouse and car garage. The film was shot on location. The dialogue provided exact addresses.

Albert Dekker plays an older doctor of dubious character. Whenever he was on screen, I wondered about his death.

The lights came up. Erik and I walked to the Yaffa Café, taking a table within its red velour cave. I thought about Ralph Meeker, about the knowingness of his big dumb face.

I lowered my menu and looked at our fellow patrons. They were so goth. Tables filled with kids from the outer boroughs and Long Island, done up in black clothes, faces smeared with kohl and greasy lipstick, black nail-polished fingers that dipped pita bread into piles of hummus.

—This place is lousy with spooky kids, I said.

—Don't be negative, said Erik.

Our waitress seemed stoned. I was sure that she got our order wrong, but I didn't bother correcting her.

—You loved the movie, said Erik.

—Who wouldn't? I asked.

—I'm tired of nihilism, said Erik. It's so done. Our culture has been stuck in this miserable loop for the last forty years. Maybe I'm too Aquarian, but I think these stories we keep telling ourselves are totally wrong. We're not in a death spiral. Things keep getting better, but everyone pretends like they're worse. *Kiss Me Deadly* is a film about how you have to be afraid of everything. About how the world is going to end at any minute through the stupidity and meanness of people. Why aren't there any films about how people are good?

—Probably because most people aren't.

—That's bullshit, said Erik. How many bad people have you actually met? Two? Three? Out of how many thousands? Most people are good. Most people value other people. We waste our lives only paying attention to the wrong ones, to the handful who don't honor the social contract. I'm not complaining. I'm just tired of squalid movies and squalid books, and I'm tired of being told that the planet's on the verge of its own doom. I believe in humanity, I believe in our future, I believe that we'll figure it out. I believe we'll be here in ten thousand years, not much worse for wear.

At least he wasn't talking about Jesus.

I couldn't help but think that we were a terrible match. He was too good. Maybe I'd been in New York too long. Maybe the farm disabuses a person from any illusion about life's sacredness. How could a person look at human history and feel anything like optimism? Our planet was a whirling mudball infested with insignificant creatures that evolution had driven to the heights of cruelty.

On the other hand, I sat in a basement café in the world's most interesting city, surrounded by kids dressed like they'd just fucked Bela Lugosi. My beautiful boyfriend's countenance shining high with dreams of human goodness.

I knew enough not to let the moment escape. If I could have that spasm of happiness, maybe there was hope. Maybe there was a way that we wouldn't destroy the planet. Maybe Erik was right. I hope so. I still do. I always hope that Erik is right.

He escorted me home, but couldn't spend the night. He was starting a new job in Midtown. He'd been bouncing between offices for years, quitting every sixteen months. He'd been hired by a group of lawyers.

Before we kissed, we looked up and down the street. An unfortunate side effect of living so near McSorley's. For 138 years, the bar had attracted a certain kind of clientele. I wasn't worried about being bashed, but I'd rather not beat a drunk senseless when all I wanted was a goodnight embrace.

Adeline was in the kitchen, cooking ramen noodles and boiling eggs. Another new habit. I'd known her seven years and never seen her buy groceries.

—Baby, she said. Did you love it?

—It knocked me out.

—Do you want to hear about Albert Dekker?

—Sure, I said.

—They found him on Normandie, between Hollywood and Franklin. His fiancé hadn't heard from him in a few days. She did as people do in these situations. She contrived a way into his apartment. When she got inside, she discovered Dekker's naked corpse kneeling in the bathtub. A noose is tied around his neck and is affixed to the shower rod. Leather belts restrain his body. He's handcuffed. Someone's taken lipstick and written all over his body. 'Whip' and 'Make me suck' and 'cocksucker.' Someone drew a vagina on his stomach. He'd been there a few days. Putrefaction had set in. There were valuables missing. And do you know the most amazing thing? Even with all of that, the death was ruled accidental. A possible suicide.

APRIL 1992

More Patrick Geoffrois and His Cacophony

I was deep in Grove Press's unfortunately idiomatic translation of Albertine Sarrazin's *Astragal* when someone cried Adeline's name. We'd lived in the same building since 1987. The landlord had yet to install a buzzer.

She ran downstairs then barreled back up. Her boots stomped the holy hell out of our unpolished kitchen floor. She knocked on my bedroom door.

—Yeah? I asked.

—Baby, Patrick's outside. Will you walk with us?

—I'll pass, I said.

—Young man, she said, don't dismiss this out of hand. You simply have no idea what kind of experience you'll be missing. You're acting like a bigot. Don't close that beautiful American mind.

Experience. The magic word. I operated from a naked and foolish belief that each experience of the writer's life would recycle into the work. The dreck and stupidity of humanity undergoing an alchemical conversion into the gold of literature. If Adeline wanted me to walk with the sorcerer, then even that could be transmuted.

Geoffrois was on the sidewalk, facing our building, leaning against a parked car. His gaunt face like a death mask lit by streetlight, ringed with the white flow of his hair, his wardrobe its usual sable. His eight points of interest dominated by gaudy jewelry.

—Patrick, said Adeline, this is Baby.

—I too have a baby, he said. But my woman and my child are not home. I thought I would show Adeline the demonic currents running through the East Village.

—I've seen you tell fortunes on St. Mark's, I said, with your finger in the palms of creeps from Jersey.

—Even pigs have a destiny, said Patrick Geoffrois. It may be the slaughterhouse, but it remains a destiny.

Geoffrois launched off the car, heading east. Adeline matched his stride.

As the evening's designated third wheel, I trailed behind, affording myself the opportunity to observe the man's frailty. His clothes sagged over his body. A true devotee of Ulysses S. Grant.

Their conversation went beyond my comprehension. Something about Crowley and the Star Ruby Ritual. I listened, wanting to understand, but the details proved elusive.

Geoffrois spoke at length about the necessity of preparing the ceremonial chamber, about the importance of set and setting in implementing the science of change.

Adeline took this seriously, responding in kind, her voice imbued with gravity. It came to me that I had no idea whether or not Adeline believed in God.

An American moment. You can know someone's outward personality better than you know your own but still lack any clear sense of their inner beliefs. There is no way of knowing if they hope for an intangible being that permeates infinity with its eternity.

Geoffrois yelled: —Witches will be released upon New York! Men and women will die, animals will come back to life. Penises carved of olive wood will propagate the wisdom of Satan. Samurais of all kinds should stay put in Brooklyn! Giant green flies will come out of the mouths of children.

—What are you talking about? I asked.

—The fate of New York, he said. The vengeance that it will suffer.

—Hasn't the city suffered enough?

—It hasn't yet begun to suffer, said Geoffrois. The suffering that the city knows is like a drop in the ocean. A great plague will come upon it, and heretics will beat stockbrokers with sorghum and fennel, and the stalks will burn like hot irons.

He babbled all the way down 7th Street, pausing only before the McKinley Apartments. Staring into the light well that split the building's two wings, Geoffrois claimed that its negative space was an intentional representation of *Le Maison Dieu*, or The Tower, the sixteenth trump card in the Major Arcana. New York, he said, is a city with too many towers. Ruin will befall them. Always beware The Tower when it is pulled in a reading. It is the most sinister of omens.

We crossed Avenue A. The park was closed, encased within eight-foot-tall chain-link fences, the result of a riot that had taken place on Memorial Day.

This most recent outburst of popular dissent wasn't nearly as severe as the one that had destroyed Adeline's ability to think about city life, but it adhered to genre conventions. Fires in the streets, bottles thrown, wild eyed nudist radicals screaming about the New World Order, dumpsters serving as barricades.

The municipal authorities became convinced that the very topography of Tompkins Square was desperately wrong. They suspected that its individual parts comprised the gears of a great machine which deranged the human mind into a fervor against civilization. The holy reliquaries of Robert Moses transmitting out energies of chaos.

A month after the Memorial Day riot, several hundred cops secured the park's perimeter while the bells of St. Brigid's pealed. The homeless went out, fences went up. Renovations announced, with no fixed date of completion.

The first act of destruction was visited upon the band shell, crushed into nothingness. They'd painted over Billie Holiday two years after I moved to the city, but I imagined that she went to dust with strains of "Strange Fruit" on her crudely rendered lips.

A key component of the park's transformation was the establishment of a constant police presence. Tompkins Square was under guard twenty-four hours of each day. But this was the East Village. The first few months were pure show. Cops making a general demonstration of force for media and the mayor, followed by the inevitable diminishing of resources and interest.

Breaches appeared along the chain-linked perimeter. These entrances did not appeal to the anarchists. Sneaking into the park offered no political theater. Why bother if you lacked an audience?

Adeline and Geoffrois scrambled through a hole along 7th Street. I crouched down and went inside, hoping that I wouldn't snag my clothes.

Geoffrois stumbled off. I was looking for the empty space where the band shell had been. Passing through the rubble, I considered it a lesson in controlling dissent. Create symbolic distractions for the vocal contingents fixated on imagery. Then destroy the symbol. Ignore the content.

Geoffrois and Adeline ran beneath the brick portico near 10th Street, stopping beside a monument that looked like an oversized headstone. Its purpose had been vandalized away. Graffiti rendered the inscriptions illegible. Its water spout, a lion's head, had been broken off and stolen. The basin blown apart by fireworks.

—This is the most mystical object in New York, said Geoffrois. It was erected in memory of a disaster, of the *General Slocum*. A passenger ship that caught fire. One thousand dead. That's the cover story, a lie designed to hide occulted knowledge. This stele sits at the intersection of at least five different ley lines that power the city's economic energies. This is the heart of all New York's money!

—Why does it look like shit? I asked.

—The secrets of ages were with the keepers of flame. When Churchill extinguished the flames, the knowledge was forgotten. Only the adept can know the truth. If this memorial disappears, then so too disappears the whole of New York's economic prowess. Good-bye, Wall Street. Good-bye, Dow Jones Industrial Average. This is why squirrels and birds congregate at its base. They sense its power. Animals are mental states. I've personally inhabited the body of a bird and my eyes were seeing through its eyes. I saw my double and I was not dead.

He ran from us, toward Avenue A.

—Isn't he simply fascinating? asked Adeline.

—I can say with honesty that I am amazed.

I could've been writing. I could've been giving my boyfriend the time. Instead I was chasing a necromancer through an abandoned park.

I'd spent too much of my life in New York, too much time interacting with its street people, with its lunatics, its mad ones, its charlatans, its would-be revolutionaries. I remember when I could be held rapt by any street preacher with a grievance against Ronald Reagan. But I knew now that none of it amounted to anything. It was all substance abuse, underlying emotional problems, and enforced commitment at Bellevue.

I found them beneath the graffiti-covered canopy of the Temperance Fountain, the word CHARITY above them, the zinc statue with her missing arms like the crippled goddess of a forgotten pantheon. Geoffrois stood over the fountain, hands extended, fingers spread. Beneath thick hooded eyelids, his eyes rolled white.

—He's about to cast a spell, whispered Adeline. He needs absolute concentration.

—A spell? Really?

—Don't concern yourself, she whispered. Nothing happens. Nothing ever happens. It's about the psychological transformation of the self.

Geoffrois grunted and threw his arms up over his head. He spread his legs and thrust back his head, assuming the shape of an X. He shouted. I worried about the volume. After all, we were surrounded by the cops.

He lowered his arms over the bowl.

—Body of fire, body of light, he said. This is how we can describe the astral body. Egyptian gods live in the astral plane. We can also find symbols and alchemists there. With the body of light, we can travel anywhere. Everything is possible. Spirit of fire, remember! Gibil, spirit of fire, remember! Gibra, spirit of flames, remember! Oh god of fire, mighty son of Anu, the most terrifying among your brothers, show yourself! Appear, oh god of fire, Gibil in all your majesty and devour all of my enemies! Appear, oh god of fire, Girra in all your might and burn the sorcerers that persecute me! GIBIL GASHRU UMUNA YANDURU TUSHTE YESH SHIR ILLANINU MA YALKI! GISHBAR IA ZI IA IA ZI DINGIR GIR A KANPA! Appear, son of the enflamed disk of Anu!

I took my leave. Neither Adeline nor Geoffrois paid me a lick of attention. I traversed the empty lunar landscape and escaped back to Earth through a hole in the fence.

No police saw me. No one saw me.

MAY 1992

Baby Goes to Erik's Hometown

Erik asked me to visit his hometown. I wanted to shout, *No, absolutely not, not now, not ever!*

—Honey, said Erik, you can meet my mother.

My beau begged. I resisted. He demanded. I refused. The barometric pressure dropped. A storm grew on the horizon. So I agreed. I said we'd do it. I'd acquiesce. I'd visit Narberth, Pennsylvania.

We picked a weekend in mid-May, after semester's end. Which was also the end of my time at New York University. Graduation loomed.

I kept this momentous event on the sly, avoiding conversations about its possible meaning, adamant in my refusal to attend the ceremony. I had no taste for the flavor of tiny American piety of the commencement address.

And mine was to be no typical ceremony.

Three weeks prior to graduation, a septuagenarian resident of Yonkers named Stella G. Maychick lost control of her Oldsmobile Delta 88 and crashed through the western entrance of Washington Square Park. Mrs. Maychick injured twenty-seven and killed five. One of the deceased was a sophomore at NYU, his bleeding body crushed atop the graves of twenty thousand.

The university always scheduled its commencements in Washington Square. There was no time to find a new location. Hallowed ground newly made, the site of a student's tragic demise.

I imagined Dr. L. Jay Oliva, our university president, offering a speech rife with the stupidities and reassurances that make unwelcome appearances at every funeral, any tragedy, all unexpected deaths. *Always remember. Better place. Never forget. Honored friends. Trusted memories. Carry on.*

Complete and total horseshit. Only time salves the wounds of loss. Year after year until failing synapses dull away the pain.

My last few nights as a student were spent writing a paper on Don Quixote and another examining Etruscan images of Lucretia. With these minor works completed, a sense of finality washed over my frame. I'd spent four years in the womb of NYU. There was no going back. Time to be reborn.

That Friday, Erik and I navigated the labyrinth of the Port Authority, climbing aboard a dingy Greyhound bus on the lower level. I hadn't been on a bus since my arrival in New York. I hadn't been outside of the boroughs in almost four years.

I'd decided to embrace the trip and the suburban weekend. Our relationship needed the time. Neutral space away from New York was an absolute requirement. It had become clear that I'd have to level with Erik about my literary output.

He knew nothing of the stories, of the publication credits, nothing about the endless span of effort.

It wasn't that I didn't want to tell him, but I was embarrassed that there was a thing in my life that mattered. I was ashamed that I'd done anything. Faced with the flaws in my writing, and the atrocious aesthetics of science fiction digests, I'd never mentioned my relative achievements.

By the fifth published story, it was easier to pretend as if it was happening to another person.

The pretense was now impossible. I'd met with Parker Brickley, the squeaks of his childlike telephone voice leaving me unprepared to encounter a middle-aged bearded behemoth trapped in the clutches of male-pattern baldness.

He insisted that we lunch upstairs at Sardi's. The portraiture was grotesque, but I loved Parker. Instantly. He was the most obscene man that I have ever met.

—I don't fucking know why it fucking happened, said Parker, but something about the way you scribble gets my dick throbbing. You're a fucking faggot, so you probably think you've mapped out the whole territory of cock. You'd be surprised about the secret knowledge of the straight pervert. Reading your stuff is like rubbing an eight ball under my foreskin and paying six prostitutes to seek the powder. Johnny fucking Cyberseed, like shitting myself in pleasure. I loved it. I've got literary clients, but only science fiction floods my erectile vessels. I'd trade five Jane Smileys for one of you. So please don't tease me. Please don't say that you're the kind of girl who lets a man buy dinner and then won't hike up her skirt. I want to see that big ass and those tender thighs. Tell me about the sweet treasures of your pussy. Tell me that you have a fucking manuscript. Give me something, buddy, give me a juicy piece to take back to William Morris and ram up their shit-stained asses.

A novel meant commitment. A novel was permanent. A novel couldn't be taken back. A novel couldn't be ignored. A novel was the past made perpetual future.

—Yes, I said. I have a manuscript. I finished in March.

—Fucking beautiful, said Parker. I'm going to piss Champagne on every woman that I meet and tell them it's Hindoo holy water from the sacred Ganges. Here's the thing, Baby. It isn't just that you're a good writer. It's not that you're an East Village prodigy. It's not even that you're young. It's that you've got all of that and you've got those looks. You're one beautiful queer. You're the full package. You're enough to turn me faggot. We'll suck and rim each other until the sun goes supernova. I can mint a million off your looks. Throw in the writing, and blamo!, okay, now we're neck deep in the churning brine of wall-to-wall pussy, now our scrotums have retracted into the pleasure centers of our own bodies. Now all systems are fucking go. Now we're relieving the vital center.

I took the manuscript from my backpack and passed it across the table.

Parker called the next day. He loved it. He told me not to change a word.

He'd decided to push the book upon multiple editors with whom he had a personal relationship, playing the heavy. We had to find the right home, he said. He wanted someone who could look beyond genre trappings.

Three weeks before graduation, Parker called again and, like Apollonius of Tyana, he preached holy wisdom.

—Harcourt, Brace and fucking Company. Michael Kandel wants you. You should be honored. This is the man who translates Stanislaw Lem. He'll publish you in hardback. These people smell the meat on your bones. They want to eat. They want to drink your marrow. The advance ain't stellar, but it's better than anyone else would get. Trust me, Baby. You've got a one-way ticket on the Brickley express. I'm like true love and nuclear war. You can never prepare for Parker. I don't stop until every hole is fucked and puddles of my kids dribble on the linoleum. We've got a lot of work over the next few months. Welcome to the big leagues, boy-o, welcome to the hot-shit hotshot misery of dealing with editors and copyeditors and book buyers and designers. You better go outside and get a good look at your little patch of the East Village. You better take it in, because nothing will ever be the same. And when you're old and I'm a fucking corpse rotted out with worms, you had better fucking remember my name. You had better remember that it was Parker Brickley who gave you this bleak gift.

I signed the contract at Parker's office in the West 50s. I didn't tell a soul. Not even Adeline.

Later, in that same office, he handed me my advance check. I stared at the paper. It is impossible to understand the true and full occult nature of publishing. If you intuit how to pull the levers, people pay you to engage in your basest fantasies, in madness. Your depravity goes out. The cash comes in.

Two drunks boarded the Greyhound bus. They started talking about being on parole, about who they knew on parole, about who'd gone back inside. I stood up and asked them if they couldn't talk a little lower. They apologized. I sat back beside Erik.

—I hate asking people to be quiet, I said.

—I'm amazed that you did at all, he said. I'd be so scared.

—What's the worst that can happen?

We disembarked at the Philadelphia Greyhound terminal, a bland institutional building filled with the poor and the bewildered, all of who bore a resemblance to the wreckage of the Port Authority. I wondered if this same scene wasn't playing out in bus stations all across the country, with the same actors simultaneously appearing in each location.

Philadelphia was limited to exiting the bus station and walking across the street to a subway entrance. Mystified by a transit system not under the MTA's control, I followed Erik's lead. He shepherded us onto the commuter rail.

The city disappeared behind us, the train making its way into the late afternoon of green suburbs. I suffered nausea beneath the fluorescent lighting.

When we arrived at Narberth, the sky was dark. We stepped away from the station and entered the dead emptiness of Main Street U.S.A.

—It's a short walk, said Erik.

Erik had neglected to mention that his mother had no idea of his sexual longing for men. This tidbit of negligence was revealed only on the front steps of his childhood home.

He said that we'd have to pretend, which meant no touching, that she was uncomfortable with hetero displays of affection, let alone the blooming of queer flowers. We could share his bed but we'd pretend that I was sleeping on the floor. His door had a lock.

Erik rang the doorbell, then knocked and called for his mother.

—Don't you have a key? I asked.

—Ordinarily, yes. But the locks were changed last month.

The house was a wooden frame two bedroom. His mother's room was right beside his own, a thin plaster wall away. Adios, my dreams of sweet suburban sex.

We still managed to go down on each other. I was a quiet lover. Erik was different. He always came loud, wailing like Cathy's wraith chasing Heathcliff back to the Grange. So our coupling tested his powers of will. An area in which he could have taken lessons from Patrick Geoffrois.

On Saturday morning, we woke with the sun, hot light slashing across the bed. I heard Erik's mom in the kitchen.

—Is she making breakfast? I asked.

—I'm sure, he said. She loves feeding people.

She'd manufactured a feast. Eggs, pancakes, fruit, toast, cereal. I hadn't eaten so well in years. I stuffed my face, watching Erik and his mother, feeling sweet on the both of them. She delighted in him. I wondered, really, why he hadn't told her about his pleasure in the company of other men.

—I saw that you slept on the floor, she said. Why'd you go and do that? Don't you know the couch folds out?

—Baby's got a bad back, said Erik. He always sleeps on a hard surface.

—It's true, I said. Back in New York, I sleep on a wooden board. Anything too soft and I'm a goddamn cripple for the rest of the day.

—Please don't swear, said his mother. It's vulgar and I don't like hearing it in my house.

Erik called his high school best friend, a woman named Liz. He invited her over. The idea gave me the jitters, fearful of an evening with someone that I didn't know. But we didn't have a car and Narberth was a two-horse town.

Liz arrived around 8 pm. She rushed inside, hugging Erik, her face scrunched into bliss. All I could think was, *Does every fag have their Adeline?* Or was she his Regina?

Erik's mother hugged Liz. They gabbed for the better part of an hour. Liz spoke about her life, about everything that'd happened in the last year. She talked about being a mother. Her son was three years old. The father was long gone. She lived at home. When Erik had called, her parents were so thrilled to hear his voice that they volunteered to babysit.

We took our leave. Liz's car was parked in front, an old Ford Maverick from the 1970s. My father had owned the same model, in lime green, before the transmission fell out. He'd given the car up for scrap.

I crawled into the backseat, adrift in a sea of wrappers from Wendy's and Burger King.

—Sorry about all of that, she said. But with a kid, you know.

—Sure, I said.

—I haven't even seen your boy, said Erik. Why don't we go see him?

—God, no, she said. There's a party in Ardmore. I never get out anymore.

Then there was the time when Liz, Erik and I went to a party in Ardmore. The party was held in a decrepit Victorian house that sat alone on a prime piece of land. Erik and Liz abandoned me as soon as we were inside.

I wandered, examining the faces. People are the same the world over. The obvious mental cases, the jocks, the alcoholics, the madly promiscuous, the wallflowers. They could be plucked from Pennsylvania and put down in Arizona. No one would notice any difference.

Everyone was old. Not geriatric, not even middle aged, but older than I expected. They were five years older than me, at least, and they were acting like teenagers. Making out for the benefit of an audience, smoking from comically oversized bongs, chugging beer from kegs.

Life had stained them, they'd been pummeled by the disappointments of their scant years, as if they knew their injuries would never mend. As if there was nothing but long decades spilling out. As if there'd been an unspoken group decision that the future could be confronted only through a descent into the banality of petite nihilism.

I was far more comfortable with grandiose nihilism. After all, I knew Michael Alig.

I opened the bathroom door, walking in on a man and woman, both shirtless, lying on a futon mattress wedged between the bathtub and the toilet. The woman's hands covered her sagging breasts.

—Shut the fucking door, said the man.

—I have to make water, I said.

—What?

—I have to make water.

—He has to piss, said the woman.

—Don't worry, I won't splash you.

There were flecks of vomit around the toilet's rim.

Michael Alig. He was somewhere in New York, flying kite high, screaming and primping and dancing. He was with women unafraid to show their breasts. These women, the ones with Michael, exposed themselves at the slightest provocation. They shoved people's face into their bosoms. That was their idea of a joke.

In the living room, three dirty men sat on the floor in front of a television. They were playing a video game on a Nintendo system that looked different than the one I remembered. The game was definitely *Super Mario Brothers*, but the graphics were too good for *Super Mario Brothers*, and besides, since when did Mario ride on the back of a green lizard?

—What game is this? I asked.

—*Super Mario World*.

—And that's Nintendo?

—It's Super Nintendo.

—There's a Super Nintendo?

—Where've you been?

—New York.

—It's 16-bit.

—Huh.

A new Nintendo with a new Mario. They'd changed the power-ups. A feather came out of the question-mark bricks. If Mario got the feather, he'd put on a cape that let him fly. Mario could fly. I hadn't played much Nintendo, but I'd wasted hours at other people's houses, staring into the abyss of the original *Super Mario Brothers*. Long philosophical discussions about the meaning and function of the Minus World, and whether or not it portended other hidden secrets within the game. It seemed infinite, like if we hit the right combination of buttons in the right location, we might discover a new, entirely unknown vista. I remember staying up late, watching my friends kill themselves over *Ghosts'N Goblins*, beating the Devil only to discover that the true conclusion required another quest. I remember people playing *Metroid* at parties in Brooklyn, desperate to get the best ending, the one where Simon takes off the suit and wears a bikini.

A Super Nintendo. If they'd released a new *Super Mario Brothers*, then there was almost certainly a new *Legend of Zelda*.

Everything was changing. I felt so fucking old.

Erik was in the basement, drunk, laughing, playing Ping-Pong. A crowd watched. They'd all placed bets. Most of the room had money on his opponent, a burly looking fat kid. I had no idea that Erik played Ping-Pong. I was learning new things every goddamn minute.

*

Liz gave us a very drunken guided tour of the streets between the party and Erik's house. She talked a mile a minute, asking Erik about people from high school. She talked about the basic unfairness of life, about how people had succeeded and left the area because of their parents, because they were born into money.

—I'm not impressed, she said. Nope, I'm not impressed.

We got home around 3 am. We crawled into bed. I was very buzzed. Erik was wasted. I took off his shirt and his pants.

Moonlight through the window. Pupils fully dilated, I surveyed the whole of Erik's room. His mother had never removed any of his things. The only additions from this decade were objects that Erik had sent back home, using the house as a storage space. Old objects upon old objects upon old objects. Like compressed layers of dead skin.

I fell asleep realizing that I hadn't told Erik about my novel. It'd have to be tomorrow before we got back to the city. I'd do it on the train. Or on the Greyhound. But it'd get done.

I dreamt of my parents' house. It started in their bedroom. I was talking to my mom about their black cabinet. Then I went down in the basement, where there was a hole in the foundation. My father and I examined it, discovering the Captain curled up with another cat.

Try as we might, we couldn't coax them out.

Erik's mother stood over the bed. Us with our arms around each other. Me in my underwear, Erik naked. My face pressed hard against the back of his neck. The gayest possible tableau. She was screaming, she was screaming, she was screaming.

He tried calming her. It didn't work. She told me to get out. The woman who'd fixed breakfast had twisted into a ruddy monster. It didn't take long to gather my things. I always pack light.

If life is a cycle, then it's the worst things that repeat. At least his dick hadn't been in my mouth.

I sat on the front steps, waiting over an hour for Erik. I'd brought along a copy of Connie Willis's *Lincoln's Dreams*. I tried to read it, but with the muffled screams, I couldn't concentrate.

The door opened. Erik was wearing yesterday's clothes. He wasn't carrying his bag.

—You should go, he said. I'll come to the city later tonight.

—Don't stay, I said. Come with me.

—She's my mother, he said.

—Please, I said. Nothing good can come of you staying.

—I'll call you when I get into the city.

—I don't even know how to get to the train.

—Walk in that direction. Just ask anyone, they'll help you.

He went inside. No goodbyes. I walked to the train station. Narbeth was tiny. The sun, the birdsong, the quiet of Sunday morning. The train ride was easy, as was the Greyhound terminal. A bus waited. It was so easy. Everything was easy.

Erik and I never spoke again. I called and called and called and called. He never answered. He didn't return my calls.

JULY 1992

David Wojnarowicz Dies

David Wojnarowicz died. Mad, delirious, brilliant, done in by the disease and its cure. I read his obituary in the *Times*. Another beautiful fucked-up faggot stolen away. I told Adeline.

She didn't say a word.

That night, she knocked on my door.

—Patrick also carries the infection, she said. Too much heroin.

—I hope to Christ you aren't sleeping with him, I said.

—Don't be disgusting, she said.

JULY 1992

Baby Goes to Disco 2000

I went back to Limelight. I called Regina, Miss Queen Rex, whom I hadn't seen in months and said, Sister, I'm fucked up and lonely and I'm sorry I put a relationship before you, but here I am, about to be a published author and I'm alone and I can't manage a love life. Let's go to Disco 2000. Let's see Michael Alig and James St. James and Kenny Kenny and Kabuki Sunshine and Jodi Jingles and Sebastian Jr. and Armen Ra and Sister Dimension and Astro Erle.

She said yes, sure, I was going anyway.

I refused to dress like a club kid. I'd gotten everything that I'd wanted and discovered that none of it meant anything. I was a young urban professional.

After the advance came in, I had attended an event hosted by Bloomingdale's Men's Store, with the very special guest of Mr. Robert Gieve, personal holder of the Royal Warrant of Appointment to HRH The Prince of Wales. I blew thousands of dollars on a black pinstripe Gieves & Hawkes. I didn't give a shit about the money.

I put the suit on before going to Limelight. For the finishing touch, I went to Duane Reade and bought their cheapest aftershave. I doused myself in the blue liquid. I smelled like Barbicide and balsamic vinaigrette. I was ready for Disco 2000.

On my first night back, I watched a man piss into a bottle and drink his own urine. The audience cheered. I watched an amputee remove her prosthetic leg and insert it into her vagina. The audience cheered. Weird bridge-and-tunnel people got up on stage. They stripped for fifty dollars. The audience cheered. I was watching Rome fall and it was fucking fantastic.

Queen Rex introduced me to ketamine, a veterinary anesthetic. Its packing reads: FOR USE IN CATS AND SUBHUMAN PRIMATES ONLY. Like a message written in hot neon, a clarion call to the world's drug fiends. This drug destroys minds and reaps souls.

In the chapel of a deconsecrated church, while Donald Trump and his bodyguard played a hand of pinochle, I snorted bumps off the key to Regina's apartment. Ketamine was like water, clear, like being disconnected and shut down from the senses, being forced into using the hidden senses to comprehend input of the primary five. The body imprisoned in one place, the soul in another. Glimpses flickered in and out. I'd be on the side of the club one moment. The next, I'd be on the other, with no memory of the distance between. Intermittent psychic visions flashing in my head, mindless insight into the world. I lived other people's lives, from birth to death. I saw myself in the distant future and the backwards past. I touched the whole of eternity and mingled with the infinite. Very stupid jokes became funny. *Knock knock, who's there? Boo. Boo who? You don't have to cry. Ha. Ha. Ha. Ha. Ha. Ha. Ha. Ha. Ha. Ha.*

When I started to come down, I snorted cocaine. When I came down from the cocaine, I snorted more cocaine. When I came down from that cocaine, I snorted more cocaine. When I came down from that cocaine, I smoked pot.

Michael treated me like a king. Regina'd told him about the book. I also suspect that he noticed the quality of my suit. Michael was a truffle hog about money. I became popular with the new club kids.

Most of the old faces were gone. Replaced by the young, the fresh, the dumb. They'd've followed Michael into burning ovens if he'd said there was a party inside.

He pulled me aside, eyes bleary with drugs, and he said: —Tell me, honey, what's the book about?

What was the book about?

I'd titled it *Trapped Between Jupiter and a Bottle,* after this time when Erik and I were lying around naked listening to a Bob Dylan album called *Street Legal.*

—I've never understood what he meant, said Erik, when he sings that she was trapped between Jupiter and a bottle.

—You've got it wrong, I said. She's torn between Jupiter and Apollo.

—I've listened to the song for nearly ten years. I know the lyrics.

—Start it again.

On the third rotation, Erik admitted that I was right. So, yes, I'd titled my novel after my boyfriend's charming error. Because I loved him.

The action is set in the year 2043, in New York City. The novel's protagonist is an ex-cop turned private gumshoe named Lucy Lucatto. For an unexplained reason, the 2010s began a vogue in which parents bestowed their male children with typically feminine names. And their female children with typically masculine names. Anyhoo, Lucy is hired by a femme fatale named Bruce to follow her husband through the New York underworld.

I borrowed heavily from my own life, making almost verbatim transcripts of my experience in clubland. I'd even based a character on Michael. Michelle Gila. The only significant difference between Michael and Michelle was that Michelle had injected his genetic code with an elephant's DNA. As a result of this back-alley procedure, the king of clubland grew a great fleshy gray head and an enormous trunk for a nose. Imagine the boatloads and mountains of drugs which might be snorted by an elephant's trunk.

The book was based on a flash of inspiration. I'd started to tire of science fiction, having exhausted the genre's possibilities not only as a writer but also as a fan. There weren't many good books left unread. I turned on to the crime novel, to the noir, to that detective subgenre, and spent months hunting down old paperbacks. My favorite writer was Horace McCoy, author of *They Shoot Horses Don't They?* and *Kiss Tomorrow Goodbye*. The prose of the latter went through my brain like a hook through the scales of a fish. I couldn't escape. I moved to Hammett and Chandler. Then I discovered Ross MacDonald and the late-period Archer books.

After *Sleeping Beauty*, I decided I'd never write straight science fiction again. In my epiphany, I saw that the bitter flavor of noir, its midnight lightning, could be married with an outrageous science fiction context, and that the push and pull of two ridiculous genres would mask the flaws of both.

And I assumed that the juxtaposition would allow its writer to be funny. I was too insecure to not build in humor. I needed to be funny.

What was the book about?

—It's about you, Michael, I said. I've written an entire book about you.

—How fabulous! I've been waiting all my life for someone to write about me! It's about fucking time! But I always thought it'd be someone good like Dominick Dunne or Kitty Kelley! But a girl can't be choosy!

AUGUST 1992

Baby's Birthday

On my birthday, I invited Adeline to Limelight, knowing that she would refuse but asking anyway. She said no. I said fine. I made other arrangements, inviting Regina and Parker Brickley.

The sacred anniversary of my advent fell on a night when Limelight was hosting Lord Michael's Future Shock. A techno extravaganza with a bridge-and-tunnel crowd. Lots of people stayed far away, but I dug it. I thought it was beautiful how a bunch of fucked-up Staten Island Italians could come together, eat Ecstasy, and lose their machismo. Countless young men without their shirts, sweating and dancing and hugging, approximating love through the chemically mandated release of serotonin into their synapses.

Parker stared at the drugged-up women, laser focused on their thick asses and even thicker accents, watching the girls strut in obscene clothing.

—If I couldn't agent, said Parker, I'd like to be a modern-day Victor fucking Frankenstein. I'd take the legs from that one and the tits from that one and the face from a third and sew them all together. I'd make the perfect mate.

—Isn't that a little *Rocky Horror Picture Show?* asked Queen Rex.

—I've never bothered watching that fruit shit, said Parker. Hey now, but what do I see over there? The most beautiful creature. Look at that ass. I'm going to see if she wants to sin on my face.

Leviathan sank into the human ocean. There came no screams, no signs of obvious violence. Maybe Parker got what, or whom, he wanted. Maybe a girl really did sin on his face.

When Parker didn't return, I converted to the nouveau theology of birthday intoxication. Regina rummaged in her purse, taking out a clear glass vial of ketamine, her compact mirror, a dollar bill, and an expired credit card.

I'd gotten worried that ketamine's dissociative states had spilled into my waking life. Away from the club, in my daily existence, I was attuned to the unreality of human experience.

I'd lost the ability to comprehend and could no longer believe my eyes. The street corridors of Manhattan were haunted. The Empire State Building was a monolith of confusion. A veil of gossamer web draped each hour. Nothing was real. Life felt thin. I felt thin.

It might have been depression. I missed Erik.

The ketamine went up my nose. I snorted it right on the dance floor, in a jangle of limbs and bodies. There wasn't much effect, so I headed toward the chapel.

I never arrived. I submerged into a world of spectral light.

An enhanced universe of rainbow gradation. There was no boundary between my body and the light, the pleasure of colors. I could go like that forever, and it went for hours and days and months and years before the shadow people arrived. Their bodies were ill defined, like compounded smoke, and they were talking to me, but they couldn't speak. They were aliens with no capacity for sound, who had developed modes of communication through the mechanism of high-frequency light manipulation. It took a few weeks, but I learned their language.

I could see what they said: —I find you obscene, unclean, and, most of all, ordinary. Your money can buy you just about anything. From what we know, Judas was the victim. He had earned more money than Christ. Twenty gets you laid, ten gets you high, three gives you death for a whole weekend.

When I reemerged into the mundane universe, I was in Limelight's bathroom, staring at a toilet. People were screwing each other's brains out in the next stall. The grunts, the moaning, the thrusting. Sounds from the predawn of history. Words on the toilet blazed: AMERICAN STANDARD.

James St. James told me that he'd seen Andy Warhol's ghost on 47th Street.

—You believe me, don't you honey? I knew Andy. I'd recognize that walk anywhere!

Regina and I left early, around 2:15 am. We both had headaches. She asked if she could stay in my apartment. Ordinarily, I'd've refused, but brain chemistry prevented any resistance. She could've asked me to hit my face against the colonnade of the Manhattan Bridge, and I'd've been there, mashing my skull against Neoclassical granite.

We walked on Broadway.

—On my very first day in the city, I said, I did this route. Times Square to the East Village via Broadway.

—You've told me before, said Regina. Let me ask you something. Do you really think that Dinkins can't beat Giuliani?

—I can't stand politics, I said. Why would you ask me about politics?

—Thirty minutes ago you were in the VIP room, screaming about how New York would be the staging ground of a Fourth Reich. You told a guy from Tompkinsville and his bleach-blonde girlfriend that Giuliani would be their new Führer.

Other people got high and screwed like a rampaging Minotaur and woke up in a gutter.

—Get out, I said. I did not.

—Even if you're super fucked up on ketamine, said Regina, you probably shouldn't talk about politics. Especially not with club people.

—Let's not talk about it now, I said.

I told her about the world of spectral light. I told her about the shadow people. I told her about their method of communication. I told her their language.

—Did I ever say anything about *Begotten*? she asked.

—No, I said.

—One night we were all at Michael and Keoki's place, and Michael put on this movie called *Begotten*. I hate horror films, but I was too high. I couldn't leave. I said, Michael, please, can't you put on *I Love Lucy*? He screamed and said it was his apartment. We were going to watch whatever he wanted. The film started and it's in black and white, and shit, Baby, I didn't understand none of it, but at the beginning it's this monster sitting in a chair, cutting open its stomach. The sound, oh mija, the sound. The monster reaches into itself and pulls out its intestines. I heard a voice in the sound, and I thought it was the voice of God, the great old man, the big one, speaking through this fucked-up film. On the screen, I swear, was the Holy Ghost.

—What did he say?

—He said *stop pretending. I am the unbroken heart and the forgotten anvil. She whosoever striketh against me shall forge unbendable steel.* I'm on mushrooms, the whole room is sparkling, all these queens are screeching about Vivienne Westwood, and here's God talking through this movie.

We arrived on 7th Street. It wasn't even 3 am. Residual traces of ketamine and comedown cocaine. We climbed the stairs.

Adeline was in her room, door open, hunched over her desk, drawing. I waved. She waved back. Regina waved too. Adeline waved back.

Regina and I talked in the kitchen, not loudly, foraging the fridge. We decided that eating was impossible. Besides, it'd be much better at the Kiev, with all the other late-night freaks and vampires. A restaurant packed with people too high and too dissolute to do anything but inhale latkes, cheese blintzes, and challah.

We sat on my bed. Regina said that she'd been watching Gene Kelly movies on Channel 13. She loved the psychological undertones of the dance numbers, how each scene contained an accidental revelation of Kelly's mental state. Plus, Cyd Charisse had the best legs that Regina'd ever seen, legs like the ideal of legs, legs that would be in heaven, legs that would inspire heroism and villainy.

The telephone rang.

I walked into the kitchen, where we kept the answering machine, and waited. Adeline came out of her bedroom and stood beside me. I thought it'd be Parker, calling to report on his conquest or his failure. I wondered why Adeline cared about Parker.

But Adeline didn't know about Parker. She didn't know about the book deal. It wasn't like with Erik. It wasn't shame. I wanted to wait. I wanted the drama, the finality, of putting the thing before her and saying, here. This is the measure of my life.

I'd fantasized about the look on her face. The joy when she understood. The self-esteem boost when she approved. It would be like I'd become the person she had always seen, the New York intellectual hidden within the doughy flesh of a scared Middle West farm boy. It was all for her. She was the reason that I even thought of writing. The reason that I dreamt of being anything other than what I had been. Without her, I would've died within six months. I would've tricked for heroin and wasted away with AIDS on the Christopher Street pier. She would always be my best friend. I remembered when she was my only friend.

The machine picked up and ran through the message. Then the beep.

—Adeline, slurred the speaker, it's your mother. I'm thinking about selling the house. I saw a place out in Pacific Palisades last weekend that's too perfect. Dahlia saw it, too, and she loves it. Charles couldn't come, but I'm sure he'd love it. But Adeline, I wouldn't dream of selling our house without your permission. I know how attached you are. Call me when you get the chance, Adeline, because I have to make an offer soon. A house like that won't wait. Just let me know.

She hung up.

—Mother is a true and genuine lunatic, said Adeline.

The phone rang again. Suzanne loved leaving multiple messages.

—This message isn't for Adeline, said the machine. Go into your room. This message is for Baby. Baby, I expect abuse from Adeline. She's never had manners. I thought that you and I had a special arrangement. You knew how much Adeline's graduation meant to me, and you know that she skipped it out of spite, and then you did the same thing. Don't you know how much I wanted to go? Why else would I pay for your degree? Dahlia is useless. Adeline's always been a bitch. She's always hated me. I thought with you I could attend a ceremony. But I'm so foolish. Nothing ever happens how you want it. Nothing good ever happens.

The unsanded and paint-speckled floorboards. Couldn't look at Adeline.

—Get out, Adeline said. Get out of this apartment. Take your drug addict with you. Come back tomorrow and get your things.

Her eyes spiraling, her flesh red. The mouth like a frown of daggers. I'd never seen her like this. Not even with Jon.

—Please, can we talk about it? I asked.

—Get the fuck out of my apartment.

Something scuffled behind me. Regina. Standing there, I don't know how long.

—How could you not tell her? asked Regina.

—It appears that I'm the only one who wasn't informed of Mother's charity, said Adeline. Get out of this apartment, Regina. Get your shoes and go outside and wait for him. The way that I'm currently feeling, I simply can't guarantee your safety.

Adeline never really understood New York's indigenous peoples. She spent her life with emigrants from other locales. Regina was native. Regina was Queen Rex of Washington Heights. No matter Adeline's infinite reserve of hurt and resentment, if she fucked with Regina, she'd end up with both arms in a sling.

—Please, I said to Regina. Do as she asks. I'll be out. Please.

Regina got her shoes and her coat, stormed out of the kitchen, slamming the door, stomping down the stairs.

—I don't want to leave, I said.

—You haven't any choice, said Adeline. We are long beyond our expiration date. You've ruined everything.

—We've known each other so long, I said. You're my best friend.

—You can't repeat the past, she said.

—What do you mean you can't repeat the past? Of course you can.

I packed several sets of clothes into my backpack, putting my unsold manuscripts at the bottom. I looked around my room. I always knew it would end like this.

Adeline hadn't left the kitchen.

—I'll call to set up a time, I said. I can't carry everything.

—Fine, she said. Do it this week. After next Sunday, I'm changing the number.

—Does it have to be like this? I asked.

—You know that it must, she said.

Only when I was halfway down the stairs did I realize that I wasn't only losing Adeline, but that I'd lost the Captain too. Adeline would never let me have him. I hadn't even said good-bye.

Regina was waiting.

—I never liked that bitch, she said.

—I don't want to talk about it.

—What now? she asked.

—I'm going to go around the corner. I've always wanted to spend a night in the Sunshine Hotel.

Regina knew the place, knew its reputation, knew that it was a disgusting fleabag SRO pit of scum. She wouldn't let me stay. Refused, absolutely. I had money, she said, why didn't I get a real hotel? I don't deserve it, I said. I should suffer, should be punished. Because Adeline was right. That's crazy, said Regina. She forced me to stay in her apartment. With her family.

We took the L to Eighth Avenue and the A local up to the top of the island. We emerged from beneath the Earth. It was 5 am. The unhappiest hour of New York life. The bleak period between night and day. There was no life on the street, only the dead silence of my first encounter with the Fort Washington Collegiate Church, a single-story building from the turn of the century. I tried to comprehend how it could be here, in Manhattan, how it looked so alone surrounded by all the apartment buildings, how it looked like someone's house, how it looked like a modest house from California. I tried but couldn't.

Like no one lived in the city. Like the apocalypse happened and only me and Regina had survived.

FEBRUARY 1993

Adeline Splits from the Big Shitty

L et us be clear. I did not flee New York City because of my former roommate. Our unspeakable schism wreaked its terrible havoc, but your old pal Adeline stood her ground, resolute and knee deep in her even-eyed imbecility. I should have fled, howling like a wounded animal. Yet I indulged the great vice of stubbornness and suffered out a long chain reaction that manifested through my menstrual cycle.

To wit, darlings, the arrival of my period. It was not merely a few days late, or even several weeks, but two solid months past its due date. Barring an actual and genuine miracle, pregnancy was beyond the realm of possibility. I'd practiced the deadly art of celibacy for almost the full annum.

When the scarlet tide washed in, I spotted for days, followed by a deeply uneven flow, as if a poltergeist haunted my insides, playing with the tap of a faucet. On and off, on and off, on and off.

Three weeks into this farce, when I presumed that the whole matter had come to its surcease, I simply overflowed, staining out every pair of underwear and most of my pants as I cried out for Jesus to make up my dying bed.

I missed my period when Bush fumbled away his presidency, and I did not cease bleeding until after Bubba Bill Clinton assumed office of the usurped king.

Around then, you see, I learned the unfortunate truth of the human body. One can spend years experiencing all manner of illness and horrible vagary and remain unprepared for how far the flesh will go. There's no end to scars and scabs in this old world, dearies, and our organs do betray.

I'm surely conflating the months, but I could swear that my crimson odyssey ended on the very same day that I left the apartment and walked to Cooper Square, snowflakes falling around my bonny red hair.

Reaching the western corner of 7th Street, I encountered an exodus from the southerly lands, a great swell of people, many with noses ringed by dark ash.

"What in the blazes is this?" I asked a woman.

"Explosion," she said. "Down at the World Trade Center. Everyone's evacuated."

February 26, 1993. For a few hours of naiveté, the world held out hope that perhaps the explosion wasn't caused by a bomb, that perhaps it was a baroque mechanical failure.

Of such things are dreams made. Boom! Pause for a moment and consider, my sweethearts, that the 1990s was a decade in which Islamic-flavored terrorists attacked the World Trade Center and the United States of America waged war against Iraq. History always repeats.

I'd long mastered the indifferent sneer at life's circumstance, curling my upper lip like a J.D. in a paddywagon on his way to the hoosegow, but over the next week, the bombing tugged on my soul, wormed its way deeeeeeeep into my consciousness.

Navigating city streets became a great difficulty. I jumped like a jackrabbit at the backfiring of cars, winced at shouts, a general nausea settled in my stomach, constantly expecting to fall victim to an unknown and unseen horror.

Then the dreams started.

Dreams of being trapped, of wandering through a blown-out basement, of being in office buildings filled with smoke, dreams of exploding cars, dreams of my skin shredded by metal fragments, dreams of fire, dreams of my body maimed and mutilated, huge holes blown into the flesh, limbless and flopping like a fish hooked out of water.

I had stayed in touch with Минерва. We spoke every few weeks through the fine art of telephony. She had suggested, ad infinitum, that I move to the Bay Area. "San Francisco is shitfest," she said, "but different flavor turd. Come learn bitter disappointment of new city."

Noodling it out, I struck upon the thought that there was no time like the present. The dreams, said I to meself, are a signal. New York is hitting you like a zonk on the head. All your old used-to-bes got their get up and went. It's time, Adeline, for a change.

I subletted away my home of six years. The sublessee was an acquaintance of Luanna's from somewhere in the great wilds beyond Manhattan. We never met. Luanna handled the details, taking her cut off the top.

Who cared? Let unknown parties trash the whole place. Let them burn the building. Any keepsake of value or meaning had been put into a dismal storage unit on Houston Street.

The Captain accompanied me, his carrying case tucked beneath my arm. For the third time in his short life, the feline hurtled at thirty thousand feet across American skies.

Jeremy Winterbloss had found his employ in Marin County, as a low-level functionary at LucasArts, an organization named with great modesty by its founder, George Lucas. The company's purpose was the production of computer games.

Each morning, Jeremy traversed a semi-mythical journey across the Golden Gate Bridge and arrived at the Skywalker Ranch, a vast expanse of land purchased with Lucas's endless *Star Wars* lucre. It was an education not only in his profession but also in the American potential for grotesque opulence.

For her part, Минерва floated through a litany of retail jobs. Her real focus was elsewhere.

She'd somehow encountered two dissolute young девушек, both escapees from the former CCCP. As all three members of this femme troika shared a mutual interest in punk aesthetics. They cohered into the nucleus of an almost all-girl band called Daddy Was in KGB.

The single masculine note in this estrogenized symphony came from the drummer, a 17-year-old high school student from San Rafael who'd contacted Минерва after she'd stapled advertisements to the city's telephone poles. WANTED: DRUMMER FOR BAND.

Минерва mailed me the flyer for every gig played by her band. The names of the other groups always amused. Lilyvolt, Cheap Vegan Cafe, Storm and Her Dirty Mouth, Honeypot, Drunk People R Loud, Homo Holocaust, Coffee Scented Come Stain.

She herself had illustrated many of these flyers, working an intentional *homage* to the Family Dog and Neon Rose posters of Victor Moscoso. At Parsons, she'd never evidenced much interest in control of her line, so this move towards psychedelic baroque represented a visual direction that was brand sparkling new.

"What you expect?" she said into the telephone. "Every creature changes or dies."

*

I landed at San Francisco International. Jeremy and Минерва stood by my gate, their wide bright smiles dispelling the ugly magick generated by the drab interiors of the American airport. All of that functional decoration, all of the white and gray paneling, the navy blue carpeting working like a slow poison on the human constitution.

"Jeremy! Минерва!" I cried.

"Adeline!" shouted they.

Our group embrace was horribly awkward. I banged my forehead against Winterbloss's spectacles, and stabbed my skin on the metal studs of Минерва's leather jacket.

I looked into their shining faces, into the radiant visages of people who were so clearly my friends. Much to my horror, my eyes began crying.

"What shit," said Минерва. "Unnecessary displays exist beneath you."

"I'm ever so sorry," I said. "It's been a hard year."

We descended like Dante to the lower level and waited beside the baggage carousel, standing amongst the rubes and zanies who'd flown with yours truly across the Great Abyss. The majority of my fellow passengers looked to be from Northern California. I imaginated their luggage, stuffed with fleece jackets and plastic Statues of Liberty and white t-shirts boldly proclaiming love for New York City.

In the backseat of Jeremy's 1986 white Toyota Camry, I simply delighted in their voices, attempting to decipher the hermetic shorthand of a long-term relationship.

"Donny's a real carpetbagger," said Jeremy.

"You meet Donny," she said to me, "you meet the world."

Whittle away enough of one's life in California and one grows accustomed to empty highways where the only visible nighttime landmarks are bodies of water and distant mountains. U.S. Route 101 was a road that I knew all too well. It had bored me for most of my childhood.

The generic landscape dissolved into growing industrial distress and we trespassed into the city. An instant disorientation settled upon my starry brow, as if the Victorian houses conspired with the hills and the uncanny quiet of the streets. Every thing, and I do mean all things, looked sinister. Great swaths of fog rolling in from the west, caught by headlights, a spectral layer haunting the world. The dark and decayed city. I wondered, and not for the last time, what I had done to my poor self, and where I was. If nothing else, the human body was not meant to jolt twenty-five hundred miles en moins de six heures.

Their third-floor apartment was located within an ancient building on Steiner in the Lower Haight and had an irrefutably San Francisco floorplan. A street-level entrance with a ridiculous staircase that led to an irregular space, the primary feature of which was the cancerous sprouting of rooms along a long hallway.

Though Минерва and Jeremy had navigated the horrors of cohabitation and the maintenance of erotic desire in the suffocating context of love, they hadn't displayed much competence in adapting to the needs of decoration and décor.

They lived beneath a worn tapestry of American pop detritus. I had no doubt about what belonged to whom. The punk metal inverted crucifixes and revolting caricatures of political figures went into one column. The full-size posters of Wolverine and *Maniac Mansion* in another.

One fixture to which I paid an especial attention was Jeremy's state-of-the-art IBM PC Compatible 486DX-33mhz computer, replete with 1024 x 768 SVGA video and a SoundBlaster 16 Pro 2. I'd never encountered a home computer that was actually in a person's home.

"It's for work, mostly," he said. "But I'm using it more and more. Have you heard about email?"

"Please, spare me the details," I said. "I have trouble enough with the regular mail."

We sat in their living room, overlooking the street, our faces illuminated by red Christmas lights. Минерва emerged from their bedroom carrying a brightly colored plastic bong, and seeing that instrument of intoxication, at last I knew that I'd landed within the borders of Californy.

We helped the Captain get his bearings and then listened to L7's *Bricks Are Heavy*. We bullshitted about the whereabouts of former Parsons students.

"Do you remember Janine?" asked Jeremy.

"Nooooooo," I said. "Whatever did this Janine look like?"

"She had black long hair, which I think she dyed, and glasses, and she always carried an unwashed grotty pink messenger bag."

"Oh, her," I sniffed. "We called her the Pink Princess of Nassau County."

"That'd be the one," said Jeremy. "Do you want to guess what she's doing?"

"I detest guessing. I'm always wrong."

"Pink Princess is dog catcher?" asked Минерва.

"She stayed in New York for a year or two," said Jeremy. "I guess she was working in fashion, but then she moved to Hollywood and now she works for Jack Nicholson. She works for the Joker."

"Whatever does the Princess do for Mr. Nicholson?" I asked.

"No one really knows," said Jeremy. "I think she's his personal assistant."

"I loved *Five Easy Pieces*," said yours truly, "but one imagines there's a singular task in which he requires the assistance of a pretty young thing. And that, my darlings, is an idea that's real horrorshow. Think of their faces twisting and contorting in the throes of orgasm. Oh, the terror, the terror."

They turned in before the clock struck midnight, retiring into the apartment's sole bedroom. It'd been decided that I would slumber on the living room couch, but sleep was beyond my powers. I sat stoned and stared into the street.

Over the rooftops, I espied the dark and ragged outline of Buena Vista Park, towering above San Francisco like Fangorn over Middle Earth. The blinking lights of Sutro Tower hovered like UFOs. It'd been so long since Jon. I hadn't seen the other one in almost six months. I'd alienated my family. The only friends who gave two shakes of a fist were in the bedroom, but they were coupled, and the mystery of every coupling is impenetrable.

I slept fully clothed, not removing a stitch, opting to ignore the blankets piled beside the couch.

MARCH 1993

Adeline Wanders Around San Francisco

I became as a pilgrim on the road to Canterbury, frittering away the weeks by wandering around San Francisco, un flaneur sans privilège du pénis.

I flitted in and out of the city's little fiefdoms, developing the mad idea that one could create a sonic map for the blind on the basis of each neighborhood's catcalls. The *hola mi lindas* and *ay gueras* of the Mission, the *pssst psst psssst sexys* of Hayes Valley, the polite honky condescension of the Marina, and then the vortex, the absolute sucking silence of the Castro.

My many years constrained within the rigid grids of New York and Los Angeles had left me unprepared for San Francisco. Why would anyone build a city punctuated by things like Nob Hill? What gin-soaked sot had believed that Market Street was best designed as a diagonal slash cutting through all rational thought? How could one explain California or Geary streets? How was I to comprehend the inexact and odd location of the Financial District? What in God's good graces were the Richmond and the Sunset?

Four years had passed since Loma Prieta shook 'em on down, but traces of the destruction were everywhere. Empty lots where apartment buildings collapsed upon themselves, the blankness of the former Embarcadero Freeway, the dead zone by Fell Street.

I haunted cafés and walked the streets and wondered how the city's residents could content themselves with living in such a jerk backwater. Everybody was stoned, everyone worked pointless jobs. Everyone was laid-back, but it wasn't the sunstroked ease of blithe Los Angeles. People in San Francisco affected strange airs, undercurrents of tension and anxiety, of an undirected madness. Perhaps it was the weather, perhaps a result of the pure heresy of living in a place with more fog than sun.

Wandering out of the Marina, I spied a grand Art Deco marquee reading METRO in red neon lights. I moseyed over and discovered that the theater was screening a new film entitled *Point of No Return*, starring Bridget Fonda.

I'd last watched the actress in a risible thriller called *Single White Female*, where she battled her ravenous Sapphic desires. That film was terrible, but I groooooooved on the dynastic implications of her flat performance. Famous family, Hollywood nepotism, the decaying of American values. I wasn't sure, but I thought that Daddy might've worked on her father's dental bridge.

The next showing of *Point of No Return* was but half an hour away.

Inside the theater, I encountered one of those majestic institutions from the halcyon days when cinema remained an event and theaters were designed to highlight the moment's monumental nature. Yes, darlings, those nouveau-riche aspirations were unmatched by the modest little films that they played, asking an audience of millions to satisfy itself with the heavy lids of Gloria Swanson, but the cinemas were like palaces.

The ceiling was Spanish Revival, the walls painted with red fairies, and the seating, mes amis, the seating was tiered. The rickety wooden chairs were an unrelenting agony, but one imagined a time when they'd been something better. I could have died there, and, like Claudius at prayer, witnessed my gentle soul transported straight to heaven.

Point of No Return was no better than *Single White Female*. I thought about drafting a letter to Ms. Fonda's agents, suggesting that they select her roles with greater care. What's the point of a famous name if it doesn't deliver a modicum of dignity?

It's the little details that stick. Not the plot, not the characters, but certain aesthetic moments rising from the mise-en-scène.

Минерва's enthusiasm for L7 was beyond my understanding, but she'd played their LP enough times that I could recognize "Everglade" when it appeared on the soundtrack. It acted as prelude to the sonic entrance of Dr. Nina Simone, a record artist with whom Fonda's character is obsessed. This musical choice is the only quirk of the entire film.

I knew of Miss Simone, coming across *Little Girl Blue* in bins of used vinyl, but I'd never listened. Upon hearing "Feeling Good," I understood that I simply must purchase her records. The song was wonderful enough to overpower any concerns about a recommendation offered by an ultraviolent multimillion-dollar spectacle.

I ambled my merry way back, taking Fillmore and cutting through Alamo Square, encountering the inevitable tourists photographing the

Painted Ladies. I watched them watching the buildings, wondering where in America they were from and what they thought about the decay of the neighborhood, if they could reconcile the houses that appeared every Friday night on *Full House* with the untreated mental illness and feces smears of the homeless.

At Recycled Records on Haight, I ran my long fingers through the vinyl. I unearthed ten different albums by Miss Simone. Working from the mystery of tactile osmosis, I picked *Nina Simone Sings the Blues* and *I Put a Spell on You.*

An unpleasant-looking creature behind the register lifted the albums, bringing the cardboard close to his pockmarked face. I worried he might extend his tongue and taste the vinyl.

"You're buying these because of that movie, ain't you?"

"Whatever do you mean?" I asked.

"That movie. *Point Break.* You're the third one this week. All of you women."

"I have no idea what you're talking about."

"Sure you don't," he said. "Fifteen bucks."

I headed home, passing beneath Buena Vista Park, trying yet again to apprehend its trees and its eldritch nature. Both Jeremy and Минерва had warned me against the park. They spoke of unknown crimes, of bodies discovered.

Yet I'm an infant in my mentality and being told not to do a thing always piques my curiosity. On my third day, I'd climbed to the park's crown. I'd repeated this journey on several occasions, never once encountering another human being, only finding indirect evidence through discarded drug paraphernalia and canvas tents pitched amongst the trees.

Jeremy was at home. Минерва was working. Jeremy was reading a comic book.

"You need to check this out," he said.

"Whatever is it?" I asked.

"*Kid Eternity #1,*" he said. "It came out last week, on Vertigo. It's by Ann Nocenti. It's the craziest thing I've ever read."

"Leave it for me when you've finished," I said. "I require a record player."

Jeremy ventured into the breach of their overstuffed closet, pulling out a cheap plastic turntable. Минерва had purchased it for $5 at a garage sale, entertaining the delusion that she was one of those punk people who cherished seven-inch records, who collected and listened to the latest releases of her acquaintances. Her dreams proved fruitless. She could not resist the sway of the compact disc.

The player had a headphone jack. I plugged in Jeremy's giant oversized plastic contraptions and sat on the living room floor, playing records. I preferred *Nina Simone Sings the Blues*. There was a consistency, not a bad song on it, though it lacked a standout. *I Put a Spell on You* was punctuated by numbers of incredible power. The title track, the aforementioned "Feeling Good," "Gimme Some," and "Taking Care of Business."

I played the records all night, headphones pressed tight against my bony skull. I didn't apprehend Минерва's arrival. Nor when she and Jeremy departed, nor when they returned, nor when they retired into their bedroom. The voice of Miss Simone bored a hole. That voice owned every word that it enunciated, bending music in its service.

Towards midnight, I took in *Kid Eternity #1*. It was the single strangest thing that I had ever read, and you know me, darlings, I've been identified by several law enforcement agencies as one of those wretched people who adorates *Simulations* and all the other borrrrrriiiiiiing books on Semiotext(e).

Kid Eternity, the titular character, can resurrect any historical or mythological figure, making them present in the flesh. An overweight Buddhist monk suggests that Kid Eternity must create a Moonchild. The purpose of this homunculus will be to bring mankind to its next state of developed consciousness. The narrative ends up encompassing the entire Greek pantheon, a group of demonic children who eat their own skin, and a Symbolist Beelzebub in hell. There's also a B-plot about the discord among the people Kid Eternity attempts to mate in the creation of his Moonchild.

At least that's what I think happens. I most certainly could be wrong. Interpretation is a fine art and Ann Nocenti is an unsung genius, a freak of nature walled within the prêt-à-porter ghetto of the comic book.

I asked Jeremy about Ann Nocenti. "She's incredible," he said. "But the comics world is too sexist. No one ever pays attention. We should bow at her feet. Vertigo is a good place for her. They're doing a lot of interesting work somewhere between the mainstream and the alternative world. She couldn't fit anywhere else. By the way, have you read *Sandman*?"

MARCH 1993

Nash Mac

The one constant of daily life is other people's inability to mind their own business. Минерва and Jeremy had drawn negative conclusions regarding my shambling around San Francisco.

Too much perambulation enclosed within tendrils of fog and woe. They'd decided it was unhealthy. Thus the picayune image of my hosts dragging me hand-over-foot to Thai House, a restaurant on Noe Street.

We walked in the shadow of Corona Heights, a rock outcropping looming over this patch of the city. Jeremy noticed my interest and said, "Do you know the writer Fritz Leiber? He wrote a great book about Corona Heights called *Our Lady of Darkness.*"

I hung my head low. "Mmmmm, uhhh, mmm, uh," I replied.

Fritz Leiber. Yes, sir, I did indeed recollect Fritz Leiber. The name filtered into my consciousness through the same route as all such trivialities, via a certain personage who possessed an unrefined taste for science fiction. I'd been avoiding all thoughts of the other one, but it proved impossible, as in the moments when our behemoth cat would crawl into my lap and insist on being hugged until he purred. The beast's gray face, his caterwauls. What had been lost.

Thai House represented a new stratagem. Jeremy took it upon himself to arrange a mutual dinner between we three and one of his co-workers, a man named Nash Mac.

"Nash Mac?" I asked incredulously. "He sounds like a gay cash machine."

"It's short for رصان محمود," said Jeremy. "His family's from Persia."

"But Jeremy," I whined, "I don't want to meet any of your dreadful computer people. I hate computers. I hate technology. I wish I could live in the eighteenth century, my tattered dress speckled with the rot of the road."

"He's not like the others," said Jeremy. "He cares about things beyond computers."

There we stood outside of the restaurant, its interior glow lighting the sidewalk. Минерва leaned against her beau, hands beneath his jacket, kissing his neck. How had they managed to keep it alive? In my humble experience, most relationships lasted two years before dissipating into contempt and mutual loathing. Yet their vegetable love grew vaster than empires.

"Why ever are we suffering this cold?" I asked.

"I told Nash Mac that we'd meet him outside," said Jeremy.

"Fine," said I. "You wait for this young man who is apparently incapable of peering inside a glass window. I'll collect a table. Минерва, will you come with me?"

"Prefer standing," she said.

I entered the establishment. It could have been any restaurant in San Francisco. Simple design and modest touches of ethnicity. I spoke with the hostess. She sat me at a table. I waited, in total boredom, for another ten minutes.

There was action outside, blur of bodies in nighttime. They rushed in with the mystery guest. I had to admit that Nash Mac was crushingly handsome, but oh so poorly dressed in his pale blue button-down and his brown khakis. Alas, his sartorial missteps made no difference. You know your Adeline. She's always believed in the fundamental attractiveness of the poorly dressed male.

Nash Mac made eye contact only to break it a moment later. He didn't ask a thing of me, preferring to speak with Jeremy about work, about the way that Ron Gilbert had left the company, about finishing touches being put upon something called D.O.T.T.

Минерва and I were boooored. She kicked Jeremy beneath the table. He stopped talking. We all stopped talking.

"So what do you do?" asked Nash Mac.

"Me?" I said.

"Yes," he said. "You."

"I'm one of those poor souls doomed to wander the night without anything like a clear idea of what it is that she does. Don't you know that I feel obsolescence creeping upon me?"

"Is bullshit," said Минерва. "Adeline is artist."

"Now, darling," I said. "You know how I hate that word."

"But it's true," said Jeremy. "She's incredibly talented."

"And that talent, Nash Mac," I said, "is why I've spent the last few years drawing pictures of women in their bras. There's a great wide world of difference between being talented and being an artist. Talent is a curiosity that one squanders or develops. It doesn't mean a single thing."

"That is misguided bullshit," said Nash Mac. "People are distinguished by natural gifts. Some people are born beautiful. Some people are born smart. Some people are born talented. It's a crime to waste your gift. If you're okay with being a criminal, you're a fool. You'll regret it. If you don't already."

The waiter brought our entrees. Nash Mac consumed his pad thai, inhaling the meal. Awkward, messy, the noodles slipping over his face and fork. I am insane enough that it appealed to something deep in my soul.

We landed at Mad Dog in the Fog, an Irish sports bar on Haight Street. Минерва and Jeremy ordered a drink and made their strategic retreat, feigning exhaaaustion, leaving me by my lonesome with Nash Mac.

"So, Nash Mac," I said. "Why don't you inform me about the relationship with your last girlfriend? Are you still friends?"

"This is distasteful," he said. "Are you making fun of me? What did Jeremy tell you?"

"Nothing," I said. "Why so nervous? Did you cheat on the girl and leave her for someone else? I'm simply curious. A person's last relationship can tell you an awful lot."

"She's dead," he said.

"What," I said.

"I don't bring it up when I first meet people," he said. "It tends to murder conversation."

In my indecency, I pressed for details. He demurred. I inquired into his life. His father and mother, doctors with deep connections to the Shah, had fled Iran during the Revolution, bringing a young دومحم رصان into the States United, where he adapted to the new culture by bowdlerizing his own name, assuming an ultra-American identity. He graduated high school in Fairfax, Virginia, then ended up at college in Bloomington-Normal, where he'd studied computer science, graduating with his BS and then heading out for the Bay Area. Everyone was making noise about the prominence of the region, about the development of new technologies, about Steve Jobs and NeXT. He picked up work and learned that he couldn't stand employment at a normal corporation, that he'd dedicated his life to an intolerable industry. He quit his job with every intention of becoming a retail wage-slave, but then a friend suggested that he apply at LucasArts. They were looking for quality-assurance cogs. A week into this position and Nash Mac realized his passion for the material. He pushed his way up, functioning as an intermediary between the technology people and the designers. Initially, that line had been blurry, as the original designers were the people who created SCUMM, the primary scripting language of the LucasArts adventures. Yet the technology had accelerated so fast that it became impossible to both design and handle the back end. Nash Mac assumed his halfway position. He'd recently been promoted, working under Tim Schafer on *Day of the Tentacle*. Nash Mac liked Tim, liked D.O.T.T., but knew that he'd missed the golden age. LucasArts under Ron Gilbert was a palace of wonder. Gilbert was a master. Nash Mac treasured even his tangential involvement with *Monkey Island 2*.

"Some games are just games," said Nash Mac. "Some designers are only designers. Ron Gilbert is an artist. *Monkey Island* is real art. But the process is collaborative."

"That's all well and good," said I, delighting in my crassness, "but tell me about this girlfriend."

They met when he moved to the Bay Area, introduced by mutual friends. She lived in San Francisco, he resided near Menlo Park. The first year went well enough that when her lease expired, she made the daft suggestion they find a place together. Nash Mac thought it was surely too soon, but worried that saying no would end the relationship. She discovered a two-bedroom apartment in the Marina. She was fine. He was fine. Things were copacetic. Then her father died. Then her mother killed herself. Nash Mac attended the funerals, driving both times to Spokane, Washington. She lost her job. Nash Mac hadn't a clue what to say. Around then, he said, he came to understand that he'd moved in too soon. She started doing speed, keeping the activity clandestine, in shadows distant. Nash Mac was an innocent. He never made the connection. He simply thought that her mood was improving. Life continued on apace. As it must. As it does. She didn't work. He paid for everything. The speed started giving her grand swells of delusion and paranoia. She turned cruel. Nash Mac asked her to move out. She refused. He told her to retain her hold on the apartment. He'd leave. She said that he couldn't. He said it was happening. She said that she'd rather die than live alone. Nash Mac didn't believe her. She did it in the bathtub. He found the body, the gory lifeless mess, the blood and the water.

"The worst part," he said, "is that we hardly knew each other."

And that, darlings, is how I ended up with the first boyfriend of my postcollegiate life. I'd dumped a nonpracticing Jew and set up shop with a nonobservant Muslim. A microcosm of American foreign policy passing through my loins, the flesh of my flesh, the bone of my bone.

APRIL 1993

Adeline and Jeremy Go to a Signing at Comic Relief

In my boredumb, I started hanging out at The Owl and Monkey Café on Ninth Avenue, which served a customer base of aging burnouts with insatiable desires for coffee and homemade quiche. On occasion, these drug casualities would gather en masse and listen to the sounds of live acoustic music.

Meself, I sat near the counter, straining for cheap stereo sounds, avoiding any critique of the artworks that hung on the white walls and dodging stories about famous musicians who'd performed at the august institution. One gent in particular availed himself of the opportunity, every single day, to inform me that the cover of a Mike Bloomfield album had been photographed in the establishment. Each afternoon, he promised to bring the LP and show me. Yet he never did.

On the topic of records, I should note the day when I walked home from The Owl and Monkey and stumbled over a cache of discarded vinyl at the corner of Cole and Cart. This harvest, which I cherry-picked, provided the soundtrack of my life on those days when I was not in the café or sleeping at Nash Mac's apartment in the Sunset District.

Entertainment came through indulgence in Jeremy's comics collection. Befitting a gent who'd worked in the Marvel offices, the boy was rife with material. Boxes upon boxes upon boxes upon boxes. The reservoir ran deep. I devoured forty or so issues of Ann Nocenti on *Daredevil,* a run marked by yearly Christmas stories and Matt Murdock's espousal of pacifism whilst solving his problems through a perpetual recourse to violence.

Jeremy initiated me into the world of Los Brothers Hernandez, into *Eightball,* into Alan Moore's run on *Swamp Thing* with Steve Bissette and John Totleben, into *Hate,* into *Elfquest.* More titles, too, that I shan't mention. Some horrible, others ridiculous. Almost none of the creators were women.

"If you're interested," said Jeremy, "come next week to Comic Relief.

There's a Vertigo signing. Grant Morrison will be there. He sort of knows who I am. I had a few letters published in *Doom Patrol*."

Минерва wanted nothing to do with the event. She dismissed it as plain madness. "What Grant Morrison does for you?" she asked. "You pay him, not vice versa. Now you stare at his face for hours like risen Messiah. Strange people."

Yet there we were, April 18th, a Sunday, trudging towards the Upper Haight at 6 pm. Gray buildings, gray sky, gray faces, gray people. Fog over Buena Vista Park with sinister intent, carpet looming above Golden Gate Park.

Regarding the trees of the former, I thought, as ever, about the hey-hey heyday of the hippie era, imaginating how much smaller the vegetation would have been during the golden years, wondering if the psychopathologic influence of their increased heights wasn't responsible for the shift away from Luv on Haight.

The human mass outside of Comic Relief produced instant repulsion, like a finger on the trigger of my latent claustrophobia.

Jeremy assumed a place in line. I wandered the store, examining the scene. Morrison sat at his signing table, dressed in a twee black leather cap, wearing red-tinted sunglasses, a white shirt, and a black leather jacket. His outfit gave him a very San Francisco look. Everyone in San Francisco wore black leather jackets.

Beside him was Jill Thompson, remarkable with her witchy mingles and waving red hair. The third guest, Steve Yeowell, was notable for the normalcy of his appearance.

I milled about, thumbing books while Jeremy ascended through the line. I smiled my way to the front when I saw that mi amigo was chatting up Morrison. Jeremy schmoozed into the man's social good graces. They talked about *Animal Man*.

Jeremy asked Morrison what he and the others were doing after the event. To my surprise, Morrison told him. It should be remembered that Jeremy had worked in editorial at Marvel. His professional livelihood had been dependent on manipulating comics creators into doing his bidding.

I thought about, of all people, my late lamented father. Daddy offered such a presence within our home that we would forget about his civilian identity. We never remembered that he was an oral surgeon who maintained a thriving practice. His celebrity clientele remained distant concepts until those ridiculous moments when we'd be out in public and Daddy would fall into a conversation with Judd Nelson or Kathleen Turner.

Daddy dominated those dialogues. World-famous celebrities deferred to him. He had the right manner, the suave calm that perpetuated his business. He was the man who gave them their prize-winning smiles.

"Ah, fuck," said Morrison, in a Scots dialect. "We're down to a fifty years of LSD rave."

"I see," said Jeremy. "Good luck with that. Nice talking with you."

Outside, Jeremy said, "We've got to discover the location of that rave. We have to be there."

"Why ever didn't you ask? He seemed amenable," I said.

"Too awkward," said Jeremy. "But if we show up, that's a challenge met."

"You tell me, then," I said. "How do we find a rave in San Francisco?"

Jeremy rustled up a copy of the *SF Weekly,* a localized and lame alternative weekly that employed the same cover template as the *Village Voice.* Spreading the paper across the trunk of a parked car, Jeremy flipped through until landing upon a list of cultural events. "Look here," he said, pointing to an advertisement that read:

FOR ALL RAVE INFO CALL
RAVE HOTLINE
1-900-844-RAVE

"There's another on the other page," he said. "Same thing, but different number. 900-844-4RAV. We'll go home and use the telephone."

At Steiner House, Jeremy telephoned and listened. "It's on Folsom, south of Market. Robert Anton Wilson will be there. It starts at 8, so let's show up around 11. We can walk. It'll take about an hour."

Минерва stumbled in and decided to accompany us, whilst making it ever so plain that she still disapproved of Jeremy's fixation on Grant Morrison and other comics professionals, asking why he would ever desire such a thing and why he acted with such subterfuge. "I don't know," he said. "It seems interesting. His run on *Doom Patrol* was exceptional, okay?"

I strung together an outfit from my own rough materials and Минерва's discards. Tiger-striped tights, purple sweater, green army jacket, knee-high brown boots.

The walk down Haight was borrrrrrrrrrrrrring. By the time our legs crossed Market, fatigue settled on my brow. Carried away by Jeremy's enthusiasm, I hadn't considered my decision. Going to a rave, embracing a scene that I'd rejected in NYC, a scene that I'd decidedly besmirched before a certain somebody. But that's very me, isn't it, darlings? Grade-A hypocrite.

I imagined him at that moment, ambling towards a club, listening to ghastly music and schmoozing with people for whom he harbored no particular affection.

Our journey was a drift through the homeless and the destitute and the indigent. People screaming with desperate cries. A miniature drama staged on every corner. The threat of violence lingered, but our individual appearances added up to a sum total that dissuaded outside interference.

Ninety-five percent of the time, it's as simple as looking weiiiiiird. Why bother with a freak when there's always another easy victim around the corner?

1015 Folsom Street was only another nondescript relic from the industrial era, a place converted into four stories of dancefloors. I'd been to Tunnel. I'd been to Limelight. I'd been to Mars. I possessed an immediate understanding of the layout.

I contemplating drinking myself absolutely stinko blotto, but decided instead on eating hallucinogens in celebration of fifty years with Dr. Hoffman's problem child. Although, I must say, that for yours truly there has always been a kind of hyperintoxication that emerges from alcohol, when the head spins, when the streets rise with power, that has struck me as very close to the experience of consuming lysergic acid diethylamide.

Don't you know, my sweet things, that for an event explicitly tied to drug use, I had a rather difficult time observing any obvious ingestion. I surveyed the scene, hunting for degenerates and dopers. No matter how hard that I searched, I seemed doomed, like the protagonist of a mildly popular country ballad, to never discover the object of my longing.

I changed my approach. Amongst the dancing bodies, the laser shows, the pounding electronica vibe, the circus, I sent out a psychic signal. Putting on my very best little-girl-lost face, I leaned against an exposed metal girder and waited for men to come and speak.

Talk they did. All manner of balderdash. I asked each one if there was any MDMA upon his person, yet each was appalled and refused my request. Finally, the last of them, a bit overweight and sweaty for my tastes, offered me two tablets imprinted with McDonald's golden arches.

Obligation hung heavy upon me. He'd given me intoxicants, so I let the man go on and on and on and on and on and on and on, tuning in and out of his monologue, waiting for the drugs to take hold. "In a truly dance-oriented shamanistic society," he said, "we would all be known by our own personalized dance as much as by name. In fact, our very names would become synonymous with our external manifestation of our inner being. And to others, these names would also take on their own personal meaning. Individual symbols of individual existence."

Unsure how to respond, I started dancing, a crazy little St. Vitus dance. I melted away towards the floor. Darlings, how I danced. Yet I wasn't listening to the music.

My thoughts were of an album that I'd rescued from trash. *Lark* by Linda Lewis. I'd picked it up assuming that it was an example of 1970s schmaltz but instead found a quiet album marked by clear production, constructed to highlight Lewis's five-octave range. She could go from a deep growl to a breathless high-pitched sound. The best song was "It's the Frame." Her voice sang within my head: *Now, Lord, well you don't wanna be alone in Heaven, do ya? Wouldn't you like me and my friends and my family for company?*

Минерва emerged from within the crowd, giving me a bottle of water. "Drink," said she. I danced and danced and danced and danced and danced but now was victim to looping drug logic. The experience of an idea imprinting itself upon your waking mind, like a dealer's brand pressed upon a pill. I could see individual dances like signatures, identifying signifiers as distinct and powerful as names. What would it be like to live within a truly dance-oriented shamanic society? How ever would dances function as repeatable signatures? The human body mutates, as does one's sense of self. The name remains unattached. I saw dances shift through constant change. Even my own. I undulated, an oddity with my arms, as if I were performing a butterfly stroke. I'd never danced like that before. I never have since. How could one maintain a style of dance long enough to establish a workable social identity? Michael Jackson had The Moonwalk, but what else was there? What would happen in a truly dance-oriented shamanic society to poor souls incapable of rhythm? I danced with the awkwardness of a white girl. Would my failure to stay on beat mark me out with the equivalent of a regional dialect? Would one's lack of ability separate one from society?

Inhaling a deeeeep breath of toxic club air, holding it within until I slowed my beating heart. I exhaled and repeated the dreary process. I'd wanted a pure drug experience, but now I was infected with this masculine taxonomy where even dance was destroyed by a man's language, by another man's insufferable need to rewrite society. I suspect that my benefactor believed himself a fellow on the cusp of a new society, of a viable alternative, but he attempted to tear down the master's house with the master's tools. Real change would come only when hordes of thick Amazon women conquered the American male, when warrioresses stormed the White House with bows and arrows, when they invaded the boardrooms of the corporate empire, when Fortune 500 CEOs were subject to processes that instilled humility.

People kept talking about CRASH WORSHIP. Every mouth in the room said CRASH WORSHIP. I asked, "What's CRASH WORSHIP?" and they said, "CRASH WORSHIP is the main event. It's why everyone's here." "I presumed that everyone was attending to celebrate the fiftieth anniversary of LSD." "Yeah, that too, but, like, we're mostly all here to, like, see CRASH WORSHIP."

You'll forgive me, darlings, but the  states that every human being is entitled to at least five experiences in her life beyond the descriptions of words, and CRASH WORSHIP was one of my personal quintet.

People together in a pit, surrounded by drumming. Fires built. Liquids thrown. Dancing, dancing, dancing. CRASH WORSHIP finished its set. The atmosphere had evaporated. We'd been moved to a different realm. Space and time no longer existed.

Jeremy talked with Grant Morrison. "I'm working on something new," said Morrison in his Scots dialect, rougher than before. "I think it's the big one. I think it might change everything."

"I've got an idea, too," said Jeremy. "We should compare notes."

"I'll give you my address," said Morrison. "You can write me a letter."

"What time is it?" I asked.

"It's almost 2 am," said Grant Morrison. "I feel like a dandy in the fucking underworld."

"How long was I dancing?" I asked Jeremy.

"Hours," he said. "Минерва took a cab home."

"Did you enjoy CRASH WORSHIP?" I asked Grant Morrison.

"Aye," he said. "That I did."

"I think I may have seen God," I said.

"Really?" asked Grant Morrison. "How do you know?"

MAY 1993

ADELINE ♥ Baby

Somehow I embroiled Nash Mac and myself within a ridiculous fight about crime rates, with yours truly staking the claim that San Francisco was a backwater compared against New York City. People can be astonishingly provincial about the homes they've chosen, taking pride in all manner of absurdity, and so the boy argued for hours, insisting that his adopted hometown was worse than anywhere in America.

When one factored in the gangs and the homeless, he said, Baghdad by the Bay was far less safe than any other locale. He spoke of how often he'd been mugged, of the time when someone had punched him in the head.

Yet I was a New Yorker of a certain vintage. Absolute knowledge of the 1990 murder rate, constituting two thousand two hundred and forty-five deaths, had been tattooed upon the neural pathways of my brain. I'd suffered the crackhead influx, swum the primordial ooze of the Lower East Side and its junkies, bore witness to untold numbers of crime. There were always more dress suits for hire. There was always another bathtub.

My anecdotal and statistical evidence meant nothing to Nash Mac. He knew everything. He always knew everything. After all, darlings, the man worked with computers.

Storming out of Nash Mac's flat, elemental heat pouring from my eyes, I leapt upon the N Judah. By the time I disembarked, I was laughing at myself, at how lunatic I'd gone with fervor.

If you can believe it, I'd never before had such a heated fight, not with any of my other boyfriends. Not even Ian fucking Covington. I hoped, with every wispy strand of my soul, that I wasn't in love.

I arrived at Steiner House in time to witness Минерва's bandmates shuffling out of the front door. I'd never spoken with any of them, not the femme chellovecks nor the San Rafael adolescent. They raised their hands to greet me. I motioned back with a royal wave. They turned the corner, heading towards the Upper Haight.

Минерва smoked from her bong in the living room, sitting beside a stack of flyers advertising the next performance of Daddy Was in KGB. Imagining the babushkas plotting official business in my de facto bedroom, I recollected again the indignities of the freeloading houseguest.

"You see girls?" she asked.

"Yes, and your pubescent with them," I said.

"Nice boy," she said. "I think loves Нина. Girl does not notice."

"That's cute," I said.

Daddy Was in KGB were scheduled to perform in two weeks' time at the Night Break, a club on Haight separated by a small space from the bowling alley. The other bands on the bill were The Mecies, Kill Sybil, and The Bottom Feeders. According to a parenthetical note on the flyer, Kill Sybil were from Seattle.

Минерва had invited me to go with her to an event at Night Break called Sushi Sundays, during which the management erected tables and set up an impromptu restaurant. The denizens of San Francisco sat devouring tekka-maki and kappa-maki and were entertained by local punk and metal bands. I'd declined.

Following a few merry-go-rounds with Минерва's bong and its sweet maryjane, I couldn't help myself. I spilled the beans about my fight with Nash Mac. "That boy is such a clod," I said. "You know New York, darling, you've been there. You remember what it was like. San Francisco is nothing."

"Wrong," said Минерва.

"What?" I asked.

"Wrong idea," she said. "San Francisco is deadly."

"We walked over the corpses of junkies! You were a Tompkins Square anarchist!"

"San Francisco is too fresh," she said. "You are tourist. Sorry, but is true."

"Two thousand two hundred and forty-five murders in 1990!" I said. "The city elected a fascist because it couldn't deal with the crime! San Francisco is a liberal paradise with a handful of muggers!"

"No argument," said Минерва. "We seek truth like explorers. Come, get your coat."

She brought me down Steiner, over to 14th, across Market on Church past Aardvark Books, over to 18th and Dolores Park, and then on to Mission Street. Our footsteps punctuated only by Минерва's color commentary. "Never eat at Sparky's," she said. "Instant diarrhea. Instant misery. But open late." Then: "You see church in distance? Where they shoot *Vertigo*.

Alfred Hitchcock. We see screening at Castro. Typical misogynist domination fantasy. Kim Novak shaped by two different men. Winterbloss loves. Says is about depth of obsession and despair. Sure thing."

The Mission was one locale that I had not fully explored. The dreary place always seemed too much a wasteland, beyond reach and without purpose. Now, in the streetlamps and headlights, it appeared not so very different from the 1980s desolation of the East Village. The human faces and bodies were different but I viiiibed on the crumbling sidewalks and broken pavement.

"We go here," said Минерва, pointing to a building at the corner of 20th. The neon read HUNT'S QUALITY DONUTS, donut-shaped letters falling into a giant coffee cup. Along the building read the ominous tag: OPEN 25 HOURS A DAY. My heart fluttered, all pitter patter, as I recalled Disco Donuts.

"An extra hour of life," said Минерва.

You needn't ask for a description, reader, to conceive of the unsavory characters hanging about on the pavement. It took all types, my sweet nothings. I steeled myself for the catcalling, but through intercession of the Virgin Mother, Минерва and I ran the gauntlet without a word. They didn't see us. We were the invisibles.

Within the warmth of the restaurant, the human comedy advanced to Act IV. To our left was the serving counter. Tables filled the rest of the restaurant, tables occupied by drunkards, by hollow men, by Latino gangsters, by drug dealers, by the criminal class, by the broken, by the miserable, by the bored, by the extraterrestrial. A layer of smoke hung over the panoply, thick like a fog shroud above the Haight, penetrated by flickering fluorescent light. Oh Lord, thought I, please let my Ruskie friend get to her point.

Минерва surveyed the customers. I ambled to the counter and ordered doughnuts. The poor boy took my order, smiling, made my change, and pushed across mi donas. They appeared day-old and stale, but one never refuses wafers in church. I bit into one of my prizes, rushing with the vile sugar and dough, the taste reaffirming what it meant to be a citizen of these States United.

Минерва extracted a doughnut from my bag. "Him," she said, biting into the cheap delight. She nodded towards an individual sitting at the back.

He had the appearance of someone's junky uncle, the kind who'd come for Thanksgiving dinner, shoot up in the bathroom, and then nod off while passing the cranberry sauce. "Man we come for," said Минерва.

She sat opposite him. I sat beside her. He looked up. The fluorescence made him ashen, a visage like the secret decade that existed between the 1940s and 1950s, where every clock's hands always pointed to the twenty-fifth hour. "Yes?" he asked.

"We need object," said Минерва. "You sold me object before, remember?"

"I think I remember you," he said. "I think I remember you."

"Yes," said Минерва. "Great friends. Amigos."

"What is that you need?"

"A knife," she said. "Special knife."

"What's so special about this knife?"

"I want knife that stabbed a man," she said. "With blood on blade. Not fresh. Dried blood."

"That could be hard to come by," he said.

"Thirty bucks," she said. "No more, no less."

He stood and left.

"Eat doughnut," said Минерва. "We wait."

"Are you quite certain this man will return?" I asked. "He almost certainly made you for a copper."

"He comes," she said, biting into the brown frosting.

Hunt's Quality Donuts. A hot-stepping hoedown where everything had gone wrong. The bloodshot alcoholic eyes of the other customers. The cheap wine. The disgraced tables. Act V. I'd spent my adult life fetishizing the outré of the urban landscape, indulging in the decay which only an abandoned city can produce, but beneath the smoke and green light of Hunt's, I experienced a moment of doubt and pain. Whoever these people were, they were not on our side. These people didn't have a side. They were as distant as the Sahara.

The man returned with a rolled-up towel. He sat across from Минерва and unrolled his package. Surely enough, there was a knife, a serrated blade, with uneven and spotty brown stains along its length.

"You didn't get this from me," he said. "I'll deny it."

"Sure thing," said Минерва. Turning to me, she said, "Pay man."

Not about to refuse a knife-wielding gentleman, I sputtered out a response that died into nothing. I wished she'd told me. I could have had my money ready. Instead, I dug through my purse beneath watchful stares of the criminal class. I counted out the bills.

"Put in purse," said Минерва, handing me the knife.

The man stood up and rushed out.

"Fucking junkies," said Минерва. "No manners."

I finished my second doughnut. We exited Hunt's. Yes, I suppose, it was impressive that one could buy a bloodstained knife in a doughnut shop. The speed certainly was remarkable, taking less time than a delivered pizza. Still, aren't junkies always stabbing each other? The North American continent was crammed full with knives caked in their victims' effluvia. Yet I wasn't about to argue the point with Минерва, knowing that it's always best to let your landlords win their pyrrhic victories. We must allow others their idiosyncrasies.

At 17th and Church, whilst Минерва occupied herself with a store window, I dropped the knife into the trash can. As I stepped away, I looked down at the gutter and saw graffiti carved into the pavement by some cad who'd come upon it while the cement was still wet:

BUCK ♥ bAbyDoll

Don't you know that it gave me the Mississippi boll-weevil blues? It took all my blossoms and left me with an empty square.

Who was Buck? Who was Babydoll? Were they still together? Perhaps they'd always be together, perhaps the permanence of cement meant that their relationship could never end, that theirs would be one of the great love stories.

Yet all great love stories end in tragedy. Héloïse and Abelard, Bonnie and Clyde, Romeo and Juliet, Sid and Nancy, Scott Summers and Jean Grey.

It wasn't Nash Mac flashing in my head. Nor Jon de Lee. It wasn't even Ian fucking Covington. Don't you know, darlings, that I thought of Baby Baby Baby?

BABY ♥ aDelINE

ADELINE ♥ bAby

I heard his voice. "Adeline, stop thinking of me," he said. "You can't repeat the past."

"Can't repeat the past? Why, of course you can."

JUNE 1993

Jeremy Makes a Proposition

Jeremy labored from home, stationed at his computer, playing a pre-release of *Day of the Tentacle*. Weeks passed bathed in the blue glow of his monitor. He reported by telephone and through email. Nash Mac still went into the office, rarely discussing the project. I asked Jeremy to show me the game, to show me the fruits of their struggles.

Using the computer's mouse, one navigated characters around a très outré mansion. I gathered from Jeremy's comments that this was rather similar to *Maniac Mansion*, the game to which *Day of the Tentacle* served as a sequel.

What separated the latter from the former was the novelty of being able to navigate the mansion through three separate historical eras, these being the American Revolution, the present day, and the far future. The player controlled one character in each time period, passing items between them via an arcane mechanism that involved the flushing of toilets.

I don't deny that the mechanism was clever, and the graphics impressed in their Tex Avery style, but I only played about as long as I could manage, which was somewhat under thirty minutes.

Jeremy found his computer sitting idle and myself returned to the living room. "You didn't like the game?" he asked.

"Darling, I didn't dislike it," I said, "but it's someone else's cup of tea. One thing did surprise me."

"What's that?"

"The attempts at humor. Are all games like that?"

"All LucasArts games are funny," he said. "Except for *Loom*. *Loom* was moody."

"How very remarkable," I said. "Nash Mac is less interested in humor than any boy that I've ever dated. Yet there he sits toiling, day and night, on D.O.T.T."

"Computer people are weird," said Jeremy, "I have no idea what I'm doing with my life."

Jeremy wasn't like Nash Mac. Technology wasn't in his blood.

"To be honest," he said, "I kind of hate it."

"Why don't you do something else?" I asked.

"I have an idea," he said.

He went in his bedroom and returned with a sheaf of papers and several notebooks. He laid them on the floor. "Look through them," he said, but I demurred, suggesting that he play docent and give me a tour. I didn't dare make my own journey through that voluminous body.

Jeremy had dreamt up a comic about a society of anthropomorphic cats. The first ten issues would follow one family through history, from primitive sabretooth origins to a late medieval period. Each of these early issues would focus on one cat interacting with the troubles of their world. Some would be high adventure, others snapshots of historical domesticity. By the tenth issue, in which we meet Felix Trill, the series' main protagonist, it is apparent that the previous cats have been incarnations of the same soul, the soul which now inhabits Trill's body.

From issue ten, the narrative follows Trill as he goes on a winding adventure through the medieval world. Jeremy had yet to plot out that adventure, but if the time ever came, he'd work off of patterns in the previous nine issues. The details, he was sure, would emerge from his cranial lobes.

"With the way the direct market works," said Jeremy, "all you have to do is publish with a splash. Everything is print to order, and the orders are nonreturnable. I know Dave Sim. He said that if I ever get anything together, he'll run a preview in the back of *Cerebus,* which means orders in the thousands, if not higher. It's like minting money, except you're also creating work. I know that I can make this happen."

"So why not?" I asked.

"I need an artist," he said, with a finality that gave me the fear.

"You should make it a love match with your lady," I said. "Her line work has gotten very fine."

"Минерва has no interest," said Jeremy. "Plus, she couldn't follow through. I was thinking about you, actually."

There was the long conversation and the hard sell. I resisted. I did not believe in art. I did not want to be an artist. As much as I had enjoyed my brief dalliance with the wonderful world of comics, I couldn't be interested in a full-time gig. I'd seen Grant Morrison, seen Jill Thompson, even seen poor old Steve Yeowell. I didn't want to be a rock star, didn't want to be surrounded by acolytes, didn't want to be stalked at raves by would-be writers. I was so old, reader. All I wanted was for the world to leave me alone. I wanted to grow aged, obscurely in obscurity, my final days spent in a nursing home flushed with golden light. I didn't want anyone to know my name. I didn't want people expecting things.

"There's no point," I said. "Art is meaningless."

"I figured you might say that," said Jeremy. "There's one last thing I want to show you."

He went back into his bedroom and this time returned with a little booklet printed on 8 x 11-inch sheets of paper, folded in half and stapled together. Right away, my peepers spotted it for what it was. Someone's zine. Jeremy pushed the booklet upon me.

I looked at the front page and in my shock I saw it. Very familiar lettering surrounded by the line drawing of a bathtub:

DRESS SUITS ON FIRE

"What in the holy high hell goddamn!" I said.

"I bought it at Bound Together," he said.

"This isn't original," I said. "It must be a Xerox of a Xerox. Of a Xerox."

"I asked at the store," he said. "New copies get mailed in every six months. You made this thing, what, five years ago? Somebody was moved enough to keep it in print. And Adeline, it's good. It's really good. You're letting everything go to waste."

There I was, back again, on the street looking up at rotting plastic and an aging tuxedo.

I attended a screening of *Sliver* at the Galaxy Theatre, a monstrosity of a building with enormous screens and a functionless yet delicious glass lobby presumably constructed as salve to the architect's ego.

When I moseyed on over to see the film, I hadn't the slightest that it starred Sharon Stone. Watching her thrash around in a bathtub, I couldn't help but think of her previous flicker, another scandal du jour titled *Basic Instinct,* which had provoked insanity in the American nation by featuring a brief intimation of Stone's outer labia. A great deal of that film takes place in a club based on Limelight.

Sliver convinced me that there were no standards for cultural products. Jeremy's hard sell had left me worried about working on a project released for public consumption, worried that if I said yes, we'd make something that wasn't up to snuff.

I'd been measuring myself against expectations of the Good. *Sliver* taught me that I had the idea backwards. It's never a matter of being good. One needn't be good. This is America! There are no standards. Nothing is good. One needn't be good, one only need be no worse than anything else. One only need be as bad as *Sliver*.

"You win, amigo," said I to Mr. Winterbloss. "I'm yours if you'll have me. Fetch me my ink and my paper."

Jeremy'd decided that the comic would be black and white, and he'd concluded that we must have at least three issues completed before he initiated the business end. Independent comic books, he said, worked best when the issues came out on a regular monthly schedule. The road to Rome was lined with promising projects that had fallen apart because of creators unable to stick to a schedule. If I drew sixty-six pages and three covers, it'd keep us from a false start.

Jeremy's scripts were an especial torture, as his descriptions were massively elaborate yet exceptionally vague.

> **PAGE ONE, PANEL ONE:** WE SEE A BIPEDAL SABRETOOTH CAT EXPLORING AN UNCONQUERED WORLD, BLEAK IN ITS EXPANSE, OVERPOWERING IN ITS ENORMITY. THE UNIVERSE SHIMMERS ALONG ITS MICROCOSMIC/MACROCOSMIC SPLIT. WE SEE IT ALL IN THE CAT'S POSTURE.

"Jeremy, darling, what in the world do you mean?" I asked. "How could a person draw such a thing?"

"You're the artist! Figure it out, Adeline!"

Much of my time was spent in the reading room of the Park Branch Library. I'd walk over to Paige Street with my paper and pencils, station myself, and dig through the tomes for reference imagery.

I reeked of ambition when I started, developing an intricate and controlled line, but soon discovered that precision made it impossible to produce pages with anything like due speed. I simplified my style, focusing on the fluidity of line, going cartoony on the figure work while maintaining a level of detail with the backgrounds. I inked in heavy blacks, the density undercutting the saccharine cuteness.

Those weeks disappeared, eaten by my process. Drawing, café, library, Nash Mac. Repeat, repeat, repeat! Repeat! Soldier on, O Dear Adeline!

One of San Francisco's street people took up late-night residence on Steiner Street. This ne'er-do-well arrived each and every around 1 am, heralded by the telltale sound of his shopping cart, and spent several hours screaming out non sequiturs. Many times he went on and on and on and on about food products. Other times he remarked upon traffic regulations.

I dreamt of drawing, dreamt of the cat people. One dream, in particular, stood out, and I included it in issue #2. You'll find the transmuted sequence, darlings, on page 13, where the cat people are standing before an obelisk.

In the dream, I watched from a far distance, their backs turned until one noticed my presence. The rest followed its lead. A sea of cats' eyes, green and blue.

What you won't see on the page, however, is that the central cat was looking at me with the eyes of good ol' Patrick Geoffrois, my dashingly bizarre Frenchman, the blackest magician in the Lower East Side.

Patrick was the greatest freak with whom I'd ever made an acquaintance, and he had arrived at the very moment when I needed a friend disconnected from my past and with whom there was a total absence of romantic tension.

Baby had taken an instant dislike to my pal, convinced that I'd turned acolyte of the dark arts, crushed by Aleister Crowley. Poor Baby! It was beyond his mortal ken that one could vibe on magickal aesthetics without believing a single word.

The people who one meets are so dreadfully boring, aren't they? Whatever criticisms you might lob at M. Geoffrois, the man never bored. He was a traveling circus, clad in black and dressed in the gaudiest baubles that ever bubbled.

Missing the man, I sent him a few postcards. He never wrote back.

JULY 1993

Daddy Was in KGB Gets a Good Review

A bright moment occurred when the *Bay Guardian* featured Daddy Was in KGB as "Demo Tape O' The Week." Минерва rushed into the apartment, her pale face flushed with ruddy color. It was the first time in our friendship where she'd displayed unbridled enthusiasm. She seemed positively American.

> With the fall of the Berlin Wall and the evaporation of Communism, it wasn't a question of "if?" but of "when?" and "where?" I'm happy to report that the when is now and the where is here. Daddy Was in the KGB, a S.F. punk outfit made up of four women who've escaped the former Soviet States, offers a headcrunching, genre-bending response to the last few years of realpolitik. Songs like "Sergey Kirov Makes Fuck in Karl Marx" and "Do It in Your NKVDs" warp the mind and offer a PhD-level education in Russian history and American consumerism. A shiver went up my spine when I heard lead vocalist Minerva Krylenko's bloodcurdling cry of "Messerschmitt fire at Leningrad, made blood in ground plan, don't have cow, man!" The instrumentation is simple but effective, reminding us that those boys from Seattle and Portland may have "rediscovered" something that never went away.
>
> ALEX LASH

> Send tapes to Demo Tape, Bay Guardian, 520 Hampshire, S.F., CA 94110.

"I hadn't the slightest that you'd recorded a demo," said I.

"Secret well kept," she said. "Band agreed not to tell. Next we press 7-inch."

We were all imbibing at Mad Dog in celebration. I watched those wild Russian girls running up and down, acting as if they'd won the Nobel Prize in economics. Even the drummer showed his chubby little face. Despite looking as if he'd crawled straight from the crib, the bartenders didn't ask for proof of his age.

Two beers into the evening and the child became sullen. Минерва and I engaged him in conversation, but it was like extracting teeth with pliers. After his fourth drink, it emerged that the article had hurt his feelings, as it had presumed that he was both a girl and a Soviet. He was especially peeved that the reviewer had misrepresented the band's name, throwing in the decidedly un-Russian definite article.

The young lad spent the night under the kitchen table, waking me at 4 am with the sounds of his vomit splattering against the ancient toilet. *Doesn't this child,* says me to meself, *have parents?*

JULY 1993

D.O.T.T. Goes Gold

Day of the Tentacle went gold and shipped. Nash Mac blossomed into a sweeter person, a massive tension released from his body, as if he'd shrugged off the terrible weight. To mark the occasion, we went to the Tonga Room, where we became unspeakably tight, and then walked back to his apartment. From Nob Hill to the Sunset, across three blotto hours. Inhaling the city, languishing under its burdens.

Near Van Ness, we met a homeless woman, reasonably well dressed, only a few years older than I. She was pressed against a building, begging for change. I slipped her a dollar. The poor thing started singing an off-key version of "She Loves You" by The Beatles.

Any song but that! What if Nash Mac read meaning into the lyrics?

I'd such a wonderful time, rutting in the Sunset, that I telephoned him at work the next day, suggesting we meet again. He told me to amble on over around 8 pm, which was fine with yours truly, as I was planning to spend the day at The Owl and Monkey.

Nash Mac's rented house was not very far from the ocean, a two-bedroom installation with a roommate who was never home. I let myself in. Yes, darlings, we'd progressed to the point where I had my own key.

The lights were off. Stepping into the living room, I presumed that the boy was not at home. Then I heard the breathing from the couch and saw him curled up like a foetus that's survived its own abortion. He may well have been crying, but I didn't dare investigate, fearful of producing emasculation.

"Nash Mac?" I asked.

"My whole life," he said, "my whole life is over."

"How's that, brother?"

He'd arrived at work, late, and come upon his co-workers playing the leaked 0.5 alpha of a forthcoming game called *DOOM*, which was published by iD Software. iD's earlier work on *Wolfenstein 3D* was revolutionary, but Nash Mac intuited from this early version of *DOOM* that a massive leap had been made. This was the big one, he said, the one that would cleave the past from the future, and it was clear that his division at LucasArts was on the wrong side of history. "No one will play adventure games in five years. No one. I don't like any other games. What am I going to do?"

Yours truly lacked the proper vocabulary to make a convincing argument. What was an alpha release? What was an adventure game? So I thought about it for a moment and then decided to work in generalities, best to discuss life at the end of the American Century.

"You must realize," said I, "that you're talking with a person who believes that we live in a society which is completely off its rocker. We've spent fifty years, at least, pretending in the supremacy of technology. All we've received in return is screens to stare into and cars that poison the environment. Technology, dear heart, will never save any of us. It may make some number of us richer, but to what end do you put that money? To buy more technology. I wouldn't worry. If you make one kind of game or another, it won't change a single thing. You're still distracting people from their lives. It's all a con. America is the greatest con, and the most perverse. America is a con that America runs on itself. I've spent my whole life being told about the things that I should want and the things that should matter. Yet I'm old enough to know that none of it matters. None of it has ever mattered. I don't care about Harvard. I don't care about wealth. I don't care about prestige. I don't care about the ambitions of the upper middle classes and those who are desperate to scramble into it. My heroes are drag queens and drug addicts. My heroes die at twenty-seven. I'm older than them now, darling, so not only am I a failure but also a full hypocrite."

In bang-on fashion, batting a thousand for sensitivity, this was the worst thing that I could have said. He withdrew even further into his protective cocoon, curling tighter.

"It's all over," he said. "It's all fucking over."

Vulnerability always was one of Adeline's turn-ons. The weaker the sob sister, the more I wanted to sleep with him, the more I wanted to help him maintain his eroding macho status.

I rummaged through Nash Mac's kitchen, making him some oatmeal with fresh strawberries and a dash of honey. I wouldn't see him this upset again until he frittered away hours attempting an install of Slackware 1.0 on his spare 386SX, only to discover that the last three of his twenty-four 3½-inch floppies were useless with bad sectors.

"Eat this," said I. "The heat will help."

OCTOBER 1993

Adeline Receives a Postcard

I should have learned from Emil. I should have learned from Daddy. I should have learned from Baby. The universe had sent me the message three times, as plain as possible. *Adeline*, it said, *Adeline, don't ever take too much pleasure in anything. It's when things seem their best, Adeline,* said the universe, *that I'll fuck you up the most. Adeline, don't get arrogant. Adeline, stay far from hubris.*

I ignored the obvious and let myself be happy. I'd finished my sixty-six pages and three covers. When I reached page 40, Jeremy started working his connections. He'd asked Dave Sim if we could preview in the back of *Cerebus*. Sim said yes, whenever we wanted, simply send him the pages. He'd even connected us with a cheap printer, Preney Print and Litho of Windsor, Ontario. Everything was set. We were ready. We even had a name: *Trill.*

Jeremy'd taken leave from LucasArts. He was checking the post every day, like clockwork, waiting to receive formal notice from several distributors. We'd developed a tiny routine, him retrieving the mail and myself waiting for the good news.

Then, on that night, he came into the living room. "I'm sorry," he said.

"What is it?" I asked. "Is it Diamond? Was there bad news?"

"No," he said. "It's this. It's for you."

It was a postcard with a picture of the Empire State Building on its front, the kind of cheap item that one bought for pennies in Times Square. I flipped it over. Patrick's wife's handwriting.

Oct. 2

Hello Adeline,

Your friend Patrick died on September 12th. He had a stroke.

"New York is calling one back home. It's time to ramble," I said, the words cutting across the roof of my mouth as they made their terrible way out. Goodbye, California, goodbye.

DECEMBER 1993

Dorian Corey

New Year's Eve is only another stitch in the great tapestry of distant drug memories, but I'm positive that I wasted my evening in a dismal club. Eyes blasted, nose aching, chemical drip leaching into the back of my throat. Christmas is the same. Only blurry intimations of jingling bells and Salvation Army Santa Clauses.

My memory of the period is very spotty. And not because of my chemical intake. The drugs goofed up my memory, sure, but the writing was way worse.

The more that I vomited out words, the less that my own life maintained its texture, the less that I remembered of my daily existence. My brain couldn't juggle two realities, couldn't maintain its focus, so I plunged further into the world that paid the bills, into the world that kept me rent stabilized.

Of that entire holiday season, only one thing stands out. A headline that ran in either the *New York Post* or *Newsday*: DRAG QUEEN LEFT MUMMY BEHIND.

The queen in question, Dorian Corey, died in August. She was famous. You may remember her from the documentary *Paris Is Burning*. You may not.

For something like twenty years, Dorian designed clothes for other ballroom queens from her apartment on West 140th Street. When she croaked, another victim of AIDS, her friend Lois Taylor inherited the wardrobe. The glory and the glitter. Word got around that if people needed outré outfits, they should get in touch with Lois.

Two straight guys asked Lois if Dorian's apartment might hold a black cape. They were going to a Halloween party, and one of them wanted to dress like Dracula. Lois said, sure, honey, come and take a look. She let them explore the bedroom-sized closet. Lois saw a bag on the floor, beneath an orange dress. She tried to lift the bag. It was too heavy. One of the men cut the bag with a pair of scissors, releasing a boggy stench.

—What is this? asked the guy. A dead dog?

And here the story goes Only in New York. One of the men identified himself as a cop. Consider that. Consider a straight cop digging through a queen's closet in Harlem, looking for a cape because he wanted to dress up like Dracula.

Anyhoo, guess what he found?

A mummified body wrapped in naugahyde. Through a disgusting process, which involved cutting the fingers off at the second knuckles, injecting them with a special solution, slipping the skin off the bone, and finally, a police technician wearing the fingertips like a glove, the corpse was identified.

Bobby Wells a/k/a Bobby Worley, born 1938. Arrested for rape in 1963. Last seen in 1968. It's possible that Dorian lived with his body for twenty-five years.

The club kids were crazy with the mummy. Who could blame them? Michael Alig loved it, couldn't stop talking about Dorian. It was the weirdest story in a long time, the old striking out against the new, a reminder that even with growing gentrification and the reign of Mayor Rudy Über Alles, the city remained the most bizarre place on earth.

A mummy in a drag queen's closet! So perfect. So New York. So beyond my imaginative powers as a writer.

—Educate me about this fucking mummy, Parker said over the telephone. Give me the scoop on Dorian Corey.

I made up a story about how Dorian charged admission to see the corpse. Back in the early '80s, when things were bleak. She only asked for five dollars. The lie satisfied Parker. More gossip to throw in his colleagues' faces. The inside scoop. The real deal.

I only hoped that he wouldn't end up the fool, bloviating about nothing. But who would challenge him? People in publishing were afraid of Parker.

He was big and he was abusive.

And he was my main man.

Parker transformed my pages into cash money, keeping me in my coffers. In this arena, none of his many efforts had matched the feat of optioning *Trapped Between Jupiter and a Bottle* to the Hollywood director/producer Alan J. Pakula.

When Pakula first started sniffing around, I rented several of his films. The best was *All the President's Men*, starring Robert Redford at the height of his beauty. Robert Redford was gorgeous. I couldn't get over it. I ended up renting *The Candidate,* a slightly earlier film where his face radiates off the celluloid, his very image imprinted upon the human brain.

All the President's Men featured two-time Academy Award winner Jason Robards in the role of *Washington Post* editor Ben Bradlee. Robards made me think of Adeline, of the time that he took her to Serendipity III. Not that I needed any excuse to think of Adeline. I thought about Adeline every stupid day.

I told Brickley that if Pakula wanted the book, and if Pakula would fork over a ridiculous chunk of change, then, please, Parker Brickley, take your twenty percent. Set up the deal. I needed the cash.

Pakula's largesse bought an incredible luxury. It gave me free time. I quit my job at Theatre 80. Partly because I'd been blessed with the imprimatur of Hollywood, Parker was able to negotiate a much bigger advance on the next book.

That's the one that nearly killed me.

JANUARY 1994

Baby Attends the Launch for Philip Levine's *The Bread of Time*

Despite it being an explicit work of science fiction, Parker had convinced Michael Kandel to publish *Trapped Between Jupiter and a Bottle* with the trade dress of a literary novel. Books are like pastry. Presentation is everything.

My trite SFisms about the future and gene splicing and robots, written with the sorry earnestness of youth, were misconceived as dense metaphorical allegories about present-day society. I stopped being a geek interested in spaceships. I became a postmodernist.

Most reviewers situated *Trapped* within a trend of new literary works encompassing the outward aesthetics of genre fiction. Comparisons included Robert Coover, Thomas Pynchon, and Don DeLillo. A sizeable minority rejected this review, believing it closer to the nihilit of Bret Easton Ellis. My favorite review appeared in *The Houston Chronicle*. This minor masterpiece suggested a link between the elephantine appearance of Michelle Gila and the Hindu god Ganesha, reading my novel as a substrata retelling of Vedic literature. Michelle Gila was the new remover of obstacles, swiping away the world's troubles with his synthcoke-encrusted trunk.

The *Voice Literary Supplement* asked for an interview. I said yes, which was a mistake, as the resulting article did not increase sales one iota but made common knowledge of my residency in Manhattan. I would have preferred my location to have been a mystery, going so far as to claim in my biographical blurbs that I was a fishmonger in London's East End.

But the secret was out. I started receiving invitations to launches and readings. Even worse, I started saying yes.

The very first outing that I attended was held at Nell's.

When I started clubbing, Nell's emanated an aura of a mystic world where yuppies and aging veterans shelled out ridiculous amounts of money on food and alcohol and high-grade cocaine. There'd never been any reason to go into Nell's.

When I did get inside, my name on the list, I didn't talk to anyone. I stood in a corner and watched as a group of women in their late thirties decayed into shrieking laughter.

For someone who haunted clubs, I'd made an inexcusable mistake.

What's the first rule? Never arrive alone.

So I drafted Regina. She feigned disinterest, but as soon as I brought her to a party where we watched Jay McInerney crying into a frozen watermelon, she engaged with the concept.

When we attended the launch of Philip Levine's *The Bread of Time*, I had my first encounter with that fat little fuck Norman Mailer. The old fruitcake stood at the bar, eyes agog at every broad in the joint, drooling in his senescent lust. Every inch the pompous ass. I watched from across the room until I was distracted by the cackling of Nan Talese.

The year previous, I'd inhaled Mailer's work, first picking up a cheap paperback of *The Armies of the Night*. It was the best book that I'd read in a long time. It hooked me on the rest of his stuff. *Miami and the Siege of Chicago. The Fight. The Executioner's Song. Of a Fire on the Moon*. Even *Marilyn*! All remarkable, all incredible!

But nothing about Mailer's writing made me want to meet the man. If nothing else, future societies will prize my ability to separate artist from art.

Regina went to the bar, with no recognition of the little troll beside her. She ordered a drink. Mailer scummed up against her. I saw his withered claw on her bare shoulder. I let out an audible gasp and stomped over.

—Come on, I said, taking Regina by the arm.

—Listen, sweetheart, said Norman Mailer, you aren't the person who'll decide whether or not she's leaving.

—I hold a great deal of respect for your work, Mr. Mailer, I said, but you had best say a prayer to your gods if you still think this is 1967 and your headbutting can help you. You aren't dealing with a Harvard faggot who'll wilt beneath the stench of your testosterone. I'm molten lava and you're smoldering embers left over from a long-extinguished fire. I'm a butterfly and a bee.

—Baby, said Regina, what the hell are you talking about?

—I'm talking about beating this old man like a dusty broom, I said.

I yanked her away. Norman Mailer never said a word. I suspect that the scene existed beyond his critical capacity. A faggoty farm boy fussing over Nuyorican tail. The triumph of multiculturalism.

Word traveled around the party that I was the guy who threatened to kill Norman Mailer. High school is inescapable. No matter how many miles from home.

This gossip attracted a contingent of younger people. Some pretended to have read *Trapped*, but I knew that they hadn't. People at literary parties never read each other's books.

But one person had. He was about thirty years old, wearing this ratty blue cardigan and black-rimmed glasses.

—Hi, he said. I loved *Trapped*. You based it on Michael Alig, didn't you?

—Are you a friend of Michael's?

—Oh no, I'm too boring, he said. I caught him on the *Joan Rivers Show*. When I saw the name Michelle Gila, and the context, I presumed it had to be about the club kids.

—You're the first person to catch the reference, I said.

—My name's Cecil.

—Have you ever read *Cecil Dreeme*?

—You must be the only other person alive who knows the book, he said.

—I went to NYU, I said.

—A fellow alumnus, he said. I graduated in 1986.

I can't remember if I screwed out Cecil's brains that night. I might as well have. You meet some people and you're doomed to come inside them and have them come inside you. Some dicks are as unavoidable as death. Some dicks are magnets to your metal.

If we didn't avail ourselves of each other's bodies on that first night, then it definitely happened on the next. And for days thereafter. Pretty soon we were going steady.

We were perfect together. Same interests, same tastes, same relative intelligence level, roughly the same level of attractiveness. Same industry. Cecil worked as an assistant editor at Vintage. He was the sweetest man that I'd dated, the most thoughtful, the only person who'd doted on me. He was always there in the morning with breakfast. The sex was great. We screwed each other's brains out seven different ways from Sunday.

I sleptwalked through the days. Cecil by my side, talking, discussing concepts, being considerate, loving, asking with actions but not words if I loved him back, talking about moving in together, talking about our future, and me, eyes blank, head nodding, noncommittal answers, barely words, hugging him when necessary, kissing him when appropriate, screwing his brains out. I didn't care. None of it mattered.

I remember obsessing over Jaime, when his presence changed the atmosphere, when the walls sparkled in his light. The same feeling with Erik. As if our entire relationship happened in Washington Square, him looking from the window of a crummy hotel, our breath making white clouds in the air. I could have died.

With Cecil it was only this thing. It happened.

Jaime and Erik were shitty people. In comparison, Cecil appeared like a divinity, like the god of boyfriends. Jaime hadn't even been my boyfriend. He screwed my brains out and refused to tell his friends. Erik wouldn't fess up to Mommie Dearest about our love. Cecil was on the phone every weekend, talking to his Ma and his sister in Chicago, telling them about me, putting me on the phone. His mother asked every weekend when I might visit. We developed a good phone relationship. She was very funny.

But I didn't have the juice. I'd closed the book on that kind of love, on that kind of obsession, on that kind of infatuation. Maybe it was maturity. Maybe not.

—Baby, said Cecil, you're the first guy who's made me happy.

—I'm happy too, I said.

—Baby, said Cecil, you're such an interesting person.

—You aren't so bad yourself, I said.

—Baby, asked Cecil, what's your favorite thing in New York?

—The Minettas, I said. What's yours?

—Cleopatra's Needle, said Cecil. Have you been?

I hadn't. Cecil let out a girlish scream, the faggiest sound that he ever made, and insisted that we take the subway. Right that minute.

We got off the 6 train at 86th and walked to the Met. I presumed that we were going inside the museum, but Cecil dashed past the building and into the park, through the greenery and across a road into a circular enclosure, stopping before a giant granite obelisk.

Its four sides were weather blasted, stained black from pollution, as if the stone was corroded and rotting with atmospheric exposure. Destroyed by the filthy air that we daily breathed into our lungs.

—What is it? I asked.

—The oldest thing in New York. It's from Heliopolis. It's three thousand five hundred years old. It's Egyptian, erected during the reign of Thutmose III.

The city's toxicity had effaced two sides of hieroglyphics. The remaining two were barely visible. The obelisk was mounted on a base, bronzed crab claws emerging from beneath its bulk.

I was transfixed, thinking of the rock. Older than all of New York. Older than all of America. Fifteen hundred years old when Jesus was born. That isn't old. That's ancient. The clouds moving behind the obelisk.

I wobbled, stumbled, caught myself on the railing.

—Baby, are you okay?

—I'm fine, I said. I don't know what happened. I was looking at the thing and it was like this sound went off in my head.

—Let's get you home and into bed, said Cecil. I'll make you something to eat.

Let me backtrack.

The Tunnel had reopened around Thanksgiving, a month after the police discovered the mummy but before the media linked the body with Dorian. Peter Gatien had purchased the club and shuttered it for renovations. The new décor looked a lot like Arena.

I skipped the reopening. I was busy. I did attend an event a few weeks later. For one night only, the club exhibited paintings by the serial killer John Wayne Gacy. I assumed that Michael Alig was responsible.

Michael had become a full-fledged drug addict, developing the mordant streak that is a common reference point among junkies. A real death trip, a modern-day Thanatos. He and the other club kids had started wearing bandages and makeup that simulated injuries. I was convinced the inspiration for this choice was a series of photos of Edie Sedgwick taken after she'd set fire to her room at the Chelsea Hotel. But no one would admit it.

Anyhoo, there I was in Tunnel, peering at the shitty paintings of a man who'd killed and raped something like thirty-five boys. I wondered what it meant.

America was always bloodstained, but serial killer chic was a new depth. A dying empire always meditates on death. Maybe Michael Alig's junky intuition was like an extended antenna, an early warning system, a radar for the great coming doom.

On my way out, I was stopped by this slutty, druggy-looking guy. I'd seen him before, at Disco 2000, talking with Michael.

—You're the writer, right?

—That's what they tell me, I said.

He'd bleached his hair out and dyed it an unpleasant shade of copper. He'd smeared kohl around his eyes. He wore a Stüssy shirt and a pair of ugly jeans. He looked too old for his clothes. By the time a person reaches that age, they should either give up or be fabulous. No one can hover in the middle.

—I read your book, he said.

—Oh really? I asked.

—It blew my fucking mind. Michael said it was good. But Michael says lots of things are good. I bought a fucking copy and I think it's just fucking amazing.

—Thanks, I said. It's nice to hear.

—Is there somewhere we can talk?

—What's your name? I asked.

—Franklin, he said.

—Franklin what? I asked.

—Franklin Perkins.

—Sure, Franklin Perkins, I said. We can go and talk. Let's get the hell out of here. I can't stand these crummy paintings.

James St. James worked the door. Honey, he said, why are you leaving so soon, aren't those paintings fabulous? I said, No, they're awful, I can't stand them, and they're beneath you, Jimmy. But James St. James just said, Honey, what isn't?

We went to Franklin's hovel in the East Village. We screwed each other's brains out. It wasn't great. It was better than okay. I spent the night. The only problem arose when Franklin broke out a wide array of dildos and harnesses.

—Sorry, I said, but I have a thing about sex toys.

—That's okay, he said. Vanilla is still fucking hot.

When we woke up, he asked me if I wanted to get some breakfast. I said, Sure, yeah, let's get some breakfast.

—I know this really great fucking place, he said. It's called the Kiev.

—Oh, really? I asked. Let's check it out.

Franklin had moved to Manhattan a few months earlier, emigrating from the middle of Connecticut. Don't think that he was an innocent. He'd grown up in suburbia and screwed out the brains of every swish young man from Hartford and New Haven, giving of his body as indiscriminately as Jesus.

He'd seen Michael Alig on the *Jane Whitney Show*. The episode with G. G. Allin, right before Allin died of an overdose at 3rd & Avenue B.

Michael's cavorting and capering struck Franklin like an epiphany.

Connecticut clubs were one thing, but the city held real action. There was a great wide world over the state border. He resolved to find Michael. Which he did, the very next week. Michael loved fresh meat.

I couldn't ferret out whether or not they'd screwed out each other's brains. I hoped that they hadn't. As far as I could tell, I'd managed to avoid sharing any of Michael's sex partners. Only Venus and Ulysses S. Grant knew what bacteria and viruses haunted that accursed bloodstream.

A few nights after my escapade with Franklin, I read an article in *New York* magazine about gonorrhea. The disease congregates in a germ pool at the back of the throat. There is no such thing as safer sex. Oral won't give you AIDS, but dip your dick into a tainted throat pool and it'll give you the clap.

I obsessed over the idea that Franklin'd given me gonorrhea. Whenever I pissed, I was terrified that it wasn't urine, that it marked the early formation of pus. But the disease never arrived.

If I were a good person, I'd say that I never saw Franklin again. But I can't. We were together at least twice a week. It went on for so long. I was screwing his brains out the whole time that Cecil was screwing out mine.

FEBRUARY 1994

Baby Sees *Schindler's List*

On the basis of *Trapped*'s relative success, the film option, a five-thousand-word excerpt, and an outline, Parker had sold my second novel to Bill Thomas at Doubleday. They were happy to have me. I was a young writer building my name. They had faith in my future.

I decided to abandon science fiction and focus on noir. My second novel's tentative title was *In She Walked, Her Legs as Long as Midnight, Her Back as Bold as Brass.*

Set in 1950s Los Angeles, the narrative followed the misadventures of Frank Fist, an ex-Marine turned private eye. He'd been hardened at Guadalcanal, soaked in the blood of a thousand Japanese. He brought his brutality home, using it to service his clients' needs.

The science fiction overlay of *Trapped* had allowed me to skirt around heterosexuality's central place within the crime novel. Now, with no practical knowledge of female anatomy or its tactile sensations, I made the leap. The neon jazz bebop of crime writers was an ultraqueer manifestation. They all tried so hard to be butch.

I wrote the most stupidly straight scenes that I could. Here's a brief excerpt:

> She swung her caboose low and easy. With a behind like that, she didn't need a smart mouth. Every conversation ended when she walked away. Her derrière taunted a man from across the room, making him want to teach peace to the conquered and tame the proud. "Miss Orrin," I said, "young ladies like you come to the big city and talk a tough game, but you dames are a dime a dozen. One spanking and you cry for papa. Get your sweet kiester over here, Miss Orrin, and let me wipe that lipstick right off your face."

I eked out twenty thousand words. Things were going fine. I could have finished the book, but I derailed myself. I attended a screening of *Schindler's List* at a second-run theater, months after its release.

Within the film's three hours, there's an absolutely brilliant work done a disservice by its director's pedagogical impulse. Over forty-five minutes are wasted making sure that the audience understands that the Holocaust was bad and that Oskar Schindler's salvation of twelve hundred Jews was good. Why the morality tale? The story is strong. Why the window dressing?

As I'd learned in my brief conversations with Alan Pakula, screenplays are based on an inherent three-act structure. Issues raised in the first twenty minutes of any film must neatly resolve within its final ten. But what about the Holocaust is resolved? There were no ten final minutes, only decades of psychological suffering and historical consequence.

I kept thinking about the German and Polish gentiles, the fathomless millions of goyim who never appear in *Schindler's List,* the millions of good citizens who kept on keeping on while their government orchestrated genocide. The average people who didn't say a word against the crimes. Who couldn't give two shakes of a stick about the Jews, the gays, the Romany, or the mentally ill.

Twelve hundred lives is a miracle, but six million deaths is cold fact. The consequence of a world placing a premium on capital and technological efficiency. Europe saw it through to its final solution.

But who was I to judge? I didn't know a thing about the Holocaust, about the suffering of its victims, or about the Nazi regime. My understanding of WWII was cobbled together from a piss-poor public education and the ongoing fiftieth-anniversary commemorations.

I ended up at the Strand, buying as many books as I could carry. Until I stood within the bookstore's sickly light, peering up at the twelve-foot-tall gray metal bookcases, I didn't have any idea how many books had been written about the war.

Books on every goddamned subject, from the obvious to the ridiculous. Books about GI rations. Books about German tanks. Stalin. Churchill. Hitler. Roosevelt. Truman. Books about obscure Japanese rituals. Books about Czechoslovakian housewives. Books about the impact of tanks on migratory patterns of North African birds. Books, books, books. Tales of the Luftwaffe. Endless books.

I stuck to titles that I recognized. *The Rise and Fall of the Third Reich*. *Night* by Eli Wiesel. Both volumes of *Maus*. *The Boys from Brazil*. *War as I Knew It*. And finally, *Eichmann in Jerusalem* by Hannah Arendt.

The balding middle-aged cashier blanched when he noticed that every book was about Nazis or the Holocaust. I didn't mind, but I did feel some sympathy for him, imagining the deranged ones who must come into the store and buy an ungodly number of titles on gruesome subjects. Feeding an obsession through bibliographic mania.

But not me! I was doing research, though by this time it was difficult to discern writing from mental illness. I'd developed the muscle to the point where it no longer required conscious thought. I sat at my computer and the ideas poured out. I could watch it happen.

To sit there and have the words flow out of you, to make characters speak, to move them like chess pieces. It was madness.

Eichmann in Jerusalem. I read it last. A mistake, as it was the best. Hannah Arendt wrote with a naked glass malice that was the only rational response to systemic Teutonic cruelty. Unflinching, without sentiment, cognizant of the paradox of trying Eichmann under the laws of a country that did not exist when he committed his crimes.

When Arendt reached the sui generis case of Denmark, she nailed me. Here is what she writes: "This was one of the few cases in which stateless-ness turned out to be an asset, although it was of course not statelessness per se that saved the Jews, but, on the contrary, the fact that the Danish government had decided to protect them."

That one sentence flipped my thinking. The story of the Holocaust was one of bad governance. I'd lived my life hearing about the evils of the gov-ernment, about the horrors of bureaucracy. A hate and mistrust of the fed-eral government was probably the sole opinion shared by East Village hipsters and farmhand yokels, proving that stupidity and ignorance are constants, regardless of your neighbors.

The only thing that keeps America from fascism is our laws, our courts, our checks and balances. Everything good about American life, and every-thing bad, is the product of the federal government. In 1787, the world's staunchest adherents of liberty wrote a Constitution that did not afford the citizenry any protection against being owned by other citizens. In 1860, four million people lived in the shackles of slavery. In 1865, the addition of thirty-two words to the Constitution released those slaves from bondage. The myth of the lone individualist is full-spectrum bullshit permeating all strata of society. It's a way of disguising personal complicity in the descent of our public life into trifles and nonsense, an excuse for what we've let ourselves become. Historically, the enemy has been evil rich people and stupid people. The latter are used by the former, trapping society within a death cycle of pretense, the great myth of an America that flourishes in spite of, rather than because of, her laws. A world in which the zombified corpse of Ronald Reagan embraces profound and systemic industry deregulation and is followed into the presidency by Bill Clinton, a backslapping Southern politician who never saw a civil protection that he didn't detest. Both men abandoned probity, abandoned good thought, abandoned rational thinking, inhaled the jargon-saturated monocultures of Hollywood and Wall Street. Both men well aware that the ability to sparkle on camera could blind an entire nation. Who cared if these rabid animals destroyed the fabric of society? Who cared if the weak and the idiotic were left vulnerable to predators and parasites? A cowboy actor with a chimpanzee sidekick and a philanderer playing his saxophone on late-night talk shows. I'd grown into an adult at the exact moment when society had abandoned adulthood. I'd become a man after everyone had agreed that manhood was a thing without use. Far better to destroy the government. Far better to eradicate the girders of American life while chasing ephemeral dreams of maximum profits and self-regulating free markets. Far better to pretend that Ayn Rand was a prescient genius, that her psychopathic doctrines possessed an actual connection with reality. Far better to shoot enormous wads of jism into dog-eared copies of *Atlas Shrugged,* an orgasmal cri de coeur for John Galt and Howard Roark. Far better to disguise every ignoble goal in catchphrases, buzzwords, and pop culturalisms that appeal to a mix of the greediest and the least educated. Far better to bamboozle the very people who need protection from the world's bad actors, those simpletons who always vote and buy against their own self-interest in exchange for whispers about which showbiz phantasm vaginally penetrated other showbiz phantasms. Far better to pander to the Business Community, a self-appointed circlejerk of low IQs in thrall to every bogus investment, who conceive of their fellow citizens as open mouths hungry for nothing but rank diarrhea and runoff, who see every vacant lot and every charming warehouse as an opportunity for miserable low-quality condominiums disguised as luxury living, who are themselves so dazzled by their own bullshit that they gladly eat the same poisons, convinced that their horrors are medicines. The spectacle reflects itself, our lives grow ever more hollow, there is no longer quality or value in modern life. The populace is so badly educated that it doesn't complain when sold toxic plastics, when goods break four days after purchase, when nothing works. The goat of the woods produces a thousand new monsters who suckle upon her and stalk into the world, their bellies filled with treacherous milk, repeating the process, producing their own young, each generation nourished on less and less substance until the edifice collapses beneath nature's gentle breeze. Everything ends when the government abandons all responsibility, when lust for power and money replaces the desire to serve one's fellow citizens. There are no natural rights, no universal and inalienable human liberties. Rights are protections granted to a citizenry by its government. A right comes into existence at the exact moment that its violation is illegal. Not a moment sooner. Laws are reality. When a nation has bad laws, its citizens live in a bad reality. We allow the worst of all creatures to position themselves as our leaders. The kind of men who swindle us, convince us that the word *bureaucracy* is a pejorative. Bureaucracy is the only thing that saves us from ourselves! Americans can't see a difference between the government and the state. The government is comprised of the corrupt scum who rule you. The state is the bureaucratic functionary that protects you until it is corrupted by the government. Without a well-functioning state, our rights are bought and sold with as much ease as a new computer. And those rights can be taken away with as little effort, particularly if the people are bewildered away from self-protection. Welcome to an economic cycle of perpetual bust and boom. Welcome to a world where education is devalued and underfunded, leaving the country with a population too stupid to remember the last catastrophe. Welcome to a world where no one can recall the taste of shit. Welcome to an America where McDonald's is an investment opportunity and a quick buck is of greater value than the people's health. Civil rights are only another product that is debased and copied and deleted and relayed until nothing remains but a blank piece of paper. Philip K. Dick was wrong. The Empire always ends. Nero's fiddling is the soundtrack of our collapse. America dies when the integration between her government and her entertainment becomes absolute, when politicians pander without shame to the famous and the few, basing public policy on the opinions of degenerate CEOs and shit-eating rock stars. When powerful men believe that conferred power is less important than naked fame, when they see their elected positions as venues for mindless self-glorification. It all comes back to clubland. America really is a club, and everyone wants to be in the VIP room. Everyone wants to be fabulous. Andy, take my picture.

European Jewry didn't need Steven Spielberg's vision of an American individualist dressed in Weimar drag. They needed the same thing that everyone has always needed.

A good government.

I went back to the Strand and bought a copy of Anne Frank's diary. It wasn't my first go-round with Annelies. My English teacher had assigned the book during my sophomore year of high school, but I'd been a dopey adolescent preoccupied with his athletics. I didn't pay attention.

With total clarity that came from having read the other books, I entered the *Diary*. The tortured cultural history was stripped away. The book made dull by bad teachers, by social piety, by shitty Hollywood adaptations. That was gone. Now the words burned with gunpowder. Her soul reached through the page. That funny voice, that wiseacre girl trapped behind a bookcase in Amsterdam, the fear of it. And all I wanted was to save her.

I called Parker and told him that I'd abandoned my crime novel. I couldn't do a book about an American who'd gone to the Pacific and came home. That wasn't the story. The only story was the Holocaust.

He tried talking me out of writing a different book.

—I admire the ambition, he said, but it's a freaking headache that neither of us needs. You know I've got hemorrhoids. They give me pain and complicated shits. I don't need you mucking about with social issues. You saw what happened to Bret Easton Ellis with *American Psycho*. People are calling in death threats to Dennis Cooper. Death threats, kid. The country's changing. No book is worth dying over. I want ambition dripping out of your scrotal sac, sure, but not like this. Have a little scale.

—If I do the book, I asked, will you stand behind me?

—I'll stand behind you whatever you choose, he said. But it's a terrible idea. It'll fuck your whole life.

—It'll be tasteful, I said. Don't worry. No one will take offense.

—This is America, you dopey fuck, said Parker. People take offense at a paper bag.

FEBRUARY 1994

Karen Spencer

C ecil introduced me to his best friend, an artist named Karen Spencer. They'd been at NYU together, both enrolled in drama at the School of the Arts. Upon graduation, Cecil descended into the mire of the publishing industry and Karen Spencer fell in with the dissolute louts of the East Village and SoHo art scenes. Her own paintings never had much success, but she'd made fabulous friends and dabbled in selling their work.

Cecil convinced me to visit Karen's loft on Spring Street. I heard Adeline in my head.

—Baby, why ever would you visit an artist's loft? Haven't you spent enough time with those dreadful people? All they do is cover the walls with their own work. Whatever will you say? You'll have to fake enthusiasm. Can you do that, Baby? Can you fake enthusiasm?

But Karen's walls were blank. She'd left her space unreconstructed in its industrial chic, not touching the exposed beams and ancient windows. As it was the dead of winter, her loft ran about the same temperature as a Frost Giant's cavern.

—Come and sit by the heat, she said.

She'd installed several wooden chairs around an oversized space heater. I pulled as close as I could. How the hell had I gotten so sensitive to cold? What happened to that farm boy hardened by Lake Superior?

Karen and Cecil talked. I couldn't follow what they said. Partly work, partly gossip about old friends, partly nonsense refined through a decade of friendship.

—Cecil says you're working on a new book, said Karen.

—Yes, I said.

—And you write science fiction?

—Not this time, said Cecil. He's writing a noir.

I hadn't informed Cecil of the new direction. I let him tell people about a book that I'd abandoned. Correcting him seemed too much effort. What did it matter, anyway? Easier to agree with whatever he said.

—I love crime novels, said Karen Spencer. Do you like David Goodis?

—Goodis is great, I said. What's your favorite?

—*The Blonde on the Street Corner.*

—I haven't read that, I said.

—It's barely a novel, she said. Mostly it's broke people who fuck and then fight and then fuck again. You'll love it.

Karen went to her kitchen and put on a kettle. She poured us cups of tea. The heat thawed my hands, the liquid warmed my innards.

—Baby, asked Karen, have you ever watched *The Bold and the Beautiful*?

—No, I said.

One thing about a life without Adeline. I'd purchased a television. A big color one. A real television. I'd watched more boob tube in my first six months of ownership than in the previous seven years. Several interesting programs had premiered on the networks. *NYPD Blue, The X-Files, Lois & Clark: The New Adventures of Superman.*

Generally, though, I kept the thing on Channel 13, on PBS. I stayed as far from *The Bold and the Beautiful* as I could. A soap opera! My god, no!

—And you, Cecil? asked Karen.

—I work an office job, he said. I'd have to tape it, which I don't.

—You can see that I don't own a television, said Karen, which makes it a rare experience. A couple of weeks ago, I was in the waiting room at my doctor's, and because you can't go anywhere without there being a blaring television, I was sitting directly beneath the noise. I ignored it, trying to read *Entertainment Weekly,* but I kept hearing my name. Karen, Karen, Karen, Karen. If you have a name like Karen, you get used to hearing it, so I ignored it. But then the television was saying my full name. Karen Spencer, Karen Spencer, Karen Spencer, and for a second, I thought that I'd lost my marbles, that I'd gone schizo and was hearing voices. I stand up and look at the television and there's a plotline about this character, Karen Spencer. I ask the receptionist what show we're watching. She says it's *The Bold and the Beautiful.* I ask her if she knows this Karen Spencer character. She has no idea who I'm talking about, so I point to the actress on the screen, and the receptionist says, oh, her, she's been on for a while. This called for investigation. I went to a newsstand and bought *Soap Opera Digest*, and it's full of plotlines about Karen Spencer! I went to the library and looked at old issues. Months and months of Karen Spencer.

She lit a cigarette. Her smoke hung at eye level, an evil cloud wafting around us.

—Then I started thinking, what if the other Karen Spencer is the real one? What if I'm the fictional Karen Spencer, and the one who appears five times weekly is the genuine article? What if my life is bogus? What if I don't exist and she does? Maybe that Karen Spencer is the one that matters. Maybe I'm a shadow projected against her wall. Maybe that other Karen Spencer is the one watching me.

When we left Karen's loft, Cecil walked me the long way to my apartment. He suggested taking a cab, but I loved New York in the winter, especially after Christmas. Even if it was freezing.

—You aren't quite there yet, he said, but when you end up in your thirties, life is different than you ever imagined. Movie stars visibly age but you feel the same. You ask yourself, how can I be getting older? I don't know anything! And your friends start changing in ways that you couldn't expect. Everyone has one or two friends who end up in the exact place for which they seemed destined, but most people go places that would have been unthinkable.

—Like Karen? I asked.

—Oddly, he said, no. Karen ended up exactly where I thought she might.

MARCH 1994

Baby Adopts the King of France

Then there was the time when Franklin came over and said that I needed to adopt a cat. I didn't want a cat, thinking that owning another pet would be a betrayal of the Captain, but Franklin wouldn't stop talking about one particular tabby kitten at the ASPCA on 92nd Street, where he volunteered.

—They found the little guy with his brothers and sisters in a garbage can. We think their mother left them to find food and never came back. Some guy was throwing away a can of soda and heard the kittens crying. They were only about a week old. But this kitten, the one you have to adopt, he was the runt, a little guy. They put all the kittens in the same cage and his brothers and sisters wouldn't stop trying to nurse on his dick, so they had to separate him and put him in another cage with a bunch of other orphans. Anyway, he's about three months old. I played with him yesterday. He's the best, but I can't have a cat in my apartment. My landlord would shit a brick. I thought of you. This guy is the sweetest fucking thing. He's got his shots. He's fixed. He's made for you, Baby.

—Why not give him to Michael? I asked.

—C'mon, be serious. Michael's got a cat. Plus it'd be fucking criminal letting this little guy live in a drug den. You're different than most club people. You're normal. You're stable.

We never know how others see us. I felt on the verge of men in white coats throwing me into Bellevue. Tormented by writing, hollowed out by words. One of literature's few salves has been the veneer of respectability it casts over its practitioners, an undue conference of reputation and status. Consider the personal history of that fat little fuck Norman Mailer, who inaugurated the 1960s by stabbing his wife and ended the decade by running for mayor of New York.

—Oh, fine, fuck it, I said. Let's go look at this cat.

We took the 6 uptown, getting off at 86th and walking to 92nd and First. The ASPCA was in a squat building near the river. A housing project loomed across the street. Franklin led me inside the building and through its minor labyrinth.

I'd only seen Franklin inside clubs, at the Kiev and in our apartments. My idea of him was as this trashy slutty drug fiend burning away his mid-twenties. At the ASPCA, he conversed with a wide range of society. Everyone liked him, seemed to value his conversation. He brought nothing but smiles. Only then did I wonder, for the first time, what the hell he did for his money. I had never bothered to ask.

The cats were kept behind bars in a room with rows of cages. Some were sullen and withdrawn. Others terrified. Many rubbed against the metal, pushing their faces between the gaps, pleading with pathetic meows. At least they weren't in abusive homes or starving in the street. I couldn't avoid thinking of my research. Humanity never stops building cages.

The kittens didn't break my heart. Kittens always find homes. The older cats killed me. Each offered a depressing story, adding to a collective weight that no person could bear. The eleven-year-old orange tabby that stank of tragedy. The death of an owner, an accidental escape, the indifference of a cruel host.

Franklin took out the kitten in question, this cock-eyed mewling thing. His head and back were gray with brown highlights. His side had swirling markings. His stomach was pure white. His legs striped with beige fur. I held him in my palm, upside down on his back, and saw that his paw pads were alternating black and pink.

—Fine, I said. Fine. You win. I'll take him.

—I knew you would, said Franklin.

I filled out an astounding amount of paperwork. I showed two forms of identification. I forked over serious cash.

The people working at the ASPCA kept telling me that I was doing a great thing and how happy life is with a pet. They put the kitten in a cardboard box. I carried him outside.

We found a cab and had it take us to the pet store near my apartment. I bought the four essential ingredients of cat ownership. Food, receptacle for food, litter, receptacle for litter.

Back at home, I freed the mewling thing from its box. It ran around my apartment in circles, climbing on every surface, sniffing, knocking things over. I tried catching him but failed until the beast realized that I only wanted to touch him. He ran to the rug and flopped on his back, displaying that dazzling stomach.

I lifted the creature.

—What the hell am I going to call you?

There was nothing in his green saucer eyes but psychosis. I hadn't adopted a cat. I'd adopted a bag of emotional problems tied with a string of lunacy. He let out a tiny little meow in his squeaky kitten voice.

—You shall be known, I said, as The King of France.

APRIL 1994

Baby's New Novel

I went back to science fiction. I figured that my reception would expand if I passed off even more watered-down genre conventions as post-pop cultural profundities. Plus, the whole thing came to me. In a moment. As if in a dream, as I wandered past Tower Records on 4th Street, cast in the illumination from the lightboxed record covers, blown up to a hundred times their original size, shining like beacons in the store's plate glass windows.

One thousand years in the future, around 3000 C.E., time travel has become a fact of life, its use regulated by the Time Travel Commission, a bureaucratic arm of the world government.

The average citizen may not travel back in time. Not on a whim. Not for any reason. Time travel is a legitimate tool of scientific and historical research performed by trained professionals.

Travel to the future is impossible. Attempts have been made. Each failed, resulting in the destruction of sensitive equipment and a significant death toll.

Our lives are narratives shaped by the past reaching into the present with unholy precision. The human race lumbers in the shadows of ghosts, is stained with the ectoplasm of its own history. The great flaw of human biology is our sensory inability to perceive the fourth dimension while being doomed to traverse through it. There is no objective truth of an event, no way to capture a moment once it has passed. Even video fails to convey the fullness of the event.

The solution to this quandary is the development of full imaging holographic technology that stimulates all five senses and extends across the three-dimensional planes for a radius of up to sixteen hundred meters. Time travel, then, is a parallel technology. The purpose of the time traveler is to bring holographic equipment into the past and make a perfectly accurate impression of an event.

The implications are massive. When a person experiences an exact replica of a historical event, myths are shattered. Thus, the death of most religions. It becomes impossible to believe in Christ's resurrection when a person can behold the man in his actuality, a charismatic street preacher crucified and then impersonated several months later by a rabid beggar. Islam lasts slightly longer, but not by much. The religions that do survive are primarily of Asian origin and so-called primitive faiths which retained an ongoing belief in animal spirits.

Monotheism was out.

With one exception, with that great exception to all things. The Jews. If a culture can survive the Egyptians, the Babylonians, the Romans, the Europeans, the Nazis, and late twentieth-century politics, then it can survive the advent of time travel.

All practitioners of time travel take a pledge based on the Hippocratic Oath, vowing to do no harm. This charming idea proves woefully inadequate. The problem is not the effects of the travelers on time but rather the effects of time on the travelers.

By any measure, 3000 C.E. is a technological utopia. Violence still erupts, but it is the small violence of an overcrowded planet adrift in luxury rather than the wide-scale bloodshed of previous periods. War and disease are relics of the past. Money is an unheard-of obscenity.

Time travelers, innocents abroad, are thrust into milieus where they must observe mass slaughter, observe millions rent asunder by incurable disease, observe cities being destroyed, observe populations wiped out, observe environmental chaos. The impossible pain of history is beyond their personal experience, yet they are forced into its middle, watching war, watching genocide on an accelerated planetary-wide scale.

Suicide rates, always high after the installation of worldwide euthanasia centers in 2731, skyrocket among those who visit the past. The biggest such center, located on the south side of Nueva Washington Square between Wooster Street and South Fifth Avenue, reports a massive spike.

The Time Travel Commission takes notice.

Many studies are conducted. Following a meta-analysis, it emerges that the only demographic of time travelers with a statistically significant variation away from suicide is the Jews. Theories are floated, several containing an atavistic resurgence of anti-Semitism, but the one with the most currency suggests that the Jews are culturally inculcated to think of history as a horror with no answer but survival.

Jews become the only people willing to do the work. The Ashkenazi prove more capable at recent history, while the Mizrahi possess an innate understanding of the distant past. The Sephardim demonstrate high competency with eras predating the advent of homo sapiens.

House scientists at the Time Travel Commission run an R&D department, hoping to develop new technologies to ease the experience. The most effective is a bioengineered bacterial strain of super gonorrhea. When collected in the throat pool, the bacteria develops its own intelligence and exerts a control over its human host's vocal cords, tongue, and facial muscles. Designed with specific limitations of emotional and intellectual range, the disease speaks with a voice markedly different than that of its host.

The first chapter opens with a dialogue between the protagonist, a time traveler named Boaz ben-Haim, and his superintelligent gonorrhea. The setting for this dialogue is a bar. Ben-Haim nurtures a cocktail of synthetic mescaline, alcohol, and methamphetamine.

—This job is pushing me toward addiction, says ben-Haim.

—the world is a wonderful place, says the gonorrhea. you need not give over to the temptations of the flesh, nor drown your sorrow. rejoice on tomorrow and remember today!

—The mescaline is making me see shapes in the artificial cloud formations. I think I can see the end of the world.

—the world never ends, says the gonorrhea. the multitudes go on forever. recall walt whitman's "sun-down poem," where the good gray bard speaks to future generations.

—Wasn't that poem addressed to future Brooklynites? asks ben-Haim.

—yes, says the gonorrhea.

—Brooklyn was destroyed in 2321 C.E.

—yes, says the gonorrhea. but the brooklyn of our hearts remains. why meditate on destruction? think of the happy rebuilding that follows!

Boaz ben-Haim stumbles home through the slick fiber-optic acid rain. He falls asleep after chasing his cocktail with a massive dose of Mandrax and barbiturates. The next morning, he is awoken by an instant video communiqué demanding his appearance at the Time Travel Commission.

When Boaz ben-Haim arrives at the Commission's epical concrete bunker beneath the Nueva United Nations, he's informed that certain higher-ups have been paying special attention to his career. His five years of effort have demonstrated his capacities. As such, he's been promoted. Boaz ben-Haim groans. Promotions only expose the traveler to historical epochs of higher psychological impact.

His new assignment is one of the worst. A genocide, the Shoah, and the Shoah at its very worst. Auschwitz in May 1944. Boaz ben-Haim is ordered to stay for three solid months. The hologram technology requires daily tweaking.

Boaz dresses in full SS regalia and poses as a camp guard. He's equipped with bewilderment technologies ensuring that neither he nor his equipment are discovered. He sleeps in the hutch of his time bubble, hidden from the outer world, but sleep only brings nightmares of his father.

Over the weeks at Auschwitz, his hyperintelligent gonorrhea takes on a disturbing aspect. Confronted by the human race at its worst, the disease begins speaking exclusively in platitudes.

Boaz ben-Haim witnesses the gassing of a hundred Jews. His bacteria tells him: —things are bad now, but remember, we're from the future! one thousand years from now, everything's fine!

Boaz ben-Haim sees a starving child, no more than eight years old, shot through her head. His bacteria tells him: —death is part of life's natural cycle. we must not consider it an absolute state of being.

Boaz ben-Haim, the stink of crematoria in his nostrils, bumps into Josef Mengele. The bacteria tells him: —even the worst people have good intentions, it's just that the biochemical makeup of their neurological pathways frustrates their ability to achieve goodness.

The bacteria speaks with ben-Haim's throat, with ben-Haim's face, with ben-Haim's vocal cords. The experience is akin to punching yourself and then apologizing to your fist.

Boaz ben-Haim questions the time traveler's first mandate. *Do no harm.* Doing no harm can be perceived, uncharitably, as not doing anything. How many children must die? What if the fundamental principle of time travel, that altering the past may prevent the traveler from being born, is little more than the kind of bullshit political practicality supposedly outmoded in the year 3000 C.E.? Isn't it chronocentricity to suggest that his life is of implicitly more value than the lives at Auschwitz? Or dying anywhere in history? If a life can be saved from needless death, then shouldn't its salvation occur? Can self-preservation be a valid argument against action?

—remember, says the gonorrhea, by the time of your birth, the human race has worked out all of its problems! history is the long process of your species making the best of all possible worlds!

Unwilling to save the blameless, the Commission gives tacit approval to the crimes of history. Time travelers aren't scientists. They aren't trained professionals. They are tourists in humanity's suffering. They are the same colonialist caste who've preyed on mankind from the advent of industrialization. People who owe their livelihoods to the distant suffering of those hidden from view. No place is more convenient than the past.

Six million deaths are not without meaning. The history of the Jewish people, the culmination of several thousand years of persecution, is Boaz ben-Haim's ancestral heritage, but when technology might save these people from their doom, how can a person fail to act?

Boaz ben-Haim isn't the first to come to this conclusion. Fail-safes are built into the technology. Nanotech filters prevent the ingress of unauthorized organic material into the time hutch. The very mechanism that allows him to witness also enforces his complicity.

Meanwhile, the gonorrhea is displaying a surprising awareness of Boaz ben-Haim's thoughts. Its platitudes have changed. It offers reassurances about the vitality of his mission. The gonorrhea may be reading his mind.

—remember, boaz, says the gonorrhea, these kinds of crises are in no way unique. the feelings you're experiencing are not new. they've been considered and addressed. there are programs in place.

As Boaz ben-Haim approaches the end of his mission at Auschwitz, he suspects that he will not be allowed to return to the past. The gonorrhea may be compiling a dossier of unflattering information about his doubts and his suspicions about the failures of time travel. If the Commission discovers his incredulity about its central tenets, he will be removed from duty.

His one chance for action is now, before the return to his own epoch. The Commission may control the future, but in the past, they're at his mercy. He has the ability to go anywhere and do anything.

His first stop is America in 1970. He breaks into the Walter Reed Army Medical Center and steals megadoses of penicillin and ampicillin.

When gonorrhea was cultivated as an aid for time travelers, the disease had not infected a single human for over four hundred years. The strain was selected because of its unique vulnerability to antibiotic doses. Its developers, EliGlaxoLily, saw this susceptibility as a method of easy removal when the disease was no longer required. Back in his hutch, Boaz ben-Haim eats the pilfered medicine.

In an ideal situation, removal of hyperintelligent gonorrhea occurs in a hospital, while the human host is under sedation. Boaz ben-Haim suffers the transition without tranquilization. The gonorrhea dies, croaking out with ben-Haim's voice, its pleas for mercy diminishing into a final empty silence.

—help me, help me, help me. help. help. help. help.

For his next destination, Boaz ben-Haim travels forward to the distant future, to the epoch when time travel technologies are first mass duplicated.

There is the distinct danger that this journey may create a paradox. The Commission has always warned every traveler about the impossibility and danger of arriving in an epoch that possesses the technology. Death is the only result. Only death and doom.

Taking the chance, he punches in the coordinates and arrives unharmed.

Nothing happens. It's like any other historical era. He interacts with people, uses bewilderment technologies upon them. Nothing changes. He's still alive. Boaz ben-Haim concludes that time travelers have been visiting the post-travel epoch all along.

Perhaps the Commission knows. Perhaps they knew from the beginning. No one informed him that the gonorrhea could read his mind.

He steals the central processing unit of an older time travel hutch, one lacking the nanotech filters that block the ingress of organic matter. He interfaces the CPU with his hutch.

For his next destination, Boaz ben-Haim travels to Mauritius in the year 1534. He captures a dodo and brings it inside the hutch. The machine does not reject the bird. For his next destination, Boaz ben-Haim travels to the year 1988 and frees the bird by Cleopatra's Needle. The creature gives Boaz ben-Haim a stupid, screwball look and then hops away, rubbing against the obelisk's base.

With evidence of the possible, Boaz ben-Haim resolves to rescue victims of the Holocaust. It is his hope that this removal, at the last possible moment before death, will create as little havoc as possible. Boaz ben-Haim plans to bring those whom he rescues into the far future. Into the year 2700. After the last great war, after massive depopulations.

He'll rescue them from the worst government known to man and deliver them to human history's most universally admired system of political representation. The Neo-Doge of Nuovo Venexia. *I am a one-man Zion.* The only question is how many. The sheer enormity of all of those deaths.

Boaz ben-Haim opens his hutch. As the dodo watches, Boaz ben-Haim climbs into the hutch. He travels to Bergen-Belsen, to March 1945. He moves among the sick, among the doomed women, among those bodies riddled with typhus. They are about five hundred in number, crammed inside a single poorly constructed wooden barracks. There are no windows or doors. The wind howls through the room. It's freezing. There are no beds. The inmates sleep on the floor.

Boaz ben-Haim stops above a young starving girl, delirious with illness, hovering near death, shivering on the ground.

—Anna? Anna?

MAY 1994

Baby Sees a Ghost

Every Wednesday, Regina and I attended every Disco 2000. The freak show had erupted into new extremes. I doubt that even the Romans under Heliogabalus, or Berliners in the Weimar Republic, experienced such tortured hedonism.

People dressed in costumes of butchered meat, anorexic midgets, amputees, piss drinkers, shit lickers, men fisting themselves on stage, people eating their own vomit, brutal S&M. The spectacle dusted with endless white powders. Ketamine and cocaine and heroin. Snow was general over Ireland.

I loved wallowing in the filth that accrues around every fin-de-siècle. That dewy moment before a new millennium when the peasantry stage orgies before the wrath of a nameless God.

One night in May, I ran into Jae-Hwa, or Sally, or Sigh. She was dressed down, looking like a young professional in her late twenties. Which I guess, technically, she might have been. She was like Franklin. I had no idea what she did for money.

I was crazy on cocaine. She couldn't get in a word. I kept talking about three Aerosmith music videos starring a blonde actress named Alicia Silverstone. A living embodiment of fresh-faced lust, appealing to the world's schoolboys. And their fathers.

The videos, released over the course of a year, were incredibly popular. People kept talking about them. The most recent, "Crazy," had debuted a few weeks earlier.

—There's a full narrative running through the trilogy, I said. Alicia Silverstone experiences a personality transformation of sexual disinclinations across an elapsed timeframe. The failures of heterosexuality and suburban rebellion in the first video leads into an escape from the phantasms and pleasures of the digital world in the second, the simulacra of which ultimately cannot sustain her interest nor salve the wound of her hetero failures, culminating at last into the petit mal climax of crime and bisexuality that dominates the third.

—Ah, Baby, said Sigh, I need to make wee.

I saw a drug dealer named Angel Melendez. He knew Michael Alig. Everyone knew Michael, especially the dealers, but Michael's relationship with Angel was inscrutable. They were junky and dealer, but Angel had allowed Michael to corrupt the natural power dynamic of the relationship.

He'd become blinded by Michael's fame. And, by now, Michael was dazzling.

He'd become a staple of daytime television. He'd thrown parties in every major American and European city. Every fashion magazine of note had done an article. His movements were tracked in gossip rags, in newspapers, in glossies.

Angel was one of those sad people who believed that if he suffered a famous person's abuses, he'd end up famous too. The reward for his naiveté? One time Michael invited Angel to a taping of *Geraldo,* but Angel had to sit in the audience.

Angel always wore a pair of wings. Hence the name. These were both a fashion choice and a helpful accoutrement of the drug trade. Potential buyers could spot the wings across even the darkest club. Some people thought he was ugly, but I found him rather handsome, if overly groomed.

Anyhoo, we didn't talk much but he did sell me something that he said was ketamine, but as soon as I snorted it, I knew that it couldn't be ketamine. The taste was wrong, a way different chemical experience. I wasn't numbed. I wasn't experiencing the failure of my human senses, but rather their heightening. Like dropping acid without the confusion. Everything shimmered. Everything seemed hyperreal.

I stumbled around, looking for Queen Rex. I couldn't remember if I'd come with her. I couldn't recognize anyone. Everyone's faces were melting. Whenever I attempted conversation, no words came out of my mouth, or theirs, only the sounds of a thumping techno beat.

—Thump, thump, thump.

—Thump, thump, thump.

—Thump, thump, thump.

—Thump, thump, thump.

—Thump, thump, thump.

I quit Limelight's cloistered atmosphere for the streets. The cars blurred into a solid state streak of traffic. Light and paint smearing above the pavement. Buildings swayed into each other, charcoal messes of breathing matter.

I must have started walking, because I stood on the far side of the West Side Highway, looking over the water at the green hills of New Jersey. There wasn't another soul present. I saw the sky, the slow liquid motion of the heavens, the stars smudging across the sky, as if it were me dislodged in time, as if I were Boaz ben-Haim and could see the twelve evening hours as simultaneous events.

—Thump thump, I said, thump thump thump?

Fog rolled off the river, thick tepid tapestry. The piers from the ocean, the streets from the buildings, the buildings from the cars. One gray mesh layer, one impossible situation. I'd done bad drugs, I'd done good drugs, but I'd never done a drug like this. The faux-ketamine had boosted my intelligence, giving my brain a massive spike in capacity. For me, the point of drugs was getting fucked up, dimming the controller, not enhancing its perceptual faculties, not being so transformed that I lost any sense of matter. There was a reason why I hadn't done DMT.

A sound came down, a sound like an air horn, a sound like buildings collapsing, a sound like the cries of a banshee announcing the death of a family, a sound like a Greek chorus of dogs heralding their owner's tragedy. The fog parted, a pathway made through the middle, and walking toward me, I swear, was a solitary figure of unknown proportions.

I trembled.

And then it closed upon me. A frail man, five feet eleven inches in height, wearing an Andy Warhol wig. Only another person who thought that if they dressed up like Andy, then they could be Andy.

—Oh, gee, said the Andy, what are you doing here?

—Bad drugs, I said.

—That's tough, said the Andy. I knew a lot of people who took bad drugs. Most are dead. Some took too much. Some took too little. The rest committed suicide. One girl was hit by a car. It was so sad.

—Who are you? I asked.

—You know who I am.

The Andy took off his black leather jacket. Andy lifted his black turtleneck, revealing the tortured area where Valerie Solanas had fired .32 caliber slugs into his exploding plastic inevitable torso.

—That's the best makeup I've ever seen, I said.

—It isn't makeup, said Andy.

He took my hand. He put my fingers inside the bullet hole. My fingers sank into his body, warmed by his inner flesh.

—Don't look surprised, Andy Warhol said. I came back before, after Valerie murdered me. If death couldn't stop me then, why would it now?

—Angel told me it was ketamine, I said. Are you a ghost?

—I'm much worse than a ghost, he said. You know what the Pseudo-Dionysius the Areopagite says, don't you? You can't define what I am, only what I'm not. Lots of kids know that I'm going to live forever and they haven't even seen me. You only believe because I'm here before you. All those people have a faith that you don't. Isn't it terrific when people believe in you? Isn't it great when they love you?

—I don't believe in anything, I said. I don't love anyone.

—Gee, said Andy, that's too bad.

Blame the drugs or the writing or the drugged writing. The next night, at Tunnel, I found some kids who'd bought ketamine from Angel, and asked if they'd had similar experiences. They hadn't. His ketamine was fine, they said. What was wrong with it?

I called Angel at his number and at Michael's, but no one answered. I didn't bother leaving a message on Michael's machine.

I found Franklin in the Tunnel basement. I suggested we amscray back to my apartment and do the things that people do when they're desperate for a flickering glimpse of intimacy. He said that he'd rather stay at the club. I reminded him that he hadn't checked on The King of France for over a month, and wouldn't it be nice to see the little guy before he wasn't a kitten anymore?

We abandoned Tunnel. Walking back to my place, I kept thinking about Andy fucking Warhol. He'd always been a sore spot, dying a few months after my arrival in Manhattan and long before I'd joined the Downtown scene. He'd haunted my years in New York, his influence lingering over every aspect of my life.

His death caused a vacuum, and then there was this evil creature Michael Alig, desperate and salivating, muscling his way into the lights and glamour. For over twenty years, those lights and that glamour were Andy's, he was the beacon for America's fucked-up and alienated and gay kids. He transformed himself into a living idea like a Tibetan tulpa, an image that self-replicated across the whole culture. But the thing about Andy, the inexplicable thing, is that in addition to being a media superstar, he was the greatest American artist of the twentieth century. I'll defend that opinion till the death. No one was better.

Someone like Michael, or the thousands of kids who came to New York each year to throw away their lives on the fable of the Silver Factory, assumed the outward form of Andy without having an ounce of his talent.

One of life's cruel facts. Talent floats you in ways that are incomprehensible to the untalented.

Ability was Andy's foundation, the bedrock on which he built everything else. When Edie was vomiting up bile, when Ondine was shooting speed into his own eyeball, when Billy Name trapped himself within a bathroom hermitage, there was the underlying stability of talent. A talent that could survive anything. A talent that could survive being shot. A talent that could survive death. A talent that could survive the 1970s.

Franklin and I got to my apartment. I took off his clothes. Then I took off my clothes. Then I screwed his brains out. Then we hung around, naked, for hours, playing with The King of France.

—Aren't you so glad you adopted this little guy? He's the cutest!

—It's probably the best thing that I've done with my life, I said. Whenever I imagine his kitten face in a trash can, rotten food on his head, I know that I've done something genuinely good.

The King of France enjoyed chasing change. I'd throw my nickels and dimes and pennies and quarters around the apartment, and he'd run after them, often leading to the spectacle of the fellow trotting around with silver currency dangling from his mouth. At any given time, my floor was littered with roughly thirty dollars in coins.

We were throwing quarters when someone knocked on my door. I heard a man and a woman giggling.

—What fucking time is it? I asked.

—Two in the morning, said Franklin.

More knocking. The woman's shrill laughter even louder.

—This building. These people must have the wrong floor, I said. Straight people can be so fucking annoying. I'm not putting on any clothes. If these people are so rude that they'd knock on a stranger's door in the early am hours, then they deserve the poet in his naked glory.

I opened the door. There stood Cecil and Karen Spencer. They'd lived through the East Village arts scene, sure, but it hadn't prepared them for the glory of my nudity, for a sudden dewy explosion of the uncircumcised human form.

I should have moved into the hallway and closed the door behind me. Instead I stood there, waiting for them to say something, waiting for them to get over the abrupt frankness of my Hellenic neo-paganism, none of us saying anything until Franklin walked up behind me, himself stark naked, his cock half erect. He put his arms on my shoulders and nuzzled into my neck.

—Hi, he said. I'm Franklin. Who're you?

—I guess I'm not the only person who lives in a soap opera, said Karen Spencer.

I tried pacifying Cecil, calming him and reassuring him, blaming myself, talking about how much he meant. His need was obvious. He wanted me to fight for him. He wanted a grand show, a pantomime to convince him that it was okay to forgive me. But I didn't have the energy. I let him slide. I let it pass.

It's taken me years to admit it, but it was a shame. Cecil would have forgiven me anything. If I hadn't fucked it up, he would be sitting behind me now, typing on his computer, happy as a clam.

Franklin didn't give a shit one way or the other.

And me?

The only thing I cared about was the writing.

JUNE 1994

Baby Turns In His Manuscript

I finished the manuscript, finished my revisions. I typed the title page:

SAVING ANNE FRANK

I put the manuscript on Parker's desk. He reached out with his thick ham hands. He read the title.

—You're fucking killing me with this, he said. How the hell am I going to make this right with Bill Thomas?

—We have a signed contract.

—Big whoop.

—Read it. Tell me what you think.

Happy to be rid of the manuscript, happy to be done with the absolute depths of human darkness, I wandered from Parker's office and ended up in Central Park, a locale that I generally avoided, ancient obelisks notwithstanding.

I walked through Sheep Meadow and across West Drive. A large pedestaled statue stood in a leafy grove, dedicated to the memory of the New York 7th Regiment, a Civil War unit. It depicted an infantryman as standing sentry, leaning on his rifle. Scattered around its base were a bunch of old chicken bones.

It's an idealized portrait but I recognized the face. The simple, dumb American face. A face that I'd grown up with, a face that had died hundreds of thousands of times because half of the country could not admit the evils of slavery. I'd spent half a year working on a manuscript, a year that I could have spent living, and soon I'd be gone, too, as dead as the 7th Regiment. Those who escaped battle had gone with old age, or with disease, or with accident. There was no way out. Everyone turned to dust. Why had I even bothered?

I had a sensation that the Civil War hadn't ended. That our world lay atop the true, older reality. We were doomed to fight out the same battles.

Look at American politics. The schism has always been the same. North versus South. White versus Black. Over two hundred years of the Republic and nothing had changed. The battle went ever on, would go on long after my death, long after my books were forgotten.

As I looked into that stupid American face, I thought, *Oh, fuck, this could be a really good book. This could be great.* I was back on the treadmill, the never-ending march of literature.

Oh, Ulysses S. Grant, you patron secular saint of addiction, how I wished you would deliver me. How I wanted a drink! I stopped at a tourist bar near the Empire State Building and downed a series of vodka sodas.

Back at my apartment, my answering machine held three messages. All from Parker.

—You miserable piece of shit, said the machine, you had better pull your dick from whatever hole in which it's stationed and ring me as soon as you get this. I'm not fucking around, you weak sister.

He answered the phone. He too had gone into the realm of the drunkard. His voice too was thick with demon alcohol.

—Parker, I said, it's Baby.

—You son of a bitch, he said. You fucking goofball queer.

—Do you hate it? I asked.

—A fat girl with a bad weave in yellow snake skin shoes and red pants. That used to be my vision of god. But now I know that god is your manuscript. I want to dress it up, name it Susan and propose blissful and fiscally rewarding matrimony. I want my dick between the pages, evenly distributed on both sides. I want to ride it. This is hot shit, kiddo. I can sell this like water to a ragheaded sonofabitch who's dying from thirst in the Saudi desert.

—So everything's copacetic? I asked.

—Things are beyond copacetic, you poof, said Parker. I had a girlfriend who couldn't pronounce epitome. She kept calling it epi-tome. Like some crazy Greek fuckbook. Things aren't the epitome of copacetic. They're the fucking epi-tome. We're set and ready to go.

—All right, I said. I'm deliriously drunk and I need to feed my cat.

—I'll call you tomorrow, he said. They're gonna kill us for this, but it'll be such a glorious fucking death.

I took The King of France into my lap. He flopped on his back, showing me his snowy gut. Having never had a mother, and being exiled from his siblings, the kitten had never learned any normal cat behaviors. He didn't enjoy being pet, but he loved being slapped on his stomach.

He purred as hard as I'd ever heard. The weakness of alcohol came upon my body. I felt so fucking lonely. I'd made it as an author, I'd gotten where I'd wanted, but in the end, I didn't have anybody. I'd fucked up my friendships, fucked up my love life. The best that I had was Franklin. Back to that dead awful sensation of my first day in New York, the complete and absolute freedom of having no human attachments. I'd escaped the American Middle West and it still felt awful. I was a member of the 7th Regiment, stationed at Petersburg, hoping not to die.

I called Franklin.

AUGUST 1994

Reunion

I'd been listening to Dion and the Belmonts. My favorite song was "Little Diane," an up-tempo number with very dark lyrics about Dion wanting revenge upon a two-timing woman, but also admitting that his desire for vengeance is the only mask that can suppress his pain. The song's unique feature comes in its instrumentation, with a kazoo as the lead instrument. You'd think that this would kill the song, but somehow a child's toy gives it an ultra-modern sound.

The *Greatest Hits* of Dion and the Belmonts was one of the first CDs that I'd purchased. I'd given over to the new technology, liking the clarity of sound and the smallness of the individual unit. I didn't own many LPs, but whenever I moved them, it was like carrying a solid ton of material.

While writing *Saving Anne Frank,* I'd bought a six-disc changer so that I could listen to solid hours of music. I'd never been particularly interested in music, even as a devotee of the club, an environment in which you were supposed to have favorite DJs and all this other unmemorable crap, but I had discovered one kind of music that I truly loved. Old pop and soul from the 1950s and 1960s. This material was being re-released on CD, so I was spending every Saturday down in the Village, digging through the racks.

Then there was the time when I was thinking about Sam Cooke. Unable to get "That's Where It's At" out of my head, I went to Bleecker Bob's with the hope of finding more material. I came across an import of a Japanese CD, *Live at the Harlem Club, 1963.* I'm not big on live recordings, and it was pricey because it was from Nippon. But what the hell, I said, it's Sam Cooke. If you can't trust Sam Cooke to be good, is there anything you can trust?

Sam Cooke is always good. "Bring It On Home to Me" was my favorite song. It's the best song ever recorded. And the saddest.

The young man behind the register, who looked as if he'd made a habit out of avoiding sex, gave me the once-over. He couldn't believe that some swish guy in gross clothes with an obvious yuppie attitude had enough taste to buy this album. I could hear the question that he wanted to ask: *Are you sure you don't want some Pearl Jam?*

I'd changed, I'd evolved past the Village, evolved past record store clerks. I was something else.

Still, I always loved the NYU stomping grounds. On MacDougal, I drank an iced espresso in Caffè Reggio, sitting in the alcove by the bathroom. Beneath a cheap bust of Nefertiti. I'd brought a book. *A Prayer for Owen Meany,* by John Irving. I read about 100 pages, going blind from the titular character's dialogue, which appears IN ALL CAPITALS. Other than this typographical oddity, I liked the novel just fine. I liked everything by John Irving.

I walked through the park, passing the homeless guys playing ultra-abusive games of chess. There were more drug dealers than I remembered. Each said the same thing. Smoke, smoke, smoke.

One of New York City's great mysteries is the fountain in Washington Square. You can never predict when it'll be turned on. As I moved toward the center of the park, I could see the water blasting skyward. It was one of the lucky days.

A crowd had formed around the pool. Half-naked teenage girls sat on the upper ring, their feet dangling into the water. Parents let their infant children splash around. A guy played an out-of-tune guitar and sang off-key.

I watched for a little while. Then I heard a girl calling my name.

—Baby Baby Baby!

I shuddered inside, not wanting to deal with a club person in the blinding clarity of late-summer sunlight. But what could I do? I turned. And there she was. And there she was. And there she was. And. there. she. was.

Adeline.

—Adeline? I said.

—Baby, she said.

We hugged. I held her too long. She tried squirming out of my arms. I wouldn't let her go. She'd put on weight. She didn't feel like a skeleton.

—Baby, she said, please. I can't breathe.

—If I let you go, are you going to run away? I asked.

—You'll remember that I'm the one who called you.

I let her go. Her face was red. She took in a deep breath.

—I don't come to the park very often, I said. I live up in the mid-30s.

—I started making my appearance only a few weeks ago, she said. It's a pleasant enough exercise. One does what one can to stave off boredom.

—Where are you living? I asked.

This question may have given away more than I wanted. It presumed that I knew she wasn't living on East 7th Street. I'd haunted the old block on several occasions, hoping to catch a glimpse of Adeline. I never did. Finally, I encountered this old Ukrainian lady who lived on the ground floor of our building and asked if she'd seen Adeline. The Ukrainian said that Adeline had moved out.

—The same old place, said Adeline. I'm serving a life sentence on East 7th.

—No kidding, I said.

Adeline couldn't even look at me. She kept staring at other people's children.

I saw the conversation ending in five minutes, with us maybe running into one another on the street every couple of years. As if we'd never been real friends. I swallowed my pride, my everything.

—Adeline, I said. I'm sorry.

—Don't be sorry, she said. I'm the one who should apologize.

—It's all my fault, I said. I fucked everything up.

—I've wasted the last two years blaming myself, she said.

I hugged her again. I didn't care if she couldn't breathe. I loved her so goddamned much.

—Put me down! she cried. For God's sake, man, get some control over your impulses.

—Adeline, I asked, can it go back to how it was?

—You can't move into my apartment, she said.

—That's not what I meant, I said. I want to be friends again. I want to go back to how we were.

—Me too, she said.

—But, Adeline, I said, you can't repeat the past.

—What do you mean you can't repeat the past? she asked. Of course you can.

Everything would be fine again, everything would resume where it left off. But that was a crazy fantasy. Things left off horribly. It was a nice thought, a reassuring moment. A point of adolescent reversion.

A child in a stroller started crying for its mother. I was about to say something to Adeline about irresponsible parents who inflicted their miserable kids on the world, but she wasn't there.

She picked up the crying child. She carried the crying child to me.

—Baby, she said, meet my son. Meet Emil Mahmoud.

AUGUST 1994

Reunion, Part Two

I'll beg your indulgences as I simply flood you with information, that new currency of our twenty-first century. Very many things transpired betwixt my San Francisco departure and the decade's halfway mark. I've gossip to dish, you lovely creatures, and I suppose that you must be dying to hear about Emil Mahmoud and his big daddy Nash Mac and my procreative urges and how yours truly found herself embalmed by motherhood.

As you might imagine, it started in simple innocent pleasure, with Nash Mac screwing out my brains. Please believe me when I say that I ain't one of those foolish simps who adopts an inactive role in her own contraception. I insisted, each time, that Nash Mac wrap his Johnny within a rubber, whilst also personally deploying many a liberal squirt of spermicidal gel.

When my period ran late, I thought nothing of it. You'll remember the dreary months following my contretemps with Baby. Only natural, wasn't it, to assume that faulty plumbing had forced another work stoppage. As it turns out, I'm one of those rare women blessed with a lack of morning sickness.

I maintained my starred-eyed ignorance until month three. 'Round then, I came to the misbegotten notion that, Great God All Mighty, I might be carrying a child!

By that point, I'd reestablished residence on East 7th Street, evicting Luanna's friend and retrieving my useless possessions. I had presumed that a return to NYC would be as pleasant as a four-automobile highway massacre, so imagine the surprise when excitement burst beneath my skin as I stomped down from the L train at Third Avenue. When I saw the dome of St. George's, why, a jolt of pure joy rose in my breast!

Luanna'd begun grumbling about how I must learn to use a computer, as daft an idea as any I'd heard. "Things are changing," she said. "It's a cutthroat business and the newest knives are digital." I'm positively certain that you'll understand why I gave up illustration and chose to focus on *Trill*.

I didn't give a jot or tittle about the business end of comics, trusting that Jeremy could handle matters. Winterbloss suggested letting a third party take care of distribution. He arranged a last-minute deal with Image Comics, a company founded by some of the biggest brutes in the whole dirty funnybook bizness, men like Todd McFarlane and Robert Liefeld.

Those boys had established Image as a response to the ghetto workhouses of Marvel and DC, focusing their new company on creator-owned projects and constructing a framework by which the individual might release her work upon the world. The company took the upfront, asking for zero stake in the intellectual property, an arrangement unprecedented in human history.

Jeremy's connection was Jim Valentino. They'd dealt with each other, briefly, whilst working on an issue of *The Official Marvel Index to the Avengers*.

Winterbloss reasoned that with our promotional debut in *Cerebus* and Image's place of pride in Diamond's *Previews* catalogue, we would establish a fairly meaningful beachhead. If business with Image proved unpalatable, then we could dump the company and self-publish on the strength of the material and the launch.

Everything was swellegant. Yet you'll remember, darlings, that when life is at its most swellegant those who are doomed to live it will most often cock the thing up.

My breasts swelled. My stomach protruded. My emotions veered into the erratic.

All of this seemed cotton-pickin' peculiar and far beyond the elementary discomfort of a long overdue period. Don't you know that the idea arrived fully formed like Pallas Athena? *Adeline,* said my brain, *what if you're pregnant?*

O, God no! says I to myself. How could it be? The only man who'd given me the time was Nash Mac, and it seemed impossible that anything about the fellow, let alone his DNA-infused spermatozoa, possessed the gumption to survive a heady mix of latex and Nonoxynol-9.

I purchased two pregnancy tests at a grocery store on Avenue A that was built into the crumbling remains of an old RKO movie house. I had no other items of acquisition. The woman behind the cash register proffered an all-too-knowing glance. A lesser person would have wilted under her disapproval, descending into all six forms of Judeo-Christian shame.

Yet you know me, darlings. I'd read somewhere about a custom during the Middle Ages called The Beggar's Tribute. Kings and other nobles took no vengeance upon any beggar who dared insult them, believing a beggar's voice to be his only coinage and his insults the only tribute that he might pay. A beggar's insults marked one as a person of distinction.

This grocer woman was no different. Let her stare down my slutting ways, let her examine the "A" branded into my cheek. That's what beggars do before their betters.

I made water upon the first test. Not examining its result, I made water upon the second. I waited a good ten minutes before consulting both.

+. The double +. +.+. ++. Ne plus ultra. My fertile womb, my jolly unborn child. ++++++++++++++++++++.

A baby was so much work. A baby was so much money. A baby would change everything. Life would never be sane again. All those dreadful little clichés. I was acting positively plebeian!

The enormous debate. Whether or not to keep the thing. Yet there ain't much suspense in that regard, is there, oh reader? You know that the babe was born. Little Emil may be many things, but we shan't count him as the sole known example of spontaneous human generation.

I'd floated through life vowing that if I ever had suffered the misfortune of being knocked up, I'd dilate-and-scrape quicker than two shakes of an epileptic's fist.

I'd known some very dubious young sophomores and juniors who conflated abortion with birth control. How many friends from Crossroads had I driven to Planned Parenthood? I never judged, never saw it as anything other than an operation. Many of the girls were shell-shocked by their visit to the clinic. Their rationality of choice could not outweigh the emotional imbalance.

They resided in a country that heaped ashes of guilt upon their heads, victims of a misbegotten religious society which framed the argument through a bogus feint towards the inherent sanctity of all life. What egregious nonsense! The sheer hypocrisy is revealed by anyone who spends twenty minutes walking through any major American city, any person who speaks with the country's destitute and its broken, with its homeless. People smeared in their own filth, reeking of acidic urine, destroyed by mental illness. Life was sacred, old boy, but only so long as it remained within a woman's womb. Once the damned creatures crawled from the primordial uterine ooze, then it was a battle for every cent and every breadcrumb. There are no handouts in America! Everyone must operate their own bootstraps! Three cheers for a decrease in the surplus population!

This says nothing of the poor abused mothers. Girls doomed by social pressure into the wrong decision. Their fragile lives ruined by the phantasmal promise of sanctified motherhood. Those who are miseducated from their early months, told of the beatific glow of motherhood, only to be thrust deep into the bowels of poverty.

Abortion is a social good, but you'll never hear tell of that particular notion. Our country is addicted to its own lies. Even the so-called prochoice wing of the national dialogue will not publicly admit the truth. At last some mouth must give it an utterance, so I suppose it shall be yours truly. Abortion is a grand thing.

For me, myself, I considered the operation in the stewing mess of my own life. I'd spent years running towards the weird, shunning the normal. And it hadn't gotten me very far, had it? I drew a comic book about anthropomorphic cats, and I spent a good many days listening to *Astral Weeks*, but there wasn't much to show, was there? What if the only path forward was through an embrace of family?

The situation itself suggested that I might not want to tempt fate's vagaries. If this particular sperm, of all the billions, had survived its many travails, then surely it must be a special thing, a creature desperate to be born. It struck me that the universe was giving me a sign.

You'll be charitable enough to remember that the pregnancy went three months without discovery. My body had flooded itself with hormones designed to cloud judgment and commandeer my thinking. The fetus protected through biochemical manipulation of its mother.

I telephoned Nash Mac.

I'd dumped him in San Francisco. That news hit with a rough shock. He sunk so low as to suggest following me to New York. I'd given this half-baked notion a complete veto. "Dear boy," I'd said, "don't you know that you're a San Francisco person? A California kid? You can't come live in New York. It simply won't do, old sport. It won't do!"

Nash Mac pointed out that Fairfax, Virginia, was significantly closer to New York than Pasadena, and that thus, perhaps, he had more of a genuine connection with the East Coast. Acrimony ensued. He accused me, as most men eventually do, of never really knowing him. It hit me as it always does, but what can a person say when they're escaping a scene and going back to their once upon a time? I cut the apron strings and said good-bye.

Now imbued with the news that he was a father-to-be, Nash Mac moved to New York. Nothing could keep him from his child, and, one supposes, myself. He asked no permission, but in fairness, the pregnancy had me befuddled enough that when he arrived at JFK, I waited by his gate and brought him into my arms and my bed.

He'd taken an extended leave from LucasArts, summoning his inner Daniel and reading MENE MENE TEKEL UPHARSIN. He'd arranged employ at Enteractive Inc., a third-rate outfit on West 40th Street. Despite the many times that he attempted description, I could not understand the nature of his job. I presumed that he was hired as a result of his infinitesimally tangential association with George Lucas.

Had it lasted, I've no doubt that he would've proposed marriage.

I managed a month and a half before his tender ministrations drove me to distraction. I cut the cord, again. In the seemingly endless fight, he held his move to New York over me, suggesting I hadn't expressed gratitude for his performance of an action that I hadn't requested.

"You imagine me some fey creature of whimsy," said I. "My only mistake was in thinking that you'd want to know about the omnipotence of your spermatozoa. Don't delude yourself. You came to this city because you wanted to live in New York. None of this was for me or for the baby."

I promised Nash Mac that I shouldn't ask a thing of him. He was appalled. He wanted to be in his child's life. I assured him that he would, leaving the details vague. We didn't know a thing about this child. Why make plans?

Yet I knew that I couldn't keep Nash Mac out forever. Every action has its consequences.

His experience at Enteractive offered enough trauma that he was soon ringing LucasArts, informing them of his imminent return. We'd passed into the year 1994. The company'd released *Sam & Max Hit the Road* and were ramping up for *Full Throttle*. "None of these games are great," said Nash Mac. "No one is as good as Ron Gilbert."

He departed through the same terminal gate by which he'd arrived. The true horror of sex spilled out, right there on the industrial carpeting of Terminal 3. The inescapable Nash Mac.

He wasn't nothing but some guy who'd given me the time in San

Francisco. I'd done no wrong, kept myself protected, but it hadn't mattered. Caught stealing from the cookie jar, we'd been sentenced to a lifetime of each other. Oh Jesus, make up my dying bed!

Goodbye, New York, said he. Goodbye, Adeline, said he. Goodbye, Nash Mac, said I, hoping that I might yet discover a path to navigate the awkwardness of our special relationship.

With Nash Mac stationed back in Californy, I didn't have another soul to help with my pregnancy. Luanna only went so far. There were many considerations. Should I move? Should I convert Baby's room into a baby's room? What of the delivery itself and the prenatal care and the vitamins and the food and all the other miseries with which Nash Mac had been helping?

Darlings, I was at my lowest. I telephoned Dahlia.

My sister, that abominable fool, that delirious idiot. She and Charles had separated and reunited on three separate occasions, never quite divorcing and somehow bringing two children into this mortal world. A daughter and a son. Dahlia was an old hand at motherhood. For the first time in her life, she knew more than yours truly.

Yet she remained Dahlia, unable to transcend herself. "Pregnancy," she said, "is like the worst flu you'll ever get. It's a nine-month sickness. It's, like, an agony. When I was carrying Deanna, it was, like, the worst time of my life. My stomach swelled up, I got so fucking fat, I retained water in my ankles, I got hemorrhoids, I was sick all the time, I got varicose veins, I peed every thirty seconds, I ate like a whale, I craved like the grossest foods, and when I did, like, give birth, the labor was thirteen hours and it felt like shitting a baby seal. You're in for it."

Dahlia arrived for the last month of my pregnancy, helping with the preparations. Her most vital role was serving as a buffer between me and Mother.

My coinage couldn't cut it. Though I still refused to speak with the old crone, I'll say one thing for Mother. She did pony up the cash that eased her third grandchild from my womb.

Emil was born at Roosevelt Hospital. The labor was as bad as Dahlia had warned. Even with all the pain and all the drugs, I kept hearing her stupid advice. There I was, darlings, experiencing the miracle of birth, and the only thing flying through my drugged brain was how dreadfully close the process felt to shitting out a seal.

When it was over, I had the child in my arms. Emil's bruised and purpled face. All was forgiven.

Dahlia remained for two extra months. She'd fallen in love with the East Village's upmarket diversity. Through the magic of telephony, I know for dead certain that both of her children and Charles were happy for an interregnum. Life without my sister's inane dialogues and meditations. I was their favorite.

Her focus fell on yours truly and my son. Yet even here I can't rightly complain, as Dahlia taught me the very basics of motherhood, and helped keep *Trill* on schedule. We never missed an issue or a ship date.

Consider it, won't you, darlings? My two great contributions to human civilization. Emil and *Trill*. In a horrible way, their success was down to Dahlia.

The very soul that had haunted my adolescent years with her manic braying and incessant preening. Dahlia! Dahlia! My wretched old sister. Now I owed her everything. She'd saved me! She was my hero. She was all that I had!

No one ever claimed that adulthood would be easy.

I saw Baby beside the fountain in Washington Square Park. Blond hair, farmfed good looks only modestly weathered by city life.

I've no shame confessing my moment of doubt. I considered gathering Emil and avoiding complications. The old bitterprick of anger about Mother, emerging from sheer hypocrisy.

Baby'd only done what anyone would, which is receive a cash infusion from the family coffers. I myself was guilty of the very same. To whom did I run when it became clear that I'd birth Nash Mac's demon seed?

That's the problem of people like Mother, people with serious money. We are bent to their wills.

I said, "Hello, Baby, how do?"

Without expectation of things playing out as they did, but that was only yours truly making herself the fool. I loved Baby. I'd always loved Baby. I'd missed him, even if I loathed admitting it to my lonesome.

So there we were, the old messy duo standing in Washington Square, a child in my arms. I invited Baby to 7th Street. Perhaps it was too soon. *Oh, Adeline,* said I to myself, *throw caution to the wind. This is Baby. Baby whose only crime was getting an education. No ill fortune can befall you. Not from Baby.*

As we walked towards Cooper Square, Emil squirming in his stroller, I said, "When I was in San Francisco, I heard a song on the radio called 'Detachable Penis.' What a preposterous name! Do you know it?"

"I heard it once or twice. I didn't really pay attention," said Baby. "The chorus is stupid."

"Baby," I gasped. "One must always listen to the verses. That's where songwriters hide the most diabolical messages. 'Detachable Penis' is about this doltish East Village denizen who makes an appearance at a party and wakes up hungover only to discover that he's lost his penis, which, as the title infers, has a detachable mechanism. He goes on a wild and woolly bildungsroman throughout this very neighborhood, attempting to find the missing member."

"Where does he go?" asked Baby.

"The Kiev," I said. "He walks down Second Avenue, right next to Love Saves the Day, and finds his penis being sold by one of the junk merchants. Imagine it, Baby! There I am, in a café in the Richmond District, hearing a song about my old neighborhood! A song about the Kiev! It's a bad omen. A cruel wind blows towards New York. People are taking notice."

Baby emerged into his old demesne and his eyes went agog-gog-gogmagog-gog with the changes that I'd wrought upon the place.

Via and viva Dahlia, I'd asked Mother for a tad more money in order to ensure that her grandchild wouldn't choke on lead paint or receive a rusty nail through the foot. Poor Emil, bless his heart, couldn't grow up in the bozo bohemia of our former lives.

Mother distributed a heavy influx. I'd refloored the place and repainted, replacing the fixtures. New kitchen and bedrooms. Nothing could be done about the bathroom. The toilet, the bathtub, and the sink remained split asunder. There still was no buzzer.

I'd transformed Baby's room into a nursery, painted light blue and filled with all manner of tasteful toys. I wouldn't let Emil touch anything plastic, so I'd scoured for vintage playthings built of solid wood.

Yet the room proved an afterthought used mostly for storage. I couldn't bear to sleep apart. Emil remained cribbed by my bed. I hadn't yet attempted sleeping together. I wasn't one to wake in a damp spot of overflowing urine, or worse, retching in the pudding of his shit.

"It's like you've gone yuppie," said Baby. "You may have become part of the problem."

"This child," I said, "will not grow up like the half-loved orphan of a drug casualty. He'll suffer all the affection that he can handle. All the stability, too. New York will not ruin him."

"Where's the cat?" asked Baby. "I've been missing the Captain for so long."

"I didn't want to say," I said, "but the animal has passed from our mortal world."

"How?" asked Baby.

"A tumor on the spine," I said. "We could have operated but it seemed cruel. That's the thing about pets, isn't it? They always break your hearts."

"I need to sit down," said Baby.

New York would not ruin my dear child, but his overactive bowels certainly might. A stench wafted through the apartment. Sitting on the floor, he looked up with a tell-tale expression beneath his shock of thin hair.

"The child's linen must be changed," I said. "I'll spare you the quelle horreur and bring him in the other room."

"Don't bother," said Baby. "I have to do something. I'll be right back. Do I still have to yell to get inside?"

"A handful of things, my dear," said I, "never change."

Whilst Baby stomped down the stairwell, I put Emil up on the counter and investigated the matter. His stool was solid, a happy digression from the previous several days. I'd grown worried enough that if he'd gone another day with looseness, I'd resolved to bring him to the doctor.

Catching my reflection in the toaster's metal as I cleaned my child, I laughed, wondering what Patrick Geoffrois might think of my fixation on Emil's stool. The science of diapers was almost petty divination, attempting to read the symbols and smears of the child's thrice-daily deposits.

The sourness passed from Emil's face. I put him back on the floor. We sat and waited. Baby cried from the street. I descended the stairs and let him inside. He carried a brown paper bag.

Baby bent over and spoke with Emil. "Hello, little guy," said Baby. "Do you mind if I pick him up?" Baby placed his bag on the kitchen table and lifted Emil in the most unusual fashion, keeping the child at a grave distance and holding the young one by his underarms.

"I can't believe this living being came out of you," said Baby.

"Welcome to a very unexclusive club," I said. "I'm fairly certain that it happened."

Baby lifted his bag off the table and brought out a book. "I bought this at the St. Mark's Bookshop," he said, handing me an odd-looking volume entitled *Trapped Between Jupiter and a Bottle*. The cover depicted a man with an elephant's head. "This is my book," he said.

"Very nice," I said, handing it to Baby. "But why show me if you haven't read it?"

"Adeline, this is my book," he said, pushing it back. "I wrote it."

The second page bore a dedication. TO ADELINE, WHEREVER SHE MAY BE ON THIS AMERICAN CONTINENT.

"I had no idea if you'd ever see it," he said. "I never told you my pseudonym."

"Baby," I said, "I've something to show you."

I went into my bedroom and pulled out all ten published issues of *Trill*. We were selling an unfathomable amount each month. I never asked for the numbers, worried that they'd give me performance anxiety, but Winterbloss said that we moved enough units that if I met all of the people buying the book, I'd occupy the rest of my life simply saying hello.

"Here," I said. "Take them."

Baby flipped through the pages.

"Written by J. W. Bloss," said Baby. "That's Jeremy?"

"Yes," I said.

"But who's the artist? M. Abrahamovic Petrovitch. Минерва?"

"Why would it be Минерва?" I asked. "It's me, Baby. It's yours truly."

"Why aren't you using your real name?"

"Jeremy believed it was best if no one knew that I'm a woman. Comics are America's most sexist industry."

"Why the fuck are you the one who has to pretend?" asked Baby.

"We're both pretending. Why do you think he's calling himself J. W. Bloss? His real name is known within the industry. I pretend that I've got a penis and Jeremy pretends that he's not Black. It's an ugly business, but it pays the bills."

NEW YEAR'S EVE 1994

Baby and Adeline Watch Television

I won't bore you with the rest of the motherhood rag, as I'm sure you all have your own terribly disinteresting friends phasing through the throes of parenthood. You know the type, don't you, darlings?

Those folks who'll telephone at any hour, simply dying when little Tommy takes his first step or utters his first nonsensical monosyllable or reaches some arbitrary milestone only appreciable by those with a direct genetic link. I'm not sitting in judgment on those souls, those friends of yours. I'm with them in Rockland. I've made a fool of myself over Emil more times than I care to admit. Yet I won't bore you, reader. I know you have better things.

I'll spare you, too, all the disinteresting little details about me and Baby and our reunification. You know as well as I that it was inevitable. If it hadn't happened, your nose wouldn't be buried within this book, would it? You'd be reading one of those sad little stories about people who spend their sour lives crying into store-bought beers.

When New Year's Eve rolled around, it was Baby and I sitting in my apartment, Emil fast asleep. I was outraged, as one will be when one's child might be woken by the sounds of nighttime revels. "These mongoloids are making a hullabaloo in the street," I said. "They have no respect for the delicate nature of a sleeping baby."

"There was a time when you stalked the East Village."

"I never ran wild with abandon, shouting out whatever market-tested non sequitur passed through my idiotic head. Advertising slogans and human degradation! Is this how they ring in the last five years of the millennium?"

If you can believe it, we had my old black-and-white television tuned to *Dick Clark's New Year's Rockin' Eve*. I lived on the island of Manhattan, and had lived here, more or less, for ten years. Never once had I been tempted by the Sodom and Gomorrah of Times Square on December 31. Yet there we were, watching it flicker on the screen.

"You need a new television," said Baby. "I can't believe this thing still works."

"When it breaks, I'm not replacing it. The radio is good enough. Emil won't grow up as one of these fat children whose best friend is the blue glow of the death box. If this contraption still functions when he's old enough to understand its purpose, I'll throw it out."

Although *Dick Clark's New Year's Rockin' Eve* focused on New York, the musical numbers were performed remotely and introduced by the comedians Margaret Cho and Steve Harvey. One watched crowds crammed into Times Square and then the camera cut away to performances at Walt Disney World.

Melissa Etheridge, The O'Jays, Jon Secada, Hootie & the Blowfish, and Salt-N-Pepa. I'd half hoped that they'd feature this reggae singer named Ini Kamoze. At that very moment, he had a huge crossover hit called "Here Comes the Hotstepper." I found it inescapable. It drifted to my ears from stray radios, from cars, badly warbled from people's mouths. One couldn't leave the house without hearing of the hotstepper and his arrival.

As enlightened as yours truly counted herself, a Buddha done up in Aveda, I remained a creature of my own era. Having come of age during the lilywhite daze of synthpop, there was a distinct decay in my understanding of popular culture. Gone down to dust was the Great White Rocker, at last replaced by the sounds of hip-hop.

Emil rendered me too distracted to give two farthings of a faker's pretense. Busy with my child, busy with my drawing. Even if I hadn't gone over to motherhood, the thing that I'd've wanted least was to be a woman on the verge of her thirties maintaining the pretense that she retained an acute comprehension of teenage tastes, hoping beyond hope for a genuine connection to evolving trends of lowbrow culture. Imagine me talking about Snoop Doggy Dogg!

A few days earlier, I'd rented an awful film from Kim's Underground on Bleecker, a location with a far better selection than the Kim's on Avenue A. The title of this awful film was *Return of the Living Dead III*. As the Roman numerals imply, *III* is the third installation in a series of zombie films possessing a tangential association to the grandsire of the genre, *Night of the Living Dead*. The original *Return* is well liked for its ultracheeze '80s punk overlay, a bit like *Jubilee* by Derek Jarman if Derek Jarman's *Jubilee* were absolutely moronic and had its theme sung by Dinah Cancer.

Don't you dare ask why I'd rent such a thing. I offer neither a sane nor

reasonable answer. I am an inveterate loather of zombie films, if you exclude my thumping heart for Bela's bravura performance as Murder Le-
gendre in *White Zombie* and my great admiration for *I Walked with a
Zombie* by Jacques Tourneur and Val Lewton. I will profess even a certain
affinity for *Night*. Those exceptions aside, the zombie remains horror's stu-
pidest trope.

With a wee bit of squinting, one can see its appeal to the American
mind. We're a militaristic society, born in battle, defining our historical
periods through war. Bloody G. W. enthroned as our first president, the
War of 1812, Baby's idée fixe of Mr. Lincoln's agony, WWI, WWII, Vietnam. Our silly little history ain't much but war history. Our entire dialogue
is a reference to war. The War on Drugs. The War on Poverty.

Link that with our present-day empire in decline, our high point hit
around 1963, and armies of animated corpses begin to make a semiotic
sense. I'm not a girl who holds much truck with allegory, intentional or
otherwise, but one can't miss the equation. War culture + societal death
trip = a nation enthralled with images of the walking dead.

Filmed in 1992, *Revenge of the Living Dead III* makes overtures toward
the perceived youth culture of its moment. Posters festoon the male lead's
high school bedroom, advertising every alternative band that one can
imaginate, including my old favorites L7. The female lead's fashion is a
hodge-podge of early-'90s clichés. Leather jackets, fishnets, dyed hair.

There's a moment when the male protagonist's life has gone tits up. His
lady's been killed, and he's transubstantiated her into a zombie, a plan that
works out rather poorly.

At his lowest moment, given over to despair, our hero is hiding in a
sewer. He engages a homeless vagabond in conversation. The young man
tells his newfound friend all about his hopes and his dreams. He wants to
go to Seattle, to join a band, to be a drummer. Everything'll be cool once
we're in Seattle, he says.

You'll recall that the film was shot during one of those appalling moments when the spectacle has found itself a new youth movement. The
world was lousy with bands from Seattle. Nirvana, Pearl Jam, Soundgar-
den, Alice in Chains, Mother Love Bone, Temple of the Dog, Tad, Screaming Trees. Sub Pop Records.

O Jesu Cristo, protect me from such demons!

What's saddest about *III* is imagining its creative fulmination, the moment when its director, Brian Yunza, and its scriptwriter, John Penney, read

an article in the *New York Times* about the latest craze with the kiddies and envisioned making their film fresh, with real cultural currency. And where did these men land? On a boy who longs for Seattle whilst his zombie girlfriend takes up the hobby of body piercing.

No one is worse than the oldest person at a punk rock show.

That was Baby. Clubbing had not been kind. It never was. The spectacle of a successful young author trapped in his own desire for relevance, believing that he must, at all costs, keep up with people ten years younger.

Since our reunification, I'd concluded that life was, indeed, a repeating cycle. I'd convinced him to stop sleeping with that mysterious little toad named Franklin, but it'd left Baby lonely, and brought us back to where we'd started. I spent my spare time wondering how I might fix Baby with a nice boy.

APRIL 1995

Baby and Adeline Go to Norman Mailer's House

During one of my more addlepated phases, I sallied forth under the delusion that perhaps one could make friends with those undergoing the same maternal experiences as one's lonesome. I even joined a support group of new mothers, following a recommendation from Emil's pediatrician.

Alack, most of the group tended to be rather booooooooring and soooo stiflingly conventional. You should have heard their complaints, reader! They fixated upon the awful jobs of their miscreant husbands. Otherwise it was sore nipples and the inability to find the right toys. Their braying wore on the nerves. I absconded after a few months, more than happy to be left alone with my comic book cats.

The only other freak of our little group was a raven-haired woman named Frances Washington, who hailed from the State of Rhode Island and Providence Plantations. Never quite confined by the smallest state's definitions of life for a poor girl living in Smith Hill, she'd graduated from Classical and matriculated to RISD on scholarship. She did her graduate degree at Parsons. Her current employ came as an in-house graphic designer for NBC, at the General Electric building in Rockefeller Center.

She too was one of those unwed mothers about whom so much hay was made in the mass media. As was I. If you can believe it, your old pal Adeline had joined the sole demographic which all of America had decided it could hate. Single mothers! Yet Frances had it worse. At least my crimes occurred within the rubric of Whiteness.

Our status as wanton strumpets provided common ground, giving Frances and I many a thing to talk about. Or tawk about, as she'd never lost all traces of her native accent.

I'd asked her if, as Baby contended, Rhode Islanders were the only people besides Wisconsinites who used the word "bubbler" as a noun for drinking fountains. To my shock, she said yes, yes, Rhode Islanders drink water from bubblers.

We shared a general paranoia about leaving our children with strangers. During the day, Frances deposited her child with an understanding aunt from Queens, giving Miz Washington two hours of daily commute.

At night, she lacked a good option. "I just can't do it," she said. "I'd rather be single the rest of my life than leave Danielle with a sitter."

One night, stuffing our faces with undercooked pizza, we examined our parallel situations and made a pact. As she was ensconced up in the badlands of Gramercy, not so very far from 7th Street, we would pool our resources and mind the other's child whenever Mommy needed a night.

Thus it was on a fated Friday, somewhere in April, when I escorted Emil to East 19th Street. Frances answered the door, clad in paint-stained clothes. "I've been back at the canvas again," said she. "I need to work on something that isn't paying my rent."

"You simply must take up comics," I said. "No one ever earns real money in my dirty little industry."

Frances showed me her canvas. A tableau evidencing deep traces of the medieval. A woman in the garret of a tiled, multitiered Moorish tower. A half-human, half-frog strapped to a table. The woman uses an impossibly arcane instrument to measure the monster's limbs. On the shelves are beakers full of variegate liquids. Twisting blue smoke rises from a candelabra made from a waxy human hand.

"Whatever is it titled?" I asked.

"Nagasaki/Hiroshima: After Remedios Varo for the Tutsi Peoples."

I hugged and kissed Emil. He'd be spending the night. Much as I loathed leaving him, I couldn't tolerate dragging the boy home at 2 am. Besides, the darling did enjoy his visits with Frances and Danielle.

"What's the plan?" asked Frances.

"Do you know, I'm not quite certain," I said. "Baby invited me to one of his literary parties. Some dreadful place in darkest Brooklyn."

I rode the 6 to Grand Central, reading the briefest snippet of Angela Carter's *The Bloody Chamber*. In the main concourse, I did as always and attempted to discern the astrological symbols on its ceiling. I caught vague intimations of the zodiac beneath the black tar, but I couldn't discern any specific shapes.

Putting on my headphones, I turned on my Walkman and listened to Bob Dylan's most recent album, *World Gone Wrong*, a clear aftershock of Dylan's laboring through a wrenching experience. Namely the 1980s.

I still picture with abject horror the middle-aged troubadour in his stonewashed blue jeans, his leather vests and white t-shirts, his crucifix earrings. I chill to the bone when I think of his unspeakable contribution to "We Are the World." Let no charitable mouth speak of the baroque horror that is *Empire Burlesque*.

Yet you've gotta serve somebody, and no soul ever recognized the pearly gates without first glimpsing fiery brimstone. The old boy had abandoned the cocaine and pastel glitz and neon of the previous decade and reconnected his self with what'd first brought him into the music biz. Those old vinyl and shellac 78s.

Race and hillbilly records flew at the man, and he decided to record a few of the ancient numbers by his lonesome. One man, one acoustic guitar, no mastering, no studio albatross. The first effort, *Good as I Been to You*, was throat-clearing, or voice destroying, because truthfully, Robert Allen Zimmerman sounded as though he'd inhaled a balloon full of helium before every take.

By *World Gone Wrong*, the follow-up, his voice had cracked. He sang with a gravel-hardened instrument. The years became evident, weighted with the backroads of American history. I couldn't cease listening. Between *World Gone Wrong* and *The Sporting Life*, a collaboration between Diamanda Galás and John Paul Jones, I had soundtracked out months of my life.

Dylan synced with 42nd Street. This excess of human glitz and greed, of flesh and lust and sinister grace. I wondered about Erik, Baby's old beau. He'd turned me on to Dylan, saying that my caricatured image of the singer did not tally with the recorded work. He lent me copies of *Desire* and *The Freewheelin' Bob Dylan*. Now Erik was gone, disappeared into the stupidity of broken human relations.

I crossed Fifth Avenue, staring at the public library and its increasingly anachronistic lions. A half-crippled fat man limped in my general direction. His was a face designed to bear disappointment. He wore a green t-shirt with white lettering that read I'M A KEEPER.

Baby had some dreadful business with his agent that occupied the early evening. He'd suggested we meet at 41st and 7th Avenue. As I came upon him, the boy stood rigid, looking into the glimmering distance of Times Square.

"It's different on television," he said. "I haven't been here in a long time. I didn't bother when they closed Club USA."

"Do you know that I haven't been since we went to McDonald's?" I asked.

"I think Outlaw Parties are well behind us," said Baby. "It feels like twenty years ago. My father used to say that time sped up as you got older, but for me, it's only getting longer. Everything seems so remote."

I considered recommending *World Gone Wrong*. Bob Dylan was a man keyed into the weight of time's passage. Yet I thought better of it. Who could fathom what associations Baby had with Bob Dylan?

"Anyhoo," said Baby. "We've got to get on the 2 or the 3. I have no idea which one is faster."

The Times Square subway station is a hideously complex subterranean world. Tunnels upon tunnels upon layers upon exposed rusting girders. The experience oppresses one's spirit. We rushed to the first available train. Baby and I didn't much ride the subway together, but whenever we did, I was grateful that his disinterest in conversation equaled my own.

We exited at Clark Street, the first stop in Brooklyn, the strangest of all the straaaaange subway stations in New York. First of all, darlings, after we ascended the platform stairs, we walked a long hallway towards a series of three elevators. Two of which were broken. Crushing ourselves into the sole functioning apparatus, we then disembarked into the converted lobby of an old hotel. Tiny stores built into its walls. Finally, in the street, there we were, standing on a corner in Brooklyn Heights beside the remains of the old Hotel St. George, a blocksized castle.

"Baby," said I, "this experience is très outré."

"Wait until we get where we're going," he said. "It'll be dynamite. I guarantee it'll fry your synapses."

"As long as I needn't employ the word manqué," said I. "Then I shall be fine."

Baby guided us towards the water. "Have you ever heard 'I Saw Linda Yesterday' by Dickie Lee?" he asked.

"No," I said.

"I was reading about it in George Plimpton's oral biography of Edie Sedgwick. I guess Andy Warhol listened to it for eight solid hours. I haven't heard it. I guess Warhol thought it contained the key to American pop culture. I guess he was right."

I rolled my eyes. Baby on Warhol.

We arrived at a four-story brownstone. Baby simply waltzed in, pushing open the unlocked front door and climbing three flights of stairs. The noise of a party drifted down somewhere around the second.

"It's not even a launch," said Baby. "This is an afterparty. I'm not sure we're welcome. Technically, we aren't invited."

"Whose abode is this?" I asked.

"It's the home of that fat little fuck, Norman Mailer," said Baby. We swept into an apartment painted a color best described as Alcatraz Green.

Amongst the bric-a-brac of a multidecade literary career, one noticed that the apartment's ceiling, being the roof of the building, had been gouged. A glass pyramid extended above, resembling the hold of a seafaring ship, nautically themed and painted white. A series of ladders led to different platforms within the triangle. People hung over its balconies. Others had stuffed themselves within its faux cabins. They were all very sophisticated literary types, most decades older than me or Baby, and, reader, we were not young. I was a mother!

"That fat little fuck just launched a book about Lee Harvey Oswald," said Baby. "I read Michiko Kakutani's review. She hated it. Boy, she really hated it."

A group of middle-agies waylaid Baby, asking him about his forthcoming novel. Publication scheduled rather soon. I knew nothing of it. "I want you to be surprised," he'd said. "I want you to read it with open eyes."

I drifted around the apartment, examining books on the shelves, fiddling with mementos. A man with an English accent approached me, asking if I'd read *Oswald's Ghost*, which I intuited was the title of Mailer's new work. I said that I hadn't. The man said, "I rather liked it until the final chapter."

"Whatever happens?" I asked.

"Mailer goes on a long transhumanist digression, positing a future in which our race will emerge from an accelerated evolutionary process. The males become translucent squids and the women become fully opaque octopuses. It's a very strange coda to a book about Oswald, don't you think?"

"Indeed," said I, considering what possible response one could make. Particularly as I had yet to read the book. The man regarded yours truly. Yours truly regarded the man.

He bumbled off in another direction. I stood, mouth open, gaping at a bookcase full of books written by Mailer. Another man approached, and this one, I do admit, was to die for. Whilst he wasn't what one might call handsome, he was extraordinarily well groomed. His appearance was spotless. His clothes well chosen.

"Did Danny speak with you about the squids?" he asked.

"How ever did you know?"

"He's an editor at Random House," said this man. "He goes to book parties and talks to people about books that they haven't read. He tells everyone, no matter what the book, that there's a final chapter about a future in which mankind has transformed into cephalopods. I've heard him say it about everything from *Fathers and Sons* to *Prozac Nation*."

"How very peculiar," I said.

"It's supposed to be a joke," said the man. "Only no one laughs."

We talked and chatted and gabbed. We commiserated. The man introduced himself as Thomas Cromwell, bearing the same name as an unfortunate historical figure during the reign of Henry the VIII. When I inquired as to the origins of his moniker, the nouveau Thomas Cromwell suggested that his mother was too poorly educated to know of American historical figures, let alone the brutal enforcer of a Tudor king. I went on and on and on and on about, of all things, the Tuesday siren in San Francisco, this monstrously annoying occurrence every week at noon when the city officials see fit to blast all quadrants with an alarm followed by a message reminding the citizenry, yet again, that the noise is only a test.

Thomas Cromwell was, apparently, another book editor. In his late 30s, gainfully employed, and not gay. I was such an innocent that I didn't look for a ring. Had I, I should have found nothing. The man was not married.

He went on about how much he loved the unicorn tapestries at the Cloisters. "It depends on how you look at them," he said. "If you walk while fixing your eyes, the tapestries can be three dimensional. They shimmer and move."

Well, well, thinks I, here is a grown man talking to a youngish woman in Norman Mailer's living room, and his chosen topics of discussion are unicorns and medieval tapestries. Well, well, says I, here's a man to whom, perhaps, one might expose a poor child.

Mark me, reader. I had not engaged in the fleshy temptations since Nash Mac's departure. Even if one excluded my prolonged period of existential crisis about the meaning of sex and relationships, it was getting on to a ridiculous number of months.

"Now, your lordship Master Cromwell," says I, "seeing as you are here, is there not somewhere a Lady Jane Grey in hiding, drifting in and out of these nautical cabins?"

Often it ain't worth asking a question if you can't bear its answer. Thomas Cromwell says back, very kindly, I thankee, "My girlfriend's somewhere around here." Then, horror of horrors, he suggests that I follow him as we go and look for his lady.

We climbed all over Norman Mailer's apartment. Up ladders, down ladders, into cabins, out of cabins. In the galley, out of the galley. On the balcony, on the roof. At one point, Thomas Cromwell pointed over the open space, and said, "Norman's very excited about something." I peered across and there was this tiny old man with a great blast of white hair rising like steam, hearing aid in each ear, encased inside a very animated conversation. His interlocutor?

My old amigo Baby Baby Baby.

"We'd better find your lady," I said, "before I'm shown the door."

She sat alone on the outdoor balcony, looking across the East River towards Lower Manhattan. One often had moments with the Twin Towers, of recognizing their incredible height and their hideousness. Yet their size transcended facade. Perhaps one could find a lesson in there. Perhaps sheer scale outweighs questionable aesthetics.

"How do you do?" she said. "My name is Aubrey."

I wanted to loathe her but simply couldn't. She charmed one, all the more so because whilst she was not by any means ugly, she was no great beauty. One thought, if nothing else, this Thomas Cromwell must appreciate women for more than their pulchritude.

She explained how she'd insisted that they attend the party. She was an inveterate reader of Mailer and not necessarily as an aficionado. Rather, she appreciated the ongoing limitations of his work. She thought it pitiable that such a radical figure believed in masculine solutions to the problems created by men.

"It's like when a farmer shoots at a rabbit and misses," she said, "but the rabbit's nervous system gives out. The animal keeps running in circles of decreasing size, getting nowhere, doing nothing. That's a bit like Mr. Mailer, I'm afraid."

By the end of it, when I saw Baby wandering beneath the pyramid, a daze on his face, done in by the old man, I'd become bosom with Thomas Cromwell and Aubrey. They gave me their phone number. Aubrey said that we should get together. She suggested that I stop by her office, in Chelsea, where she worked as a lawyer. We could lunch. Thomas said the same.

"It's so difficult," I said. "I have a son, don't you see, and I hate exposing him to a sitter."

"Bring him along," said Aubrey. "Tom's great with kids."

Down in the streets of Brooklyn Heights, I asked Baby what he and the old man had discussed. "If you can believe it," he said, "we argued about boxing."

"Why ever were you talking about that?" I asked. "You don't know a thing about boxing."

"I read his book *The Fight*," said Baby. "I thought I could wing it. Boy, was I wrong. That fat little fuck really put me in my place."

"What did he say?" I asked.

"I guess he read my book," said Baby. "*Trapped,* I mean. Boy, say what you will about that fat little fuck, but he's a hell of a literary critic."

Poor Baby. He'd traded one club for another.

APRIL 1995

Trouble in Club Land

As it's fallen to yours truly to document the dread year 1995, it must be remarked that it was an annus horribilis for clubland.

Our dear old mayor Rudy bulldozed into office shouting promises to clean up the great unpoliceable city. The reign of terror kicked off pre-election style on 16 Septembre 1992, when Giuliani appeared beside the Brooklyn Bridge, addressing a crowd of off-duty NYPD officers. The boys in blue had gathered to protest then Mayor David Dinkins's attempts at police reform. Some held signs that read, "Dump the Washroom Attendant." Many had drunk themselves stinko.

Rudy summoned his inner fascist and delivered a hellwinder of a speech, twice employing the word bullshit. *I will bring law and order. I will bring an iron fist. I will oppress those who misbehave.* Given the context, and what followed, it's impossible to ignore the fact that Those Who Misbehave were earmarked as poor folks, disgraceful queers, and people of color.

The new mayor came into office with a list of targets. Clubland was one of his biggest.

Club USA sat not far from the corner of West 47th and Broadway. Owned and operated by Peter Gatien. Cyclops had pumped eight million dollars into the club's construction. Barely two years later, in the early weeks of 1995, he shuttered its doors. Only another casualty of the New Times Square.

The one-eyed man had demonstrated weakness before a bloodthirsty beast, enraging the animal. The NYPD declared war. The next casualty was Sound Factory, sending Junior Vasquez, the resident DJ, into a tailspin of ennui and depression. More losses mounted.

Undercover officers infiltrated the clubs. Imagine all the junior cops from Far Rockaway induced to glam up and dress in feather boas.

I was repulsed by Rudy's efforts to clean up the city. Yes, the crime had been terrible, but the solution upon which he'd fallen was full authoritarian fantasy. Let us not forget that the man was a former prosecutor raised in a deep Catholic household. Four of his uncles were cops. He was hardwired for punishment.

When he looked over his throbbing domain of New York City, the man simply quivered with the sense that someone somewhere might be committing a Grade E misdemeanor.

New York is Alexander Hamilton's town. The rich have always ruled, but I hearken to the velvet glove. I preferred that our overlords exhibit some sense of shame and proportion.

On the other hand, I believed that Baby would be served best by the evaporation of his grotty little scene. He might yet progress into the warm light of adulthood.

I must admit that Baby'd begun a gradual withdrawal. The defining moment was in April, on Michael Alig's birthday, when Alig threw a party at Limelight called Bloodfeast, named after an atrocious Herschell Gordon Lewis film. The flyer for Bloodfeast depicted Alig with his brains bashed out, a hammer beside him. One of his gaudy little club kids, a completely baldheaded young lady named Jenny Talia, holds up a fork with ersatz brain matter suspended a few centimeters from her mouth. She's covered in blood, as is Alig. Above her right shoulder red text reads: LEGS CUT OFF!

Baby attended this dreadful party alone. Even his she-beast Regina had begged off from making an appearance. She'd started her own removal, having finally graduated from NYU and entered into a serious relationship with a lesbian from the Bronx.

People attended in outfits smeared with fake blood. Giant knives hung from the ceiling, suspended above the blood-smeared coffins and beds in which some of clubland's lesser denizens reposed for the entire evening.

Baby didn't say much other than that he'd found the event distasteful. Even with the drugs that he undoubtedly consumed, he was unable to delude himself into appreciating the strange vibes. Shortly thereafter, his attendance dwindled. He was going, at most, once a month.

Even if I did desire for the scene to evaporate into thin air, putting faith in petite dictators isn't the best way to serve one's friend. I'd watched the NYPD beat the stuffing out of the homeless. How could I not side with those dreadful club people? I lamented the changing of the city. "Detachable Penis" played like a message from the gods.

The sense of impending doom only grew stronger. Great change was looming. Soon the city would be only a plaything for the moneyed, and I'd be one of them, darlings. I'd be condemned to suck the marrow until the bones broke.

MAY 1995

Adeline Has Lunch with Thomas Cromwell,
Touches the Berlin Wall (Again)

I made plans with Thomas Cromwell for lunch near his office in Mid-town. Keeping faith with Aubrey's words, I brought Emil, pushing his stroller forty blocks. When we reached Mr. Cromwell's place of work, he stood in front, perfectly groomed. He held a lead attached to an astoundingly wrinkled brown dog.

"Sorry," he said, "but I have to take a rain check. I had to bring Oscar into work. We're having our carpets cleaned."

That was more than fine with yours truly. I worried about bringing Emil into a restaurant. I'd spent some great percentage of my years judging those mothers who insisted on bringing their screaming children into unfamiliar situations. With my own offspring in tow, I'd become hypersensitive to re-creating any situation that'd driven me bonkers.

"Let's get some coffee," said Thomas Cromwell. "We can go over to a park not far from here. It's a hidden gem."

We stopped at a deli. I left Emil with Thomas Cromwell and Oscar, buying two cups of coffee. I'd rushed in and out, terrified to leave my child with a stranger and his dog.

The fear was baseless. Cromwell hadn't absconded with my child. He was bent over the carriage and talking in a sublingual babble.

I handed Cromwell one of the cups. How I admired the hideous faux-Hellenic design printed on the cardboard! I took a swig from my own, imbibing the vilest brew that I'd yet tasted.

We talked about nothing in particular, about his job in publishing, of which I understood very little. I spoke of *Trill* and its relative success, about the grind of churning out twenty-two pages a month plus a cover, about how I'd received offers for other work. Some of which I'd be insane to refuse, as work for Marvel and DC was ridiculously lucrative, but how I was having trouble managing my schedule and was unwilling to delay an issue of my own book.

The park was a green sliver wedged between two buildings. At its rear, water cascaded down, drowning out the city's clamor and din. Add to that the trees, and one could delude herself into believing she was somewhere beyond the city. If one was the sort of person who wanted to be somewhere other than the city. Which one was not.

Emil climbed out of his stroller and chased pigeons before targeting his affections on Oscar, lifting the dog's ears and hugging it around the neck. Cromwell said the poor thing was a Shar-Pei, purebred. I dared not inquire as to the cost of buying a dog created by pointless eugenics.

Dogs in the city evoke my pity. All of them, Oscar included, have a faraway look in their eyes, as if overexposure has leached away any possible emotion or thought.

I couldn't help myself. I inquired about Aubrey, about how they met.

"At college," said Thomas Cromwell, "which is a long time ago, now that I think of it. We didn't start dating until years later. We've been together now seven years. I think she wants a ring, but my parents divorced before I was born. Neither of them remarried. I don't know about marriage. The word doesn't mean anything."

I whistled. "Seven years," I said. "How about that. That's perfectly swellegant. And you've never been tempted to stray?"

"I've strayed," he said. "I'm not proud. It happened. Two years ago. I started seeing a girl from 143rd Street in Flushing. I liked the odd-couple aspect. Uptight white boy makes a play for Latina who doesn't care about his industry or his profession."

"Does Aubrey know?"

"Aubrey knows," said Thomas Cromwell. "We spent a year in couples' therapy."

"What happened to your mistress?"

"Someone on MacDougal Street stabbed her in the thigh. I took it as a message against my unfaithfulness and repented the next day. I told Aubrey everything."

Emil hugged my leg. I brought him into my lap. All the while I drank that vile coffee. I liked Aubrey, had taken to her, but oh, Thomas Cromwell, how I liked you, sir. How you moved me way inside with your hideous dog and your tales of tail from Flushing.

He mentioned the Elizabeth Murray exhibition up the street at the MoMA. Cromwell had seen it and liked it. I hated tearing another sister down, but I truly disliked Murray's work. I said that I planned to avoid it.

"Give it a chance," said Thomas Cromwell. "Aubrey still hasn't seen it. If you want, we can all go together."

"I'd be delighted," I said.

Cromwell looked at his watch. "I can't believe we've talked this long," he said. "I've got to get back to work."

"I'll walk you," I said, "it's the least that I can do."

"Before we go," he said, "take a look at this."

He brought me over to three slabs of freestanding pieces of concrete. I'd noticed them when we'd come in, but hadn't particularly cared for the mural. Public art gives me a bad case of the shivers.

"This is the Berlin Wall," said Thomas Cromwell.

"¿Qué es?" I asked.

"These are parts of the Berlin Wall."

"I'll be," I said, running my fingers across the concrete. I'd witnessed the thing when it stood in Berlin, as a young girl on a continental tour with Daddy, Mother, and Dahlia. My father insisted that his daughters touch the wall, despite neither of us understanding its import. I was too young. Dahlia, you'll not be surprised to learn, was too dense.

"That's Manhattan for you," said Thomas Cromwell. "I need to get going."

I strapped Emil into his stroller. We pushed through Midtown in silence, determined, comfortable. Oh so comfortable, darlings.

Two blocks before his building, Cromwell said to me, "The next time, you'll have to tell me all about Baby. I read *Trapped Between Jupiter and a Bottle*. It's surprisingly good, especially for a book with an elephant-headed man on its cover. How long have you known each other?"

"For almost a decade," I said. "We ceased speaking for some while, but things are back to normal. Our lives are hideously entwined. He's as much my blood as Emil."

"How do you account for it?" asked Cromwell. "What keeps the friendship going?"

"That's the simplest thing," I said. "Both of Baby's parents are dead. I've never asked the details, but I gather it happened with great tragedy. As in murder. My brother committed suicide. When you meet another person with that same awful gift, you never let them go."

JUNE 1995

Dinner at Tom and Aubrey's

Aubrey telephoned on Wednesday, inviting yours truly to Saturday dinner. "I'm trying a new recipe," she said. "Garlic brown sugar chicken. You eat meat, don't you?"

"I only abstain from the ruddy stuff," I said. "Chicken is fine. Tell me, do you often cook?"

"Hardly ever," she said. "My grandmother sent the recipe, so I thought I'd try it."

I asked if she wouldn't mind extra guests, meaning Baby and the baby. Aubrey said the more the merrier. She'd be delighted to meet Emil. He'd made quite an impression on Thomas Cromwell. The man couldn't stop singing my son's praises.

After hanging up the receiver, I contemplated whether Aubrey and Cromwell had attempted creating their own child. Perhaps the option was tabled for future days.

As I'd soon be within the warm embrace of their home, I considered a surreptitious examination of the medicine cabinet, a hunt for evidence of Ortho Tri-Cyclen. The appalling fantasy passed. I'd ceased raiding toiletries somewheres around high school graduation.

You may be asking, *Oh, Adeline, why ever would Aubrey be calling you?* Well, darlings, in my unfathomable perversity, as the weeks had passed, I'd experienced many more lunch dates with Aubrey than her fella.

Why, just a week earlier, we'd met at an exceptionally sterile restaurant on Seventh Avenue. The name escapes me but rest assured that it was bleedingly bourgeois.

Our mouths moved, the proper words came out, but as always the cut of her suit and the shape of her hair transfixed my human soul. I'd seen thousands and thousands and thousands and thousands of women like her, young professionals clawing their way through the world, women who believed that New York offered them profound and infinite opportunity. I'd always fantasized about their lives, imagining what they'd done and where they came from. Now I was friends with one! There she sat, eating arugula and talking about politics.

Could these women be happy working for the sole purpose of accumulating capital that afforded them certain luxuries, the maintenance of which required the further accumulation of capital? Where did it all go? Where would it go? Must we all own property?

Aubrey mentioned her disappointment in President Bill Clinton. "I voted for Jerry Brown in the primaries," she said, "but we saw how that turned out, so I held my nose and went with Clinton, hoping that he'd be the lesser of two evils before he proved that he didn't understand the job. Now the Republicans have Congress with their Contract with America. None of the issues that I care about will be addressed for twenty years."

I said something noncommittal, a pleasant nothingness. Our conversation drifted elsewhere. I wasn't so naive as to express my political opinions in polite conversation, particularly not to a woman who did legal work for major corporations.

By any measurable American spectrum, my ridiculously far-left convictions ranked me as amongst the certifiably insane. No one wanted to hear my opinions. Not even my own self.

We'd drawn each other further into the net, moving from acquaintance into friendship. When the idea of a mythical garlic brown sugar chicken came upon her, she telephoned.

They resided on the East Side, on 56th Street, on the twenty-eighth floor of a drab building constructed within the last decade. If you're surprised that Aubrey in all of her proper taste would ever consent to such a nondescript building, please remember that New York remains New York. Every soul makes the devil's bargain in the matter of living quarters. Even Norman Mailer.

In the elevator, riding towards the sky, questions danced through my head, tormenting me like visions of sugarplum fairies. Adeline, why are you dining at the apartment of an unavailable man? Adeline, why are you regularly lunching with his common-law wife? Adeline, what is wrong with you?

I'd not expressed my depth of feeling for Thomas Cromwell, not even to Baby, but I knew that I needn't. Not with the young author, trained with a novelistic predilection for detail and human squalor. He'd been kind enough not to inquire after the obvious.

Aubrey opened their door, a clean white apron over her perfectly casual outfit. She hugged Baby, whom she had not met, and examined Emil. "Isn't he lovely?" she said. "Tom's getting dressed. Make yourselves comfortable."

Like the New World, some realms are better left unexplored. The décor lacked any defining feature but was so of its very moment, hovering at the exact edge of a taste. Faddish technology du jour and reproduction posters from the Art Nouveau.

"Their television is fucking enormous," whispered Baby.

"It's far worse than yours," I said, "which is an astounding sentiment."

The bedroom door opened and out ran the great wrinkled beast. I put Emil on the ground. My toddler tumbled towards the animal, throwing his stubby arms around the dog's neck and kissing its folds of flesh.

Baby cooed at the image, but even Emil's joy couldn't mask the cruelty of a fifty-pound Shar-Pei trapped in a two-bedroom apartment. We are all prisoners of our environs but typically the bars are not so visible.

Thomas Cromwell sauntered out, wearing a modest shirt and khaki pants. He still looked like one of America's best-groomed men.

"I thought that I heard the buzzer," he said.

"We've been here for a while," said Baby. "We've been judging you and Aubrey by the books on your shelves. It's something that Adeline and I do. You can learn a lot by what books people keep in their living room. The book's physical presence is pure wish fulfillment. It's a marketing device, like your identity refracted through a misreading of the author's intent."

"Baby," I whispered. "Stop being a dick."

"If you're interested in my insecurities," said Thomas Cromwell, "then you'll want to examine the shelves in the other room. These are only the ones that I've worked on professionally."

That simply set the tone, didn't it, darlings? Baby mildly aggressive and possibly autistic whilst he and Tomás del Pozo talked shop. I'd whittled away enough time with literary people to know that soon enough Baby'd start spreading gossipy rumors about Jay McInerney and frozen watermelon, so I went out on the balcony, which wasn't much more than a little 8 x 3-foot rectangle.

One could see across the East River, staring straight at Queens and Roosevelt Island, a view that one never caught in the East Village. The 58th Street Bridge, the tram, the United Nations headquarters, and the Pepsi-Cola logo blazing through the darkness, stationed atop a squat factory that bottled ghastly soft drinks.

Aubrey called us in for dinner. As these things go, which is the distance from plate to mouth, the food was delicious. "Your grandmother's recipe really knocks me out," said Baby. She served wine with the meal, a Sauvignon Blanc.

Baby and Thomas Cromwell talked more shop. Boooooooooooring. They descended into that most dismal of all masculine quagmires, trying to discern the future of their industry. How would writing change with the rise of things like the Internet and AOL? What did it mean for the role of the author?

"In twenty years, no one will read on paper," said Baby. "It'll be digital, on our computer screens. You can't fight the future, so why not embrace it?"

This was not the first time that I'd heard Baby lay this jive turkey rap. I'd asked that he refrain from discussing it, but he had no self-control. He'd gone native in Nash Mac territory, subscribing to *Wired* magazine and trading his typewriter for a computer. He spent time on chat boards dedicated to his own work. He received email from his fans, discussing the finer points of his narrative strategy. It all made me gag on my own vomit.

"I hope not," said Thomas Cromwell. "It's like what you were saying earlier, about the book being a physical ideological point. What's the point of owning a book if you can't show it off?"

"You can't fight change," repeated Baby. "You can't repeat the past."

"Can't repeat the past?" I asked. "What do you mean you can't repeat the past? Of course you can. I'm always telling Baby that if I have to read on a screen, then I'll simply stop. Electric books can take a flying fuck at a rolling doughnut. They can take a flying fuck at the moooooooooooooon. Paper is radical. Paper will always be radical. Computers are conservative. Computers are a tool by which the rich pen in the poor. Obviously there'll be an attempt to put books on computers. Why wouldn't there? Corporations love computers. Yet print culture shall never die, if for no other reason than no one will ever screw out another person's brains for a computer. Well, perhaps some people will, but imagine those ghastly beasts. Imagine how ugly they'll be. Imagine how poor their taste. There will always remain acres of beautiful lithe bodies willing to drop trousers at the sight of a smarmy boy with his copy of *Franny and Zooey*. The problem is that the dopes like you, you great stupid woolly mammoths of publishing, you market yourselves as if reading were an ennobling act of high culture or a passing amusement. When it is neither. You have debased the rush and throb and gob of it. Personally, I'd strike posters of sexy young things sitting in darkly lit Parisian cafes, dressed to the nines, face in a classic, and the text would read: 'BOOKS. THEY GET YOU LAID.'"

Aubrey was too interested in Emil to engage our malarkey. She helped him with his food. She talked to him. She rubbed his head. "He's so cute," she said. "Tom, you never said he was this cute."

"All babies are cute," said Baby. "But Emil really is the cutest."

"Having spent more than my fair share amongst a gaggle of recent mothers," I said, "I'll have it known that some babies are quite ugly."

We moved back to the living room. The distance was only about ten feet. Thomas Cromwell talked about gentrification and the East Village. He spoke of things that existed before my arrival in the city, like Colab, the Mudd Club, Tier 3, and Club 57.

"There was an art installation in the back of the Mudd Club," he said, "which was called *The Talking Head of Oliver Cromwell*. The name caught my eye. As it would. There was an artist's statement, hand-carved into a wooden plaque. After Charles II regained power following the brief reign of Tumble Down Dick, the newly enthroned King had all of the regicides dug up and beheaded. He had their heads put on stakes at Westminster. Cromwell's sat for thirty years before a storm knocked it down. The head circulated in the hands of private collectors for centuries. For a while it was in a traveling circus. They only reburied it in the '60s. The artist claimed that the buried head was a fake, and that he'd stolen the real head from the Knights Templar and put it on display in the East Village. The Templars had cast a spell upon it, giving it immortal life and the ability to engage in discourse. People would go to the Mudd Club and ask questions of the head. It gave practical advice. There was something very fascinating watching New Wave kids asking a mechanical talking head about their sex lives."

We drank more wine, a drug lacking in social stigma, and chatted about absolutely nothing. I promise you, dearies, that I didn't make too much a fool of myself, paying Aubrey equal time.

Emil fell asleep in my arms. I suggested that it might be time to depart, as the poor boy needed his rest. Aubrey and Thomas Cromwell protested, but what could one do? The child took precedence.

Aubrey had stored our coats in their bedroom. She suggested that she and I retrieve them. I thought the request mildly odd. Surely she devoted enough time to the gym that two adult garments couldn't weigh her down. Yet I said nothing. In the right frame of mind, I'll agree to any old thing.

The bedroom was dominated by the bed and very little else. A paperback book rested atop the polished wood of a very marginal bureau. I couldn't help myself. Blame Baby! He planted the idea. I examined the book. Behind me, Aubrey fiddled with our jackets.

Entitled *WANT-AD WANTONS*, the book was a piece of old-time erotica, one of those bizarre works that flourished for several decades before the publishing industry discovered how to mask its pornography within the confines of literary fiction, before the advent of the XXX feature, before home video.

The author's name is Drew Palmer. The cover depicts a suited man with his hands around a blonde moll's waist. They're inside an apartment, both looking towards a fiery redhead who stands in a doorway. Her thin white slip hugs a voluptuous figure. Over the suited man's shoulders is yet another doorway from whence peers a beady-eyed couple. The advertising copy reads: "Wanting to avoid eventual boredom with each other, Terry and Lou teamed up with other broad-minded couples." Published by National Library Books, the cover price is but 95¢.

"What a charming piece of kitsch," I said. "It's my understanding that none of the authors used their real names."

Aubrey had a curious expression, giving one the impression that her eyes had been staring through the back of one's head.

"You know that Tom and I have been together for a while," she said. "It hasn't always been easy."

"No relationship is," said I. "They're all a kind of lingering misery. It takes true grit."

"He's hard to deal with," she said. "I don't know why I'm still doing it."

The woman was asking for advice about the man that she loved. Yet he was the very object of my fantasy, a fantasy based on his unavailability, on the fact that Aubrey bulwarked against hanky-panky. I could deliver the worst possible advice, telling her to abandon the man. I could reap what I'd sow. I wanted none of it.

"Is it wrong to do what you want?" she asked.

"Getting older seems to be the process of weighing what you want against the interests of the people that you love," I said. "It's almost never worth hurting anyone."

"You're probably right," she said. "But what if he wasn't hurt? What if he never knew?"

"That way madness lies," said I. "They always find out."

She picked up my drab green coat. Motherhood had murdered my interest in fashion. To think that once my clothes fascinated an entire neighborhood.

Aubrey put her hand on my wrist. O Lord, thought I, this woman is unstable. We barely know each other, why ever would she need this kind of support?

She leaned towards me. Must I hug her? thought I. This is punishment for involving yourself in the affairs of others.

She leaned further in, pushing her mouth against my own. My lower jaw fell slightly open. Her tongue was in my mouth. It felt like a soft robot.

I stepped away.

"There's been a misunderstanding," I said. "It isn't that I object in principle."

"Oh my god," she said. "I'm sorry."

Aubrey picked up Baby's coat and left me alone with *WANT-AD WAN-TONS*. I gathered the remnants of my composure, put on my jacket, hid the book in one of the pockets, and followed her into mixed company.

Baby was buttoning his coat. Thomas Cromwell held Emil. You might wonder if your old pal Adeline was discombobulated by boudoir events. Most certainly, but please remember that I was raised by parents with very active social lives. My first lessons were in the maintenance of social graces. Always repress, always fake it.

We said our goodbyes, Aubrey not meeting my eyes. As we rode the elevator to the ground floor, Baby said, "That was some kind of evening. Those are some kind of people."

"I hope you enjoyed it," I said. "I very much doubt that we'll see them again."

NOVEMBER 1995

Suzanne Comes to New York City

November landed upon us, bringing the confusion of daylight savings revoked.

Even in New York, where mankind's arrogance illuminates the sky, the canopy was darkness. No stars, no moon, no clouds, nothing but pitch.

One thought of antiquity and eras before the advent of modern conveniences. Human history reducible to an elementary fear of darkness, a quirk of evolution providing us with ocular apparatuses incapable of vision beyond a verrrrry limited spectrum.

Some nights, I'd sit with Emil while he attempted speech, hoping that he'd be safe in the world. My only desire was to keep the child from harm, to keep him from corruption, to shield him from unnamed horrors. That was the measure of parenthood, the sensation of your own helplessness. One took hope in the fact that he would not live in total darkness.

Somewheres in this maudlin period, I received a ring a ding-ding from dear old Dahlia. Generally, one preferred for her to babble into the answering machine, but this time, I lifted the receiver.

"Mom's coming to New York," she said. "She's flying in tomorrow."

"Is that so?" I asked.

"You should see her."

"For which sideshow rube have you mistaken me?" I asked. "My feelings about Mother are explicit."

"She paid for you, paid for Emil. She's not getting any younger. Do you really want him growing up without knowing his grandmother?"

I telephoned Baby and asked his advice.

"You might as well," he said. "She's not all bad."

I telephoned Jeremy Winterbloss, with whom there was a long-overdue conversation about the latest developments in *Trill*. The script for issue sixteen featured an overblown story in which Felix Trill undergoes a *Yojimbo* moment and involves himself with two warring cat tribes. Winterbloss had asked for an ungodly number of double-page splashes involving the machinery of war. One side employed giant battering rams that resembled dogs. Jeremy had written endless pages of description. I'd winced in advance for the strain on my drawing hand.

I'd registered my displeasure on his answering machine, protesting the insanity of his design. He'd telephoned back, leaving a message on mine, suggesting that we speak soon and discuss strategies for simplification.

My latest call, then, was not unexpected, but I had no particular interest in the script, preferring to speak of Mother. He asked me why I wouldn't meet with her, why I would keep her from Emil. As I spoke, I discovered that I had no obvious objection beyond our tortured family history. You know me, darlings. I'm as stubborn as a mule on Easter.

"There's no good reason to avoid her," said Jeremy. "What if she died tomorrow? How would you feel then? Would you be happy?"

"Nooooo," I said.

"Then what's the problem?"

"Put Минерва on the phone."

I repeated myself for the third time in less than an hour. Say what you will about Минерва, but the girl displayed more patience than either Baby or Winterbloss. She listened without complaint or interjection.

"Family is not happiness," she said. "Family is misery only. Why expect coldness from fire? Don't fight river. Meet with woman. If she disappoints, keep from son."

I telephoned Dahlia.

"Tell that ad hominem harridan that I'll meet her," I said. "I presume she's staying at the Plaza?"

"Mom wouldn't stay anywhere else," said my sister. "I don't think she even knows the name of any other hotel in New York."

"Inform her that I'll be at the Oak Room. In two days at noon. Ask her if she'll do me the kindness of not getting too drunk prior to my arrival."

"I'll let her know," said Dahlia. "Adeline?"

"Yes?"

"I'm happy."

I telephoned Baby for the second time and told him that I'd agreed. I asked if he couldn't watch Emil whilst I visited with the Old Shrew.

"Don't raise your hopes up high, buster," I said, "but if things go well enough, I may bring her back to meet my son. You can hang around if you want. She'll be delighted."

"Are you sure?" he asked. "Wouldn't you rather have Frances?"

"Tell me one thing," I said. "Have you talked to Mother since that fateful day?"

"Not a word," he said. "I learned my lesson. You have no idea how terrified I've been that she'd find my number and call me."

"Am I so terrible?" I asked.

"You're the scariest person I've ever met."

I wasn't sure whether to be proud or mortally offended.

He hung up. Emil had fallen asleep in my bed, atop the covers. I crawled beside him, my arms around him. I would not allow the child to be sucked into the bad craziness of my family.

You know the routine, don't you, my pets? A cab to Central Park and William Tecumseh Sherman. My cabdriver was a man named Balwinder Singh. I spent the ride in a reverie about his amaaaaaaaazing name. Balwinder Singh was possibly the best name that I'd ever heard.

I walked into the hotel with a stab of stomach anxiety, wanting to turn and go back home, but I'd come this far and couldn't fathom a surrender to cowardice.

Mother waited at the bar, her back turned to me. She'd changed the color of her hair, giving it an age-appropriate hue.

"Mother?"

"Adeliiiiiiiiiiine," she said, resisting the urge to throw her arms around her daughter. She gripped the bar with both hands, holding herself steady. "Adeliiiiiiiine, how nice to see you."

I sat beside her and ordered a Cape Cod.

"Whatever are you drinking?" I asked, eyeing the clear liquid in her glass.

"Soda water," she said. "Dahlia said if you saw me drinking that you'd run away."

"That wasn't quite what I said, but our messages are sometimes relayed by faulty wires."

Mother looked older. The torture of plastic surgery still contained her face, but there's only so much restoration that can be done before it's ruined forever. Even a woman as depraved as Mother would hesitate before surrendering herself to a fish-eyed blankness.

I'd gone through the Cape Cod with an astounding speed. We hadn't spoken a word. I ordered another drink.

"Alcohol has always been our family's curse," she said. "Your grandmother had great thirsts."

I never met Mother's mother. She expired long before my birth. I'd never been told the reason. Unexplained ill health. Mother's father had lasted until my tenth birthday, but I couldn't recall anything about him other than his craggy visage, a California face escaped from the Dust Bowl.

"How have you been, Adeliiiiiine?"

"Fine, I suppose," I said. "I've no complaints."

"Dahlia's shown me copies of your little book. The one with the cats?"

"I didn't realize that Dahlia was a collector."

"It was all she could talk about when she came back," said Mother. "She drove Charles crazy. She gave me an issue. Ever since, I've been forced to make monthly visits to a store on Melrose that only sells comic books. I'm on a first-name basis with the strange young men who work there."

Mother was reading *Trill*. The horrors!

"But one thing, Adeline," she said. "Whenever I tell them that M. Abrahamovic Petrovitch is my daughter, they tend to laugh. Why would you hide yourself behind such a silly name?"

"By cock," I said, "I'm tired of explaining the purpose of a pseudonym."

"You shouldn't hide," she said. "The art is too good, Adeliiiiiine."

I ordered another Cape Cod. Despite my intake, I couldn't feel the slightest bit of intoxication. This had happened once before, when I was fifteen years old and we'd attended a wedding for the daughter of Mother's friend Mildred. I'd spent the evening with an endless supply of White Russians, yet never once experienced a moment of drunkenness.

The woman hadn't asked word one about my child.

"Mother," I said, "are you at all interested in meeting Emil?"

"Yes, Adeliiiiiine," she said, very carefully, masking her emotion. "I'd love to see him."

"He's back at my apartment with Baby," I said. "You remember Baby, don't you? The young man to whom you played benefactress?"

"Adeline," she said. "Do you really want to revisit that unpleasantness?"

I pondered the question.

"No," I said.

"Can't you forgive me?" she asked.

"I must have," I said. "Why else would I be here? Besides, I was much angrier with Baby. And we're back to being the best of friends."

"Do you know that I saw his boyfriend?" she asked. "A year or two ago, on Colorado Street. What was his name? Hymie? He didn't recognize me, or if he did, he didn't acknowledge me. He looked rather sad. He hasn't aged well."

"I wouldn't mention Jaime," I said. "Baby's grown tetchy. He's a novelist now. They're all barking mad."

"Has he published?" she asked.

"More books for your collection."

I stepped away from the bar. It often takes a rush of blood before the intoxication washes over. Yet there was no such effect. My nerves had rendered me invulnerable. *Adeline,* said me to myself, *if you're ever going to attempt freebasing cocaine, now is surely the moment.*

The doorman hailed us a cab. We climbed into the back seat. Mother barked at the driver. "Second Avenue and 7th Street!"

I sensed that she wanted to talk more, to babble about the inessentialities that comprised her worldview, but she remained afraid that at any moment I might revoke the privilege of meeting Emil. There'd been a time when she possessed the power, when I was the one who followed orders. Now the authority was mine. There'd be a distant day when the same thing should happen to me, when Emil would venture into his own life and I would lose my hold. God help me, darlings, but I had empathy for the woman.

The driver let us off on Second Avenue. Mother said, "Well, nothing seems very different on your block."

"A few new things," I said. "Did you ever see Burp Castle? I've never set foot but I'm told that they dress like monks and only serve beer. This building here, if you can believe it, is an NYU dorm. I've resided on this street for years and never knew. Not until a few months ago."

Dread settled upon me. We walked up the stairs. There was déjà vu about the experience, about Mother on my steps, about Mother on 7th Street, about Mother invading my apartment. In San Francisco, one would climb a hill and sweat buckets of liquid whilst a cold wind blew through one's clothes and a disgusting drip of mucus smeared down one's face. I wanted to stop, to cry out, to put a halt to the madness. I expected the worst. That, darlings, is my tragic flaw. Adeline always expects the worst.

Baby and Emil were on the kitchen floor, playing with an ancient wooden Fisher-Price circus set that I'd scavenged from the Salvation Army.

The toys looked pathetic. I worried, and hated myself for it, that Mother would observe their paucity.

She came in behind me, shutting the door. Baby tilted his head up, smiling. Emil didn't look up at all, preoccupied with the giraffe.

"Hello, Suzanne," said Baby. "It's nice to see you."

"Baby!" she said. "And look at this darling child!"

She scooped Emil from the floor. He didn't struggle against her. She held him to her breast, practically smothering the boy. He didn't make a noise.

There was my best friend, whom I loved more than I could possibly say, and my child, for whom I willingly would be set ablaze on a pyre of my own bones, and my mother, that ever-complicated being, standing with only a slight tinge of lunacy.

Mother put my son on the ground and then she was on the ground beside him, her hands on him, her hands on Baby. What could I do, darlings, but get down on my own knees and join them?

"Emil," I said. "This is your grandmother. What should he call you?"

"He can call me whatever he likes," said Mother.

MARCH 1996

Baby Explains How the World Works

This is how the world works.

A young man comes to New York City with hopes of studying architecture at Fordham University. Architecture is the chosen profession of his distant father. Having escaped from South Bend, Indiana, from the nowhere armpit asshole middle of Bumfuck USA, this young man ingratiates himself into the *de rigueur* world of clubland. He starts off as less than nothing, a busboy at Danceteria, and works his way up. He becomes famous. His name in gossip columns, his face in magazines, an object of televised fascination.

He adopts several overlapping drug habits. It starts with the easier stuff, the quicker stuff, the harmless stuff. He passes beneath the influence of Ulysses S. Grant. It ends with daily doses of crystallized cocaine and injected heroin. He descends into babbling incoherence, into cruelty and mean spirits. The glamorous act corrupts into the sallow image of a thirty-year-old junky infected with hepatitis nodding off in his own drool, pissing from balconies on the people attending events that he's orchestrated. His brain twists from years of ketamine and Rohypnol.

This is how the world works.

A small boy and his family move from Colombia to New York City. The boy grows up with ambitions of becoming an actor, or maybe a filmmaker. He discovers his gayness and consorts with certain social scenes. In his early twenties, he is sucked into the Downtown demimonde. He meets famous people. Everyone is fabulous. Everyone is glamorous. This small boy, now a man, gains attention from the famous by supplying their drugs. He ends up unexpectedly close with one of our era's great junkies. He crashes at the junky's apartment, storing many of his possessions in the junky's care, including money and a drug stash.

This is how the world works.

A young man moves to New York City at eighteen years of age, desperate to abandon the American Middle West. He walks to Alphabet City, where a vague acquaintance resides in a squat. The experience turns out badly. While he is in the squat, the young man meets a girl. On his first night in the city, he moves into her dorm. They become best friends. They become inseparable. This friendship is one of great consequence, leading to the young man's attendance at New York University, leading to his career as a writer. The young man ends up well regarded, preparing for the release of his new novel in the fall of 1996.

This is how the world works.

On March 16th, 1996, Angel Melendez heads to the corner of 43rd Street and Eleventh Avenue. He struts up to the Riverbank West, a luxury high-rise where Michael Alig lives in an apartment paid for by Peter Gatien. The rent is $2,400 a month. Angel floats through the courtyard, past the fountain. He is waved in by the doorman and rides the elevator up to Michael's floor.

Melendez has fallen on hard times. He had a brief burst of glory, dealing drugs in the Limelight and Tunnel. He'd been on Gatien's payroll. When the hammer of the NYPD began pounding the clubs, Gatien fired Melendez. Angel bummed from place to place, with no fixed address. One of these temporary homes was Michael Alig's apartment. He kept his money and his drugs in a junky's home.

Michael ripped him off, stealing a few thousand dollars and some unknown amount of drugs. A story went around that when Angel realized what'd happened, he'd taken off his shoe and battered Michael Alig's head. This may or may not be true.

Angel exits the elevator and confronts Michael Alig. The two-bedroom apartment is stocked with a wide library of VHS tapes. Michael has all two hundred of MPI's *Dark Shadows* compilations. He has every episode of *I Love Lucy*. He has a wide collection of horror and slasher films. Before the drugs destroyed his life, Michael Alig was making ten thousand dollars a week. He could afford anything.

In one of the bedrooms, a club kid named Freeze is sleeping beside Paul Auster's Son. Freeze is a junky. Paul Auster's Son is also a junky. Earlier that day, Paul Auster's Son overdosed. Michael recognized the symptoms. He gathered cocaine from Angel's stash and blew it up Paul Auster's Son's nose. Paul Auster's Son woke from the black oblivion of death. The bells of cocaine rang in his head.

Angel and Michael argue. Angel strangles Michael Alig. Michael is bashed against a glass curio, which breaks and gouges a deep wound into his neck and shoulder. The noise rouses Freeze. He enters the living room. He sees the mayhem, hears Michael crying out for help. Angel is on top of Michael. Angel is biting Michael, teeth sunk into the junky's chest.

Freeze's dope-saturated primary motor cortex sends out neural impulses to his body. He picks up a hammer. He hits the back of Angel's head. Three times. The final blow breaks bone.

They gag Angel. They believe that Angel is dead from falls of the hammer, but it is the suffocation which kills him. The body is brought into the bathroom and put into the waters of the bathtub. Michael Alig pours Drano into Angel's mouth. Or injects it with a syringe. Freeze asks why. Michael says that he is trying to embalm the body. There is a bloodied, destroyed mess of a human, filled with Drano, in the bathtub. Throughout this process, if a corpse can retain ownership of anything, they are stealing drugs from the corpse's stash.

Michael Alig calls a bevy of acquaintances. He tries to call me. I'm not home. He doesn't leave a message. Michael tells everyone that he talks to about having killed someone. He says that he has a body. He asks for help with disposal of the corpse. No one offers any aid. No one calls the police.

They leave the apartment. They visit the queen Olympia. They get very high.

Days pass. The body stays in the bathtub. It bloats with water. Michael takes Angel's money and refurnishes his apartment. People visit, Michael entertains. The bathroom is blocked from guests. There's something wrong with the toilet. This is believed, in part, because of the odor.

After a week, Michael Alig tells Freeze that he'll take care of the body if Freeze gives him ten bags of heroin. Ten bags of heroin is a bundle. Freeze agrees. Michael sends Freeze to Macy's. Michael tells Freeze to buy the proper cutlery. Freeze returns with two large knives and a meat cleaver. Michael injects heroin. Michael goes into the bathroom and dismembers Angel's corpse. He cuts off the legs. After a week of being under water, the meat is disgustingly tender. He cuts off Angel's genitals. Just because.

Michael and Freeze put the legs in two garbage bags. They throw the legs into the Hudson River. The bags sink.

In the basement of the Riverbank West, Freeze finds an empty box. The box was used to package a television. Michael and Freeze tape Angel's leg-less body inside the box. They ride with the box in the elevator. In front of the building, they hail a cab. The cabdriver helps lift the box into the car's trunk. The driver brings them to 25th Street and 11th Avenue. They are very close to Tunnel. They wait for the cabdriver to pull away. They carry the box to the Hudson River. They throw the box in the water.

Unlike the legs, the box does not sink. Angel's torso floats away.

This is the official story, which will calcify after confessions and transform into convictions. There are other versions. Paul Auster's Son, whisked away by Paul Auster after the murder, will later meet with family friend Robert Morgenthau, the septuagenarian District Attorney of New York. Paul Auster's Son will tell Morgenthau that Freeze and Michael Alig plotted to rob Angel. Paul Auster's Son will tell Morgenthau that Michael lured Angel to the apartment. The invite for the previous year's Bloodfeast party, featuring a hammer and a club kid with his brains bashed out, along with text about legs being cut off, will be remembered.

Paul Auster's Son will plead guilty to stealing $3,000 of Angel's money. Morgenthau will not put Paul Auster's Son on the stand to testify against Michael Alig or Freeze, believing that junkies make unreliable witnesses. In 2003, Siri Hustvedt, the stepmother of Paul Auster's Son, will write a baldly autobiographical novel touching upon Angel's murder. Titled *What I Loved,* Hustvedt's fictional analogue speculates that the fictional analogue of Paul Auster's Son has never been truthful about the murder.

Four men are present in Michael Alig's apartment on March 16th. The poorest person receives three hammer blows against his skull. The best-connected person receives five years' probation.

This is how the world works.

APRIL 1996

Peter Gatien Fires Michael Alig

In April, Peter Gatien fired Michael. I discovered this by reading "La Dolce Musto" in the *Village Voice*. Item #1: Alig was locked out of his apartment at the Riverside West. Item #2: Alig blamed Gatien's wife, Alex. Item #3: Alex hates Michael and thinks that he slept with Gatien. Item #4: Michael went to rehab on Gatien's dime. Item #5: The Limelight is still hosting Disco 2000. Item #6: Michael is starting a second Disco 2000 at Expo.

I had no idea how to get in touch with Michael. I called James St. James at his place in Alphabet City. I asked if he'd seen Alig.

—Girl, he said, you don't want anything to do with Michael. You were right to get away. Trust me, Baby, that is one itch you do not want to scratch. Things are so dark right now that I won't even gossip. Go back to your books and pretend like you never met us.

—Are they really doing Disco 2000 without Michael?

—You remember his assistant, Walt Paper? That annoying little bald-headed bitch? Guess who's running the show? Anne Baxter for the new millennium!

—Thanks, Jimmy, I said. I'll see you around.

—Oh, Miss Thing, you will. I'm a heavenly fixture.

We hung up. I didn't call anyone else. When James St. James warns you off, you stay warned off.

But I did decide to go to Disco 2000. I was curious about the spectacle without Michael. Besides, it was Tuesday. I only need wait a day.

I attempted for the fifth time to read David Foster Wallace's *Infinite Jest*. Two months earlier, the thousand-page magnum opus had been published to broad acclaim. Much of the praise centered on Wallace's postmodern mechanism, employing over three hundred footnotes, which apparently ruptured the text.

That was the 1990s. The publishing industry spent the first half of the decade attempting to incorporate outside voices into Literature. Homos, women of color, the poor. When the great game proved resilient, New York City's editorial class retooled and published straight white guys who'd intuited that postmodernism was only a return to the same old bullshit disguised through cloying formalist devices. Five full years of footnotes and drawings of staplers.

Infinite Jest came like the tablets of Moses, a prefab masterpiece acknowledged well before its appearance in stores, as unavoidable as the political candidates produced by a two-party system. I'll admit to slight jealousy.

Saving Anne Frank was not manufactured for that particular success. It wasn't in my blood. I was from the wrong family. I was too queer, too fucked up, too science fiction. An unfortunate lack of a Masters of Fine Arts in Creative Writing. The only things that I had going were my pair of gonads and a dangling cluster of erectile vessels.

For David Foster Wallace, the role of serious writer was an irrevocable birthright. People think of Literature as if it were a natural occurrence revealed through the honesty of post-Enlightenment expression. Horseshit. Literature is a long-standing market construction of the late 1800s that details the social progress of the upper middle classes.

In America, this means WASPs. Any deviation is judged with modifiers. A woman who wrote *Infinite Jest,* word for word, comma for comma, superfluous adjective for superfluous adjective, couldn't have had the same reception. She would have been a Woman Writer who produced a fascinating oddity. Much discussed among a certain academic class. The same is true of Black Folk. *Infinite Jest* would have been shelved in African American fiction and lost to the world.

This mirrors the text of *Infinite Jest*, a book that never fails to identify its racial and cultural minorities by their deviation from whiteness and straightness. Black people are so black that they're blue. As long as David Foster Wallace cared to write giant books about young honky geniuses who played metaphorical tennis at academies run by their overeducated parents, the mechanism would receive his output.

I'd been asked to review *Infinite Jest* for *Sloat & Taraval,* a San Francisco literary journal. The editor was Bob Glück, the New Narrative poet and novelist. Glück liked *Trapped.* Given the vague science fiction overlay of both books, Glück was curious about my thoughts on Wallace's masterpiece.

When I told Parker about the review, he threw a chair across his office.

Brickley thought that one writer reviewing another writer's work was nothing but trouble. Publish something negative and suffer the social consequences. Publish something positive and you're lumped together for life. If Parker Brickley understood only a single thing, it was the impossibility of predicting a writer's path. Why dilute your brand through association with an unknown commodity?

But I was flattered that Glück had asked. I said yes. I'd engage with David Foster Wallace. I'd been trying since February. I'd even asked Adeline if she'd attend Wallace's reading at Tower Books.

—Baby, replied Adeline, I simply can't stand these authorial events. It's more than enough steeling one's self for the inevitability of your dreaded moment, so why in the blazes would I listen to the half-baked yammerings of a dude in a bandanna?

No matter how hard I tried, I couldn't get past the first few paragraphs. I'd stumble on the atrocious second sentence. "My posture is consciously congruent to the shape of my hard chair." Consciously congruent! How could I go for a thousand pages? But I must make the effort.

By Wednesday morning, after about two hundred pages, I realized that *Infinite Jest* couldn't be read. The thing could be apprehended only as an object, as an ultra-kitschy, giant-sized pastiche of *The Crying of Lot 49*.

If you excluded the timeless books, the special ones, then the reception of writing was little more than a contest of dick size. An atavistic component of the human psyche is always overwhelmed by the huge. We loved the biggest houses, the biggest cars, the biggest skyscrapers. Why not the biggest book? The longest cock. Quality is irrelevant. The reading public are a bunch of size queens. And I know size queens. All that matters is length and girth.

I left a message for Regina, saying that I'd be attending Disco 2000. I hadn't seen her in months, not since she'd started going with this bull dyke from the Bronx. I assumed that Regina was embarrassed by either me or her girlfriend. Possibly both. Queen Rex wouldn't make her appearance at Disco 2000, but what was the harm in asking?

Limelight was a ghost town. I didn't even see Walt Paper. The clueless few in attendance were candy ravers in their phat pants. Phat pants. Whither gone were the boiler suits of my youth?

I left after ten minutes, standing on Sixth Avenue, waiting for a notion to strike. There wasn't even a line. No one wanted to be at Disco 2000.

—Hey, Baby!

It was a friend of Michael's, a blonde junky named Gitsie. She was nineteen years old and from Miami. Gitsie saw Michael on *Geraldo* and ran away to New York City, showing up somewhere around 1992. She'd come fresh faced, a bit on the chubby side. A goofy teenybopper in questionable leather vests. Every town in America had a Gitsie.

The drugs ate away the weight and her youth. I'd heard stories about how she made her money. They were unpleasant.

—I've been looking for Michael, I said.

—I haven't seen him for a few days, she said. He's staying with Brooke at the Chelsea.

—Too bad he got fired.

—It's so unfair, she said. How could Peter do that?

—It happens to everyone, I said. Employment is the socially acceptable term we employ to describe the state of waiting for the axe.

—Are you looking to score? she asked.

—What do you have?

—I've got diesel, she said. I'll sell you two bags for forty dollars.

I had no particular moral objection to the drug, but heroin always seemed so scummy. Buying it from a nineteen-year-old with visible track marks did not lessen this impression. Still, why not? It wasn't like I'd shoot it.

Twenty dollars a bag was criminal, but I always was an easy mark.

Back at my apartment, The King of France had eaten all of his gourmet food. He'd been put on a special diet after developing an allergy to store-bought brands. Anything with too much grain and he'd vomit. Before we found a prescription brand that he could digest, the cat lost two pounds. The vet said this amount was significant.

I scooped the wild thing into my arms and flipped him on his back. He purred and put his paws on my mouth.

For all of the moments in my life that I'd watched people doing heroin, my strongest impression was from the film *Bad Lieutenant*. Harvey Keitel empties his heroin onto strips of tinfoil. A prostitute lights the bottom. Keitel, using a straw, sucks the smoke into his mouth.

He's a really bad lieutenant.

I went across the hall. I rarely talked with my neighbor, but whenever we did speak, she seemed more than pleasant. Her name was Deborah. I think she'd said that she worked for David Letterman.

—Do you have any tinfoil? I asked.

—How much do you need?

—Two or three sheets.

—What are you cooking?

—I've got my grandmother's recipe for garlic brown sugar chicken.

She closed her apartment door and came back with three sheets.

—When's the next book coming out? she asked.

—A few months, I said. You'll have to come to the release party.

—I'll definitely go for sure, she said. Let me know.

—Thanks again, I said.

I balanced a sheet across my knees and poured out the powder. I bent over the tinfoil, straw hanging out of my mouth, and flicked my lighter. The smoke tasted like the odor of street vendors selling cashew nuts. Burning tinfoil.

The drug bubbled and turned a tarry black. I smoked the first bag.

An immediate rush at the back of my temples. Unlike any other that I'd experienced, like a warm hug from the inside. I returned to the familiar place of doing a drug and liking the first five minutes and then realizing that I'd be like this for hours. Unsure what to do with myself, I decided to watch a film that I'd rented at Kim's. *Blow-Up* by Michelangelo Antonioni.

Motor control issues getting the tape into my VCR. My quest was not aided by The King of France, who rubbed against my ankles and mewled, drawing my attention from the task at hand.

I was outside and inside myself. I'd always presumed that nodding off was the result of a loss of will, that being on the nod was a weakness. Now I couldn't keep my eyes open. I caught glimpses of the film, flashing in and out. A fashion model on the floor. Other fashion models. A man in a car. Mimes. Very white pants. Cubist paintings. Stoners in an overly ornate house. A junk shop. Black-and-white photography. Jimmy Page. Silent tennis. Wind in trees.

Each time that I'd catch a glimpse, I'd go back on the nod. I could see everything, perfectly. Me on the couch. The King of France beside me. The television playing, but the scenarios would shift. David Hemmings stared at me from inside the television, saying, *Oi, Baby, you poof, where's your poodle?* Then I saw black dogs, running through the apartment, stomping on my body, tormenting my cat.

I couldn't make it to the bathroom. I leaned over the side of my couch and projectile vomited. It landed in a spot where The King of France had previously thrown up. My expulsion was consciously congruent to the shape of his mess.

I woke around eleven in the morning. The phone was ringing. My head was killing me. I answered the phone. It was Parker Brickley, my literary agent.

—Lazarus rises from the tomb, he said. I've been calling all morning.

—I went to Disco 2000, I said. This girl sold me heroin.

—Nail me to the cross, said Parker. I didn't bet the farm for you to overdose. Are you one of those assholes who can't handle the godawful stress of an audience that loves their writing? Heroin? Holy fucking shit.

—I only smoked it, I said. I'm afraid of needles. Can you be a little less loud? Why are you calling anyway?

—Slake my thirst, gorgeous, and tell me of *Infinite Jest*.

—I vomited last night in the same spot that my cat vomited, I said. I'm not of the proper caliber to write about David Foster Wallace.

—Thank fucking god, said Parker. My balls have been retracting with the fear. You can't be trusted. Knowing you, you'd go and give it a bad review. Remember that you're a professional. The days of truth are long over. Welcome to the big leagues. Every professional writer learns to be a fucking liar. That illusion of writers who tell the truth at all costs? It's a child's dream. I'm a fucking liar, too. Do you think I enjoy the work that I represent? Only you and Jane Smiley. One day, Parker Brickley will write an autobiography and call it *A List of Things and People That I Pretended to Like*. Each chapter will be about some hack whose book I said that I loved. The first chapter will be about Mona Simpson.

APRIL 1996

Baby and Adeline Go to the Mars Bar

After the reconciliation between Adeline and her mother, Suzanne became an increased presence in our lives, a happenstance once as likely as a return of Caesar's Comet.

With the focus of madness transferred to Emil, the sudden slackening of attention gave Adeline a newfound tolerance for her dear old mère. She didn't even object when Suzanne flooded Emil with plastic toys. The only downside was the elder woman's increasingly regular residencies at the Plaza Hotel.

Adeline made hay while the sun shined, playing off Suzanne's love for the grandchild and making her mother babysit whenever she was in town. The Grande Dame would decamp on 7th Street for hours, while Adeline ventured outside and experienced, for the first time in years, an adult life.

Within limits. Adeline wouldn't travel too far from home, so we settled on routines and outings contained within the East Village's borders. Typically this meant dinner at Around the Clock followed by drinks at the Mars Bar.

Of the establishments in old scumbag New York, it was the Mars Bar that best weathered the waves of gentrification. They only demolished the thing in 2011, when its walls were so covered in graffiti and filth that I wondered if any plaster remained. The toilets were works of art, little closets filled with broken bowls, every centimeter covered in ink, spray paint, and human effluvia. I once met a woman who said that she'd had sex on the pinball machine. I have no idea if it's true. It seems credible. I pray for her soul.

Anyhoo, back in '96, the bar was not quite the mess of its later years. The exterior was surprisingly clean, and its glass brick windows were intact. The name was painted in white letters above the entrance: MARZ. Above the name: CHECK YOUR MIND AT DOOR.

Which is exactly what Adeline and I did, coming in after dinner. Part of the appeal was the clientele, rock 'n' roll relics from the punk scene passed over by circumstance and time. It only took about ten minutes before some hapless Mad Tom started screaming about how Richard Hell was a cocksucker or Bobby Steele was a prick or Patti Smith was a fucking stuck-up fucking bitch who needed to be fucked.

Adeline and I ordered gin-and-tonics. The bartender was a young punk girl. Every bartender at the Mars Bar was a young punk girl. She gave us our rotten drinks. We sat on stools, attempting to ignore the taste and the assault on our stomachs.

—Baby, said Adeline, tell me, do you know of the band The Gits?

—Don't talk about bands, I whispered. You don't know who is listening.

—Are you still worried about that dreadful man?

The previous time that we were in the Mars Bar, I'd gotten drunk enough that I shouted about how much I hate Led Zeppelin. *Every time there's a song on a radio that's playing too fucking low,* I screamed, *I always mishear it as fucking "Good Times, Bad Times." It's such a shitty song! Led Zeppelin is such a fucking shitty band!*

My outburst attracted the man sitting beside me, a middle-aged guy with unfortunately long hair. He told me how much he hated Led Zeppelin too, and then told me about his idea for a screenplay, a film about vampires that lacked any plot. All he had was the opening scene. The camera is focused on a puddle. Pedestrians step around the water, keeping their feet from getting wet. We see their reflections as well as their feet. Finally, a foot stomps into the puddle. There is no reflection. The camera pans up and reveals THE VAMPIRE, wearing reflective sunglasses and a black leather trench coat.

In response, I made the mistake of talking about a club person only rumored to exist, this kid from Bombay. No one had seen him during the day. Supposedly he drank blood and slept in a coffin in the abandoned subway station on the 6 line, the one at 18th Street between Union Square and 23rd Street. Michael had dubbed him the Vindaloo Vampire.

The guy in the Mars Bar loved it. He suggested that we go to a show at Coney Island High. I was preparing to leave before Adeline saved me from my own intoxication.

—I'm still worried, I said. These rock 'n' roll people are terrifying.

—Cease your nancy boy prattling, said Adeline. Have you ever heard of The Gits?

—Alas, no, I said. I've never heard of The Gits.

—I purchased their debut at Sounds. *Frenching the Bully.* Baby, do you know, it's absolutely brilliant? The production is rather crude, but the song-writing is strong and the vocalist is exceptional.

—I'm glad you liked an album, Adeline, I said.

—I went back to Sounds and asked the disagreeable employee if they had any other albums by The Gits. He said there was another album, but it was not in stock. Then he told me the most horrible story.

I ordered another round. Adeline waited before continuing. A deaf mute named Felix came in through the entrance. He sat at the bar, a few stools down, pointed to his mouth, and emitted a squealing whimper. He was a regular.

—The vocalist of The Gits, said Adeline, was this woman named Mia Zapata. One night, she was hanging around with what I gather were a group of other musicians. She said her goodbyes and headed home. She stepped out into the night and promptly disappeared. The next morning, a jogger discovered her body. She was raped and beaten and strangled. She was young and beautiful, but now she was battered and dead. Her murder remains unsolved. The mystery remains. The killer at large. Isn't that simply the way things are, Baby? Imagine the web of her death, all the inflicted pain, spreading from person to person to person. I'm not one of those delusional fools who believes it's ever so much sadder when a talented person dies rather than an ordinary plebe, yet there is something to be said for Mia Zapata working for years, playing shows, writing music, and recording only to have it stolen away before she reaped the rewards. Those are the moments that terrify yours truly, life's irrevocable instances. What cannot be taken back. Most such moments are self-inflicted. Yet even in a life of repulsively clean rectitude, one can still be attacked in the street. Identity is porous. It isn't simply who you are. It's the damage that others inflict upon you.

A woman raped and strangled and beaten. I knew where the evening would end.

—I'm working on a new short story, I said. It's called "White Walls." I'm back to science fiction, to pure genre. The action takes place in the far future, in a Neo-Marxist Utopia. The human animal has rejected capitalism, but class and social distinctions prove persistent. A law is passed. People may not fuck each other than in very specific, controlled circumstances. Sexual partners must have sex in white rooms, completely naked, wearing no makeup or accoutrement beyond bathing caps that disguise hairstyles. Only through sexual communication without the normal markers of class identity can the socialist revolution move forward.

—That's a concept, said Adeline. Where's the story?

—I don't have it yet. I think it'll be a love story. Who are the perverts in a society that regulates sex according to Neo-Marxist dogma? It'll be people who break the sex laws of the white walls. People who dress like different social classes. Poor dress as rich, rich as poor, and they screw like animals. It'll probably be a Romeo and Juliet thing. A poor man and a rich man who wear each other's clothes.

Felix slapped his hands against the bar. The bartender shouted, telling him to calm down or get out. He calmed down. I wondered how he understood.

We left. Adeline rushed to the east side of Second Avenue, then north toward the Anthology Film Archives. I knew where we were headed. I followed anyway.

As we moved closer to the address, I couldn't remember a single time that Adeline and I had visited together. I'd seen her zine. I'd heard her talk about the Incident. I'd watched her nervous breakdown. I'd passed the address almost every day of my life. I could not remember a single time when we'd gone as a duo and peered up at the filthy tuxedo and that pathetic neon.

But there we were, standing on the pavement. After the emergence of Adeline's fixation, I'd asked around. Several people said the place was haunted. People had witnessed ghosts moving behind the tailor's dummy. I hoped that a specter would come upon us. At least then it'd be for something.

—I've tried speaking with her family, Adeline said. The woman who was murdered. Every time that I start, I halt myself before getting out a word. I'm appalled by the idea that the pain inflicted upon them is something in which I feel a personal involvement. I'm appalled that I know the name of the woman. Why should I know anything about it? All the world's murdered women. Helen Sopolsky. Mia Zapata. We must abandon our childish beliefs. There is no such thing as justice.

APRIL 1996

Michael Musto Breaks a Story

The next Tuesday, I checked "La Dolce Musto." There was more about Michael Alig. Word around town, wrote Musto, is that Michael was planning to move to Germany, to live with Rudolf, who used to run Tunnel. Musto implied that Rudolf had no idea that Michael was on his way.

A week passed. I was in a celibate period. Adeline had convinced me. She'd gone through several phases herself, eschewing the arts of pleasure, and thought it might be interesting if I gave myself a break from screwing.

Life became very boring, the pointlessness of existence driven home during the blank hours that I couldn't fill with the chaos of human relationships. My brief heroin interlude excepted, I'd also stopped using drugs. I wasn't seeing any club people, so how would I even score? Again, this de facto choice only made the boredom that much more palpable. At least I had my cat.

The next week, the next Tuesday, the next "La Dolce Musto." The world fell apart. April 30th. The column itself was ultranormal, Musto writing about John Waters and Billy Wilder and Madonna and Sid Caesar and Nathan Lane. What caught everyone's notice was a sidebar on the right side of the page.

NIGHT CLUBBING

Here's the latest story going around about what supposedly happened in that recent clubland scandal; Mr. Mess was fighting with Mr. Dealer about money Mr. Dealer was owed. It escalated to the point where Mr. Dealer was choking Mr. Mess. Just at the moment when Mr. Mess #2 happened to walk in. Mr. Mess #2, a quick thinker, promptly hit Mr. Dealer over the head with a hammer. Not happy with that, he and Mr. Mess decided to finish Mr. Dealer off by shooting him up with Drano—a trick even the twisted twosome in *Diabolique* didn't come up with. After Mr. Dealer died, the other two set to work chopping the body into pieces and throwing them into the river. "But I didn't actually kill him," Mr. More-of-a-Mess-Than-Ever has allegedly remarked (but he's unavailable for comment).—M.M.

There was no reason to assume that it was Michael. But of course it was Michael. No one else in clubland would warrant the space. Even murder has its hierarchy. If Gitsie had killed someone, it'd be a five-hundred-word story about her arrest and then a three-hundred-word story about her conviction. It wouldn't be gossip. Everything with Michael Alig was gossip.

Gitsie'd said Michael was staying at the Chelsea with Brooke. I went across town to the hotel. Entering the lobby, it came to me that I hadn't been inside since Regina and I visited Christina. Another dead denizen of clubland. That was six or seven years earlier. It felt like twenty thousand. The steady pounding of time kept beating against me.

When I told the desk attendant that I wanted to see Brooke, he went slightly pale but then examined my wardrobe. I was dressed like any other respectable young professional. He gave me her room number. I took the elevator up to the third floor. I knocked.

I didn't know Brooke very well. We'd only talked for a few minutes. I'm sure she knew me by sight and, I suspect, writerly reputation. Not that any of the club kids read my book. Only Michael and Franklin read books.

Brooke was a mountain of a girl. She regularly dyed her hair a rainbow spectrum of color. There were a ton of piercings in her face.

—Hi, Baby, she said.

—Is Michael here?

—No, she said.

—Can I come in?

—Okay, she said.

Other than a chair and a little table, Brooke had no furniture. Eight mattresses lined the floor, covered with piles of clothes and the unconscious bodies of two drugged-up kids. They couldn't have been more than seventeen years old. Ashtrays were everywhere, overflowing with cigarette butts. A few black trash bags were wedged between the mattresses. It was like being back in David's squat.

—Take a seat if you want, said Brooke.

I sat on the least disgusting mattress. It was like stabbing yourself with the dullest knife.

—What's up, Baby?

—Did you see the *Voice*?

—I only just woke up.

—Michael Musto. There's a piece about a certain someone killing a drug dealer and then chopping up his body. I got the distinct impression that the certain someone was Michael.

—Oh fuck, she said. Fuck. Fuck. Fuck. Fuck Michael fucking Musto.

—Where's Michael? I asked.

—I haven't seen him for a few days. Fuck. Fuck. He's staying with this guy he met at Future. Fuck.

—Did Michael do it?

—I don't know. It's Michael. Who knows if it's true?

—Did he tell you that he did it?

—Yes.

—What are you going to do? I asked.

—I don't want Michael to get in trouble. I'm not going to be the one who gets him in trouble. I'm not the only one who knows. Everyone knows. He's told everyone, Baby. No one's sure whether or not they believe him.

One of the kids stirred.

—But don't worry, said Brooke. It's not like he killed anyone that matters. It was only Angel.

—The drug dealer?

—If you can call him that.

I stood up.

—I'm going to try and find Michael, I said.

—Before you go, said Brooke, do you want to buy any coke?

MAY 1996

Baby and Parker Play Pool

Other articles followed. In daily tabloids that did not hesitate to name names. Michael was outed in the news media as a murderer. There was no police investigation.

As a victim, Angel offered multiple deficiencies. Brown skin, Hispanic last name, gay, drug dealer. These comprised a mathematical formula for official indifference. The NYPD didn't care.

Michael split town, embarking on a grand journey through the American Middle West. Denver, Chicago, even back to South Bend. A drug-fueled odyssey in a rented van through the badlands. He brought Gitsie as his copilot.

Back in New York, I dealt with the inevitable chaos of forthcoming publication, obsessing over every little detail. There were arguments about the cover. There were arguments about copy editing. There were arguments about typefaces. There were arguments about blurb quotes. There were arguments about jacket copy.

For the nine thousandth time, I thanked heaven for the angelic cataclysm of Parker Brickley. He rallied to even the most minor concern, screaming and cursing until it felt as though he'd shatter every window in Midtown.

The official indifference didn't extend to Peter Gatien. In the early morning hours of May 15th, the DEA raided his apartment. Gatien was indicted on two charges of conspiring to distribute MDMA in Tunnel and Limelight.

At the obligatory press conference, Zachary W. Carter, the U.S. Attorney for the Eastern United States, remarked: —Dealing Ecstasy was not just lucrative, it was the centerpiece of the operation. These clubs existed to distribute these substances. The drugs were the honey trap that attracted these kids to the clubs.

Despite their owner's incarceration, both clubs remained open.

I couldn't be bothered checking out the scene. Disco 2000 run by Walt

Paper while Michael Alig was in South Dakota. Peter Gatien rotting for two weeks in the Metropolitan Detention Center before making bail. It was the definition of threadbare.

A few days after Gatien's arrest, A. J. Benza published an article in the *Daily News*. Entitled "The Curious Case of the Club-Land Canary," it detailed the hammer affair between Michael and Angel, but with a very specific twist. Benza insinuated that Michael had turned informant against Gatien, and that Alig's exodus wasn't about escaping his own heat but rather that he'd been tipped off by the DEA about the coming raid. The idea turned out to be prescient.

Some literate wag or another realized that Michelle Gila was based on Michael Alig. As an intellectual with an apparent insider's view, I became a hot property. I fielded phone calls from beat reporters. Even Michael Musto called. A reporter for the *Post* asked me if the rumors about orgies were true.

—The orgies? What orgies? I asked.

—Word is, said the reporter, that Alig set up massive drug orgies for Gatien. These took place in hotel rooms. Sometimes they'd last a few weeks. Sometimes a few days. It'd be Alig and Gatien and hookers. Piles of cocaine, crack rock, Special K. You name it. They blew thousands each night. An unnamed source told me off the record that Alig overdosed at one of these parties. A different unnamed source said that Angel supplied the drugs. Can you confirm or deny?

—No comment, I said.

The indictment, and the subsequent reporting, focused exclusively on Tunnel and Limelight. I experienced a wellspring of pity for the Palladium. Gatien still owned it, but it was so incredibly passé that not even the DEA cared. I couldn't hazard a guess about its regulars. Yet the club remained.

From nothing more than morbidity, I wanted to look at the club. I didn't want to go inside. I wanted to observe it, to see what could possibly be happening at New York's least interesting club while its owner sat in jail.

I called Adeline and asked if she wanted to play pool at Julian's, the billiards hall that occupied the second floor of the same building as Palladium.

—Oh, darling, said Adeline, you know I'd simply die watching you be hustled by sharks, but I cannot. Honest and for true. I'm watching Frances's daughter. Plus I have a suitor set to pay a visit.

—What? Who?

—Do you remember Jon, Baby? He and I ran into each other on St. Mark's. I was walking with Emil. Jon was ever so pleasant a conversationalist, and he was quite taken with my son. Can you believe it? The punk virtuoso finally completed his degree at CUNY. He takes his employ in a lawyer's office, working for a bleeding heart on cases that no one else will touch. It's positively cinematic!

We exchanged pleasantries and hung up. Life wasn't anything but complications. The last time that I'd seen Jon, I'd beaten him with the hardcover debut of a polymorphous pervert while a Bengali waiter cursed us.

But was that as bad as throwing period blood at his shoes? Somehow he and Adeline had reconciled. They'd collapsed back into each other. Maybe good faith can remove any obstacle. Anything is possible.

I called Parker and invited him to the pool hall. When he'd discovered the media's interest, he'd wet himself in joy, encouraging me to dribble every tidbit of gravied information into the gaping maw of news journalism. Any publicity, said Parker, that occurs before a book's release is a welcome thing. Get your name out there before the reading public.

I'd explained how very little I wanted my name associated with Alig's. I needed time to figure it out. Parker wasn't interested.

—Go hog wild, he said. If you want your book to succeed, you had better get acquainted with the media. You better get real good at using them before they use you. Otherwise those fucks'll leave you as sore and sorry as a two-dollar whore who ran out of condoms. They'll leave you banged and raw, Baby boy.

Parker agreed to meet. I arrived before him, standing beside the neon-lit entrance that read JULIAN BILLIARDS. My agent's perpetual lateness afforded me time to watch all the has-beens and would-bes of clubland flowing into the Palladium. There was no door policy. It was all cash now, born of a desperation to raise Gatien's bail.

Leviathan surfaced on 14th Street, trudging east from Union Square and maneuvering through the crowd of smokers. He ambled up and put his arm on my shoulder, his meaty paw buckling my knees.

—Let's play some fucking pool.

Julian's was one of those New York establishments where time itself has sunk into the surfaces, where the floor is a carpet of cigarette butts and the reeking smoke of decades has browned the paint. Photographs of Minnesota Fats hung on the walls. If ever there was antiquity in New Amsterdam, we'd found it.

There were a handful of the requisite old timers, the crazy gone ones who'd hustled pool since the '50s. They drank from brown paper bags, nicotine clouds hanging above their heads. Most of the tables were occupied by the young. Not just men. Lots of women, too, playing flirtatious games with their dates.

Parker paid for our table, getting one by the windows. I racked the balls and Parker broke. He sunk a striped ball. I hadn't played pool since my days in the American Middle West.

A guy on the track team had a table in his basement. Everyone had shot pool in the hours after practice. It became a social obligation.

To avoid boredom, I intentionally overread the game's phallic symbolism, all those sticks and balls, and fantasized about my fellow runners. Yes, I was that guy, the one about whom Republicans warn us. I abused the locker room shower. I fantasized about the dicks that appeared before me.

—I don't like giving advice, said Parker, because advice is like the past. It always comes and haunts you. But you had best prepare yourself for all eventualities. Your book could bomb. I've seen great books fail, and I've seen stuffed turkeys take flight and soar to the land of milk and honey. What if your book doesn't tank? What if it succeeds? What then? I'm not sure you understand the effects of true success. Success can be a worse killer than failure.

—It's still a few months away, I said.

—These days will pass like all your useless hopes and dreams. It might as well be tomorrow.

—I don't even know why I started. Maybe failure won't be so bad.

—No man but a blockhead ever wrote except for money, and money is leaking out of your pockets. Speaking of, how's the next book coming?

I hadn't yet told Parker that I'd abandoned my novel of the American Civil War. I'd eked out about thirty thousand words before flying the white flag of surrender.

The idea had been to write from a grunt-level perspective that stripped away the bullshit glory of war, stripped away the mystical bullshit with which this country imbues every battle. It would be about the misery of shitting yourself before a skirmish, about having your legs amputated by nineteenth-century quacks, about your blood soaking into the soil of a country atoning for other blood. I wanted to calculate the exact cost of a human life in 1861, down to the dollar.

I couldn't make it work. The research killed me. World War II was nothing compared to the Civil War. The books people've written.

—So you're working on short stories? asked Parker.

—Yeah, I said.

—We can always sell a book of stories as a holdover between novels. Certain people are suckers for short fiction. Personally, I can't give two fucks. What are you working on now?

I'd finished "White Walls," and was putting together a new story called "Decimal Notation." It's about a printer named Solomon Prower who for years has produced single-run forgeries of Ludwig Wittgenstein's *Tractatus Logico-Philosophicus*. Prower's editions are perfect replicas of the preexisting editions, with only slight modifications to the original text.

Using Wittgenstein's method of decimal propositions, Prower locates a particularly boring part of the book and inserts nonsense phrases that undercut its central premises. For instance:

> 4.4662   The tautology of all things suggests that which is not the case is made of atomic facts unapprehended through the internal sense of a proposition. Thus anti-fact becomes fact.

In each volume, Prower includes an Ex Libris bookplate with his own address. This has gone on for ten years. He's never been contacted. In some instances, his forged propositions have snuck into low-level scholarly literature.

On August 8th, 1974, a Thursday, our protagonist receives a letter. It reads, "I know what you are doing. I am coming to see you tomorrow." Prower sits around on Friday, awaiting the arrival of his mysterious correspondent. He's so overtaken with nerves that he misses Richard Nixon's resignation. In the early evening, there comes a knock on his door.

I hadn't gotten any further. I was sure it was a love story.

—It sounds suspiciously literary, said Parker.

We played another few games, as I kept an eye on the street through the windows. Grotesque human travesties stumbled out of the A&P in the Zeckendorf Towers and passed into the Palladium. It was like watching an undertaker put a body down. Everything changes. Everything dies.

Parker won every game. Pool required a level of engagement that I had never possessed.

When our two hours were up, Mr. Brickley went to the bathroom. I waited by the windows. If I craned my neck, I thought I could see the copper-ringed roof of 31 Union Square West. I wondered if Thomas M. Disch still lived there, wondered if he'd read *Trapped,* wondered if my whole life was the product of his indirect influence. If I could talk to him again, I'd have endless questions. That fey little boy from a Podunk little town was long gone, effaced by a full decade in New York City, replaced by a brand-new creature. It happened to me, I had been in it, but I still didn't understand how I'd gone so far from home.

A sound from the far end of the room. Parker was in an argument with two guys about my own age who looked like genuine-grade Italians from Staten Island, dressed up in Wu Wear, bomber jackets and the hottest stocking caps. Parker hollered in the face of one, going red, distributing spittle. I ran toward them. The second guy hit Parker across the back with a pool cue.

The thing about hunting Leviathan. That harpoon had better pierce the hide. Otherwise it's liable to wrap a line about your neck.

Parker turned to face the one who'd hit him, exposing his back. The original adversary was in the process of picking up a pool cue.

—I wouldn't, I said.

I threw myself on the original adversary, knocking us both to the ground. I pinned his arms with my knees, and hit his face with a billiards ball that I'd grabbed on my way over. I'd been in too many fights to hit with my hands. I couldn't deal with the swelling and pain.

It took a few strikes before I drew blood. Parker's attacker swooned into the sweet blackness of the unconscious. I stood up, ready to beat out the stuffing of the other guy, but he and Parker were watching in mutual horror. Everyone had stopped playing pool. Everyone stared at me. I dropped the bloody ball.

—Come on, I said to Parker.

One of the old timers said to another: —I been here twenty-four years and I ain't never seen nobody make nobody else eat a seven ball.

Worried about cops, I rushed Parker along the east side of Union Square. He labored beside me, the heaviest of breath.

We hit 18th Street and got drinks at the Old Town Bar. I couldn't imagine that many Staten Island thrill seekers were interested in the low-key atmosphere of New York's ninth-oldest bar.

—Is it always like this with you? asked Parker.

—He hit you with a pool cue. Something had to be done. What started it, anyway?

—I bumped into them as I was coming out of the bathroom. One of them missed his shot.

JUNE 1996

Baby Looks for Michael

Gatien posted bail, but the clubs were crippled. We all lived in Rudy's world. I wasn't the only person obsessed with getting the latest *Voice*. People wanted peripheral resonances of catastrophe. It was the last cool summer that I can remember, the last summer before global warming thrust us into endless sweltering. We never broke 90 degrees.

On June 4th, Musto wrote about Michael Alig's escapades across America. Alig was spotted in Chicago then ended up in Denver, where he was planning Disco 2000 parties. Innuendo oozed from each consonant and vowel, seeping into the reader's pores through the transferences of print osmosis.

On June 11th, Musto claimed that Michael was masterminding a remake of "If I Had a Hammer." The latest rumors had Angel surfacing in one piece. Could it all be a hoax?

On June 18th, there wasn't any mention.

On June 25th, it exploded. A front-page photograph of Angel wearing his white wings. The accompanying headline: A MURDER IN CLUBLAND? Some say promoter Michael Alig killed Angel Melendez. Some say it's a hoax. FRANK OWEN investigates.

Frank Owen knew James St. James. I'd never met him, but he'd written a few clubland pieces for the *Voice*. Someone said that he had an English accent. I turned to page 29.

Looking for Angel: Did King of Club Kids Michael Alig Really Kill Angel Melendez? Or Is It All a Hoax?

Owen's opening was human interest. He followed Angel's brother, Johnny Melendez, while Johnny journeyed around New York, seeking information about his missing sibling. He posted flyers. Johnny'd last seen Angel outside of the Riverbank West. He and Angel had kept in contact through their beepers. When it became clear that Angel was not returning his pages, Johnny'd gone through clubland, asking people if they knew anything about his brother's whereabouts. No one knew anything. Johnny received the distinct impression that everyone knew everything.

The article reproduced the flyer:

MISSING

$4,000 REWARD

POSTED BY FAMILY FOR THE
WHEREABOUTS OF ANGEL

**IF YOU HAVE ANY INFORMATION PLEASE
CALL (917) 290-9012 OR (908) 629-9110**

Multiple unnamed sources told Owen that Michael Alig had killed Angel. Only Screamin' Rachel went on the record. Alig had visited her in Chicago. He'd broken down and confessed.

Owen had the entire story. The hammer, the body in the tub for a week, the dismemberment, the elevator, the taxicab. And he had the orgies. He had Angel on Gatien's payroll. He even had Freeze on the record, denying that he'd murdered Angel. Owen had everything except for Michael.

My answering machine was blinking. I had two messages from reporters. Only at this moment did I realize that the story would never go away. I would be answering questions about Michael for the rest of my life.

My phone rang. Another reporter.

—No comment, I said.

The phone rang. I let the machine pick up. Another reporter.

I left my apartment.

Owen's piece wasn't written overnight. He had talked to Freeze. Alig must have known what was coming. Michael must be back in town. I couldn't imagine him missing this defining moment in his own myth. Cover stories were too fabulous.

A club kid named Jenny Talia worked on St. Mark's at Trash and Vaudeville, a store from the early punk movement reduced to supplying mawkish clothing to bewildered teenagers from Nassau County. The latest and the last. Like an aging film star watching her starring roles in a darkened room.

Jenny Talia was another of the ones that I barely knew. Crop of more recent vintage. Four things stood out. Her piercing blue eyes. She'd modeled in a CK Jeans campaign. Her dimple piercings. Her bald, bald head.

When I arrived at Trash and Vaudeville, Jenny Talia wasn't there. A dopey kid behind the counter said that she worked part time and hadn't been taking many shifts. I asked if he knew Michael Alig.

—No, he said. But I heard he's back in town.

I started out the door. The kid called me back.

—Hey, buddy, he said, you wanna score?

As I was in the East Village, I figured that I'd visit Adeline. I stood beneath her window and hollered.

She popped her head out, waved, and retreated inside. The weirdness of not having a key never disappeared, no matter how many times that I visited. She opened the front door.

—Emil is all slumber, she said, so we must be reasonably quiet.

—You know me, I said.

—There's another issue, she said.

—Which is?

—Jon's upstairs. He's on his lunch break.

—Should I leave?

—You'll have to remake his acquaintance at some point, she said. When better than the now?

Anyhoo, there was no escape. He'd heard me shouting in the street. I had the uncharitable thought that straight women could be such incredible fools. Taking back Jon. He'd screwed the brains out of her childhood best friend!

Jon sat at the kitchen table, a pained expression on his face. Maybe he was worried that I'd beat out his stuffing. Maybe he was disgusted that he too must make nice. Who can say with people?

Jon stood and shook my hand.

—Baby, he said. Let's not think about what happened.

—Fine with me, I said.

With the fantastical exception of Thomas Cromwell, Adeline's men had always come in two varieties. She liked them filthy, as in East Village scum, or she liked them awkward. She'd shown me a picture of Emil's father. His appearance was of no particular surprise, him being one of those men incapable of experiencing comfort within their own flesh. He was handsome enough. Her men were always handsome. But Nash Mac looked as if he'd bought his clothes two sizes too small and then, through sheer use, expanded them two sizes too large.

The rediscovered Jon was in neither category. Beclad in a suit, he was a new man. It wasn't a good suit, but it was a suit and it fit. His tattoos were hidden beneath a button-up. His hair, once the staging ground of grime and grit, was washed and combed and held in place by chemical products.

He sat down. Adeline sat beside him. He touched her hand.

—We've been reading this book, he said. It's incredibly funny.

A small paperback on the kitchen table. A piece of erotic kitsch called *WANT-AD WANTONS*.

—Jesus, I said, why?

—Baby, said Adeline, don't you know that these works are hilarious? This one is rather a delight. It's about a terribly bitter man named Lou who picks up a bored divorcée named Terry. The pickup occurs only a few hours after he's mailed out responses to personal ads in a swinger's magazine. Lou's had a drought, but Terry brings the rain. They go wild in his basement bachelor apartment. Then couples start answering his letters, so Lou goes and makes love to a woman named Rita while her submissive husband watches. Rita and her hubby invite Lou to an orgy and suggest that he take Terry. Lou asks Terry and Terry agrees. They go to the orgy and, good lord, Baby, does Lou ever get lucky. As does Terry. From there, as you might imagine, matters ensue.

—Tell him about the orgasms, said Jon.

—The book has a delightful little vernacularism, said Adeline. Whenever a character achieves orgasm, they 'shoot over the top.' We thought it was coded language for ejaculation, but soon enough Terry and Rita are shooting over the top, too. Simply everyone in Lou's world shoots over the top.

—How does it end? I asked.

—We haven't gotten that far, said Jon. We're only at the part where Terry and Lou make it with a liberated Black couple.

I urinated in the closet and pulled the chain. Back in the kitchen, I sat in the only empty chair. I'd spent ten years thinking that I knew everything about Adeline, but Jon must know things about her that I didn't. It was a strange thought.

Emil yelled from Adeline's bedroom. Jon was up before me.

—Don't worry, he said.

He disappeared into Adeline's bedroom. The walls were thin enough that I could hear him talking with the child. The boy's laugh carried through the closed door.

—Jon's very capable with Emil, she said. They've taken to each other. Things are going so very well.

—Have you met his family yet? I asked.

—His mother and his brother, she said. The mother was cold. The brother loved my child.

—It's good for Emil, I said. Between you and Frances and your mother, he's probably overdosed on secondhand estrogen.

—I do hope it isn't too awkward.

She flipped through the pages of WANT-AD WANTONS.

—What a silly book, she said.

—Adeline, have you seen today's *Voice*?

—I attempt to avoid that rag, she said. I become ever so depressed by the constant stream of new films that I'm missing. If I'm lucky, I can manage one flicker a week, and rarely am I lucky.

I opened my messenger bag and took out the *Voice*.

—What in the name of Jesus Cristo? she asked.

—Read the story, I said.

She pored over the pages.

—Baby, she said, what are you going to do?

—This has nothing to do with me, I said. I haven't seen Michael in over a year. I have a new book coming out.

SEPTEMBER 1996

Baby and Adeline See *Freaks*

Summer disappeared, bleeding into September, into the month of publication. I spent August in paralysis, worried about the meaning of another book in the world. I hardly wrote, barely saw anyone, barely even bothered with gossip about Michael Alig.

It was impossible to ignore the travails of Peter Gatien. On August 20th, the US Attorney hit him with new charges. Conspiracy to distribute cocaine. On August 24th, the NYPD arrived after midnight and shut down Tunnel and Limelight. When the police arrived, both clubs only had about three hundred attendees. Cop symbolism. Public theater. It'd all gone away a long time before.

Parker convinced me to be interviewed by Mim Udovitch about Michael Alig. Udovitch was writing an article for *Details*. As I wanted to maintain the illusion of reclusivity, I insisted that we speak by telephone. I thought that I'd acquitted myself well, but the article wasn't coming out until the end of the month, about two weeks after *Saving Anne Frank*. My release date was the 17th.

The only relief from my nervous stupor came in the form of Adeline's suggestion that we go to the Film Forum.

—What's playing? I asked.

—A hot property in which I suspect you'll have the greatest of interest.

—It's not *Pink Narcissus,* is it? I can't stand another screening of *Pink Narcissus.*

—Nein, fräulein. It's a work by your great enemy. Better known as Tod Browning. They're showing *Freaks.*

—I can't, I said. I'm haunted.

—We must face our fears, she said. Besides, Jon's watching Emil. You wouldn't deny a girl the right to see a rare film on the big screen with her best friend, would you? Please say you ain't that sort of dude, dude.

I relented. I always relented with Adeline. I'd spent ten years relenting. The Film Forum had relocated from Watts Street to West Houston.

Right off Varick, about a block and a half from the Dover Bookstore. I considered leaving an hour early and then browsing the stacks but had come to the conclusion that my apartment was overflowing with unread books. At the very least, I refused to buy any more until I'd read one particular volume that I'd lugged around for years. A verse translation of *De rerum natura* by Lucretius.

Adeline arrived well before me. Thoughts of *Freaks* slowed my pace. Those little pinhead children had doomed me for the better part of four years. Why would I subject myself to them again? For the same reason that I subjected myself to so many things.

Adeline had whined. I couldn't say no.

I walked into the lobby.

—Fancy seeing you here, she said.

—Someone invited me. It wasn't my idea.

—Cease being such a stick-in-the-mud, she said. I bought your ticket.

Freaks had attracted enough of a crowd that people lined up against the lobby's right wall. The middle-aged couple behind us talked about optimizing language design. I had no idea what they meant, but their voices kept me from meditating on the forthcoming experience.

The film played in the smaller second screen. Despite my predilection for hanging on aisles, Adeline insisted that we sit in the middle seats of the middle row. We ended up boxed. Leaving was impossible, but I comforted myself with the thought that the runtime was only sixty-two minutes.

The theater lights darkened. There it was. Tod Browning's *Freaks*. All the horror that MGM could offer the year of 1932. I was prepared for anything but what I saw, which was a badly acted melodrama about life among circus performers.

We open with a full-size trapeze artist named Cleopatra trying to seduce a midget named Hans. Hans is engaged to Frieda, another midget. This does not deter Cleopatra. She's interested in Hans because Hans, flattered by her attention, lavishes her with gifts.

The film's focus is primarily anthropological, offering vignettes of its titular characters. The cast is comprised of about twenty different freaks. The pinhead girls are given the most prominence, but this takes nothing away from a limbless man lighting his cigarette, a woman without arms using cutlery, a legless man's graceful agility, or Koo-Koo the Bird Girl.

Frieda takes her concerns to Cleopatra, warning the gargantuan blonde away from her man and accidentally letting slip that Hans is the heir to a great fortune. Cleopatra and Hercules, the resident strongman with whom she is making whoopee, conspire to get Hans's money. This culminates in an off-camera wedding.

We jump forward to the wedding reception. Hercules, Cleopatra, Hans, and the other freaks sit around a banquet table. As she's married Hans, the freaks decide to initiate Cleopatra into their coven of deformity. A midget brings out a loving cup, which they fill with wine and pass around the table while singing a song that goes: *Gooble, gobble / we accept her, we accept her / one of us, one of us!*

If I could have left, I would have. But we were boxed.

Cleopatra is horrified by possible membership in this club. She grabs the loving cup and throws its wine at the freaks. She storms away.

From there, it all ends in horror.

On our way out of the Film Forum, we passed by Gilda's Club, an establishment with a very prominent red door. I couldn't imagine its purpose. I asked Adeline. She had no idea, but suggested a social club for the nouveau riche.

—That was less disturbing than I'd imagined. The pinheads gave me waves of acid resonance until I saw them for what they were. True innocents. But goddamn it, that song. Gooble gobble.

—Have you ever heard "Pinhead" by The Ramones?

—When did I ever care about punk?

—If by some quirk you do develop an unhealthy interest, listen to "Pinhead." The Ramones sing the gooble gobble song, but they've got the wording wrong.

—I'll consider it, I said. I've had enough of little pinhead girls for one lifetime.

—You do realize, asked Adeline, that the lead pinhead, the one they call Schlitzie, was a man, don't you? They put the creature in a dress because he couldn't control his bodily functions, but that pinhead was a man. He used to dance in MacArthur Park for money.

It was around the three Brutalist towers that comprise NYU's faculty housing. That's when Adeline told me.

I was looking at the buildings and thinking how hilarious it was that the ol' alma mater forced its professors to live within failed modernist experiments. They were probably lovely inside, but from the exterior, it seemed as if the university housed its faculty in projects. They were designed by I. M. Pei.

Anyhoo, it was around there that Adeline let loose her revelation.

—Baby, she said, I've asked Jon to move in with me and Emil. Technically, it's taken place. Technically, he's resided on 7th Street for the last week.

—Please say that you aren't getting fucking married.

—Dear lord, no, she said. I'd never consider that barbaric rite.

—You're going to live in sin?

—Jon and I won't simply live in sin, she said. We'll wallow in it until we drown.

When we neared the Angelika, I read the marquee and noted that *Trainspotting* was playing. All of New York was talking about *Trainspotting*. People on the street, reviews, television. I hadn't seen it.

—So Jon's watching Emil?

—Yes, she said.

—Let's see *Trainspotting*.

—My child expects his mother.

—*Freaks* was only an hour long! What's the point of a live-in boyfriend?

We saw *Trainspotting*. It's about junkies in Scotland who shit the bed and overdose. These junkies accidentally kill a baby, get drunk, spew blood everywhere. I understood why it drove people wild. The movie was terrible, but terrible in its moment. A new wave of filmmaking, a hyperkinetic style scored with perfectly curated songs selected from the last thirty years of white people's popular music, highlighting fundamentally lower-income concerns in the high-camp titillation of the ruling classes. An after-school special disguised as hard living. A sermon on the mount delivered not by a radical firebrand but from the mouth of a baby boomer who believed in his ability to separate hepcats from squares.

—What a bore the '90s are, said Adeline. No wonder Michael Alig killed his drug dealer.

SEPTEMBER 1996

Baby Does an Event at the Union Square Barnes & Noble

I agreed to a book tour. Doubleday asked if I wanted a launch party, to which I replied that I'd do it only if they could guarantee the attendance of that fat little fuck Norman Mailer. I had visions of a banquet table and passing around a loving cup and singing about accepting the great toad into our fold.

Inquiries were made. Mailer refused. I said no launch party, but a book tour, okay, fine.

My inaugural event took place on the fourth floor of the Barnes & Noble in Union Square, about one hundred yards away from the front door of 31 Union Square West. I don't know what it was. Without fail, my life came back to Union Square.

Doubleday's publicist met me outside. She introduced the people from Barnes & Noble who'd be helping with the event, and then they all went and gossiped about Jay McInerney and frozen watermelons.

I stayed on the fourth floor, hanging around by the biography section, worried that no one would come. Then I worried because so many people filled the seats. A horde waiting to see me talk. I'd been convinced that no one would show. I hadn't prepared a single word. I hadn't even chosen passages to read.

One of the handlers pulled me to the side. I endured the grueling experience of hearing my fake biographic blurb being read aloud. I ran up to the microphone. There was a sea of pink faces, staring into me, staring through me. I could only talk, so I talked. And talked. And talked. And talked. And talked. And talked.

I said so much that I'm not even sure what the hell I said. Forty minutes later, I figured that I'd done enough. Adeline was in the front row. She went from the proud to the enthralled to the disinterested to the utterly bored.

I asked if the audience had questions. I said that I'd answer anything. A great silence as people shifted in their seats. Someone in the back raised their hand.

—Yes?

—I really loved *Trapped Between Jupiter and a Bottle*. With the recent coverage, I couldn't help but remember Michelle Gila. I went back and re-read the book and realized that you'd written an allegory about the club kids.

—Is there a question in there? I asked.

—I guess what I'm asking is, uhm, how much of that was based on original research? Do you really know Michael Alig, and if you do, do you know if he really killed Angel Melendez?

Adeline perked up. I said a few words about Michael Alig. I said a few words about Angel. I rambled and ended on a joke, or at least something like a joke, because people laughed. It could have been from discomfort.

I said thank you to the audience. People applauded.

A handler escorted me to a table behind the dais. Adeline sat beside me. Jon was working late. Frances had Emil. Half of the audience stayed. Enough that I wanted to burst into tears.

Most were nice, asking silly little questions. A few mentioned science fiction or Anne Frank or clubland, looking for a validation that I couldn't deliver. I tried my hardest.

After an hour, there were three people left.

I wish I could say that I'd noticed him in the crowd, or in line, but I hadn't. His was only another brunette face in a sea of white people congregating through their interest in literary fiction.

—Do you remember me? he asked.

—Should I?

—Look close, he said.

I recognized the smile, even through the years, even with the aging, even with the wrinkles.

—Abe? I said.

—That's right, he said.

We hadn't spoken since the day that his mother coitus interrupted us. His dick had been in my mouth. Our lack of communication was no mean feat, considering the size of our high school and our Podunk little town. If nothing else, I should have thanked him for not exposing me, for not forcing me to leave in shame.

—Can you wait a minute? I asked. I'd love to catch up.

The next person presented me with a book. I had no idea how I'd do two weeks of events. Each copy of *Saving Anne Frank* felt like a rebuke for having written the thing.

—Baby, whispered Adeline, whoever is this Abe?

—Do you remember my one and only sexual experience back home?

—Not him!

—The very same, I said.

When I finished with the line, the Barnes & Noble handler asked if I would sign more books for stock. I worked my way through the pile.

Adeline and I went to Abe.

—How'd you find me? I asked.

—They had your picture in the newsletter, he said. I recognized you as soon as I saw it, no matter what name you're using.

—I'm amazed. I can't even recognize myself.

—You look about the same, he said.

Abe lived in New York, having himself abandoned the American Middle West. He'd taken a few years off before getting a degree in economics at Chicago. He presently worked in a nebulous analyst position on Wall Street. I received the distinct impression that he'd come to the city so that he could live as a queer.

We exchanged phone numbers and promised to be in touch. I presumed that we wouldn't, that at best we might have a handful of chance meetings but make no particular effort to spend time in each other's company. Until he saw me, he'd forgotten how much he needed to forget.

—One thing, he said, before I go. I'm really sorry about your parents.

—Don't mention it, I said.

—I can't imagine it was easy, said Abe. Not with them dying like that. Not with them dying in that way.

—Time helps, I said. I don't think much about it.

—I always liked your mother.

—She was a good person, I said.

—I tried to find you when I heard. By then you were gone.

—I always was a runner.

Abe disappeared down the escalator. Adeline and I waited, talking with the publicist, talking with people from Barnes & Noble. We waited until I felt sure that Abe was gone.

—I need a drink, I said to Adeline. Can you drink?

—Any human soul requires a tall order after that encounter, she said. Wherever shall we go?

—The Old Town, I said.

*

Ensconced in the bar, I ordered a Jean Harlow. Adeline ordered a Cape Cod. I stared up at the tin ceiling. I knew the question that was coming but hoped it could be avoided. I sipped my drink, dreaming that she'd say something, anything. She didn't.

—What's wrong? I asked.

—It's only that I've realized, she said, I haven't a clue what happened with your parents. Will you ever tell me?

So I told her.

I have two siblings, an older brother and a younger sister. Our childhoods were scored by the sounds of our parents' constant argumentation. Some fights were ridiculous, about absolute nonsense. The way that my mother looked at my father in the kitchen. The color of new drapery. Some fights were serious. How much my mother hated the way that my father acted around her children. Money, always money.

Every altercation occurred at the same volume. EXTREMELY GOD-DAMNED LOUD.

Divorce was out of the question.

An incomprehensible bond connected them, a thing as real as conjoined flesh, as if they were one entity. To be blunt, our parents loved sex.

They were obsessed with giving each other the time. Excluding moments of intense pregnancy or illness or menstruation, I doubt that a single day passed without them getting down to business.

My own unearthing of the situation was Freudian. One night, I awoke with an overwhelming urge to urinate. Rushing to the bathroom, desperate to empty my bladder, I heard the sounds of my parents' lovemaking.

Peeking through their slightly ajar door, I saw them naked, lit by moonlight. My ghost father atop my shadow mother. The sounds of their grunting, eavesdropped in darkness, augmented by the slap of skin against skin.

Had there been better illumination, I would have witnessed more of their bedroom's décor. Years earlier, my father had affixed an American flag on the ceiling, announcing the primacy of the red, white, and blue over their private lives. No one asked why. My father was a peculiar man. Who knows? Maybe he liked looking at it while he shot over the top.

Other than the bed, the only piece of furniture was a giant black metal cabinet. This steel onyx rectangle, always locked, was the subject of great speculation among us children. We'd pushed the heavy wardrobe on its wobbling casters, hoping that its mobility would confer a sense of its contents. My brother came up with the most plausible answer, suggesting that it was a gun cabinet. My father threatened to shoot us at least once every couple of hours, but other than a shotgun used in the routine needs of farming, we'd never seen him brandish a single firearm. Ipso facto, his guns must be in the box.

Fighting. Screwing. Fighting. Screwing. Fighting. The trochaic pentameter of our lives. I was an ingénue lacking any sense about the meaning of sexual activity spread across decades. I found my parents incomprehensible. Their marriage mystified.

These days, I've been down in the groove myself, lived through long relationships and know that the best sex only occurs once people give themselves to another. That weird growth sprouts only from the soil of familiar love.

We move now to the summer of 1986. I'd graduated high school and had no determinate future. There'd been talk about an athletic scholarship at a state university, but this had not panned out. My parents could not afford tuition.

The previous May, my kid sister had become an Evangelical Christian, washed in the blood of Christ. This unexpected conversion was the result of her friendship with the Rentmeester family, a wholesome American clan who'd invited her on a church ski trip. She returned from the snowy peaks and was born again, having called Jesus into her heart.

Many criticisms can be hurled at my parents, but give them their due. At least they hadn't raised us religious. Our family didn't believe in anything, a state of affairs that stoked my sister's evangelical fires.

She witnessed to us. She spread the Good News. We begged her to stop, but this only renewed her dedication. She gave each of us a Bible, copies of the Authorized Version of 1611 with the words of Jesus in red ink. Her church was one of those perverse institutions that believed in the incorruptibility of King James's version.

The most unfortunate aspect of her zeal was the application of Biblical quotations to our daily lives.

When my father slaughtered cattle, she said: —Hither comes the fatted calf, to be killed. We shall eat and be happy.

When our parents got into an oversized argument that ended with my mother saying that she could never forgive my father, my sister said: —Likewise shall my heavenly Father do to you also, if ye shall not forgive all of his trespasses.

When the yield of our crop was less than expected, she said: —And other seed didst falleth upon good ground, and yieldeth fruit that springeth up and increaseth.

I inquired as to the origins of these quotes. She supplied me with chapter and verse. Armed with the Good Book, I discovered that all her bon-mots of Biblical Wisdom were jumbled and mutilated. She garbled the early seventeenth-century syntax, omitting words and rearranging their order. Let us say nothing of the context.

There came a fantasy in which I would confront my sister about her abuse of the inky red words of Christ. Hey, sis, I'd say, how's about you don't misquote that there Bible no more? If you must rub our faces in shit, please do make certain that it's textually accurate shit. Verily, I doest beseecheth thee.

But I never did. There are times when a plague must be suffered.

Anyhoo, the summer of 1986. A night in August.

We'd all gone to bed. I was half asleep, thinking of a world beyond my world, wondering if I'd ever leave the farm. My older brother had moved to St. Paul. He'd sent several letters reporting on life in his new environs. Life was much harder than he'd expected. He missed home, thought often of our haystacks.

My sister was asleep. If everyone has at least one innate skill, hers was falling aslumber. The family joke was that you could lay her across any surface and within five minutes she'd be in the arms of Morpheus. It doesn't seem funny now, but at the time it was hilarious. We always broke up into laughter.

As I stretched into blackness, there came an enormous crash. Our house quivered with reverberation. I thought, for a moment, that I'd dreamt it. Then I thought it was an earthquake, but we never had earthquakes. My sister opened her bedroom door.

I went into the hallway. She stood confused in her nightgown.

—Did you hear that? I asked.

—I think it came from their room.

I knocked on my parents' door. They didn't answer.

—Mom? Dad?

No answer. I took a deep breath and pushed into their room.

Their sex must have done it. The deep emanations of repeated pelvic thrusting. They were as naked as cherubs. We could only see their limbs, the hands and the feet.

The cabinet had fallen upon their bed, taking the American flag with it. The twin doors were splayed open, spread across their bodies like the wings of a great flightless bird, as if my parents had been destroyed by an aberration of evolution. Their skulls were crushed and emptied, brains on the floor.

My parents hadn't been keeping guns.

There was nothing in the cabinet.

Then my sister misquoted the Bible.

—And by their fruits ye shall know them.

OCTOBER 1996

Baby Goes on a Book Tour

Before I embarked upon my tour of America, I bought a new computer, an IBM ThinkPad 560 with an 800-megabyte hard drive and 100mhz Pentium processor. The total cost, tax included, was a steal at $2,300. I'd gotten a deal through a friend of Parker's. Compared with models of similar power, the cost was exorbitant, but I'd been assured that the ThinkPad offered a durability missing from other models.

—You can beat the living shit out of the thing, said Parker. Everything else is a toy.

Besides, *Saving Anne Frank* was doing well. I'd avoided the reviews. Parker read them with the devotion of a monk at vespers. The most significant was by Michiko Kakutani, the great enemy of that fat little fuck Norman Mailer. By Parker's unhappy tones, I could tell that Kakutani had unsheathed her blades.

What the hell, I thought, *I'm just a farm boy whose parents were crushed to death by a cabinet.* Even a negative review in the *Times* accusing the author of Holocaust trivialization was a serious destination. It was way more than I had any right to expect.

I traveled by train. I went and saw the Eastern Seaboard.

My best event was the first, in Boston, at the Harvard Book Store.

The next event was the worst. Providence, the College Hill Bookstore. Only three people showed up.

In the hours before, I took the opportunity to wander through H. P. Lovecraft's old neighborhood. I sat for an hour in Prospect Terrace, a small park overlooking the whole of downtown Providence, and then walked over to 10 Barnes Street, where the old racist Gent wrote the lion's share of his substantial work.

One of the blessed three attendees was this weird straight kid, dressed in black with makeup smeared all over his face, his lips the color of dead snails, his eyes ringed with kohl.

You wanted to meet your audience, I thought. Well, here they are, here are the people who read science fiction. Apparently, they look like they just fucked Bela Lugosi.

I talked, I read, and I took questions. I avoided eye contact with the embarrassed customers who wandered in for reasons of commerce and found themselves confronted by the spectacle of a corn-fed homosexual addressing an audience of empty chairs.

The kid who looked like he'd fucked Bela Lugosi took advantage of the Q&A to ask about Michael Alig and daytime television. He didn't speak with a regional dialect, which was odd, because everyone else in Rhode Island had an accent so thick that it sounded as if they'd been dropkicked in the jaw.

And then it was over. The store manager was all apologies.

—Usually we get a bigger crowd. Some of the kids at Brown love sci-fi. George Takei was supposed to do an event last year. He canceled at the last minute but he still got about fifty people.

—So what you're saying is that an actor who didn't even show up still somehow drew a crowd over ten times the size of my own.

—I guess you can see it that way. I wouldn't take it personal. It's a television culture. The whole country's a real toilet.

The weird straight kid was the last to get my signature, which meant that he stuck around while I signed stock, asking me questions. Mostly it was about Michael. I was curious how a weird straight kid in Rhode Island was so in the loop on the scandals of New York's demimonde.

—I saw that article, he said. In *Details*.

—I can't imagine you as a regular reader of *Details*.

—Billy Corgan was on the cover. Have you heard the new album? "Zero" is a great song.

The day before I left New York, a new issue of *Details* had appeared on newsstands. The cover photo did indeed feature the grim image of Billy Corgan, bald as Jenny Talia, dressed in a leather jumpsuit, his stained hand wrapped around a glass star.

The cover lines advertised articles about the male g-spot, inline skates, and Mim Udovitch's piece about Michael and Angel. The article appeared on page 168. They'd gone classy and titled it *CLUBBED TO DEATH?*

Page 169 was a full-color photograph of Michael in his underwear, standing inside an oversized Jack-in-the-Box. Udovitch referred to Michael as a genius, remarked upon his childlike innocence, and entertained the notion that Angel wasn't dead. There were quotes from the usual crowd,

Gitsie included. Everyone said how impossible they found it that Michael, of all people, could have killed someone. Michael was too much of a child, they said, he was too simple to remove the corpse. Michael? He couldn't've!

There were other photos, snapshots of club life. I wasn't in any of them. A small miracle. The saddest was a black-and-white portrait of Michael taken at Coney Island, standing before Dante's Inferno. A fiberglass devil hovers above his head. Michael wears a pair of children's pajamas. His stomach fat oozes between the top and the bottom. The twisted expression exudes psychopathia. He doesn't look very fabulous.

There I was, on page 172, beside Dante's Inferno. Two paragraphs. I'd talked to Udovitch for an hour:

> But Disco 2000 wasn't only a place for dispossessed young things, attracting any number of New York's slumming intellectuals. [Baby], a well-regarded novelist, is a prominent graduate of Michael's circle. His most recent novel, *Trapped Between Jupiter and a Bottle,* is a science fiction detective tale bearing a surprising resemblance to the Downtown scene. There's even a club promoter with the head of an elephant named Michelle Gila.
>
> [Baby] denies that his novel is about Michael, but speaks fondly of his time in the darkened arenas. "It was like this demonic Disney World with Michael as Uncle Walt. He made the whole thing happen and we were all his cast members." When I ask [Baby] if he thinks Michael is guilty, he evasively replies, "Lots of people are guilty of lots of things, but the only people who really know what happened are Michael, Angel, and Freeze. None of them are talking. Until then, I'm withholding judgment. What does guilt even mean anymore?"

I'd rather be savaged by Michiko Kakutani than give idiotic quotes to *Details,* but there it was. The words like unrevised prose. I came off moronic, like a stupid club kid who didn't know that Angel was dead. It sounded as if I didn't believe Michael and Freeze had killed Angel, but Michael and Freeze killing Angel was the only thing that I did believe.

Uncle Walt? What does guilt even mean anymore? Why the fuck had I tried being clever?

And now some kid who looked like he'd just fucked Bela Lugosi was asking about Michael.

—Michael killed Angel, I said. Obviously.

—That's some sick shit.

—It always is with Michael. It always was.

—So you're still into that stuff?

—Not especially, I said. The most exciting thing happening these days is that sometimes I'll go out and have mixed drinks on the rare evenings when a single mother can find a babysitter.

—It's just because there's a show tonight at the Strand that I thought you might like. I have an extra ticket if you want.

My hotel room was in the Providence Biltmore, one of the Beaux-Arts monstrosities that you can find in any old city. They're always beautiful and ornate and ornately beautiful and built just before the Great Depression. My room had a nice view of Lovecraft's College Hill and as I looked out through the glass, with a view exactly opposite that of Prospect Terrace, I thought about how much of what I did for money had come from Providence, from this shitty little city with its shitty little writer who was afraid of everything.

When the hour grew long, I went into the streets of Downtown, trying to find something called the Strand. Even though the venue was close, I got lost wandering through the park next to my hotel. This brief detour gave me a chance to inspect the indigenous peoples.

Their accents were jaw-kicked. There were less homeless than I'd expected, but way more junkies. It was heroin city. I thought about scoring but then remembered the last time I'd chased that particular dragon. Without The King of France and his vomit, what was the point?

I saw two girls dressed in black, their baby-fat faces smeared with black makeup. I figured that if I followed from a polite distance, I'd end up at the show. Some things never change.

I'd done the same thing back in Los Angeles, that night when we'd gone to Scream, the night that I'd met Jaime. It wasn't even ten years but it felt like another person, another life.

When we got to the Strand, there were a thousand kids dressed in black. They were wearing t-shirts which said MARILYN MANSON in red and *antichrist superstar* in yellow. Behind the lettering, there was a photograph of an angel in front of some tenement windows, for all of its supranatural life looking like it'd just shared some intimate time with Bela Lugosi.

The image conveyed a visceral shock rock thrill, but I fixated on the words. Both MARILYN MANSON and *antichrist superstar* were in serif typefaces. With the professional élan of someone who'd argued with Doubleday over a dustjacket, I wondered whether or not a serif typeface appropriately communicated the idea of a spooky angel shooting over the top with Bela Lugosi. Wasn't sans more sinister?

The opening act was on stage, a band fronted by a blonde woman. Three notes in and I knew what they were. An East Village band, a relic of that brief moment in the early '90s when all of our neighbors sounded like the Velvet Underground had fathered a child inside Joey Ramone, right before everybody who was anybody discovered electronica.

The song ended.

—Thank you, said the vocalist. Thank you. This next song is a bit of a New York story. This is about a girl who jumped off the Empire State Building. In New York City.

No matter how far you go, you can't escape.

Keep on running, Baby.

I tuned out and wandered through the crowd, which was a general admission pit, and oh god everyone looked so innocent. All of those cherubic visages and all of that belief in the power of black t-shirts.

And then, somehow, I bumped into one of them. He wasn't like the other kids. There was no makeup, his t-shirt read HOLY COW, and his curly hair was long and unkempt.

I started a conversation, joking that he seemed like the only person in the place less interested than me.

—I'm with a girl, he shouted over the New York story. I don't know if you've seen her, she's the palest person in here. She lost a kidney half a year ago and just got out of the hospital. And she has no eyebrows. Well, she shaves her actual eyebrows, I think, and then glues on these vinyl replacements.

—I'll keep an eye out, I said.

—I'm not even her boyfriend. She has a boyfriend. He's from Boston. He's here, too, wearing a dog collar and some spiky bracelets. And a mesh shirt. But she won't fuck him. And she won't fuck me. She won't even touch me. The only person she fucks is Twiggy Ramirez.

—Who?

—The bassist. In the band. Not this band. The next band. Marilyn Manson.

—Why are you here?

—She asked me along. So I came. All it takes is one look. Maybe it's the missing kidney. Maybe the eyebrows. But one look, man. When the band's in the Northeast, all she does is follow them around and fuck Twiggy Ramirez. And I guess all I do is follow her.

—Sounds rewarding.

—It's not, he said. But I'll figure it out.

—Can I ask you something?

—Go ahead, he said.

—Are you from here? From Rhode Island?

—Yeah, he said. Chepachet.

—What do you call the things that water comes out of? The things that you drink from, the things you find in the hallways of high schools and airports?

—Bubblers? he asked.

The lights went down and then there was a great noise and then Marilyn Manson was with us. Anyhoo, there it was, Baby, there you saw the way of all flesh.

The lead vocalist, who shared a name with the band, was dressed in a corset that doubled as a straitjacket, straps akimbo and loose. Half of the band was in drag. Boys in dresses! And the crowd was singing along with them, and then they were chanting along with Manson, shouting "We hate love! We love hate!" and then the band was covering the Eurythmics, singing "Sweet Dreams" which I remembered hearing when I'd gone to a pool party at Cave Canem. MDMA resonances ripping through time. And then Manson was up on a podium, with the rest of the band dressed like Nazis, and he was ripping up a Bible and making some statement against God or Jesus or the Kanaim or whatever, and I think that's when I left, pushing my way through the crowd of kids, through all the black makeup, through the Bela Lugosi post-coital bliss.

Out into the streets of Providence.

I'd written two books about the future but now I could see it. All culture in America flowed up from below, from all the fucked-up queer kids cowering in clubs, from all the Black people whose intellectual and artistic legacies had been robbed for decades, and it was copied and copied and copied until all the alienating detail had been lost. Until it was smooth and marketable product.

Marilyn Manson was like watching someone's little brother wearing hand-me-downs. Everything was there. The cross-dressing, the outrageous costumes, the shock antics, the vague horror film overlay, the Hollywood glamor and the serial killer amok culture, the attempts at the sacred and the profane, the transgressive.

And now it was for straight people! Fucking heterosexuals in black lipstick! In the Tunnel Basement and at Disco 2000, there'd been no delineation between attendees and the stage. You could come up and drink your piss and be a star. Yes, everyone knew Michael ran the show, but he wasn't the show. Everyone was the show.

Marilyn Manson was signed to Interscope Records, a division of MCA Records, itself a division of Seagram. With that lineage, you knew the exact circumference of the magic circle and who it kept out. Artist. Customer. Artist. Customer.

Sometimes in New York, when everyone was telling you New York stories about girls jumping off the Empire State Building, you forgot what the rest of the country was like, forgot how disconnected most people were from the livewire, even if they were only two hundred miles away, forgot how there was a world of people whose lives and tastes were controlled by other people, controlled by people that the kids in Providence would never meet, people who didn't think of the kids in Providence as anything other than customers, as pieces to move around a chessboard, controlled by people who worked in offices and created aesthetic experiences that could define hundreds of thousands of millions of lives, and that the people being defined had no idea that this was happening, had no idea that culture didn't arrive via spontaneous generation, had no idea that they were being used by the assholes of New York, by the assholes of Los Angeles, by the assholes of D.C., by the assholes of London, by the assholes of Paris.

By assholes like me.

These Providence kids, who all looked like they'd choked into orgasm while being held by the arms of Bela Lugosi, couldn't imagine the complex processes required to bring their flesh into the Strand, couldn't comprehend the countrywide manipulation that dominated their dreams.

Back at the Strand, not even Marilyn Manson was drinking piss, and there was only one star and his name was on the marquee, and he was making serious money for some very serious people while his bass player fucked a girl with one kidney and no eyebrows.

The king was dead. Long live the king.

Back in my hotel room, I finished a short story. After learning that I wouldn't review *Infinite Jest,* Bob Glück wrote to me, saying that I should still submit. Send anything you like, wrote Glück. Included with his letter was a copy of *REAL: The Letters of Mina Harker and Sam D'Allesandro* by Dodie Bellamy and Sam D'Allesandro.

Bellamy's letters were written while possessed by the spirit of Mina Harker, the unmoved mover of Bram Stoker's *Dracula*, detailing a hyper-poetic rendition of psychogeographical sexual wanderings through San Francisco. My yarn was a response to the book. I called it "The God Hole." It's a love story.

The *Daily News* ran an article by A. J. Benza speculating that a body found in the Harlem River might be Angel. The paper's fact checkers had not bothered to ascertain that the Harlem River runs along the top of Manhattan, separating the island from the Bronx. The fact checkers at the *Daily News* had not bothered to ascertain the direction of the Hudson.

Yet the article was Michael's undoing. Its appearance jogged the memory of a police detective who'd taken a call on Staten Island. Some kids discovered a body in a box. The autopsy showed head trauma and asphyxiation. There were no legs.

Official channels were worked.

I had a message from Michael Alig. He said that he was throwing a new Friday night party called Honey Trap in Hell's Kitchen, at the Mirage. He'd invited me to the grand opening, on October 11th.

I returned too late. Michael didn't call again, which meant that I didn't need to invent excuses. That I needed excuses may offer a sense of the bizarro world of New York in 1996. Michael had murdered Angel. I knew it. Everyone knew it. It'd been aired in the press. Why the hell was anyone letting him throw a party? Why would I apologize to a killer for not attending his soirée?

Attribute my disinterest to exhaustion. I'd undergone the great open expanse of America. I was drained from meeting hundreds of people who read literary novels.

My events were variations on a theme. I'd talk and talk and talk. Some people in the audience feigned interest. Others couldn't hide their boredom. No matter what city, one or two wits asked about Michael.

The tour ended. I headed back home.

I wanted to be alone, and there is no better, and no worse, place for solitude than Manhattan. I loved every stupid street, every ugly face, every disgusting high-rise apartment building. I loved the old New York erupting from the past. I loved the new New York pointing toward the future. I didn't care that the island had gentrified. I didn't care that Rudy was destroying the fabric of society.

The configuration of the street grid, and the sordid tangle of streets below 14th Street, and the insanity of millions crammed into a small space, and the weekday surge when millions more poured in from the surrounding area. The weird angle of the Empire State Building from Bowery. Everyone desperate to bilk the last dollar. These are the ingredients of a witch's brew, the undeniable black magic of Manna-hatta.

I too lived. I walked the streets of Manhattan Island and bathed in the waters around it. I rode the subway. I invented excuses to make photocopies at the Kinko's on 12th Street and gorged myself on overstuffed burritos at the Big Enchilada. I hung out at the public library. I haunted parks, greatly amused by the appearance of a mobile NYPD station on Washington Square South. I traipsed along St. Mark's, watching kids shop at Freaks, watching kids shop at Religious Sex. I delighted in the block between 1st and A, where the Jamaican drug dealers were under the command of a lanky white dealer in rave clothes named Nev. I wandered through the four floors of Irreplaceable Artifacts. I spent hours at the Met. I saw films in Kips Bay, in Times Square, on 19th Street, at the Cinema Village, at the Quad, beneath David Wojnarowicz's old studio, on Third Avenue, at the Music Palace.

Manhattan! My one true love. Never leave me!

NOVEMBER 1996

Baby Goes to Honey Trap

On November 2nd, Adeline telephoned.

—Baby, she said, there's an article in the *Daily News*. They've identified Angel's body. Page 16.

I ran out and bought a copy. In black and white, in newsprint, written by John Marzulli. BEACHED BODY IS MISSING CLUB KID.

I had to go to the Honey Trap.

November 8th. Friday night. I made my way over to West 56th Street, between Eleventh and Twelfth avenues. There was barely a line. I talked to Kenny Kenny, who worked the door. Michael is upstairs, said Kenny, the party's on the second floor.

I dressed to the nines, putting on my Gieves & Hawkes and a deerstalker hat that I'd bought for five dollars on Canal Street from a guy with unrepentant body odor.

The Mirage was like a warp through time and space into someone's New Jersey living room. The DJ was Whillyem Ikillyou, one of Michael's final acolytes. I'd never heard of him.

A mixture of gawkers, onlookers, and last-generation club kids. The regulars, part of the retinue for years, were missing. One guy talked to me, identifying himself as a reporter for the *Guardian*. I thought he'd taken me for another reporter, but he knew who I was.

—I have your little book about Michael, he said.

—Have you read it?

—Not yet, he said.

—It's not about Michael.

—That's not what Mim Udovitch suggests in *Details*.

—That goddamned article will be the death of me, I said. The book is a noir set in the distant future. There's a character based, vaguely, on Michael. The connection is fleeting.

—I understand, said the reporter for the *Guardian*. Everyone is distancing themselves now that judgment is coming down. You know that he's working with the DEA, don't you? He's going to testify against Gatien. That's why he hasn't been arrested. He's worked out a deal. He's going to get full immunity.

—Poor Peter, I said.

—You know the one-eyed man? Are you willing to go on the record?

—No comment, I said. Where is Michael, anyway?

—He's floating around, said the reporter for the *Guardian*. He had a bottle of Champagne the last that I saw of him.

The dancefloor was anemic. The tables were empty. Most activity came from security, shining their flashlights, looking for drugs. A microcosm of entropic heat death. Maybe this was how everything went, with a dissolution into irrelevance. It felt thin, as if I could see through it, as if I'd lost whatever quality had allowed me to haunt clubs and not care about terrible people. Not care about shallow experiences. Maybe change is the only way a thing can survive. I always knew it would end like this.

Michael was in a little enclave near the dancefloor, lying on a disgusting pink bed. It'd been a year since I'd seen him. He looked like a dead man. A picture of Martin Luther King Jr. hung above the bed. I thought about nonviolent civil disobedience as a discipline of social protest, I thought about King's eventual realization that the problem wasn't a racial one, but rather one of class, that poor white people and poor Black people had more in common than poor white people and rich white people. I thought about the Poor People's Campaign shattered by an assassin's bullet at the Lorraine Motel.

Michael didn't even see me. He was too high. What did I expect? That he'd croak at me and we'd have a conversation?

In an English accent, a guy was saying: —Do you have any comment about the fact that the police have identified Angel's body?

Michael didn't hear him. He snorted a line of drugs up his nose and crashed back onto the bed, supine before us.

It was the last time that I saw him.

DECEMBER 1996

Michael Alig Is Arrested

Amonth later, on December 5th, Michael was arrested for the murder of Angel Melendez. The cops picked him up at a motel in Toms River, New Jersey. The next Tuesday, he was the *Village Voice* cover story. They went for it: THE PARTY'S OVER. THE END OF MICHAEL ALIG.

I didn't bother reading.

DECEMBER 1996

Adeline Breaks the News

Adeline called me on the pretext of making plans for Christmas dinner. I agreed to eat with her and Jon and Emil. As I'd done on Thanksgiving.

I'd started dating again, set up with a few guys that knew friends of Parker, but nothing serious enough to warrant shared holiday misery. Things were bleak enough that I considered getting in touch with Abe and seeing what an old boy from the American Middle West was doing for Christmas. I was curious to see if he'd be going back home.

Adeline said there were matters of serious import that needed discussion. As in a tête-à-tête. We met for dinner at Around the Clock. I ordered a hamburger. She had a Caesar salad with grilled chicken.

—Baby, she said, there's something we need to talk about.

—I know that tone.

—We're moving, she said.

—Where? I asked.

—California, she said.

—Please tell me you're not moving to Los Angeles.

—Holy moly, she said, you're potty. Much as I've rekindled the friendship with Mommie Dearest, I'm not yet that far gone.

—So where?

—San Francisco.

Winterbloss was pressuring Adeline to come back in the hopes that they could step up production on *Trill,* still selling in pamphlets but doing unusually well in trade paperback. He envisioned real capitalization. Adeline had resisted his entreaties, particularly on the basis of not wanting to screw up Jon's work life. But Jon had spoken with a few people from the old punk days, and they'd assured him that he could get the same gig in San Francisco. Under the reign of Mayor Willie Brown, Baghdad by the Bay's prosecutorial establishment found no shortage of poor bodies that needed shafting.

Besides, Jon'd taken the LSAT and was thinking about applying to UC Hastings.

And there was the issue of Nash Mac, who'd rattled sabers about never seeing his son.

—When? I asked.

—January 15th.

—What about the apartment?

—I was thinking that you might reassume control, she said. You could sublet your current abode and then you'll be back on old 7th Street, where you've always wanted to be.

—The only place that I want to be is 31 Union Square West.

—You can't repeat the past, she said.

—Can't repeat the past? Of course you can.

But I agreed. I always agreed. Anyhoo, Adeline was right. I did want to move back into 7th Street. I missed the East Village. I'd have the second half of January to move my stuff.

DECEMBER 1996

Baby Attempts a New Book

I started a thinly veiled fictional memoir about our eleven years in New York. Each chapter constituted one year, told in the first person either by the Baby analogue or the Adeline analogue, and rather than attempt the fullness of that year, most chapters would be biopsies of events and people. We had met bizarre characters and lived in the right place at the right time. I could scribe things as they happened, act the amanuensis. I even devised a title.

Burning for the Holy Immaculate Fix.

The holy immaculate fix came from a short story by Uncle Bill Burroughs. "The Junky's Christmas." I'd read it in *Interzone,* but the text didn't hit until I heard the spoken-word version on *Spare Ass Annie and Other Tales.*

I eked out a few thousand words about my first day in New York. The squat, Adeline, Bobby, Second Avenue Theatre, 31 Union Square West.

I abandoned the project. If I had judged *Infinite Jest* for its crimes, then it was sheer hypocrisy to think a book about my life, or a book about Adeline, could be different. We were only another group of rich white people on drugs.

I thought about the production of novels, wondering how a book akin to Literature could be produced without segregating into identity. My other novels had avoided the great white hole by virtue of science fiction. But I didn't want to spend my professional life writing about depressed robots who mainlined drugs with names like Substance D and CHEW-Z.

I considered the things that fiction never addresses. Like the way that culture bubbles up from below. Like the way that form is more important than content. Like the way that free speech is the booby prize of democracy. Like the way that assumptions about universal human rights reveal more about the person who assumes than anything universal to the human experience. Like the way that the hardest part of any political position is not navigating the people opposed to your ideas but rather suffering the ones who are on your side. Like the way in which foreign intervention never works, regardless of its purpose. Like the way in which books are the deadliest weapons devised by the human race. Like the way in which air travel is an abhorrence that destroys the soul. Like the way in which plastic saps a percentage of joy. Like the way in which fluorescent lights have poisoned the modern experience. Like the way in which no specific action by any individual person or group of persons achieves anything and yet somehow life continues on apace. Like the way in which society breaks apart when confronted by mental illness. Like the idea that the best way to deal with great evil is not to recoil in horror but rather to laugh in its face, regardless of its human damage. Like the way in which we fetishize emotional suffering as an attempt to avoid our erotic impulses. Like the way that Jesus Christ was a White Magus in the fashion of Apollonius of Tyana, both of whom conquered death through a shared system of ritual magic involving seminal fluid. Like the way we'd constructed World War II as a Great Honest Battle in which the forces of Good took on two despotic regimes and won, but in fact we'd only beaten one anti-Semitic genocidal abomination by allying with another anti-Semitic genocidal abomination, the consequences of which would haunt us for fifty years. Like the way in which the things that any society believes are its most important are invariably its least. Like the way in which stupidity and ignorance can be wiped out through constant education. Like the way in which the only hope for the future is that this education will render each member of the species subject to stunting neuroses that cripple our ability to hurt each other. Like the way in which the very idea of being a gifted person, or a genius, is a social construct benefiting children of privilege. Like the way in which being labeled a child genius leaves the labeled person in a state of profound incapacity, unable to understand the simplest things that everyone else figures out by the time they are sixteen. Like the way that women are smarter than men. Like the way that the concept of intelligence was devised by men to exclude women. Like the way that every competing theory about human advancement is proffered by someone with a dollar to make and never encompasses even the smallest fragment of being alive. Like the way in which these theories cause people to misunderstand their role in this world. Like the way in which the human animal is wired to pay equal measures of attention to the loudest jerks and the most hysterical women. Like the way in which every powerful man that I've ever met was a reeking transparent bag of insecurities. Like the way other people fell over with dumbstruck awe and admiration when given a whiff of that reek, despite the odor being indistinguishable from the smell of shit. Like the human need for leaders who cannot lead. Like the way in which the measure of offense should never be the feelings of the offended but rather a lack of thought in the offender. Like the way in which America is a country broken from its inception, a country founded by the richest men in the service of an immoral regime of multiple genocides and how the ideals enshrined in our fundamentally flawed constitution are undercooked banalities that we bully on to the rest of the world. Like the way in which an entire society, regardless of individual affiliations, can internalize and metastasize bad ideas as solid actualities despite all the evidence to the contrary. Like how if there is a hell, every American citizen is going there and when we arrive we will see these images projected on rocky walls in a random and repeating order: a manacled slave, a Cherokee walking on bloody stumps, the charred flesh of a woman throwing herself out of the Triangle Shirtwaist Factory, a Vietnamese girl inhaling Agent Orange, a queen being bashed at the corner of Sullivan and Houston, and a ten-year-old Chinese boy building a television. Like the way my mother used to tuck me into bed when I was eight years old. Like the way that my father hugged and kissed me. Like the way that my family wouldn't tell me that my grandmother was dead until she was buried. Like the way that one unexpected death causes decades of suffering. Like the way that you looked when first I saw you. Like the way that I loved you for eight years and came in you ten thousand times and now can't remember a single thing about you. Like the way that drunk drivers ruin the world. Like the way that Adeline gave me my life and saved me.

And yet people keep writing. And yet the words keep coming.

CHRISTMAS DAY 1996

When Christmas rolled around, I walked to my once and future apartment. They were celebrating the holiday for Emil. An East Village punk turned legal assistant and his comic artist girlfriend had settled into an offbeat vision of middle-class life.

I called from the street. Jon let me in. We said our hellos. I asked how the packing was going. He said it wasn't much of a problem, at least when it came to his own stuff, as he'd only moved in a few months earlier.

—I haven't even unpacked, he said. Not really. So it's easy.

—And Adeline?

—Adeline's another story.

The apartment was festooned in Xmas kitsch. Adeline's apron gave her a beleaguered look. Emil ran around, clutching shitty plastic toys sent by Suzanne. Shreds of torn-up wrapping paper were scattered like bodies at Chickamauga.

—Many apologies for the catastrophe, she said, but that's Christmas. I remember when Mother and Daddy would give us presents and we'd carpet the house with trash. Yet here we stand, repeating their sins with a new generation.

—Baby, said Emil, come look.

I followed the child into his room and sat on the floor. He picked up this stuffed doll. It looked like a character from Sesame Street.

—What's his name? I asked.

—Elmo, said Emil. Look.

He tickled the toy's stomach, causing the thing to laugh and shake.

—That tickles! said the toy. Oh boy!

Emil tickled the toy again, causing another round of violent paroxysms. I watched for as long as I could, but the squealing thing gave me a headache. I went into the kitchen.

—You're going to go insane with Elmo, I said to Adeline.

—Mother sent it, she said. I'm hoping that Elmo breaks soon. He's been screaming all morning.

—Clearly, I said, we live in the best of all possible worlds.

We went into her bedroom. Soon it would be mine. If I wanted. Or maybe I'd stick with my old room and turn Adeline's into a study. Both rooms were the same size. It didn't matter.

—As I'm packing up the entirety of my life, all manner of odd things have made reappearances.

—I can't believe you're leaving.

—Baby, she said, don't exasperate. Don't act like a parvenu. If you miss us, buy a fucking plane ticket. You're moneyed. You can stay whenever you want. I'm always Adeline. You're always Baby. That much never changes. Location is irrelevant.

—I'll miss you, I said. God, why did you choose California? There's so many places to live. Anywhere but California!

—That's very well, she said, but we must all cultivate our own gardens.